FUTURE
PASTIMES

FUTURE
PASTIMES

Edited by

Scott Edelstein

AURORA PUBLISHERS, INC.
Nashville/London

Contents

An Introduction

Time On Our Hands

As the world becomes increasingly mechanized, man (or at least industrialized man) will find himself with more and more free time. A problem that is already upon us and is likely to become more difficult to solve as the years pass is how to make meaningful use of this leisure time. Although we already have multi-billion dollar industries devoted entirely to recreational pursuits, in many cases we simply don't know what to do with ourselves. Thus, as our capacity for entertainment increases, so will the arts, the media, and other forms of recreation develope and advance. Old forms are being refined, or discarded, and new forms developed. The categories of entertainment themselves are growing in number: the arts, the media, sports, contests, competitions and games, travel and tourism, the artificial worlds-within-worlds of amusement parks, and so on and on. As a culture, we are expanding our senses and our awareness as the very sensory inputs we have available to us increase at an ever more rapid pace.

How will all these forms of leisure change in the next ten, twenty, hundred or thousand years? What new forms will come into being, and which of the old forms will die?

In *Future Pastimes* are twenty-eight possible futures, twenty-eight views of tomorrow's leisure pursuits. The stories are arranged chronologically: Steve Herbst's "An Uneven Evening" and Elizabeth A. Lynn's "We All Have To Go," for examples, could quite easily be parts of our lives a very few years from now; Dave Bischoff's "Heavy Metal" and Edward Bryant's "The Poet in the Hologram in the Middle of Prime Time" look toward the year 2000 and beyond; Alan Brennert's "Skyghosts and Dusk-Devils" and Gerald Page's "Waygift" envision forms of entertainment in the far, far future, when mankind lives in very different manners, in vastly different environments.

In sum, they are twenty-eight most unusual visions which I hope you will find exciting, intriguing, and moving.

—Scott Edelstein

STEVE HERBST

An Uneven Evening

Peter's back had been bothering him again; when he reached for the newspaper on a nearby table, he stiffened. There was no crick of pain this time. I am swiftly becoming an old man, he told himself.

"Peter, how's your back feeling?"

"It's all right."

Nancy read her *McCall's* on the sofa, ignoring the television set, which she had turned on to play the early evening news. She seemed content to keep her body still and move only her eyes. The magazine's pastel advertisements held her attention completely.

My wife is a boring woman, Peter thought. See how her fat face never alters its expression. See how her body rests slackly against the cushions and how her arms lie at her sides. See how the magazine on her lap is her evening plaything. See how I am left to fill a chair silently and become boring also.

And how boring I feel, he thought. What an incapable person I am. A dead weight suited to living-room chairs. On Wednesday nights I hit pool halls and drink beer, for of that am I capable. That is, when I ride in the car with Teague and Marvin Sapello. With Marvin and Teague I am a functioning organism, but when I am home I fill chairs.

Peter filled his chair and rested his paper until the doorbell rang, to his great relief. Teague and Marvin came into the living room after wiping their feet on the floor mat.

"You look bored, old buddy," said Marvin jovially and lowered himself into a chair.

"Hey, hey," Teague said at the same time, sagging against a wall and hanging his jaw. "Ready to go?"

My evening of boredom. Peter thought, is giving way to one of virile entertainment. I now reject studied inactivity and uneasy introspection for the security of my friends, old games, and a more forceful and satisfying social role. An escape from air-conditioned purgatory into culturally competitive paradise.

"Fuckin' mellow," he said. He hit Teague in the arm. "Let's get out of here."

They were in Teague's small Plymouth, Teague and Peter in front and Marvin in the back. Peter looked out the window. He kept his lips pressed tightly together as usual, betraying a minimum of emotion.

"How many games we gonna play tonight, eh?" Teague smiled, looking straight ahead into traffic.

"We can play until the owner throws us out," Marvin answered, his cheeks bulging when he talked. "Wear us out a pool table, ain't that right?"

"Yup," said Peter.

Teague drove impatiently, barely avoiding the night people in the streets, watching his headlight beams play on storefronts when he turned corners. His big arms rested fully on the steering wheel most of the time; he seemed to be embracing the car and the power it gave him.

2

"I told Willie Amberay and Sam Orr I'd pick them up. We're gonna fill the car tonight, hey," said Teague.

So he pulled up at Sam Orr's house and ran up to ring the doorbell. Sam and Willie were outside immediately, loping down the stairs side by side. They got into the back seat, craning their necks and darting their eyes about.

"Hi, Pete. Marvin."

"What's up?" said Peter.

Sam pulled the door closed and Teague pulled away abruptly. Willie lit a cigarette, scenting the inside of the car.

"*Hey,* Teague, guess what we found out today," Sam began.

"Yeah?"

"Get this, there's a new torming hall just opened on East Andrew Street, they got twenty-five tubes and strong alignment. What do you think of *that?*"

"Twenty-five, huh? Pretty neat, y'know?"

"Listen, Teague, if you and everybody wants to go there tonight instead of the same old pool game? Huh?"

Peter wasn't at all sure that he had heard that exchange correctly. What was Sam talking about, "torming"? What kind of term was that?

But Teague seemed to know.

"That's fine with me," Marvin said. "I haven't shot rings in, oh, a long time. Are they full-sized fields, do you know?"

"Yeah, right," said Willie. "Ten rings, oh, maybe sixty degrees up and down. That's what I heard."

"Shit, man, fuck," exclaimed Sam gloriously. "It's been so long. So long. Get the old form back, long dives, everything. Jesus!" He waved his arms in the air, grinning. "Jesus, such a long time."

Peter began to worry. What in hell was torming? He considered asking and admitting his stupidity.

"Hey, Pete," called Teague. "A good torm okay with you? We'll let the pool go tonight."

Peter decided to play it cool. "Yeah, great. How far is the place?"

"Oh, a few blocks down Andrew. I think fourteen hundred east."

Peter nodded and turned his gaze back out the window. He was just the least bit worried.

The outside of the torming hall was a storefront with a small

3

sign—TORMING/25 TUBES—printed in neon. Then an unobtrusive doorway, and then a long escalator going down. Peter
and his friends filed in neatly and descended to the front lobby.

The lobby was surprisingly big and modern. Gleaming metal
arches spaced every twenty feet around the ellipsoidal room
soared upward to a ceiling mabe fifty feet high. Carpeting on the
floor and on walls between the arches was light-green and very
thick. The pattern of metal and green was unbroken on all sides,
except for washroom portals and a food concession at one end
of the ellipse, and a counter set in the wall at the other end. The
carpeting helped to absorb the noise made by the hall's patrons
and by a powerful air-conditioning system. A fragrant odor filled
the place, and bright fluorescents overhead illuminated every
square inch evenly.

Peter and his friends were standing in front of a long, polished
desk in the center of the room behind which were banks of tiny
lights, knob controls, and two receptionists. Teague murmured,
"I've gotta use the john; get us a tube, okay?" Teague and Sam
left.

Peter tried to hang back, hoping that either Marvin or Willie
would take care of any arrangements. But, unfortunately, he
found himself up against the desk, and one of the receptionists
asked him, "Yes?"

He thought fast. If this place was anything like a bowling
alley, then he was supposed to reserve a lane. Or, in this case,
a *tube*.

"A tube?" he said casually, and the receptionist handed him
a bulky plastic key with number 5 embossed on it. Peter wasn't
sure whether there was anything else to ask for, but the girl
said, "Get belts over there," and she pointed with her arm toward
the opposite end of the lobby.

Belts?

Marvin and Willie were already at the belts counter, and
Peter watched the man behind the counter select their sizes and
hand them belts. So he went to the man and asked for a belt, got
a belt, and put the belt around his waist.

The belt was heavy plastic half a foot wide and it had weights
built into it. Three weights, evenly spaced around him.

What could the belt be for? A handicap of some sort? A thing
to hold equipment? Peter walked as easily as possible under the
added weight, trying to look as if nothing was new to him.

"What number, Pete?" asked Marvin.

Peter announced the number and said, "Where do you suppose that would be, eh?"

Marvin pointed toward the back side of the lobby and said, "Over there, probably."

At least Marvin didn't know everything for sure.

When they had walked behind the lobby, what Peter saw completely took his breath from him.

"Oh, no. OH, no."

They were standing on a balcony. In front of them the floor dropped a hundred and fifty feet in a long, slow curve. Fluorescent lights at the top of the huge torming room illuminated the smoke-filled air and set off dramatically the distance between balcony and floor, between balcony and opposite wall. Along this distance, down a seventy-three-degree angle, stretched the tubes.

"What was that, Pete?"

"Oh, uh, they're fuckin' small, that's what. Don't you think?"

"Regulation size, I dunno," said Willie.

The tubes were rows of ten soft plastic hoops about six feet across, and looking through them one could see the far diagonal end of the chamber. The tubes were a couple of hundred feet long.

But that wasn't the worst of it, Peter saw.

People were torming in the tubes.

All down the line, men, women, children were leaping with abandon head first into the upper ends of the tubes and with their arms pressed against their sides, they were falling through the hoops. As they fell they collided with the hoops and glanced off. On and on, fast, ricocheting down and disappearing at the bottom.

"Did you get an egg, Pete?" Willie said, examining knob controls by the side of tube number 5.

Peter looked wildly about the room, back into the lobby, to find a place to get eggs. He couldn't see any counter besides the one for belts, nor anything that should be called an egg. What was an egg?

"Here, these guys have one," said Marvin, and he walked over to the tube numbered 7 where three small children and their parents were torming. The children jumped into the rings fearlessly, touched several times, and disappeared at the bottom of the tubes, while a conspicuous green display registered a number from zero to ten beside the topmost ring.

The "egg" was resting on the floor behind them. Marvin asked the father of the family, and then he stooped to pick up the egg. The egg was a light, foot-long metal ellipsoid, perfectly feature-less except for a hole in one end. After turning the tube on with the numbered key, Willie took the egg and centered it in the topmost ring; a magnetic field drew it to the exact center and held it there. When Willie reversed a switch, the egg dropped slightly down the tube.

"A little too far to the left, I think," said Willie.

"Aligned pretty well, I'd say. Just a touch off."

"Too far to the left," Peter said with conviction.

So Willie played with two knobs until the path of the egg satisfied him. Then he said quickly, "Who wants to go first?"

Peter nearly panicked when he thought about jumping into the rings and practically free-falling two hundred feet head down. Very nearly panicked. He couldn't see what was down at the bottom of the huge room, but he did see the tormers come up each time through doors in the floor. He tried to assure him-self that if he were to jump into the tube, he too would come up through a door in the floor.

"Wait for Teague and Sam," he said.

"Is it aligned?" Teague asked when he came back.

"Fairly well," said Willie.

"Well then, go ahead."

Willie stepped up to the tube without a word, tossed his watch and car keys to Teague, and leaped gracefully down the tube. He touched four times and then they lost sight of him. The exhibition took a little under two seconds. Then it was Marvin's turn.

Marvin slicked back his hair, waved his meaty arms, and dove in. He collided right away with the third ring, which event through him off balance and caused him to touch five more times on the way down. At this point Willie came up through the floor.

Now it was Peter's turn.

My friends are unafraid, thought Peter. That, at least, has been proved to my satisfaction. Also, this is a fancy establishment. I think it is amazingly strange, but definitely fancy. Also there are children falling down the tubes, and none of them is getting hurt, and no one is worrying about them. Therefore, in all prob-ability, I am perfectly safe.

What I must be concerned with, then, is being skillful. The

score is based on the number of rings touched, that much is clear. If a person's aim is accurate initially, he will touch fewer rings. If his corrections are adequate when he touches a ring, he will touch fewer rings afterward. What I must do is . . .

"Go, Pete," said Sam. "It looks to be aligned all right from the way Willie went."

Skill, Peter realized, should not concern him in the least until he had satisfied himself about the matter of safety. He realized also that he wasn't satisfied. He was still scared to death.

"Don't you want to take your watch off?"

He took off his watch.

He held his breath involuntarily and jumped into the tube.

The dive was a bad one. He hit the second ring at the top of its curve, solidly, and it bounced him off and sent him spinning. The tube's magnetic field swung him around and he found himself soaring up into space, outside the rings. He flew straight up, head over heels, terror-stricken, until a secondary field caught him and fastened him on the ceiling.

"No!" he cried, trying to sound as annoyed as possible instead of scared. He looked down dizzily at the floor below.

"Grab a hand rail!" Sam called. Teague was coming up through the floor and when he saw Peter on the ceiling, he burst out laughing.

"Hey, that's pretty neat," he chuckled.

Peter found a railing and pulled himself back to the balcony. He dropped down to the carpeted floor. "Yeah," he smiled, checking his heavy breathing. His miscalculation had been an honest one, he realized, one for which he would not be ostracized.

"Try again, man."

No, not again, he thought. "Yeah," he said. "Yeah." He grinned.

No, no. He hopped in more gingerly this time, plummeted into the third ring, and clung to it for dear life. Below him seven more rings hovered vertiginously against the pale-green background of carpet a hundred feet down. He crawled along the rim of the ring, then, to face toward the middle. Stretching his hands in front of him and letting go with his feet, he fell, and hit every remaining ring on the way down.

A long curved ramp and a magnetic field stopped him at the bottom. As he lay sprawled on the wide, smooth floor, he saw a series of conveyors curving upward and disappearing into the walls. He stepped onto one. The ride was quick. At the top, a trap door opened and he was lifted onto the main-floor balcony in time to see Teague drop off into a three-touch fall.

"You okay, Pete?"

"Yeah, Marvin. What's wrong?"

"An eight-point, shit!" said Sam. "Outa practice, huh?"

"Yeah, maybe," he answered. "Field isn't, uh, very strong, is it?"

"Strongest field I've been in, myself."

"Yeah."

Peter made a seven-touch the next time and flew around the outside of two rings on the way. He came up through the door in the floor and wrote "7" on his score sheet. Willie caught his error and explained to him: "You went outside on the way down, Pete. Twice."

"Yeah, right."

"That's an extra two points, you know. Tryin' to cheat yourself?"

Peter made the correction, and Willie asked, "You ever do a torm before, Pete? Honest now."

"Asshole! You think I'm trying to impress somebody or something?" He grinned, slapping Willie on the back.

"I know," said Willie in a low voice, "that you tend to do that."

Peter lined up his next jump carefully, sighting all the way down and then listing forward in what he thought was a professional-looking posture. He swung his arms to take off, and a muscle went in his back.

He went tense from the momentary cramp, stiffened from head to foot, and fell seven rings without touching.

When he hit bottom he turned over once and stopped short on his knees, still tensed. An older man lay near him on the floor, and before he could get up the man called to him.

"Are you hurt?"

"No, shit, I'm all right," Peter smiled coolly.

"Well, *I'm* hurt," the man said, and propped himself up on one knee.

Peter helped the man to the up conveyor while the man explained. "I've got a trick knee, see, and I got it locked up on the way down. No fault of the equipment, understand. The equipment's perfectly safe."

Peter remembered that afterward. The equipment's perfectly safe.

The man thanked him when they reached the torming balcony above and a place to sit down. Peter said, "It's all right," and left to get his wrist watch from the tube 5's scoring desk.

I am a very misdirected person, he thought. I waste my energies. I find no joy in social paradise.

He said good night to all his friends, gave them some money for the torming, returned his belt, and took the bus home.

He found his wife still reading *McCall's* on the sofa. The television was still on, and the late evening news was playing. He waited for a greeting from her; anything, but she ignored him and continued to read the magazine.

Finally, he volunteered: "It was okay, we had fun."

She turned a page and continued to read.

"Nan?"

"Yes, Peter?" She looked up.

"Are you watching television? I'm going to shut it off."

"Go right ahead, I'm not watching." She returned to the page.

Peter watched her in the silent room for a long time, thinking about boring evenings and dull purgatories and culturally competitive paradises and wives.

And then his face brightened up all at once. He went over to Nancy on the sofa, bent over her from behind with his hands on her shoulders and his face close to hers.

He said, "Hey, honey, tomorrow night I'm going to take you torming."

She looked up this time.

"Oh. Great," she said. "Strong alignment?"

ELIZABETH A. LYNN

We All Have To Go

Eight A.M., Friday morning in Chicago, Jordan Granelli sat
at his desk, reading the Corpse Roster. High above the street, on
the two-hundreth floor of the Daley Tower, he escaped the noise
of city sirens and the chatter of voices: here there was only the
rustling paper and the click of computers, and a blue, silent sky.
He read the print-outs slowly and carefully, making little piles
on the desk top. Out on Madison there was an old wino dead;
they named him King of the Alkies—he never let a man go without a drink if he had a drop in his flask . . . the bums are sober-
ing up for his funeral today . . . On Sheridan Road, in the heart
of the Gold Coast, there was a crippled girl whose rich family
bankrupted itself to keep her alive; she died this morning, 4
A.M. . . . On Kedzie the hard-working mother of three just died
of DDT poisoning . . . All good, heart-breaking stories. In Evans-

11

ton, a widower's only son just got killed swinging on a monorail pylon, 10 P.M. last night . . . He frowned and tossed that one aside. They'd done a dead child Tuesday. He flipped back and pulled a sheet out, and buzzed for a messenger.

"Take this to the director's office," he told the boy, and swiveled his chair towards the window. He gazed out at the light-filled sky, at the lake, at the morning sun. There was no place in the world he felt more alive, unless it was in front of the camera's eye. "In the midst of life we are in death," he said to the sky, rolling the words like honey on the tongue. They loved it, his idiot public, when he poured clichés on their ears. He wrapped the dead round with sweet words, and the money came tumbling in. Power rose in his blood like fever. Noon was his hour. He waited for the earth's slow turn to noon.

Noon, on a Friday in Chicago: means it is 1:00 in New York, 11:00 in Denver, 10:00 in Los Angeles. In L.A. the housewives turn off their vacuums and turn on the TVs, and the secretaries in San Francisco and in Denver take their morning half-hour break in a crowded lounge. In New York clerks and tellers and factory workers take a late lunch, and the men in the bars, checking their watches, order one last quick one. And in Chicago the entire city settles into appreciative stillness. On the lunch counters and in the restaurants, up on the beams of rising buildings jutting through dust clouds and smog like Babel, even inside the ghastly painted cheerfulness of hospitals, mental homes, and morgues, TV sets glow.

Jordan Granelli looked out at them all through the camera. "It's a sad thing," he said, his voice graceful and deep, "when the very young are called. Who of us has not, would not, mourn for the death of a child? But it is doubly sad when young and old join in mourning for one they loved, and miss. Today, my friends, we talk with Ms. Emily Maddy, who has lost her only daughter, Jennifer. Jennifer was a woman in her prime, with three young children of her own, and now they and her own mother have lost her."

The camera swung slowly around a shack-like house, and stopped on the face of a bent, tired woman looking dully up at Jordan Granelli. "The kids don't understand it yet," she said.

12

"They think she's comin' back. I wish it had been me. It should have been me."

A woman in a factory in Atlanta rubs her eyes. "She looks like my mother. I'm voting my money to her."

"Look at that hole she's living in!" comments a city planner in San Diego, watching the miniature Japanese set on his secretary's desk. "Mary and I just bought our voting card last week. I wonder if we'll get to see the kids?"

A man on a road construction crew in Cleveland says, "I'm voting for her."

"You said Tuesday you were gonna vote for the guy whose son was killed by the fire engine," his neighbor reminds him.

"Well, this old lady needs it more; she's got those kids to look after."

"I don't know how you can watch that stuff," a third man says fiercely. "It makes me puke." He walks ostentatiously out of earshot of the TV. They stare at him in wonder.

"His wife died in June," someone volunteers. "Left him with two kids. He hates to be reminded."

"Jealous?" the first man nods. "He would have liked a little cash himself, I bet. He's got no feeling for other peoples' troubles, that guy. I wouldn't vote a cent to him, not a cent."

On their big wall screen in Chicago, the network executives watch the woman's tears with pleasure. "That son-of-a-bitch sure knows how to play it," says a vice-president. "I'm damned if I know why no one ever thought of it before. It's a great gimmick, death. He'll top last week's ratings."

"Ssh!" says his boss. "I want to hear what he says."

The woman's sobs were at last quieting. She bent her head away from the bright lights, and they touched the white streaks in her hair with silver. One shaky hand shaded her eyes. Jordan Granelli took hold of the other with tender insistence. The camera moved in closer; the button mike on Granelli's collar caught each meticulous word, and resonated it out to eighty million people.

"Let your grief happen," he said softly. It was one of his favorite remarks. "Ms. Maddy, you told us that your daughter was a good person."

"Yes," said her mother, "oh yes, she was. Good with the kids and always laughing and sunny——"

"There's nothing to be ashamed of in tears for youth and grace and goodness. In all your pain, remember—" he paused histrionically, and she looked up at him as if he might, indeed, comfort her with his precisely rounded sentences, "remember, my friends, that we are all in debt, and we pay it with our sorrow. Ms. Maddy, there are millions of people feeling for you at this very moment. We live by chance, and Dame Fortune, who smiles on us today, cuts the thread of our lives tomorrow. Mourn for those you love—for you may not mourn for yourself—and think kindly of those that death has left behind. In life we are in death. And we all have to go."

Poetic, smooth, slimy bastard, Christy thought. She moved even closer in, catching his craggy expressive hand holding the woman's worn one, the dirty dark furniture, the crinkled photograph of the dead daughter on the table, the stains on the floor —*push that poverty, girl, it brings in the money every time—* and, as the light booms drew back, the play of moving shadows across white hair. *That ought to do it.* The sound had cut out at Granelli's final echoing syllable. She cut out and stepped back; simultaneously, Leo, the set director, standing to her left, sliced his long fingers through the air. The crew relaxed.

Granelli stood up briskly, dropping the old woman's hand. He brushed some dirt off his trousers and walked towards the door. As he passed Christy he inclined his head: "Thank you, Ms. Holland."

She ignored his thanks. She would have turned her back, except that would have been too pointedly rude, and even she, his chief camerawoman, could not be rude with impunity to Jordan Granelli. One word from him and the network would break her back down to children's shows. She simply concentrated on taking her camera from its tripod and storing it in its case. Her arms ached. Ms. Maddy, she saw, was looking after Granelli as if he had left a hole in the air. Christy hated it, that look of beaten bewilderment. *Did you think that sympathy was real, lady? He fooled you, too. He's a ghoul. We're all ghouls.*

Zenan, the second cameraman, strolled over to her, from his leaning place behind her on the wall. She could smell the alcohol on his breath. He stayed drunk most of the time, now. "You okay?" she asked him.

"Another day, another death, right, Chris?" he said.

"Shut up, Zen," she said.

"Tell me, Christy, how much do you think the great-hearted American public will pay the lady for her sterling performance? Friday's death has an edge, they say, on the ones at the beginning of the week. If ten million people vote a dollar a week, take away the network cut, and Mr. Granelli's handsome salary, and what you and I need to pay our bills—hell, I was never very good at arithmetic in school. But it's a lot of money. Weep your heart out for Mr. Death, and win a million!" he proclaimed. "Does *she* know it's a lot of money?" he asked, jerking his thumb at Ms. Maddy.

"Zen, for pity's sake!" She could see Jake leaning towards them from his place near the door, listening, with a concentrated, big cat stare. Is there danger? those eyes asked. She caught that directed gaze and shrugged. *After six years working for "We All Have To Go," I'll be a drunkard too.*

"For pity's sake?" he repeated. He looked down at her from his greater height. "Here am I, a sodden voice crying in the wilderness, crying that when Jordan Granelli walks, in the dark nights when the moon is full, the deathlight shines around him!"

And Jake was there, one big hand holding Zenan's arm. "Come on, Zen, come outside."

Leo came striding in. "What the hell happened?"

She smiled. "He called Granelli 'Mister Death.'"

"You think it's funny? Some day Granelli's going to hear it and frown, and his guards are going to take Zenan to an empty lot and smash his windpipe in."

She was jolted. "Jake wouldn't do that!"

"You like Jake? Well, Cary or Stew. That's what he pays them for—that's what the network pays them for," he amended. "Ah, Christ. He's got seniority. They can't fire him. He's our reality check." He scowled. "I've been here too long myself"

Have I really only been here two years? She lugged her case and tripod over to Willy, manager of Stores. "See you Monday," he said cheerily. He'd been there eight years, longer than anybody. But nothing seemed to touch him.

She ducked out of the tiny house to get a breath of air. Granelli's big limousine, pearl-white with its black crest on the side, sat parked at the curb. Around the house, in a big semicircle kept back by the police, a crowd had gathered to watch. She heard the whispers start. *What are they waiting for? Granelli?* But they could all see him, he was there in the car, and besides, they all knew his face. They saw him five afternoons a

15

week on their TV screens, much closer than they would ever get to him in reality. *They're waiting for death,* she thought morbidly. The Grim Reaper himself, striding out of the house with jangling fingers, hoisting his scythe on his clavicle.

Jake came round the corner. "What'd you do with Zenan?" she asked him.

"Locked him in the crew trailer," Jake said. "It doesn't matter who he talks to, in there." He looked worried. "Christy, you a friend of Zenan's? Tell him to shut up about Mr. Granelli. If he starts upsetting people, Mr. Granelli won't like it, and the network won't either."

"I don't know what he has to complain about—Zenan, I mean," Christy said. "Any TV show that gets eighty million people watching it every day, can't be wrong."

He started to answer, and then the car motor rumbled and he ran for his seat, riding shotgun next to Cary, who drove. Stew sat in the back next to Jordan Granelli. *Does he ever talk to them?* Christy wondered. *Does he know that Jake used to be a skyhook and Cary paints old houses for fun? Or are they merely pieces of furniture for him, parts of the landscape, conveniences bought for him by the grateful network, like the cameras and the car?*

Leo came walking out of the house as the long white car pulled away. "Another week gone," he said.

"Jake stuck Zenan in the crew trailer," Christy said.

Leo wiped a big hand across his eyes, and shrugged. "I don't want to deal with it," he said. "I think I'll just go home. It's Friday. Want to walk to the subway?"

"I'd love to!"

"Good. Let me tell Gus to go without us." He strolled down the uneven sidewalk to where the crew trailer was parked, and leaned his head in to talk to the driver. The engine was idling softly, like a patted drum, as Gus played with it. Gus was nineteen, born thirty years too late, he said. His Golden Age was the world of the sixties and early seventies, before the banning of private cars from cities all over the world, when the motor was king, and all you needed was three dollars for a license to drive a car. His childhood memories were an improbable nostalgia of freeways and shiny beetle-like cars with names like Pinto and Jaguar and Matador. He even owned a monster old car ("we were born the same year") and raced it, for pleasure, along the old Lake Shore Drive. The club he belonged to paid terrific sums to keep the unused roadway in repair. Right now its current project was to convince a skeptical city government to let them use Wrigley Field for something called a Demolition Derby. In it you smashed cars against each other until they all broke down.

"All right," said Leo. "Come on."

They walked down Kedzie Street to Lake and turned east. The sun was hot; Chris felt her shirt starting to stick to her back. She hummed. The show was behind her now, and with all her will she would forget it; today was Friday, and she was going home, home to two days with Paul. Leo's head was down, as if he were counting the cracks in the broken concrete. She could just see his face. He looked tired and bothered. *I wouldn't want his job,* she thought, *not for all the world.* Maybe he was worried about Zenan. *We've been friends for a long time. Maybe he'll talk to me.*

He surprised her. "Do you ever think about Dacca?"

I never forget it, she thought.

Once, she had tried to tell Paul about it, what it had been like for her, for them all, that summer in Bangladesh. For him it was barely remembered history; he had been fourteen. He stopped her, after five minutes, because of what it did to her eyes and mouth and hands. *But Leo remembers it just the way I do.* Scenes unreeled at the back of her mind. Babies, crawling over one another on slimy floors, dying as they crawled, and bodies like skeletons with grotesque distended bellies, piled along dirt roads, the skitter of rats in the gutters like the drift of falling leaves, and flies numerous as grains of rice—and no rice. No food. The Famine Year: it had killed fifty million people in Bangladesh. And she and Leo had met there, on the network news team in Dacca. "I remember it. I dream about it sometimes."

He nodded. "Me, too. Thirteen years, and I still have nightmares. The gods like irony, Christy. When I came home, all I wanted to do was to get the smell of death from my nostrils. I *asked* for daytime TV, to work on soap operas and childrens' shows and giveaways. And here I am working for Jordan Granelli. Mr. Death."

"You too?"

"I sound like Zenan. I know why he drinks. We are the modern equivalent of a Roman circus. Under the poetry and Granelli's decorum, the audience can smell the blood—and they

17

love it. It titillates them, being so close to it, and safe. Death is something that happens to other people. And when it happens—call an ambulance! Call a hospital! Tell the family, gently. And be sure to bring the camera close, so we can watch. And don't, don't even try to *help*. You'll spoil the scene—and we all have to go." He mimicked Jordan Granelli with a bitter smile.

"I have Paul," Christy said. "What do you do, Leo?"

"I take long walks," Leo said. "I read a lot of history. I try to figure out how long it will take for us to run ourselves into the ground—like Babylon, and Tyre, and Nineveh, and Rome."

"Are we close?"

He shrugged. "I own a very unreliable crystal ball."

They had reached the subway line; Christy could feel beneath her feet the secret march of trains. "I'll take the subway here, Leo," she said. "See you Monday."

"I shall take a long walk and contemplate the city. See you Monday."

As she went down the stairs to the subway, Christy looked with curiosity at the people around her. Was there really such a thing as a mass mind? The faces bobbing by her—some were content, some discontent, thin, fat, calm or harried, bored or excited—what would they do, each of them, if she were to collapse at their feet? Observe, in an interested circle? Ignore it? *Call the police or an ambulance, maybe—the professionals who know how to deal with death. Death is something that happens to other people. All we, the survivors, need to do is to mourn.*

Damn it, I don't want to think about it! She interposed Paul between her mind and the faces, and it quickened her breathing—two days! Two days with Paul. *Fool woman! Grown woman of thirty-four, no adolescent, so suffused with plain physical passion that people waiting near you are staring at you!* She raised her chin to meet their eyes. Under her shirt her nipples were stiff. *I wonder if Paul ever thinks of me, and gets a hard-on riding home from work.* The thought delighted her.

She quivered like an antenna to the presence of the people around her, and to the city. She was riding on the city's main subway line. It ran from south to north under the city, passing beneath its vital parts—city hall, business district, the towering apartment complexes of the rich, the university—like a notochord. East of it lay Lake Michigan, with its algae and seaweed beds, like green islands, set in a blue sea. West of it the bulk of the city sprawled, primitive and indolent in the summer heat, a lolling dinosaur.

And Paul was out there, high in the smoggy sky, a mite on the dinosaur's back. She had first seen him through a camera's eye. She'd been shooting a documentary on new city buildings, six years back. He had been walking the beams of a building sixty stories up, dark against the sun, his hair blazing gold, his hooks swinging on his belt. She had asked one of the soundmen, "What are those hooks they carry?"

"Those are the skyhooks. They're protection. See the network of cables on the frame?" Through the camera she could see it, like a spiderweb in the sun. "If a worker up there falls, he can use those hooks to catch the cables and save himself. Experienced workers use the cables to get around. They swing on them, like monkeys, hand over hand. The hooks don't slip, and the cables are rough, so they fit together like two gears, meshing." He made a gear with the interlocking fingers of his two hands.

"But I thought the name for the *people* was skyhooks," she said.

"It is."

Human beings, she thought, *with hooks to hold down the sky . . .*

She opened the door to the apartment. Paul was sitting in a chair, waiting for her.

He jumped up and came to her across the room, fitting his hands against her backbone and his lips to hers with the precision of anticipation. His lips were salt-rimmed from a morning's sweating in the sun. She leaned into him. At last she tugged on his ears to free her mouth. "Nice that you're home. How come?"

"Monday's Labor Day. Dale gave us the afternoon off. Said to get an early start on drinking, so we'd all get to work Tuesday sober."

"That was smart of her." Dale was the crew boss on the building.

"So we have three and a half days."

"No," she said sadly, "only two and a half."

"Why?" he demanded sharply, pulling away from her as if it were her fault.

19

"The show doesn't stop for Labor Day. Think of all those lucky folks who could be home to watch it! Makes more money. Christmas, New Years, yes. Labor Day, no."

He grunted and came back to her arms abruptly. "Then let's go to bed now."

They went to bed, diving for the big double bed and turning to each other with the hunger of new lovers. They rode each other's bodies until they lost even each other's names, calling in whispers and groans and laughter, and ending half-asleep in each other's arms, soaked and surfeited with loving.

Christy woke from the drowse first. Paul's head lay against her breasts. She tongued his forehead gently. He stirred. The camera eye in her came alive: she saw him curled like a great baby against her, looking even younger than his twenty-seven years, chunky and strong and satiated, his skin dark red-bronze where the sun had darkened it, fairer elsewhere, his hair red-gold . . . *How brown I am against him*, she thought. A thin beard rose rough on his cheeks and chin, his chest was hairless and well-muscled, his hands work-callused . . . He opened his eyes. *He has blue eyes,* she completed, and bent to kiss his eyelids.

"What do you see?" he asked her.

"I see my love," she answered. "What do *you* see?"

"I see *my* love."

"Thin brown woman."

"Beautiful woman."

It was an old dialogue between them, six years old. It amazed Christy that, in their transient world, they had survived six years together. *I love you,* she thought at him.

Suddenly, as if someone had spliced it into her mind, she heard Zenan, drunk and sardonic. "If Jordan Granelli had a lover," he said, "and that lover collapsed in front of him, dying, he'd first call the ambulance, and then call the cameras."

What the hell? Angry, she thrust Zenan, the show, Granelli, from her mind, and like a shadow on a wall they crept back at her. "What is it?" Paul said.

"Ah. Come with me to work Monday," she said suddenly.

"Why?"

"So that I can see you sooner." *So I can hold you in front of the shadows,* she thought, *like a bright and burnished shield.* "Please."

Sunday night, the shadows turned to nightmare black.

She was in Dacca, standing in front of a wretched yellow brick tenement. It was falling apart; there were even gaping holes in the shoddy walls, and it stank. The dust stung Christy's eyes. She looked around for a landmark, but all she could see clearly was this one building; the dust clouds obscured the rest. *I want to go back to the hotel,* she thought, but, impelled, she went towards it. *I don't want to go in.*

Close to the entrance something moved. Dog pack? She looked around in haste for a brick or a stone to pitch. But the dust drew aside for a moment and she saw: it was a woman, bending or crouching, close to the open door.

Her thin flowing robes were mud-stained, and she hunched like a flightless withered bird on the ground, holding something protectively to her breasts. The whites of her eyes were as yellow as the building. Jaundice. She stared at Christy and then turned her head away, making a crooning wail. A fold of cloth fell away from her, and Christy saw that she was holding a baby. With terrible feeble movements of its lips it tried to suck, and then it cried, a whimper of sound. The woman's breast was a dun-colored rag. *She has no milk,* Christy thought. The mother wailed again, and looked at Christy with huge imploring eyes.

I must have something. Christy reached for the little pack she carried at her hip. She pulled out a small can of goat's milk with triumph, and pried it open with her knife. Hunkering down beside the woman, she held out the can. "Here."

The woman sniffed at the milk. Then she took the can from Christy's hand and tipped it towards the child's mouth. The infant coughed, and the milk ran out, down its cheek and neck. The woman tried again. Again the baby coughed, a minute weak sound like a hiccough, and gave a gasp, and was still. The woman peered at it and let out a moan. "What is it?" Christy said, and then she saw that the child was dead. It had died as they tried to feed it. She touched its forehead with one finger and pulled her hand away quickly from the ferocious heat.

She started to cry, and with tears on her face, she stood up and stumbled away from the mother and the dead baby. She turned away from the building, and not three feet away from her, directly in her path, stood Jordan Granelli. He was carrying a tripod and a camera, and his face was the face of a skull. It grinned at her, and his hand patted the camera. "Thank you, Ms. Holland," he said.

21

When Paul woke her, she was making small crying sounds in her sleep. He rocked her and stroked her. "A Dacca dream?"

"Yes—no. Come with me tomorrow, Paul, please!"

"I'll come," he promised.

"Love me. I need you to love me." In the dark morning they made love, like two armies battling for a hilltop, intent on the same desire; sighted, grasped for, won.

They woke late that morning. It was hard to dress: they kept running into one another in the way to the bathroom. Paul shaved, standing naked in front of the mirror. When he pulled on his pants, he stuck his skyhook sheaths on his belt, like a badge of office, and thrust the hooks into them.

Christy glared at him. "You're coming with me."

"I said so. But I want to make damn sure that nobody asks me to do anything. I won't look like a cameraman in these."

That's for sure, Christy thought. He looked like an extra from a set. She suspected, with envy, that he was going to visit his building, later, just for the fun of swinging around it. *I wish I could love my job like that.*

They arrived late to the studio. The equipment van, which carried the cameras and the lights, the cable wheels and the trailing sound booms, was parked outside on the roadway, its red lights flashing. The trailer sat behind it. Christy and Paul stepped up into it. "Sorry we're late," she said to Leo.

"Hello, Paul."

"Hello."

"Okay, Gus. Let's go."

Gus played race car driver all the way to the South Side, flinging them happily against the sides of the crew van like peas in a can. "Christ," muttered Zenan, "it's a good thing I didn't eat my breakfast."

"Why don't you let Gus drive the equipment van tomorrow?" Christy asked Leo plaintively.

"Because he'd break all the lenses doing it," Leo said.

Zenan added, "Us he can break."

They stopped at last. Jordan Granelli's limousine was parked up the street. He was standing outside it, with his three guards around him, waiting for them. "Next time," Leo suggested gently, "maybe you could go a little slower? Even if we are late. Tom doesn't seem to know Chicago as well as you do, even though he's forty-seven and has lived here all his life."

Gus mumbled and bent over his steering wheel as if it were a prayer wheel. Jake walked across the street to them. "Mr. Granelli's getting impatient," he said. Leo shrugged. Jake looked at them uncertainly. He eyed Paul.

Christy said, "Jake, this is Paul; he's a friend of mine," Christy said. "Paul, this is Jake. He's one of Jordan Granelli's bodyguards."

They nodded at each other. "Skyhook," Jake said. "So was I."

Paul was interested. "Were you? Where'd you work?"

"Lot of buildings. I worked on the Daley Towers."

"Did you! I didn't," Paul said with regret. That massive building, Chicago's monument to its most famous mayor, was still the tallest in the city, though it was six years old.

"Last year I was working on the new City Trust building when a swinging beam hit me—so." He made a horizontal cut with the edge of his hand against his right side. "Knocked me off. I hooked the cable—but it had cracked some ribs, and my back's been bad ever since. I had to quit."

"Tough luck," said Paul sympathetically.

They waited. "Which house is it?" Christy asked. Leo pointed to a white frame house across the street. Christy saw the flutter of curtains in the house next door. A woman with a baby on her hip was standing at her window, staring out at the black van, and at the white car with its black device.

She shivered suddenly. Paul put an arm around her shoulders. "Cold?"

"No—I don't know," she answered, irritated.

"Goose walking on your grave," commented Jake.

The equipment van came screeching around the corner then. Tom pulled it up past them, and backed with a roar of his engines. "Cars," Zenan muttered. "Oh, watch it!" Paul caught Christy's arm. The doors of the van, jarred by the forceful jerky halt, came flying open, and something black came careening swiftly out.

For Christy the events resolved suddenly to a series of stills. She sprawled where a thrust of Paul's arm had put her. The cable wheel bounded high in the air as it hit a projection in the ill-paved road. The thick cable unwound like a whip cracking. Paul seemed to leap to meet it. She heard the sound as it struck him, saw him fall—and saw the wheel roll past him, stringing cable out behind it, to hit the curb, where it shattered and sat.

Cable uncoiled like a snake around the jigsaw wreckage of wood.

She stood up slowly. Her palms and arms and knees and chin hurt, and the taste of gravel stung her lips. She walked to Paul. It took her a long time to reach him, and when she did her knees gave out suddenly, so that she sat thudding to the ground.

The cable had lashed him down; there was a black and purple bruise across his right cheek. His eyes were open, but he looked up at the sky without seeing it. She interposed her face between his eyes and the sky. Nothing changed. In one hand his fingers were clenching a skyhook. *He tried to hook the cable,* she thought. She touched his hand. The fingers lolled loose. The hook rolled free with a clatter. She reached for it, and used it like a cane, prying herself up off the street.

Leo came round in front of her, hiding Paul from her. He took hold of her shoulders. "Come away, Chris," he said. "We've called the ambulance."

"He doesn't need one," she said. "And I don't either." They circled her: Leo, Zenan, Jake, Gus.

"Christy," said another voice, a stranger's. The circle broke apart. Jordan Granelli stood in front of her, his fine hands extended to her. "Christy, I'm so sorry."

"Yes," she said.

He stepped up to her and took her hand. "Don't be afraid to mourn for him, child," he said. "I know what grief is. We all do. Chance takes us all, and she gives nothing back. There's no way to make the weight any lighter. We feel for you." He stepped back, spreading his arms in supplication and sympathy. Christy felt the first tears thicken in her eyes. She stared at him through their distorting film.

Behind him, in macabre mime, Zenan cranked an ancient imaginary camera. From a distance came the high keening of the ambulance.

Granelli turned his back on her as one of the sound men approached him. The man asked him something, pointing at the loose cable. She heard his answer clearly. "Of course we'll shoot! Get someone to help you move that thing back. And wipe it clean, first." Leo turned, his face whitened with anger. Jake looked shocked.

"Mr. Granelli," Christy whispered, to herself, to Paul. "Mr. Death, who always happens to other people." She walked towards him. The metal skyhook was cold and hard and heavy in her palm. She swung it: back, forth, back, forth—and up.

At the last minute Jake saw her, but Zenan was in his way. Jordan Granelli turned around, and screamed.

They reached her by the third blow—too late.

NORMAN SPINRAD

The National Pastime

The Founding Father

I know you've got to start at the bottom in the television
business, but producing sports shows is my idea of cruel and unusual punishment. Sometime in the dim past, I had the idea
that I wanted to make films, and the way to get to make films
seemed to be to run up enough producing and directing credits
on television, and the way to do *that* was to take whatever
came along, and what came along was an offer to do a series
of sports specials on things like kendo, sumo wrestling, jousting,
Thai boxing: in short, ritual violence. This was at the height (or

the depth) of the antiviolence hysteria, when you couldn't so much as show the bad guy getting an on-camera rap in the mouth from the good guy on a moron western. The only way you could give the folks what they really wanted was in the All-American wholesome package of a sporting event. Knowing this up front—unlike the jerks who warm chairs as network executives—I had no trouble producing the kind of sports specials the network executives knew people wanted to see without quite knowing why, and thus I achieved the status of boy genius. Which, alas, ended up in my being offered a long-term contract as a producer in the sports department that was simply too rich for me to pass up, I mean I made no bones about being a crass materialist.

So try to imagine my feelings when Herb Dieter, the network sports programming director, calls me in to his inner sanctum and gives me The Word. "Ed," he tells me, "as you know, there's now only one major football league, and the opposition has us frozen out of the picture with long-term contracts with the NFL. As you also know, the major league football games are clobbering us in the Sunday afternoon ratings, which is prime time as far as sports programming is concerned. And as you know, a sports programming director who can't hold a decent piece of the Sunday afternoon audience is not long for this fancy office. And as you know, there is no sport on God's green earth that can compete with major league football. Therefore, it would appear that I have been presented with an insoluble problem.

"Therefore, since you are the official boy genius of the sports department, Ed, I've decided that you must be the solution to my problem. If I don't come up with something that will hold its own against pro football by the beginning of next season, my head will roll. Therefore, I've decided to give you the ball and let you run with it. Within ninety days, you will have come up with a solution or the fine print boys will be instructed to find a way for me to break your contract."

I found it very hard to care one way or the other. On the one hand, I liked the bread I was knocking down, but on the other, the job was a real drag and it would probably do me good to get my ass fired. Of course the whole thing was unfair from my point of view, but who could fault Dieter's logic; he personally had nothing to lose by ordering his best creative talent to produce a miracle or be fired. Unless I came through, *he* would be fired, and then what would he care about gutting the sports department, it wouldn't be his baby anymore. It wasn't very nice, but it was the name of the game we were playing.

"You mean all I'm supposed to do is invent a better sport than football in ninety days, Herb, or do you mean something more impossible?" I couldn't decide whether I was trying to be funny or not.

But Dieter suddenly had a 20-watt bulb come on behind his eyes (about as bright as he could get). "I do believe you've hit on it already, Ed," he said. "We can't get any pro football, so you're right, you've got to *invent* a sport that will outdraw pro football. Ninety days, Ed. And don't take it too hard; if you bomb out, we'll see each other at the unemployment office.

So there I was, wherever *that* was. I could easily get Dieter to do for me what I didn't have the willpower to do for myself and get me out of the stinking sports department—all I had to do was *not* invent a game that would outdraw pro football. On the other hand, I liked living the way I did, and I didn't like the idea of losing *anything* because of failure.

So the next Sunday afternoon, I eased out the night before's chick, turned on the football game, smoked two joints of Acapulco Gold and consulted my muse. It was the ideal set of conditions for a creative mood: I was being challenged, but if I failed, I gained too, so I had no inhibitions on my creativity. I was stoned to the point where the whole situation was a game without serious consequences; I was hanging loose.

Watching two football teams pushing each other back and forth across my color television screen, it once again occurred to me how much football was a ritual sublimation of war. This seemed perfectly healthy. Lots of cultures are addicted to sports that are sublimations of the natural human urge to clobber people. Better the sublimation than the clobbering. People dig violence, whether anyone likes the truth or not, so it's a public service to keep it on the level of a spectator sport.

Hmmm . . . that was probably why pro football had replaced baseball as the National Pastime in a time when people, having had their noses well rubbed in the stupidity of war, needed a war substitute. How could you beat something that got the American armpit as close to the gut as that?

And then from the blue grass mountaintops of Mexico, the flash hit me: the only way to beat football was at its own game! Start with football itself, and convert it into something that was an even *closer* metaphor for war, something that could be called—

!!COMBAT FOOTBALL!!

Yeah, yeah, Combat Football, or better, COMBAT football. Two standard football teams, standard football field, standard football rules, except:

Take off all their pads and helmets and jerseys and make it a warm-weather game that they play in shorts and sneakers like boxing. More meaningful, more intimate violence. Violence is what sells football, so give 'em a bit more violence than football, and you'll draw a bit more than football. The more violent you can make it and get away with it, the better you'll draw.

Yeah . . . and you could get away with punching, after all boxers belt each other around and they still allow boxing on television; sports have too much All American Clean for the anti-violence freaks to attack, in fact, where their heads are at, they'd *dig* Combat Football. Okay. So in ordinary football, the defensive team tackles the ball carrier to bring him to his knees and stop the play. So in Combat, the defenders can slug the ball carrier, kick him, tackle him, why not, anything to bring him to his knees and stop the play. And to make things fair, the ball carrier can slug the defenders to get them out of his way. If the defense slugs an offensive player who doesn't have possession, it's ten yards and an automatic first down. If anyone but the ball carrier slugs a defender, it's ten yards and a loss of down.

Presto: Combat Football!

And the final touch was that it was a game that any beer-sodden moron who watched football could learn to understand in sixty seconds, and any lout who dug football would have to like Combat better.

The boy genius had done it again! It even made sense after I came down.

Farewell to the Giants

Jeez, I saw a thing on television last Sunday you wouldn't believe. You really oughta watch it next week, I don't care who the Jets or the Giants are playing. I turned on the TV to watch the Giants game and went to get a beer, and when I came back from the kitchen I had some guy yelling something about today's professional combat football game, and it's not the NFL announcer, and it's a team called the New York Sharks playing a team called the Chicago Thunderbolts, and they're playing in L.A. or Miami, I didn't catch which, but someplace with palm trees anyway, and all the players are bare-ass! Well, not really bare-ass, but all they've got on is sneakers and boxing shorts with numbers across the behind—blue for New York, green for Chicago. No helmets, no pads, no protectors, no jerseys, no nothing!

I check the set and sure enough I've got the wrong channel. But I figured I could turn on the Giants game anytime, what the hell, you can see the Giants all the time, but what in hell is *this?*

New York kicks off to Chicago. The Chicago kick-runner gets the ball on about the 10—bad kick—and starts upfield. The first New York tackler reaches him and goes for him and the Chicago player just belts him in the mouth and runs by him! I mean, with the ref standing there watching it, and no flag thrown! Two more tacklers come at him on the 20. One dives at his legs, the other socks him in the gut. He trips and staggers out of the tackle, shoves another tackler away with a punch in the chest, but he's slowed up enough so that three or four New York players get to him at once. A couple of them grab his legs to stop his motion, and the others knock him down, at about the 25. Man, what's going on here?

I check my watch. By this time the Giants game has probably started, but New York and Chicago are lined up for the snap on the 25, so I figure what the hell, I gotta see some more of this thing, so at least I'll watch one series of downs.

On first down, the Chicago quarterback drops back and throws a long one way downfield to his flanker on maybe the New York 45; it looks good, there's only one player on the Chicago flanker, he beats this one man and catches it, and it's a touchdown, and the pass looks right on the button. Up goes the Chicago flanker, the ball touches his hands—and pow, right in the kisser! The New York defender belts him in the mouth and he drops the pass. Jeez, what a game!

Second and ten. The Chicago quarterback fades back, but it's a fake, he hands off to his fullback, a gorilla who looks like he weighs about two-fifty, and the Chicago line opens up a little hole at left tackle and the fullback hits it holding the ball with one hand and punching with the other. He belts out a tackler,

31

takes a couple of shots in the gut, slugs a second tackler, and then someone has him around the ankles; he drags himself forward another half yard or so, and then he runs into a good solid punch and he's down on the 28 for a three-yard gain.

Man, I mean *action!* What a game! Makes the NFL football look like something for faggots! Third and seven, you gotta figure Chicago for the pass, right? Well on the snap, the Chicago quarterback just backs up a few steps and pitches a short one to his flanker at about the line of scrimmage. The blitz is on and everyone comes rushing in on the quarterback and before New York knows what's happening, the Chicago flanker is five yards downfield along the left sideline and picking up speed. Two New York tacklers angle out to stop him at maybe the Chicago 40, but he's got up momentum and one of the New York defenders runs right into his fist—I could hear the thud even on television—and falls back right into the other New York player, and the Chicago flanker is by them, the 40, the 45, he angles back toward the center of the field at midfield, dancing away from one more tackle, then on maybe the New York 45 a real fast New York defensive back catches up to him from behind, tackles him waist-high, and the Chicago flanker's motion is stopped as two more tacklers come at him. But he squirms around inside the tackle and belts the tackler in the mouth with his free hand, knocks the New York back silly, breaks the tackle, and he's off again downfield with two guys chasing him— 40, 35, 30, 25, he's running away from them. Then from way over the right side of the field, I see the New York safety man running flat out across the field at the ball carrier, angling toward him so it looks like they'll crash like a couple of locomotives on about the 15, because the Chicago runner just doesn't see this guy. Ka-boom! The ball carrier running flat out runs right into the fist of the flat out safety at the 15 and he's knocked about ten feet one way and the football flies ten feet the other way, and the New York safety scoops it up on the 13 and starts upfield, 20, 25, 30, 35, and then slam, bang, whang, half the Chicago team is all over him, a couple of tackles, a few in the gut, a shot in the head, and he's down. First and ten for New York on their own 37. And that's just the first series of downs!

Well let me tell you, after that you know where they can stick the Giants game, right? This Combat Football, that's the real way to play the game, I mean it's football and boxing all together, with a little wrestling thrown in, it's a game with *balls.* I mean, the *whole* game was like the first series. You oughta take a look at it next week. Damn, if they played the thing in New York we could even go out to the game together. I'd sure be willing to spend a couple of bucks to see something like that.

Commissioner Gene Kuhn Addresses the First Annual Owners' Meeting of the National Combat Football League

Gentlemen, I've been thinking about the future of our great sport. We're facing a double challenge to the future of Combat football, boys. First of all, the NFL is going over to Combat rules next season, and since you can't copyright a sport (and if you could the NFL would have us by the short hairs anyway) there's not a legal thing we can do about it. The only edge we'll have left is that they'll have to at least wear heavy uniforms because they play in regular cities up north. But they'll have the stars, and the stadiums, and the regular home town fans and fatter television deals.

Which brings me to our second problem, gentlemen, namely that the television network which created our great game is getting to be a pain in our sport's neck, meaning that they're shafting us in the crummy percentage of the television revenue they see fit to grant us.

So the great task facing our great National Pastime, boys, is to ace out the network by putting ourselves in a better bargaining position on the television rights while saving our million-dollar asses from the NFL competition, which we just cannot afford.

Fortunately, it just so happens your commissioner has been on the ball, and I've come up with a couple of new gimmicks that I am confident will insure the posterity and financial success of our great game while stiff-arming the NFL and the TV network nicely in the process.

Number one, we've got to improve our standing as a live spectator sport. We've got to start drawing big crowds on our own if we want some clout in negotiating with the network. Number two, we've got to give the customers something the NFL can't just copy from us next year and clobber us with.

There's no point in changing the rules again because the NFL can always keep up with us there. But one thing the NFL is locked into for keeps is the whole concept of having teams represent cities; they're committed to that for the next twenty years. We've only been in business four years and our teams never play in the damned cities they're named after because it's too cold to play bare-ass Combat in those cities during the football season, so it doesn't have to mean anything to us.

So we make two big moves. First, we change our season to spring and summer so we can play up north where the money is. Second, we throw out the whole dumb idea of teams representing cities; that's old-fashioned stuff. That's crap for the coyotes. Why not six teams with *national* followings? Imagine the clout that'll give us when we renegotiate the TV contract. We can have a flexible schedule so that we can put any game we want into any city in the country any time we think that city's hot and draw a capacity crowd in the biggest stadium in town.

How are we gonna do all this? Well look boys, we've got a six-team league, so instead of six cities, why not match up our teams with six national groups?

I've taken the time to draw up a hypothetical league lineup just to give you an example of the kind of thing I mean. Six teams: the Black Panthers, the Golden Supermen, the Psychedelic Stompers, the Caballeros, the Gay Bladers and the Hog Choppers. We do it all up the way they used to do with wrestling, you know, the Black Panthers are all spades with naturals, the Golden Supermen are blond astronaut types in red-white-and-blue bunting, the Psychedelic Stompers have long hair and groupies in miniskirts up to their navels and take rock bands to their games, the Caballeros dress like gauchos or something, whatever makes Latin types feel feisty, the Gay Bladers and Hog Choppers are mostly all-purpose villains—the Bladers are black-leather-and-chainmail faggots and the Hog Choppers we recruit from outlaw motorcycle gangs.

Now is that a *league,* gentlemen? Identification is the thing, boys. You gotta identify your teams with a large enough group of people to draw crowds, but why tie yourself to something local like a city? This way, we got a team for the spades, a team for the frustrated Middle Americans, a team for the hippies and kids, a team for the spics, a team for the faggots, and a team for the motorcycle nuts and violence freaks. And any American who can't identify with any of those teams is an odds-on bet to hate one or more of them enough to come out to the game to see them stomped. I mean, who wouldn't want to see the Hog Choppers and the Panthers go at each other under Combat rules?

Gentlemen, I tell you it's creative thinking like this that made our country great, and it's creative thinking like this that will make Combat football the greatest goldmine in professional sports.

Stay Tuned, Sportsfans. . . .

Good afternoon, Combat fans, and welcome to today's major league Combat football game between the Caballeros and the Psychedelic Stompers brought to you by the World Safety Razor-blade Company, with the sharpest, strongest blade for your razor in the world.

It's 95 degrees on this clear New York day in July, and a beautiful day for a Combat football game, and the game here today promises to be a real smasher, as the Caballeros, only a game behind the league-leading Black Panthers take on the fast-rising, hard-punching Psychedelic Stompers and perhaps the best running back in the game today, Wolfman Ted. We've got a packed house here today, and the Stompers, who won the toss, are about to receive the kickoff from the Caballeros. . .

And there it is, a low bullet into the end zone, taken there by Wolfman Ted. The Wolfman crosses the goal line, he's up to the 5, the 10, the 14, he brings down number 71 Pete Lopez with a right to the windpipe, crosses the 15, takes a glancing blow to the head from number 56 Diaz, is tackled on the 18 by Porfirio Rubio, number 94, knocks Rubio away with two quick rights to the head, crosses the 20, and takes two rapid blows to the midsection in succession from Beltran and number 30 Orduna, staggers and is tackled low from behind by the quick-recovering Rubio and slammed to the ground under a pile of Caballeros on the 24.

First and ten for the Stompers on their own 24. Stompers quarterback Ronny Seede brings his team to the line of scrim-mage in a double flanker formation with Wolfman Ted wide to the right. A long count—

The snap, Seede fades back to—

A quick hand-off to the Wolfman charging diagonally across the action toward left tackle, and the Wolfman hits the line on a dead run, windmilling his right fist, belting his way through

one, two, three Caballeros, getting two, three yards, then taking
three quick ones to the ribcage from Rubio, and staggering right
into number 41 Manuel Cardozo, who brings him down on about
the 27 with a hard right cross.

Hold it! A flag on the play! Orduna number 30 of the Caballeros and Dickson number 83 of the Stompers are wailing away
at each other on the 26! Dickson takes two hard ones and goes
down, but as Orduna kicks him in the ribs, number 72, Merling
of the Stompers, grabs him from behind and now there are six
or seven assistant referees breaking it up. . .

Something going on in the stands at about the 50 too—a
section of Stompers rooters mixing it up with the Caballero
fans—

But now they've got things sorted out on the field, and it's
10 yards against the Caballeros for striking an ineligible player,
nullified by a 10-yarder against the Stompers for illegal offensive
striking. So now it's second and seven for the Stompers on their
own 27—

It's quieted down a bit there about the 50-yard line, but
there's another little fracas going in the far end zone and a few
groups of people milling around in the aisles of the upper grandstand—

There's the snap, and Seede fades back quickly, dances
around, looks downfield, and throws one intended for number
54, Al Viper, the left end at about the 40. Viper goes up for
it, he's got it—

And takes a tremendous shot along the base of his neck from
number 18 Porfirio Rubio! The ball is jarred loose. Rubio dives
for it, he's got it, but he takes a hard right in the head from
Viper, then a left. Porfirio drops the ball and goes at Viper with
both fists! Viper knocks him sprawling and dives on top of the
ball, burying it and bringing a whistle from the head referee
as Rubio rains blows on his prone body. And here come the
assistant referees to pull Porfirio off as half the Stompers come
charging downfield toward the action—

They're at it again near the 50-yard line! About forty rows
of fans going at each other. There goes a smoke bomb!

They've got Rubio away from Viper now, but three or four
Stompers are trying to hold Wolfman Ted back and Ted has
blood in his eye as he yells at number 41, Cardozo. Two burly
assistant referees are holding Cardozo back. . .

There go about a hundred and fifty special police up into the midfield stands. They've got their mace and prods out. . . .

The head referee is calling an official's time out to get things organized, and we'll be back to live National Combat Football League action after this message. . .

The Circus Is in Town

"We've got a serious police problem with Combat football," Commissioner Minelli told me after the game between the Golden Supermen and the Psychedelic Stompers last Sunday in which the Supermen slaughtered the Stompers 42-14, and during which there were ten fatalities and 189 hospitalizations among the rabble in the stands.

"Every time there's a game, we have a riot, your honor," Minelli (who had risen through the ranks) said earnestly. "I recommend that you should think seriously about banning Combat football. I really think you should."

This city is hard enough to run without free advice from politically ambitious cops. "Minelli," I told him, "you are dead wrong on both counts. First of all, not only has there *never* been a riot in New York during a Combat football game, but the best studies show that the incidence of violent crimes and social violence diminishes from a period of three days before a Combat game clear through to a period five days afterward, not only here, but in every major city in which a game is played."

"But only this Sunday ten people were killed and nearly two hundred injured, including a dozen of my cops—"

"In the *stands,* you nitwit, not in the streets!" Really, the man was too much!

"I don't see the difference—"

"Ye gods, Minelli, can't you see that Combat football keeps a hell of a lot of violence off the streets? It keeps it in the stadium, where it belongs. The Romans understood that two thousand years ago! We can hardly stage gladiator sports in this day and age, so we have to settle for a civilized substitute."

"But what goes on in there is murder. My cops are taking a beating. And we've got to assign two thousand cops to every game. It's costing the taxpayers a fortune, and you can bet *someone* will be making an issue out of it in the next election."

I do believe that the lout was actually trying to pressure me.

Still, in his oafish way, he had put his finger on the one political disadvantage of Combat football: the cost of policing the games and keeping the fan clubs in the stands from tearing each other to pieces.

And then I had one of those little moments of blind inspiration when the pieces of a problem simply fall into shape as an obvious pattern of solution.

Why bother keeping them from tearing each other to pieces?

"I think I have the solution, Minelli," I said. "Would it satisfy your sudden sense of fiscal responsibility if you could take all but a couple dozen cops off the Combat football games?"

Minelli looked at me blankly. "Anything less than two thousand cops there would be mincemeat by half time," he said.

"So why send them in there?"

"Huh?"

"All we really need is enough cops to guard the gates, frisk the fans for weapons, seal up the stadium with the help of riot doors, and make sure no one gets out till things have simmered down inside."

"But they'd tear each other to ribbons in there with no cops!"

"So let them. I intend to modify the conditions under which the city licenses Combat football so that anyone who buys a ticket legally waives his right to police protection. Let them fight all they want. Let them really work out their hatreds on each other until they're good and exhausted. Human beings have an incurable urge to commit violence on each other. We try to sumblimate that urge out of existence, and we end up with irrational violence on the streets. The Romans had a better idea—give the rabble a socially harmless outlet for violence. We spend billions on welfare to keep things pacified with bread, and where has it gotten us? Isn't it about time we tried circuses?"

As American as Apple Pie

Let me tell it to you, brother, we've sure been waiting for the Golden Supermen to play the Panthers in *this* town again, after the way those blond mothers cheated us 17-10 the last time and wasted three hundred of the brothers! Yeah man, they had those stands packed with honkies trucked in from as far away as Buffalo—we just weren't ready, is why we took the loss.

But this time we planned ahead and got ourselves up for the

game even before it was announced. Yeah, instead of waiting for them to announce the date of the next Panther-Supermen game in Chicago and then scrambling with the honkies for tickets, the Panther Fan Club made under the table deals with ticket brokers for blocks of tickets for whenever the next game would be, so that by the time today's game was announced, we controlled two-thirds of the seats in Daley Stadium and the honkies had to scrape and scrounge for what was left.

Yeah man, today we pay them back for that last game! We got two-thirds of the seats in the stadium and Eli Wood is back in action and we gonna just go out and *stomp* those mothers today!

Really, I'm personally quite cynical about Combat; most of us who go out to the Gay Bladers games are. After all, if you look at it straight on, Combat football is rather a grotty business. I mean, look at the sort of people who turn out at Supermen or Panthers or for God's sake *Caballero* games: the worst sort of proletarian apes. Aside from us, only the Hogs have any semblance of class, and the Hogs have beauty only because they're so incredibly up-front gross, I mean all that shiny metal and black leather!

And of course that's the only real reason to go to the Blader games: for the spectacle. To see it and to be part of it! To see semi-naked groups of men engaging in violence and to be violent yourself—and especially with those black leather and chain mail Hog Lovers!

Of course I'm aware of the cynical use the loathsome government makes of Combat. If there's nastiness between the blacks and P.R.s in New York, they have the league schedule a Panther-Caballero game and let them get it out on each other safely in the stadium. If there's college campus trouble in the Bay Area, it's a Stomper-Supermen game in Oakland. And us and the Hogs when just *anyone* anywhere needs to release general hostility. I'm not stupid, I know that Combat football is a tool of the Establishment. . .

But lord, it's just so much bloody *fun!*

We gonna have some fun today! The Hogs is playing the Stompers and that's the wildest kind of Combat game there is! Those crazy freaks come to the game stoned out of their minds, and you know that at least Wolfman Ted is playing on something stronger than pot. There are twice as many chicks at Stomper games than with any other team the Hogs play because the Stomper chicks are the only chicks besides ours who aren't scared out of their boxes at the thought of being locked up in a stadium with twenty thousand hot-shot Hogger rape artists like us!

Yeah, we get good and stoned, and the Stomper fans get good and stoned, and the Hogs get stoned, and the Stompers get stoned, and then we all groove on beating the piss out of each other, *whoo*-whee! And when we win in the stands, we drag off the pussy and gang-bang it.

Oh yeah, Combat is just good clean dirty fun!

It makes you feel good to go out to a Supermen game, makes you feel like a real American is supposed to, like a man. All week you've got to take crap from the niggers and the spics and your goddamn crazy doped-up kids and hoods and bums and faggots in the streets, and you're not even supposed to think of them as niggers and spics and crazy doped-up kids and bums and hoods and faggots. But Sunday you can go out to the stadium and watch the Supermen give it to the Panthers, the Caballeros, the Stompers, the Hogs, or the Bladers and maybe kick the crap out of a few people whose faces you don't like yourself.

It's a good healthy way to spend a Sunday afternoon, out in the open air at a good game when the Supermen are hot and we've got the opposition in the stands outnumbered. Combat's a great thing to take your kid to, too!

I don't know, all my friends go to the Caballero games, we go together and take a couple of six packs of beer apiece, and get *muy boracho* and just have some crazy fun, you know? Sometimes I come home a little cut up and my wife is all upset and tries to get me to promise not to go to the Combat games anymore. Sometimes I promise, just to keep her quiet, she can get on my nerves, but I never really mean it.

Hombre, you know how it is, women don't understand these things like men do. A man has got to go out with his friends and feel like a man sometimes. It's not too easy to find ways to feel *muy macho* in this country, *amigo.* The way it is for us here, you know. It's not as if we're hurting anyone we shouldn't hurt.

Who goes out to the Caballero games but a lot of dirty gringos who want to pick on us? So it's a question of honor, in a way, for us to get as many *amigos* as we can out to the Caballero games and show those *cabrones* that we can beat them any time, no matter how drunk we are. In fact, the drunker we are, the better it is, "¿tu sabes?"

Baby, I don't know what it is, maybe it's just a chance to get it all out. It's a unique trip, that's all, there's no other way to get that particular high, that's why I go to Stompers games. Man, the games don't mean anything to me as games; games are like *games,* dig. But the whole Combat scene is its own reality.

You take some stuff—acid is a groovy high but you're liable to get wasted, lots of speed and some grass or hash is more recommended—when you go in, so that by the time the game starts you're really loaded. And then man, you just groove behind the violence. There aren't any cops to bring you down. What chicks are there are there because they dig it. The people you're enjoying beating up on are getting the same kicks beating up on you, so there's no guilt hang-up to get between you and the total experience of violence.

Like I say, it's a unique trip. A pure violence high without any hang-ups. It makes me feel good and purged and kind of together just to walk out of that stadium after a Combat football trip and know I survived; the danger is groovy too. Baby, if you can dig it, Combat can be a genuine mystical experience.

Hogs Win It All, 21-17, 1578(23)-989(14)!

Anaheim, October 8. It was a slam-bang finish to the National Combat Football League Pennant Race, the kind of game Combat fans dream about. The Golden Supermen and the Hog Choppers in a dead-even tie for first place playing each other in the last game of the season, winner take all, before nearly 60,000 fans. It was a beautiful sunny 90-degree Southern California day as the Hogs kicked off to the Supermen before a crowd that seemed evenly divided between Hog Lovers who had motorcycled in all week from all over California and Supermen Fans whose biggest bastion is here in Orange County.

The Supermen scored first blood midway through the first

period when quarterback Bill Johnson tossed a little screen pass to his right end, Seth West, on the Hog 23, and West slugged his way through five Hog tacklers, one of whom sustained a mild concussion, to go in for the touchdown. Rudolf's conversion made it 7-0, and the Supermen Fans in the stands responded to the action on the field by making a major sortie into the Hog Lover section at midfield, taking out about 20 Hog Lovers, including a fatality.

The Hog fans responded almost immediately by launching an offensive of their own in the bleacher seats, but didn't do much better than hold their own. The Hogs and the Supermen pushed each other up and down the field for the rest of the period without a score, while the Supermen Fans seemed to be getting the better of the Hog Lovers, especially in the midfield sections of the grandstand, where at least 120 Hog Lovers were put out of action.

The Supermen scored a field goal early in the second period to make the score 10-0, but more significantly, the Hog Lovers seemed to be dogging it, contenting themselves with driving back continual Supermen Fan sorties, while launching almost no attacks of their own.

The Hogs finally pushed in over the goal line in the final minutes of the first half on a long pass from quarterback Spike Horrible to his flanker Greasy Ed Lee to make the score 10-7 as the half ended. But things were not nearly as close as the field score looked, as the Hog Lovers in the stands were really taking their lumps from the Supermen Fans who had bruised them to the extent of nearly 500 take outs including 5 fatalities, as against only 300 casualties and 3 fatalities chalked up by the Hog fans.

During the half time intermission, the Hog Lovers could be seen marshaling themselves nervously, passing around beer, pot and pills, while the Supermen Fans confidently passed the time entertaining themselves with patriotic songs.

The Supermen scored again halfway through the third period, on a handoff from Johnson to his big fullback Tex McGhee on the Hog 41. McGhee slugged his way through the left side of the line with his patented windmill attack, and burst out into the Hog secondary swinging and kicking. There was no stopping the Texas Tornado, though half the Hog defense tried, and Mc-Ghee went 41 yards for the touchdown, leaving three Hogs unconscious and three more with minor injuries in his wake. The kick was good, and the Supermen seemed on their way to walking away with the championship, with the score 17-7, and the momentum, in the stands and on the field, going all their way.

But in the closing moments of the third period, Johnson threw a long one downfield intended for his left end, Dick Whitfield. Whitfield got his fingers on the football at the Hog 30, but Hardly Davidson, the Hog cornerback, was right on him, belted him in the head from behind as he touched the ball, and then managed to catch the football himself before either it or Whitfield had hit the ground. Davidson got back to midfield before three Supermen tacklers took him out of the rest of the game with a closed eye and a concussion.

All at once, as time ran out in the third period, the 10-point Supermen lead didn't seem so big at all as the Hogs advanced to a first down on the Supermen 35 and the Hog Lovers in the stands beat back Supermen Fan attacks on several fronts, inflicting very heavy losses.

Spike Horrible threw a five-yarder to Greasy Ed Lee on the first play of the final period, then a long one into the end zone intended for his left end, Kid Filth, which the Kid dropped as Gordon Jones and John Lawrence slugged him from both sides as soon as he became fair game.

It looked like a sure pass play on third and five, but Horrible surprised everyone by fading back into a draw and handing the ball off to Loser Ludowicki, his fullback, who plowed around right end like a heavy tank, simply crushing and smashing through tacklers with his body and fists, picked up two key blocks on the 20 and 17, knocked Don Barnfield onto the casualty list with a tremendous haymaker on the 7, and went in for the score.

The Hog Lovers in the stands went Hog-wild. Even before the successful conversion by Knuckleface Bonner made it 17-14, they began blitzing the Supermen Fans on all fronts, letting out everything they had seemed to be holding back during the first three quarters. At least 100 Supermen Fans were taken out in the next three minutes, including two quick fatalities, while the Hog Lovers lost no more than a score of their number.

As the Hog Lovers continued to punish the Supermen Fans, the Hogs kicked off to the Supermen, and stopped them after two first downs, getting the ball back on their own 24. After marching to the Supermen 31 on a sustained and bloody ground drive, the Hogs lost the ball again when Greasy Ed Lee was rabbit-punched into a fumble.

But the Hog fans still sensed the inevitable and pressed their attack during the next two Supermen series of downs, and began to push the Supermen Fans toward the bottom of the grandstand.

Buoyed by the success of their fans, the Hogs on the field recovered the ball on their own 29 with less than two minutes to play when Chain Mail Dixon belted Tex McGhee into a fumble and out of the game.

The Hogs crunched their way upfield yard by yard, punch by punch, against a suddenly shaky Supermen opposition, and all at once, the whole season came down to one play:

With the score 17-14 and 20 seconds left on the clock, time enough for one or possibly two more plays, the Hogs had the ball third and four on the 18-yard line of the Golden Supermen.

Spike Horrible took the snap as the Hog Lovers in the stands launched a final all-out offensive against the Supermen Fans, who by now had been pushed to a last stand against the grandstand railings at fieldside. Horrible took about ten quick steps back as if to pass, and then suddenly ran head down fist flailing at the center of the Supermen line with the football tucked under his arm.

Suddenly Greasy Ed Lee and Loser Ludowicki raced ahead of their quarterback, hitting the line and staggering the tacklers a split second before Horrible arrived, throwing them just off balance enough for Horrible to punch his way through with three quick rights, two of them k.o. punches. Virtually the entire Hog team roared through the hole after him, body-blocking, and elbowing, and crushing tacklers to the ground. Horrible punched out three more tacklers as the Hog Lovers pushed the first contingent of fleeing Supermen Fans out into the field, and went in for the game and championship-winning touchdown with two seconds left on the clock.

When the dust had cleared, not only had the Hog Choppers beaten the Golden Supermen 21-17, but the Hog Lovers had driven the Golden Supermen Fans from their favorite stadium, and had racked up a commanding advantage in the casualty statistics, 1,578 casualties and 23 fatalities inflicted, as against only 989 and 14.

It was a great day for the Hog Lovers and a great day in the history of our National Pastime.

The Voice of Sweet Reason

Go to a Combat football game? Really, do you think I want to risk being injured or possibly killed? Of course I realize that Combat is a practical social mechanism for preserving law and order, and to be frank, I find the spectacle rather stimulating. I watch Combat often, almost every Sunday.

On television, of course. After all, everyone who is anyone in this country knows very well that there are basically two kinds of people in the United States: people who go out to Combat games and people for whom Combat is strictly a television spectator sport.

RICHARD HILL

The Agent

The first week in November a gigantic saucer appeared overnight in People's Park. It was Wednesday morning, but everybody was on strike, so the crowd gathered quickly. They held meetings to decide who would greet the spacemen and to plan defensive moves to keep the military-industrial complex from making first contact. Obviously, it was argued, the aliens wished to contact the People; otherwise why would they have appeared here? But arguments broke out among various groups—Maoists, Trotskyites, Marcusists, Buckleyites, the three splinters of SDS, Black Panthers, Hell's Angels and others—all claiming to represent the People best.

The arguments became so violent that defenses were breached before anyone noticed and the saucer was surrounded by members of Berkeley's elite Paratroop Police Vice and Insurrection Squad. The People looked at the Parapolice flamethrowers and realized it was too late. Allen Ginsburg arrived and led them in chanting "Om" but nobody really felt good about it.

Inside an hour, every news medium in the country had it covered, from CBS to the *Oregonian Philatelist*. A State Department team was on its way, the Hot Line lit up and Japanese students demonstrated spontaneously, demanding their government give Okinawa to the saucer people.

Then Sam Grossmar gave the word.

Smoke gushed from beneath the saucer and otherworldly noises came from inside. Light panels began to flash beneath the aluminum foil. One Parapoliceman incinerated another in his haste to escape destruction of the aliens. The saucer slowly opened.

To reveal: ALIEN CORN! The band was already playing and an announcer's voice rose above their whoops and vibrations. "LADIES AND GENTLEMEN," the announcer said, as slowly the crowd realized they were not being invaded, "INTRODUCING ALIEN CORN AND THE AGE OF SPACE ROCK!" Then Alien Corn really began to wail and minds were blown from Berkeley to Benares.

It was Sam Grossmar's biggest coup and took the country completely by surprise. While in October hardly anyone had heard of Space Rock, by late November nobody talked of anything else. There had been a few hard core fans before then, in Oakland, at the Einstein Intersection where the Corn played. But nothing like this. Until Sam Grossmar.

Sam had seen Space Rock coming, as he had seen other movements. Or, more accurately, Sam had made it come. He had come by on a Thursday night, unannounced and unrecognized. The audience had been small and the Corn playing without their usual energy, but they had been enough for Sam Grossmar. He listened to Benny on drums, Ian on electric flute, Yarmolinsky on wind harp and moog synthesizer (the group's major expense which Benevolent Finance would have repossesed long ago had they known what to do with it) and Brendan, the group's lead vocalist and hydraulic ukulelist. Sam decided to make their fortune and offered to be their agent.

A week later Alien Corn appeared on Johnny Carson, Merv

Griffin, the Galloping Gourmet, Mike Douglas, and a Dr. Joyce Brothers Special. The week after that they made three movies (the four of them running, slow motion, down the Milky Way, Brendan in comic battle with a Martian Prune Man, Benny, the lovable dumb one, hanging from Saturn's ring—that sort of thing.) By early December, they recorded 13 albums which were all Gold Records by Christmas. They had a *Time* cover. They played London and met the Queen. They had it all.

They reacted differently to success. Benny, an eighth-grade drop-out, was content to buy the Jack London Oyster Palace, where he once had shucked, and to fire his old employers. That and a dayglo Honda, and he was happy. He put his fortune in the Hashbury National where it drew a meager five percent. He smiled at everyone.

Yarmolinsky, an unattractive lad who had been an involuntary virgin until the group's sudden success, gave himself over to pleasures of the flesh. He surrounded himself with groupies of every possible persuasion and complexion and seldom left his room at the Mark Hopkins except to perform. Caterers were astonished at the quantity and variety of things he ordered—carloads of grapes (union, of course), freezers full of chicken liver, cases of champagne, boxes of Tangerine Kool-Aid—the things he'd never had enough of before.

Ian was the creative one. In a language nobody could decipher, he wrote an opera which was performed at the Met. He also wrote a novel, using musical notation and an autobiography composed of photographs of fingernail clippings and sunburn peelings. People said he was a genius. People said he was on something stronger than STP, stronger than anything known on earth. He was given honorary degrees at Berkeley, Wayne State and Harvard.

Brendan underwent an existential crisis. He began to wander the streets in his performance costume—olive body paint and somebody's idea of Martian wings and antennae. He began to read science fiction and feel guilty about what he was doing. He toyed with various forms of the occult. He prophesied the discovery of Atlantis on Christmas, then disappeared in a black depression when Christmas came and Atlantis was not found. On New Year's Eve he turned up at the Essalen Institute, asking to be committed. People worried about Brendan. People said he was on something stronger than Ian was on. Timothy Leary wrote him a letter.

Everybody wanted something from Alien Corn. They hired bodyguards and even then found investment brokers on window ledges and reporters in closets. And they found Krim.

Krim had appeared one day in a new batch of Yarmolinsky's groupies, though how he got in nobody could guess. He was a misshapen imp of a man, with the most obvious toupee anyone had ever seen and a face that looked constructed of Silly Putty. His features were pulled permanently into an artificial grin.

Yarmolinsky called the guards as soon as he saw Krim, and the groupies gave little squeaks of confusion as the little man stepped forward. But before the guards could grab him, he began to talk. Yarmolinsky was so fascinated he waved the guards away.

"Your chicks make the groove," Krim said. His mouth seemed out of synch with his voice and Yarmolinsky could not believe what he was saying. "You gas it, babe."

"Wha?" said Yarmolinsky, trying to revive himself after weeks of dissipation.

"You're bossy," said Krim. "You mothers really split the scene and I dig to manage you. I'm the freakiest agent in the universe."

Now Yarmolinsky was laughing too hard to talk, and the groupies giggled with him. Every time he looked at Krim's grin, he burst out laughing again. Finally he was exhausted and reached for the phone. "Wait," he said to Krim. "The other guys have to see this." Krim waited and grinned.

The others were not easy to locate. Grossmar always got them to a gig on time, but otherwise they had come to see less and less of each other. But Yarmolinsky kept trying. He finally reached Benny at the Oyster Palace. One of the guards found Brendan giving away his money on Telegraph Hill and persuaded him to come. Ian, it turned out, was lecturing to the California Legislature, but would drop by later. Finally they were together.

"All right, King Farouk," said Brendan. "What's so damn important?" Benny smiled and Ian looked around as though anxious to be in the purer air of academe.

"Listen to this guy," said Yarmolinsky.

Krim stepped forward, grinning of course.

"You studs wig my skull and blow my cool," said Krim. "I want to manage you."

For a while nobody spoke. Then Yarmolinsky giggled. Soon they were all laughing. The groupies were laughing with them and Krim kept grinning.

"I'm a Freak City manager," he said, "and I'm going to make your scene."

"He's a goddamn narc," said Brendan with some impatience, and Ian nodded in agreement.

"If he is," said Benny, "he's the worst I've ever seen."

"Narc," said Kirm, in genuine puzzlement. "Narc out?"

Krim was convincing. They decided to keep him around for laughs. Nobody who talked like that could be dangerous. He couldn't manage them, they explained. They had a manager, Sam Grossmar. But they liked having him around.

Krim grinned unchangingly and stayed. "You'll dig my jive some day," he said.

Krim was great at parties. The groupies especially liked him, with his synthetic-looking face and his vocabulary like a linguist's jumbled note cards. Grossmar didn't like the idea until he met Krim and saw he was no threat. "The guy ain't in this world," he said.

Alien Corn's careers continued to climb into February, though there was hardly anywhere left for them to go. They had imitators now all over the world—Michael Valentine Smith and the Strangers, The Water Brothers, The Martian Chronicles, Childhood's End and others—but they were no threat to the originators of the form. Now and then one of them would come up with a new instrument, but Sam Grossmar would buy it and somebody in Alien Corn would learn to play it.

The commercial possibilities were overwhelming. They ran a line of boutiques, they endorsed toothpaste in their space costumes, they sold the rights to a cartoon series and a cereal called the Alien Cornies, they lost track of their corporate enterprises. Of course, Sam Grossmar didn't.

Some people worried that Space Rock was being watered down, that impure influences were creeping in. Some bands were already playing Soul-Space Rock, Space Acid, and other combinations. Even the Corn made an album imitating earlier groups. Some parents became worried and ministers denounced them. Brendan was in several scrapes with the law. But they were still on top in March and everyone was sure they'd stay there. Fan mags were calling them elder statesmen of pop music.

Then in early April, when some of the snow was melting in Central Park, a workman found a large mound that had not been there before. Crowds gathered. Groundskeepers began digging. Reporters came and soon the park was crowded and spilling into adjoining neighborhoods. Finally a workman broke through. And out of the hole came five of the strangest looking creatures New York had ever seen—three-eyed, lizard-scaled, playing rocks and blowing on long machete-like knives. The crowd shrank back and lenses zoomed in. An announcer's voice came from nowhere. "LADIES AND GENTLEMEN," he said, "THE MUTANTS!" And Post-Bomb Rock was born.

Sam Grossmar, it turned out, managed them.

Alien Corn couldn't believe it at first. Could Sam really have betrayed them like that at the height of their careers? Ian was the group's spokesman, but the secretary told them Mr. Grossman was out of town. He would get in touch with them.

Mr. Grossmar stayed out of town, with the Mutants. He never called them and they called him less and less. Yarmolinsky's last groupie disappeared three days after the Mutants' debut. They were alone, they and Krim.

The crisis had drawn them close again and they spent many nights together in Yarmolinsky's hotel room. They watched the Mutants on Ed Sullivan, Brendan afterward throwing a Gold Record through the screen. They commiserated. They waited. They still had money coming in but no careers. June went by, then July.

On the first of August Krim made his move.

"You hippies ready to cool it?"

"Come on, Krim," said Ian, "you're a funny cat, but you ain't no manager. We're washed up." The others nodded sadly.

"I can guarantee you work every night, at twice the cabbage you been making."

"How can a poor creep who calls bread cabbage guarantee anything?" said Brendan. "Lay off, Krim. Give us a break."

"If no other way, I'll pay you myself," said Krim, still with that permanent grin. He pulled out the largest roll of hundred-dollar bills any of them had ever seen.

They all sat up. "Christ, Krim," said Yarmolinsky, "where'd you get that?"

"Secret," Krim said. "Is it a deal, bosses?"

They were all nervous anyway and hysteria wasn't far. At Krim's remark Benny began to giggle, then Yarmolinsky, then Ian, then Brendan. Soon they were all laughing, eyes full of tears, stopping only to look at the smiling Krim and begin again. As they laughed, Krim went to the kitchen and came back with champagne.

"Let's cop a pot of sauce," he said.

Benny was rolling on the floor now and the others held their sides. Krim poured their champagne.

Somehow the mood lasted, even after the laughter stopped. They were, against overwhelming evidence to the contrary, optimistic again. Ian more sociable than he had been for months, left long enough to bring his own stuff to share. They shared it and still the mood lasted, only better. They looked at smiling Krim and somehow believed in him. "He's going to manage us," said Brendan with a kind of mystical conviction in his voice.

Then Krim also produced some stuff and everybody went under.

Benny was the first to awaken. He shook his head, then regretted it. "Where the hell am I?" He was not in the Mark Hopkins, he knew. Krim, seated in a strange metal chair, was facing him. Grinning.

"Got a hang up, Man?"

"Hangover," Benny corrected. "Damn right. What'd you give us? Where are we?"

Behind Krim was a panel with lots of dials and switches.

Ian began to groan and Benny, wanting the others awake, shook Yarmolinsky and Brendan. They came up slowly, not fast enough for Benny, who had been looking around some more. He had seen their instruments piled in a corner near a window, porthole, what the hell was it?

Krim handed Benny a pill, gave the others the same as they came awake. "Hangover pill," he said, correcting his earlier error. "Square you right up."

Brendan lurched to his feet.

"Where—"

"I don't *know*," whined Benny, who'd been awake longer and was more alarmed. He had been the first to see the metal walls and the porthole.

Brendan stumbled toward the porthole, the others following.

By the time they were there Brendan was white and speechless. They too looked out and saw stars.

"Sweet Jesus," Benny moaned and dropped to his knees.

"Momma," said Brendan softly.

The others said nothing.

"No sweat, heavies," said Krim, apparently worried about them and trying to make it easier. "You'll groove these bookings I got you. Fans who never jived a sound like yours before. I mean like you'll be a crash where I'm splitting you."

Krim was really upset now and talking faster. His linguistic programing broke down further as though the harder he tried to communicate the worse he did. His head jerked from one to another of them, his agitation increasing. The dime-store toupee went awry, revealing where the face mask stopped and his real head began. Ian hit a high note, the others filling in the chord a half beat behind him. They filled the ship with the sound of their fear, voices joined once again.

Krim tried to console them, continued to try to talk their language in the midst of their din.

"Listen, you mates," he said, then jerked the face mask away for greater freedom to speak. The Corn's performance grew even louder. "Don't rap so strong," Krim begged. "You're cutting the rug, fruggers. Gas it man, work it, baby. Please, daddyos . . . come *on,* hep cats . . . you're the cat's pajamas . . . twenty-three skiddoo . . ."

But he just wasn't getting through to them. "I promise," said Krim at top volume, with all the conviction his electronic brain could muster, "you cats will be freaks where I come from."

PG WYAL

The Hotsy-Totsy Machine

George the inventor took his wife Ethyl down into the basement and showed it to her.

"What is it?" she said.

"I call it a Hotsy-Totsy machine," George replied proudly.

"Oh. What does it do?"

He whispered in her ear.

"Too much," she said, flicking ashes off her cigarette. "What
are you going to do with it?"

He thought for a moment. "Well, I was thinking of trying it
out on you."

Ethyl looked at him with a smirk. "You're crazy."

"It won't hurt," he said defensively.

"I wasn't thinking about that," she muttered, staring at the
machine. It was a large crinkle-grey metal box with a heavy

hatch which had a seal-type lock—the kind with a wheel, like on submarines in old World War II movies. Inside was a stool.

"You get inside, sit down on the stool, and then the operator closes the door and pushes the button," George explained. "It's over in a few seconds."

"And you want me to get inside that thing, huh," said his wife. She inhaled grey smoke and blew it out through her nose, squinting. "Why don't *you* try it first?"

George cleared his throat. "I, uh, have to operate the machine." He paused. "Anyhow, I'm not really sure it will work."

"Yeah," said Ethyl.

They stood silently, looking at the Hotsy-Totsy machine and thinking.

"Hey," said George after a moment.

"What?"

"I've got it."

"Good. What is it?"

George took the cigarette out of her hand and sucked on it shrewdly. "That kid next door. Jimmy or Billy or whatever his name is. We could ask him. He might do it."

"Yeah," said his wife. "And what if it doesn't work?"

"Then it doesn't work," George shrugged. "Nothing ventured, nothing gained."

Ethyl bit her lip. "Okay," she said, "go and ask him. Maybe it'll be interesting. There's nothing much else to do."

She took the cigarette back and flicked ashes on the dirty linoleum floor.

Jimmy, the kid next door, wiped back his very blond and slightly greasy hair and put his hands in his pockets. "It's weird-looking," Jimmy said.

"Yeah, kind of," Ethyl murmured.

"I think it's rather attractive," George said contritely. "Look at the craftsmanship."

"It looks like a washing-machine," said Jimmy. "What's it supposed to do?" Jimmy was twelve, and suspicious of everything.

"Well, uh," George said, forcing himself to smile. "That's kind of a surprise. It's called a Hotsy-Totsy machine, if that gives you any ideas."

"Not really," said Jimmy, a bit snidely. "What'm I supposed to do?"

"You get inside," interjected Ethyl, who was by now out of cigarettes.

"And then I push the button," George explained.

"Oh," said Jimmy, offering Ethyl a cigarette. "I see. I guess. What happens then?"

"That's hard to explain," George said firmly.

Jimmy looked at both of them suspiciously. "Will I have to take off my clothes?" he asked, licking his lips nervously.

"No," George replied emphatically, as though that were some kind of wan joke. "Now, why not get in and give it a whirl?"

"I guess I will," Jimmy said in a bored voice, and sat down on the stool inside the Hotsy-Totsy machine. "Ready," said Jimmy.

Ethyl closed the door and spun the wheel. George hovered above The Button, which was on a console at the end of a thick black cable snaking to the machine. Ethyl nodded.

George pushed the button.

The Hotsy-Totsy machine vibrated faintly for three seconds, then resumed its inscrutable silence.

"Okay," said George excitedly. "Open the door and let him out. Let's see what happened."

Ethyl spun the iron wheel in the opposite direction, and swung the heavy door open. Jimmy emerged from the machine with a delighted grin.

"That was far out! Let's do it again."

"Only one try to a customer," said George solemnly. "Now. Tell us what happened."

Jimmy looked perplexed. "That's kind of hard to explain. But it *was* far out."

George's face dropped. "That's all?"

"That's about it," replied the boy, with half a shrug and half a wiggle.

"Okay," said George, looking at his wife with an embarrassed and disappointed expression. "I guess you can leave now."

"Okay," said Jimmy, and left. Ethyl stood smirking at George and the Hotsy-Totsy machine, dripping borrowed ashes on the floor.

"Nice-looking boy, don't you think?" murmured George. His eyes crossed back and forth over the floor, as if searching for some tiny missing detail.

"A little on the snotty side," replied Ethyl. "What're you going to do now?"

"I was thinking of trying it out on the neighbors. Jimmy seemed to like it, anyway. Maybe it'll be a hit."

"Could be," remarked Ethyl rather idly, feeling herself for a package of cigarettes that wasn't there. "Maybe you could charge admission."

"That's an idea," said George. "Start calling up the neighbors. First ride is free . . ."

"Sure. And the second one costs fifty cents, the third, two dollars . . ."

"It's nothing like that," George said aggravatedly. "Nothing like that at all."

He pushed the button, and the Hotsy-Totsy machine buzzed briefly. Ethyl went upstairs to call the neighbors.

So people started queueing up to experience the Hotsy-Totsy machine.

Most of them were delighted.

Ethyl operated the machine by herself from 10 A.M. until 2 P.M. every day while George was at work. George managed a gas station in Covina; he was naturally endowed with mechanical ability, so it had come as no surprise to Ethyl when he got interested in inventing. The surprise was when anything worked. Aside from the Hotsy-Totsy machine, very few of George's inventions had worked, so Ethyl felt she had put up with a great deal. The Hotsy-Totsy machine was his first real break; Ethyl had to make the neighbors swear not to reveal anything about the machine until they had made enough from it to afford a patent search and application.

This didn't take too long. The Hotsy-Totsy machine was a real hit. And it was unique.

"How many customers today?" asked George, returning from the gas station.

"I dunno," Ethyl replied, leaning back on the Castro sofa and breathing tobacco fumes. "Enough. We took in about two hundred dollars."

"Hear anything from the attorneys?" George asked, dropping into an armchair and flicking the remote control switch. The telly erupted into color and sound; George flipped the set randomly from channel to channel, finding nothing that interested him.

"You got a letter," said Ethyl. "Here." She picked up an envelope and handed it to him, then walked back and forth across the worn yellow carpet, dropping ashes.

George opened the letter expectantly. "It's from the patent attorneys. They say the search has turned up nothing—but if we want to secure rights of patent, we have to explain what the machine is supposed to do."

"That's tough," muttered Ethyl. "That'll be hard to do."

"Maybe if we just tell them it's a little hard to explain."

"Yeah."

"I could tell them it's self-explanatory," George surmised. "Like, that's why I called it that. A Hotsy-Totsy Machine. It's kind of alliterative. Suggestive."

Ethyl had a sudden thought. "Why not interview the customers and see if we can get them to agree about what it does?"

"Good," said George. "We'll do that. You can start tomorrow."

"I'll bet," muttered his wife, depositing ashes on the divan. "While you do the shopping and cook the meals."

"Let's not get testy," responded George abstractedly. "After all, division of labor is what a marriage is all about."

She shrugged, and they both fell silent.

None of the customers agreed about what a Hotsy-Totsy machine did.

"They just said it was kind of hard to explain," said Ethyl. "Maybe you should talk to them."

"We could have them fill out a form," George suggested, without conviction. "Like Marx and Engels."

"That's no good. They have nothing to say. Just, 'It's kind of hard to explain.' The only reaction they really have is that it seems to make them happy."

"That's it!" George jumped up from his recliner and stood almost spread-eagled in front of the TV. "We've got it! We'll just say that it's a machine intended to make people seem to be happy."

His wife blew cigarette smoke through half-smirking lips. "It sounds lame to me, honey, but we might as well try it. We don't have anything better to go on."

So they registered a patent application for the Hotsy-Totsy machine, under the title, "A Device Appearing to Produce a Semblance of Humor."

It was good enough for the Patent Office, anyhow.

Thus, George and Ethyl went into business.

They did quite well.

Several large corporations offered to buy George's invention from them for very large sums of money. Walt Disney Enterprises offered $250,000, cool.

"Not enough," said George at breakfast. "Not nearly enough."

"I don't think we should sell it," remarked Ethyl, blowing out smoke and squinting. "It's a goldmine."

"Everybody wants to ride in the Hotsy-Totsy," said George expansively. "Everybody."

"We could sell a franchise," said Ethyl. "Open a chain of Hotsy-Totsy booths. Put 'em in amusement parks and airport terminals."

"Fantastic idea!" George exclaimed. "We sell a franchise for $25,000, cool, and twelve percent of the gross."

"Gross is what it is," snickered Ethyl.

"We'll be so rich we won't even have to pay taxes," George said.

Ethyl looked abruptly sober. "Honey," she said, almost pouting.

"What?" George said with a concerned look.

"It's just . . . George, honey, are you completely sure this is a good thing? I mean, it don't have any bad effects or anything, does it? And I'm afraid . . . well, things like this, all that money and everything, things like that can ruin a marriage, if you know what I mean."

"Naw," said George. "Maybe money doesn't buy happiness— but poverty sure won't make you belch with glee, either."

"Yeah," said Ethyl, meditating on smoke-rings and a cold half-cup of morning coffee.

They opened a chain of franchised Hotsy-Totsy Rooms. Giant Hotsy-Totsy machines, large enough to enclose an entire night-club full of people in a convincing semblance of euphoria. They also leased smaller one-man machines to bus terminals, airports, bowling alleys and gas stations. They took their place alongside the two-bit photo-booths and condom dispensers. At Disney-land, long lines waited for days to sample the eight-second sani-tary thrill of "Hotsyland," a 300-meter geodesic Hotsy-Totsy machine.

George invented a new version of the machine—a Hotsy-Totsy *projector,* that could evince acres of amiable emana-tions. That, too, was an instant hit. He leased it to all sorts of enterprises for a fat percentage of the gross. It went fastest to drive-in theatres and sporting arenas. The owners said they sold more popcorn and hot dogs with the customers bathed in Hotsy-Totsy rays. All in all, it was quite a little empire they had there.

George and Ethyl got rich.

It didn't ruin their marriage.

Like many men of genius, George had married a woman of only average talents. This was not so much because George had bad taste in women, or liked to feel superior and have some-body to boss around due to some frustrated inward fearfulness —or even because he was broke, and a plain, average girl was all he could get. George wasn't really all that smart, anyhow.

There was also the fact that one cannot judge by appearances alone. George was neither as brilliant, nor Ethyl as dumb, as both bystanders and they themselves liked to think. Each had certain positive and negative traits, and these happened to bal-ance nicely within the structure of the relationship. Or—as George liked to put it—*everybody* is dumb. George was just a little bit *less* dumb than most other people. But this does not mean the less dumb people can *think* for the more dumb. There-fore, everybody should mind his own business and keep his mouth shut.

This philosophy had avoided George many a fight. George didn't like to argue, he didn't like to compete, and he wasn't concerned with looks. George just liked winning. George's only vanity was a conviction that he could score, and a certain mani-fest pleasure in doing so.

Ethyl liked being married to someone who liked to win and finally won. In return for this, she cooked George's meals, spent George's money, and gave George a bad time when he needed one. This is how mature people relate.

It proved a workable relationship.

The cumulative effect of the Hotsy-Totsy machine was astonishing. Aside from engendering great wealth and social prestige for George and Ethyl, it made others happy too. Or seemed to. It was the ideal machine, no rough edges.

Everyone jumped on the Hotsy-Totsy bandwagon. Even the police bought in—using it for riot control, and to pacify students and prisoners. The Army had a secret "Project Hotsy-Totsy" . . . you couldn't even find a congressman to leak what it was all about. The Communists were rumored to be building an *anti*-Hotsy-Totsy (or perhaps the Ultimate Hotsy-Totsy), being the killjoys that they are, and for what sinister portent none dared guess. Perhaps they feared it might "abolish the abolishers," as one clandestine wit punned eruditely.

The personal effect of the Hotsy-Totsy machine was no less remarkable. George and Ethyl were now rich and contented and successful. Indeed, they became *so* rich, they didn't have to pay taxes at all. "The 100 percent bracket," as George was fond of calling it. They were accepted in parts of society which would once have passed them nose-high on the street, openly snubbing them. George and even been interviewed by *Media; Media* approved of the Hotsy-Totsy machine and all it stood for, and thus touted George (and Ethyl) as examples of what good, successful capitalist entrepreneurs should be like. There weren't very many capitalist entrepreneurs left to go around anyway, so the press had to find something good to say about George and Ethyl whether it really liked them or not; they were practically all that was left of the American Way of Life. All in all, George and Ethyl were becoming respectable folks.

"And rich, too," reminded Ethyl, watching herself smirk a little self-consciously on the Seven O'clock News.

"Rich," repeated George, respectfully. "We're just about the only people left on our block who're rich."

"Christ," murmured Ethyl, and flicked feebly at the remote control.

Several months later, George and Ethyl sat in El Club Hotsy-Totsy (you needed a passport and a special key to get in), surveying the lush lavish fruits of their labor.

"It sure is nice being rich," sighed Ethyl, screwing a Sherman Long into her platinum cigarette holder. She struck a match with a languid slash of her wrist (as rich people do in George Cukor movies) and breathed luxuriously of the silver fumes.

"Yup," agreed George. "It sure is." He counted out a 25 percent tip for the nude waitress hovering nearby like a lascivious tinkerbell. The girl's eyes glistened with awe and respect—and a little fear. Ordinary people—"the little people," as George was fond of calling them—trembled in an apoplexy of respect and admiration at people like George and Ethyl. People who had *made* it, that is, and didn't have to get jobs walking around naked waiting tables in nightclubs.

"The vibrations are pretty good tonight," Ethyl remarked, utterly ignoring the shivering, naked girl who waited nearby like a starving puppy-dog.

"Yes," George said. "They are."

They both dragged on their scented cigarettes. Then they both took a sip of rare Fuegian coffee.

"Ahh," said George and Ethyl together. The whole room seemed to sigh with them.

Underneath the nightclub noises, an indescribable buzz permeated consciousness, projecting an aura of peacefulness and empathy . . . modulated at will by the proprietors.

Across the Earth, a strange change came down.

It mellowed out. It *relaxed*.

Or seemed to.

Slowly, by a few degrees each month or so, as George and Ethyl grew steadily richer, the violence and fear of the old world seemed to ebb away. Less and less was said of wars, disasters, famines and fights. More and more tranquility and freedom were observed. At least it *seemed* that way. Especially to George and Ethyl.

One fine spring day, George and Ethyl stood before the very first Hotsy-Totsy machine, still intact in their basement. They had turned the basement into a museum—a shrine, almost—and charged two dollars to file quickly past the original Hotsy-Totsy. Business was brisk here, too.

"It really was a beaut," exclaimed George. "I'm still proud of it."

"Yeah," said Ethyl. Her Sherman dribbled ashes on the new carpet. "At least this one paid off."

"Hey," said George, thinking a sudden thought.

"What?" said Ethyl.

"I just thought of something. You remember that kid next door—the one called Timmy or something."

"Jimmy," corrected Ethyl. "What about him?"

"He didn't evaporate or go crazy or anything, did he?"

She looked at him, half smirking. "You've got to be kidding. Look, he's fine. I saw him the other day, riding a minibike. He's got pimples all over his face. No after-effects, as far as I can tell."

"Oh," said George, a little sheepishly. "Well, that's good. Don't want the FDA on our backs."

"Yeah."

They stood there for a minute, staring at the wonderful machine.

"It sure is something, the way kids grow up," George remarked absently.

"Uh-huh."

They stood silently, contemplating the Hotsy-Totsy machine. It just sat there, completely inert and undramatic, looking somewhat like a front-loading washing-machine with a little stool inside, or a steam-bath for masochists.

"You know something," George said after a minute.

"What?"

"We're lucky, that's what. Lucky to be us. Lucky to be Americans. And above all, we're certainly fortunate to have a machine that seems to solve all our problems for us."

"Yeah," said his wife, dragging on her cigarette. "It's really nice." She patted the original prototype fondly. "Nice machine," Ethyl murmured softly. "Nice, nice, happy machine."

George pushed the button and it buzzed loyally.

"Maybe a little habit-forming, though," reflected George.

"You gotta lean on something," his wife proclaimed. "Might as well be a Hotsy-Totsy machine. Anyhow, the Hotsy-Totsy is about the only thing that makes anybody feel any damn good these days."

"Or seems to," her husband corrected blandly.

"Uh huh," said his wife. And flicked ashes into a tall silver ashtray with a sign above it that said, "Please do not drop ashes on floor."

And so.

Thus it came to pass that George the Inventor and Ethyl his wife became incredibly rich, and peace and happiness at last descended to the four corners of the round Earth. The

Hotsy-Totsy machine flooded the world with good vibrations; hunger, war, killing, greed, uptightness and paranoia all rolled away from the lumbering path of history. Everybody seemed to feel good most all of the time. There was nothing to get shook about . . . and if there had been, the Hotsy-Totsy machine would have quickly taken care of it.

"If this isn't Utopia," said George, machining a sword into a plowshare on his new multi-purpose lathe, "I don't know what is."

"Yeah," said Ethyl with a benign little smirk. "Everything is all down cool at last."

That's pretty much where things stand. We owe it all to the Hotsy-Totsy machine, and of course to George and Ethyl, who made it all seem to happen. The Hotsy-Totsy machine is perhaps the greatest invention of all time; it probably saved the world, if you remember the way things used to be. You know— war, famine, greed, killing, uptightness and paranoia. Before the good vibrations oozed into every nook and cranny of human existence. But that was then, and this is now. If you can't remember, or don't understand why people used to do all those crazy things, there really is no way to convey it to you. You just have to be patient, and thankful to George and Ethyl for the universal blessings of the Hotsy-Totsy machine, and leave the reasons up to time and circumstance. Nobody really understands why *anything* has to happen.

It's all a little hard to explain.

BRUCE BOSTON

Tarfu's Last Show

Tarfu's last and most infamous living sculpture occupied the entire three floors of a deserted warehouse on the lower East side. Though the show was filmed and photographed thoroughly for posterity, and its aesthetics have been discussed at length in my daily column, I feel that a description of the particulars is once again in order for the story I wish to relate.

Upon the night of the opening I was among the first guests to arrive. I had hoped to dash off a preliminary review, or at least a comment, for the morning edition. Little did I know that I would devote my entire five hundred precious words and more to the events which were to follow.

The large building appeared dark and deserted at the time scheduled for the show to begin. Several persons in the gathering crowd suggested that perhaps the posters and handbills had been printed incorrectly and we had congregated at the wrong address. As for myself, I suspected that Tarfu was merely preparing us, invoking a sense of anticipation and mystery as he had often done in the past. Unlike the body of his contemporaries, he believes that in this day and age the practicing artist needs to become a showman and entrepreneur. Not only must he assume such roles, he should strive to make them an essential element in the expression of his creative energies. To quote: "Art is eternal; the part played by its makers remains constantly in flux."

Tonight, his timing was perfect. At the precise moment when the crowd's peaking confusion was about to plummet into disgruntlement, the door of the warehouse slid open, squealing on its worn runners, and a man stepped smartly from the shadows within. He was attired in the elaborate livery of a nineteenth century British footman. We knew the show had begun.

Closing the door behind him, this actor-servant informed us that spectators would only be permitted to view the exhibit in groups of twenty. Once each group had passed through a given floor, another twenty would be admitted. With my usual élan, spirited yet courteous, I managed to pass forward so as to be among the first selected to enter. We were escorted along a narrow alleyway at the side of the building. We then mounted an ancient cage-like lift which creaked slowly upward, open to the air. Apparently the progression of acts, or stages, was to be from the third floor down. As we rose, the grimy brick walls were within view, nearly within reach, and provided a striking contrast to our spotless and affluent evening dress. A sense of expectation, of something special about to occur, condensed among us.

The third floor of the building, the first of the exhibit, immediately impressed me as a new progression in Tarfu's development. Or was it a regression? Stylistically, he had come full circle—back to the stark simplicity which had characterized his "ghetto period." Of course all of his more recent shows had been total environments in which the observers, by their very presence, became involved in the creation. Often the perceptions would be totally bombarded; or at other times, lulled and deceived. Yet inescapable participation, in art and in life, had been a recurrent theme.

In the scene which I now confronted, the dichotomy between spectator and object was clearly, even physically, defined. We stood at one end of a long room, cut off from the remainder by a low iron railing with staunchions which had been bolted to the floor. We could only watch; there was no way to enter the action taking place before us. And what we were watching . . . was a dancing class.

Although it was night outside, lights had been cleverly installed behind the glassed-over ceiling to give the impression of early midday. There was no music: in fact, a muffling device must have been operative since the silence remained uncanny. The dancers, perhaps thirty-odd men and women, shifted gracefully through stylized poses. Markings chalked upon the floor, white bars and *L's,* assured the easy perfection of their movements. But no, these lines were not chalk, rather strips of white adhesive, their grain dirtied by the passage of many feet and thus creating, from a distance and at first glance, the rough, textured appearance of chalk. The dancers wore black leotards, faded. Their feet and legs were bare, and though firmly muscled, the flesh held a lifeless tone in the attentuated illumination, a tone which suggested . . . mannequins? Dust had gathered visibly in the corners of the room. The planks of the hardwood floor shone dully, offering up a compressed and distorted image of the scene before us.

At a short distance from the dancers, though distinctly separate from the changing pattern they traversed, a stout, older woman stood watching. She also wore a black leotard. Her legs were thick and she leaned upon a long, thin stick of mottled wood. Clearly, this was the instructress of the class. If she was also intended as a muse figure, a symbol which has manifested itself in one form or another in nearly all of Tarfu's work, she was a stern and righteous muse, one who would bridge no nonsense.

Notwithstanding its simplicity, the effect of the scene was imposing. Space and light had been used well. The fact that the dancers outnumbered the watchers, that the area in which they performed covered more than three-fourths of the room, made our own group seem insignificant by comparison. None of us spoke, almost as if we had been intimidated into silence. In a sense, Tarfu had involved us even as spectators, causing our reaction, or in this case the lack of one, to further contribute to the effect he wished to create. And once again, timing was a key factor. The pattern of the dance proved complex enough to hold our attention, yet not so difficult that our interest wandered before we could grasp its order and form. Once the moving figures were taken as a unit, they could be perceived as akin to the changing pictures of a kaleidoscope, shrinking and pulsing in their circle, each figure no more than a fleck of crystal bound to the laws of gravity, still always in perfect symmetry with its mirror image. With comprehension, the pattern became regular and beautiful. Yet once we understood, still we continued to watch in appreciation and fascination. For here, from the most progressive proponent of modern living sculpture, we had the work of a strict traditionalist.

My absorption was so complete, my attempt to wring meaning from this radical departure on the part of Tarfu so intense, that I lost all sense of the passing minutes. Shortly, we were informed that it was time to move on.

No longer were we escorted by a liveried footman; our initial guide had slipped away unnoticed. The figure who now led us was bearded and blond, his more-than-shoulder-length hair ill-kempt and beribboned. The sleeves of the denim jacket he wore had been crudely scissored off and his lanky arms were scarred with tattoos. I recognized this man. He was one of the many young people—artists and would-be artists and ordinary charlatans—who had congregated about Tarfu in recent years. I had always viewed Tarfu's acceptance and tolerance of these hangers-on as the major weakness in his character. Now, I feared, it had spilled over into his art. This fellow was no more than a minor wood-poet. Lacking his association with Tarfu, he would have remained in the relative obscurity he so richly deserved. Because of the moderate success he had been able to achieve, he had now become puffed up far beyond his actual importance. His manner was vulgar and overbearing and reminiscent of some inept sidewalk barker.

As we descended the stairwell, he warned us against the second level. He informed us nonchalantly that we should stay close together and perhaps hold hands if it became too overwhelming. The lout was trying to throw a scare into us. I suspect that if our interest had been less, and an exit readily available, a few of the less hardy might have deserted right there.

70

We entered and the door clanked shut behind us. At first, the darkness was complete.

Light came slowly, a reversed twilight glimmering across the entire rim of the horizon as if the sun were about to rise from all directions at once. We were given the illusion that we were standing upon a vast and level plain. In the far distance we could see low clumps of dark green (vegetation? forests? gathering armies?). Already, I anticipated what was to follow—as one expects the swell of emotion in a symphony by Tchaikovsky, yet for all that expectation the impact of the moment, when it arrives, can be heightened rather than diminished. I knew that we had faced order; now we must confront chaos.

Unrecognizable noises (music?) taunted the edges of our hearing at super and subsonic frequencies. Our small circle moved forward aimlessly, peering through the insufficient light for a sign of something . . . anything. The limitations of language force a linear exposition upon me: what happened next, happened all at once.

Flash! Explosion! Ambush! Assault upon the senses! They fell from trapdoors in the artificial sky, shot up out of burrows from the artificial earth. Clowns! A hundred of them, seemingly a thousand. Beggar clowns and monster clowns. Whooping, laughing, screeching. Surrounding us on every side in every imaginable costume, shape, color and face. Our group clustered together, reeling from the onslaught. The world became painfully bright as the sun actually rose from all directions at once and coalesced to a fiery magma at high noon—only its rays were heatless and green, a fluorescent whitegreen that turned our flesh a sickly hue as unnatural as the painted skin of the apparitions cavorting about us. The music-noise was instantaneously loud, dense, discordant. Crescendo and decrescendo walloped against one another, sent shattered notes like glass splinters tinkling to the horizon and oblivion. The recorded laughter of asylum madness warred with the live laughter on every side. Tarfu had opened the gates and let down all the stops. More than delivering us into chaos, he had catapulted the entire sum of our awareness into ultimate bedlam. No sense had been forgotten: the smell of burning meat filled the air.

We moved forward now just to move, but our prancing ring of captors would not let us free. They pretended to talk to us in garbled tongues which could surely be no more than nonsense; they pulled at our clothes; they made insulting signs to our

71

faces. Painted smiles became broader with the real, malicious smiles beneath. If there was a muse figure among this gyrating pack, she had become totally wanton and submerged to the level of any other fool. The sun blinked, stroboscopically, polychromatic. Arms and legs rippled in backward multiplications of their own images. In the instants of sudden blackout, while the tumult roared on unabated, we glimpsed our beacon of salvation: the simple red-orange tubing of an exit sign glowing in the distance. Cringing, shrinking, we pushed on, our direction momentarily lost each time the painful brightness returned again and again. Unbelievably, the floor itself seemed to be tilting, spilling us onward. We had entered the domain of some lunatic god and become playthings at the mercy of his caprice.

I was the first to attain freedom. My hands were trembling, my knees about to buckle. Thankfully, the door swung open without effort. The others scurried through after me and I quickly swept it shut behind them as a jeering, white-lipped, shoeblack face loomed up before me. As suddenly as it had all begun, the storm was over.

I counted our number to make sure that all had escaped. Several women were crying. Despite the normal light of the corridor in which we stood, a number of faces still possessed a greenish tinge. In his inimitable style, Tarfu had once again made more than one enemy on an opening night—though in the past it had always been more the result of his barbed tongue than the barbs of his creation.

At this point we were left without a guide. But there could be no question of turning back. We advanced down the corridor and another flight of stairs.

We found ourselves in a small movie theater, carpeted, furnished with exactly twenty rocking chairs. What a relief it was to sit down. To relax. It occurred to me that Tarfu had gone too far. The show was not yet over and already the majority of our group seemed close to emotional exhaustion.

He did not leave us to ourselves for long.

From somewhere a plunkety, off-key piano began playing. The lights dimmed and the screen lit with a black and white countdown of number flipping this way and that. The movie began without titles. A man was walking down a city street. The film was silent, amateurish (surely intentional, given Tarfu's technical expertise), the motions of the character overly-rapid and mechanical like those in ancient silent movies. The man approached. Tall, large-boned, craggy features, dark unruly hair, the Meher Baba moustache another slab of darkness above the full lips. It was Tarfu, himself.

The scene changed. He was outside the warehouse, riding up the same lift we had taken; his eyes gazed about uneasily. Now he entered the building and here were the dancers. The entire effect was diminished by the lack of color, the size of the screen, the jerky movements. Yet our own memories were recent and vivid enough so that all we needed was this slight echo of reality to re-invoke the experience. Tarfu watched as we had watched, only he was not silent. He began talking. He yelled at the passing figures. The instructress advanced toward him as the dancers moved on oblivious to his calls. She talked back to him. Tarfu began to lift one leg over the iron railing, as if to enter the dance floor, and she raised her stick in a threatening gesture. He turned away, his lips in a grimace.

Change again: the room with the clowns. The film did even less credit to reality here. No matter, it was enough to call back the nightmare for us. Tarfu moved through that world, beleaguered by the same grotesque faces, suffering the same indignities. He attempted to join the clowns in their antics, rolling about on the artificial turf, twisting his features so as to imitate their exaggerated expressions. They would have none of it. He remained apart, an object of ridicule, as they pulsed and milled around him. Finally they began to beat at him with large stuffed pillow-clubs and he retreated, driven out the exit.

The screen blackened and the piano notes petered away. What next? Would Tarfu appear before us and lead us through the rest of the show in person? Would we see him again upon the screen, entering this theater, watching a movie of himself until the point where he was watching a movie of himself watching a movie and so on, in an endless cycle? Or perhaps we had been filmed thus far on our journey and through some magical instant processing, the play and the players would be reversed, and we would watch Tarfu as he watched a movie of us.

The screen lit up once again. The scene was entirely different. Tarfu stood alone in a room we had not been to tonight, though I recognized it as his studio in the Village. Assorted canvases covered the walls; work materials were scattered about. The camera panned slowly. Centered upon one bare table lay a large hypodermic needle and syringe. Tarfu crossed to the window, stared down into the street. The camera panned back to the needle, back to Tarfu's face, creased with lines of tension. The needle, the face. The face, the needle. This melodramatic juxtaposition occurred faster and faster until Tarfu rushed to the table and picking up the needle, plunged it into his forearm. In the sped-up, jumpy eight-millimeter action it seemed to enter his vein like a knife thrust. The plunger was depressed and the fluid drained into his body.

Suddenly, even in black and white, it became clear that all of the color had vanished from his face. Although the individual features remained the same, his alteration of expression was so complete that he was unrecognizable as the same person. He had become any stranger on the street or in the subway: a tall, rather homely man with a menacing shock of straight, yet unruly, hair.

Next, his body began to tremble and convulse. In a way the action was comic, yet at the same time his movements appeared so real that it was also horrifying. Was this a part acted out, a sobbed openly. The effect upon me was numbness, withdrawal. role which would cease once the cameras stopped turning? Some premonition told me that it was not, that we were actually watching the death throes of a fellow human being. Yet the quality of the film was so poor, it was impossible to be certain. As Tarfu's body crumpled to the floor, the screen went black once again and the lights came on.

We arose from our seats slowly, more puzzled than ever. What could it all mean? Was there any purpose behind the chain of events to which we had now been exposed, or had Tarfu finally crossed the line into totally random creation? We milled about uncertainly. The exit door was clearly marked, but dared we go on?

That final room was the room which we should have been warned against. As we stumbled out of the theater, once more into sudden brightness, what perhaps all of us had known and dreaded at some level appeared before us. Several people, both men and women, fainted. Others, who had been close to Tarfu, sobbed openly. The effect upon me was numbness, withdrawal.

Scattered about the small enclave were the awards and honors Tarfu had received during his stormy and meteoric career. We hardly noticed them, for in the center of the room he lay upon a glass-encased bier of plain, dark oak, ensconced and displayed in death like Lenin or Ho Chi Minh or other men who have made their mark upon history. The mortician's craft had returned his face to a semblance of its living self. The long, broken crag of a nose. The shaggy moustache rounding the lips, a few individual white hairs standing out in stark contrast to its blackness. His high cheek bones over cheeks sunken from missing back teeth, pitted with the lifelong scars of adolescent acne. His message came through to me with sickening clarity. Order had confronted chaos irreconcilably and the artist had succumbed.

So it was that Tarfu's last living sculpture had become a sculpture of death.

The ensuing furor raged for several weeks. The newspapers had their field day. Tarfu's past mistresses and alleged mistresses were dredged up and interviewed in depth: his true sexual preferences were never revealed. Any five-minute sketch he had once penned and signed his name to became a collector's item. The reasons behind his suicide, so clear to me, were debated endlessly. Certain cynics even argued that it had something to do with the massive amounts of back taxes he had owed the government. Inevitably, sadly, the transformation began: the Tarfu of memory became a far different man than the Tarfu who had walked among us.

It was nearly a month after the show had closed that I received the phone call. The man at the opposite end of the line claimed to be Tarfu—the rumbling baritone of the voice was surely the same, yet hadn't I seen him lying dead, struck down by his own hand? He said that because I had known him for so long (since before he'd changed his name), that because we had once been close friends (yes, even more), he had now chosen me as his confidante.

We met that night in a café whose name I will not divulge. He waited for me in the dimness at the rear of the room; as I approached, he struck a match. A misshapen candle perched atop an empty Chianti bottle illumined his face with a yellow light. The moustache was gone, the hair cut so short that it bristled and the natural oil of his scalp shone through. Yet the dark,

fiery eyes still blazed their genius at me. Indeed, it was none
other than Tarfu!

In a strained voice he explained that the entire thing had been
a hoax, an attempt to erase his living presence from the public
consciousness so that he could go underground in peace. He was
troubled, and if words can be feverish, his words were that
night. When he touched my hand, his palm was damp with
sweat.

He said that he needed time to think, to experience once
again the life of the common man, to move amidst the "nameless masses" so that his future creations could "embrace both the
salt of the earth and the heights of the stratosphere." He told
me that he was through with living sculpture, that he felt he had
exhausted its possibilities completely. He wanted to move on to
another medium for his expression. Perhaps cinema. He even
toyed with the idea of writing an epic, multi-charactered novel,
totally American yet in the grand Russian tradition of Tolstoi
and Solzhenitsyn. He would say no more. After a few moments,
swiftly, he was gone.

An empty cup of espresso, its syrupy grounds spilled within
the saucer. A half-smoked menthol cigarette stubbed out in the
ashtray. Had he been there at all? In my mind's eye he truly
seemed a phantom, dancing at the very edge of existence.

SCOTT BRADFIELD

Halcyon In A Mirror
At Midnight

Later, employing a memory which often lapsed, necessarily, into imaginary reconstruction, Magni examined the events which had predicted Arrington's intrusion.

Returning from the gallery and his bizarre trial beneath the new machines, he had been climbing the steps to his room when he glanced up the interminable stairwell which passed through the dismal tenement. Roosting just above him, a pair of thin, pale hands, frightened by his sudden approach, flashed open and disappeared from the railing. Magni was almost certain he had seen a blur of blond hair unfocus into the shadows. There was a faulty attempt at silence as the familiar sentinel sprinted back to his hidden post.

Again: he was waiting.

Magni halted at the third floor. He waited cautiously for a

few moments, leaning back against the long abandoned custodian's closet. He reached automatically to his shirt pocket for a cigarette, finding only a worn business card with an unlabeled phone number printed on its back. He dropped the scrap of paper to the floor.

Cobwebs hung about the closet's frame. He had once picked open the lock, searching for a broom. There were still sharp metallic scars where his penknife had scratched the knob. The fact that the closet was empty had not bothered him at the time —he had even expected it to be—for his actions were mostly the results of boredom and not necessity.

He looked up at the ceiling, as if expecting to discover a window that could reassure him that the floor above was empty. He remained terrified and still, hands clasping each other in moist patterns of fingers wrapped about fingers, listening for the clues of creaking floors and occasionally glancing up the slender stairwell until, out of a suicidal need for the confines of his own room, he stepped hurriedly up the remaining flight.

His door was unlocked and he was grateful to the efficiency of his poor security; he would not have to stand there helplessly fumbling for the key as he was tracked down. Shutting it behind himself, he heard the menacing tread of other footsteps in the hall. He leaned back against the door, hands meeting behind him where they grasped the doorknob nervously, stroked it with sweat. The filth of his room nearly turned him away until he remembered what was waiting for him in the hall.

Torn canvas, decomposing orange rinds, crumpled cigarette packages, and dully reflecting paint tubes shuffled beneath his feet. Ochre, amber, onyx . . . Beside his bed an old end table lay broken upon the floor, its legs folded in upon themselves. Above this was a fresh, deep indentation in the plaster wall. He could not even remember what had prompted such pent-up anger, for earlier, he had actually expected a good score from the machines. Possibly, he thought, I had a good premonition what was going to happen; at the time, I must have blamed my anger on petty annoyances.

But he could not be certain. There were no clear memories of that morning.

He stood midway across the room like some brutal god amidst its destruction of the evil within its creations. A paint-splattered easel bearing an unfinished portrait was propped against the far corner, unmolested. It appeared to huddle there, awaiting his final decision. He stared menacingly at this only survivor of his carnage: Noah, after the flood. Fists clenched sweat at his sides, relaxed, tightened again. Even in his earlier, intense rage, Magni could not produce the courage to complete his self-destruction with this.

It is easily the best thing I've ever done, he thought. It held the closest attachment to him, though little more than a simple portrait of a girl he had seen years ago. She had passed before him for only a few seconds and her subtle beauty had affected him irreversibly. He did not understand why a writer even attempted to describe a woman's face with words; that was an effect destined to be provided by the painter, if by anyone at all. She had been disembarking with her family from the same train that would carry him farther away from his own. Staring out the window from his seat, he had hoped to catch her eye, but she had dissolved, ignorant of his existence, into the engulfing crowds. Though the precise details of her features had slipped gradually away, time gently scrubbing them into inaccuracy, it was his interpretation that remained with him now in what he considered middle-age. He had since harshened the texture of her skin, exaggerated the depth and reflections of her eyes, until a myriad of tiny erasures had created a truly different girl. But to him, both aware of and pleased with his inexactness, he felt he had captured her original composure.

Easily the best thing he had ever done, or ever would do, he thought again. And with a fully renewed and distorted sense of purpose, he crossed the room and removed it from the easel, crushed it between cupped hands like newspaper destined for the fire, and, in controlled, maniacal hysteria, dropped it to the unswept floor and ground it beneath his feet. Scarcely dried paint stained the floor. A door opened behind him. He turned.

Arrington stood nervously at the door, which was still swinging slowly open. Hesitant to cross the threshold of the room, his hand still grasped the outer wall.

"Your door was unlocked . . . I was wondering—"

"Get the hell out of here!"

"I just thought—"

"Get out!"

After Arrington left, Magni lay across the crumpled blankets of his unmade bed with a deep bowled ashtray overflowing with cigarette butts placed in his lap. One at a time, he removed each stub with its repugnant odor of stale nicotine, straightened the charred tip, and smoked it down to a sizzling filter. His sheets were stained after months of unwashed use. There was a time when such filth had disgusted him.

So annoyed was he by Arrington's persistent intrusions and parasitic guardianship of his movements, Magni could not sleep. Plotting his revenge carefully, he pushed away the covers and moved to the cupboards. He found a cracked drinking glass, wrapped it in a towel, and struck it against the washing sink, placing the shattered fragments in an electric blender he once found in the basement trash. The violent chatter of the grinding was not even smothered by a pillow. Then, quietly, gruesomely aware of his neighbor's barefoot habits, he went out into the hall to spread the ground shards before his door. He paced the hall loudly until he heard Arrington jump from his bed, and then ran quickly to his room, lying propped up in bed until he heard the opening door and a cry of pain. He fell asleep to the rushing of water from the bathroom shower and the whimperings of a man too immature to curse.

The heat of the sun at its zenith pried open his eyes. He tried to escape into the fortress of a dream already dissolving, but sleep was lost.

Humidity smothered the room. It grew damper and thicker the closer he came to the window. Reluctantly, he dressed.

Berkeley lay before and around him like some abominable haze of delirium. The college was tearing down portions of Telegraph Avenue in order to protect its students from decadence and provide room for growth. Pneumatic hammers broke open large sections of asphalt. The city was a furnace. Streets were still paced by students with long hair and ragged clothes; walls were still plastered by worn pamphlets of revolution. The city seemed to him an Iron Maiden of education, its citizens the misplaced fossils of 1965.

He had intended to look for work. Instead, he wandered through used book stores, thumbed mangy paperbacks and even stole a few he knew he could never read. He couldn't concentrate enough to even read a comic book, anymore. He stopped in a diner for coffee. Before leaving, he checked the bulletin board half-heartedly for a job. None appealed to him.

Taking a detour at sudden impulse, he stopped by the gallery to re-examine his exhibit. He had thought he would be afraid to go there again.

The building was a tumbled form of architecturally misplaced blocks, bleak cement walls that revealed color inside. He hoped to sell a few paintings before the ratings became a permanent fixture of Americana.

"Hey, I'm sorry, Don," the manager said. There was a purposeful expression of sympathetic condescension obscuring the manager's true thoughts. "No one has sold much of anything these past few weeks. The economy is hard on us all."

"All right. Maybe tomorrow." Magni laughed nervously, attempting to surmount not only his frustration but the annoyance of the manager's steady insincerity.

As he turned to leave, he was called back.

Magni observed the manager as if he were across a wide and bewildering crevasse—the two of them had been friends once; the manager had once had a name. But Magni realized they had been turned away from each other, alienated by the strange consequences of technology: masked pride and an abrupt metamorphosis of artistic morals were now their opposing stands.

"You'll have to remove your exhibit sometime this week."

Magni glared back with practiced anger; the manager did not acknowledge his gaze. He began to curse vehemently, acting out some pitiful role of his own devising.

"I thought you said you weren't going to take those damn machines seriously. That is it, isn't it? The machines?"

"I'm sorry, Don. I really am." The manager accepted Magni's anger with necessary apathy; he did not know how to expose the falseness of past truths. And then, "You won't sell anything here. We both know that." He appeared both frightened and impatient to utter those last words, as if he were equally afraid and curious to observe the artist's wrath. He turned completely away and faced the artist's exhibit.

"Of course it's the machines," Magni muttered. He glanced over at his paintings, only then recognizing the numbered card which had been recently place above his name. It was only slightly larger than the lower letters; he knew what it read more from memory than perception.

107

He cried out involuntarily, and, despite the manager's startled protests, ran forward and tore it from the wall. He was possessed by furies, drunken and broken by an anger that was beyond the

81

reach of his destruction. The manager summoned the guards before he could complete the impulse—ripping his own canvases from their frames and littering them across the floor.

"Don . . ."

"What do you want?" Magni reassured himself that this would be the last time he left his door unlocked. Unbolted, it left him vulnerable.

Arrington removed the stool from its position at the far corner of the room where it rested against the refrigerator door, propping it shut.

"Put that back before you leave."

"Yeah, sure."

Magni had decided, out of the kindness of his heart, to let him stay. For a moment.

The refrigerator door opened slowly, released by lifeless springs. A faint echo of chill reached out towards Arrington as he moved towards the bed. He shivered. The sounds of the refrigerator increased until they dominated the room with a low, persistent drone, like the muffled chatter of an electric toothbrush.

Arrington dragged the stool over and sat down beside the melancholy artist. "Dave was looking for you today. He told me to have you call him."

Arrington pretended to be familiar with Magni's friends. Socially, he was intensely unattractive, and enjoyed the opportunity to mention another by their first name as if they were friendly with him. Magni disliked such an understanding of Arrington's actions, for they were actions consistently instigated by loneliness. It was difficult hating someone you knew so well.

"Thanks for telling me," he said, his tone yielding to warmth as he knew it would in his sympathy. He could easily revert to sympathy when facing this man; only in the dark, faceless night could he find the strength to exact his revenge.

"Why are you so down? Ma-machinery trouble?" Arrington's face twitched beneath the grin. His attempts at humor caused Magni to cringe with embarrassment as he remembered times he himself had said words equally inappropriate. He communicated, silently, that the remark was unappreciated.

"I'm sorry. I was only kidding."

"Will you quit saying that. You're always saying you're sorry."

"I'm—"

Magni hesitated. "Forget it."

Arrington almost thanked him.

Reward and punishment; Magni suddenly realized how he could control this man with only brief, addictive boosters of friendship. It made him for the first time fully aware of his power: he could mold or shatter someone's behavior, even re-create an image of himself in this man.

The room fell defenselessly to the onslaught of silence. The refrigerator connection had shorted out, but, silence being such a direct manifestation of their thoughts, neither of them noticed.

After a few moments: "Are you still looking for a job?"

"No."

"You sell anything?"

"Yeah, sure."

"Come on, what happened?"

"The manager decided to take everything down. He was right to do it, too. They can't make anything off me." Magni also realized how self-pitying he could be with a man he disliked, with a man who had no connections with anyone else. It was like talking to himself.

"You could still sell. A lot of people would still buy your paintings."

"Yeah. Old couples can give me two bits to do a picture of a clown or something they could hang in their bathroom. Or I could sit out on the streets and draw caricatures of tourists. They aren't rating that." (Then, as the painter turned fully towards him in the dim, half-light of the room, Arrington noticed that Magni had shaven his light beard.)

Magni stared across the empty room and saw something which increased his anger. "They've hung the rating on my exhibit. Hung that bastard number on my paintings."

"A machine can't do that. Shit." Arrington stuttered with the curse, uncomfortable with it, yet impatient to sound like his friend.

When Arrington again mentioned the machines, Magni glanced at him curiously, wondering how he had learned about them. Perhaps it had been in the papers.

"Of course it can. Get out of here."

"But Don—wait a second—"

"Get out." There was no exclamation to his words, no accompanying curse. He spoke evenly, repetitively, like a command to a trained pet.

The stool lay on its side on the floor.

A memory, distorted.

He was part of the machine.

Lights, whirling figures, glorious computations, the winking of cat's eye . . .

He melted from the machine. The machine exploded into an absurd caricature of reality. Its dark suited somber master contorting, accepting guise of mad scientists and distant capitalist gods . . .

—Rating 107, Mr. Magni, the madman wheezed, cigarettes dangling in a long row from his mouth. That's what the machine says. That's what we've been told. It looks like you're too smart for your own good, because you can see what you want but you're not smart enough to get it. No use refuting the machine, though. It could get angry. The distorted face came up close to his own, focus lost. He stifled a scream.

His mouth slobbered onto the pillow. He woke up thinking that a character from his dream was in the room, waiting for him.

Artistic I.Q., he had thought.

He lay quite still for a few minutes, trying to quell an immediate surge of energy within himself. What he had once considered, ironically, an artistic drive. He attempted to restructure the memory of his dream, and only when it was eternally lost did he try instead for sleep.

In the end, the energy threatening to overcome him, he had had to masturbate himself to sleep.

The sun entered hot and bright, refracting around the thick burlap curtains into his eyes. Steady, strong sunlight.

The room stank of stale tobacco, and it increased his hunger for a cigarette even more. He pushed the covers from the bed, searched for change under the mattress and in the pockets of old clothes. There was also no coffee. He would go to the bank today.

He shaved quickly, getting only the rough spots about his chin and lips with a bare blade. He spent a little more time than usual before the mirror, gazing into the depths of his eyes, searching out and defining the reflections he found there.

And then he dressed. Left the filth of his room behind, stepping hastily down the steps hoping to avoid the spectre he knew was lurking.

Arrington was waiting for him on the porch.

"Morning, Don," he said, looking dramatically up from his mailslot. "What're you doing?"

It terrified Magni to think that Arrington might have been waiting there for him all morning.

"Nothing." He ignored Arrington's eyes and stared down instead at the weeds that struggled up out of the cracked recesses of concrete.

"Yeah? Hey, listen, let's go to breakfast or something. How's that sound?"

Magni knew the senselessness of argument by now; his hatred warred with his daylight pity.

Walking side by side down the quiet morning street, Magni found that Arrington was stepping as fast as he could so that he might not lag behind, obviously impatient to prove to anyone that might watch that he now walked at the side of another man. Magni also noticed his companion's complete euphoria, for these few moments, at having abandoned loneliness.

"Slow down a bit, Don. I can't move too fast. I think I've still got a few pieces of glass stuck in my feet."

Arrington returned to the table from the cigarette machine. He circumcised the plastic wrapper with the strip of inlaid gold ribbon, and handed Magni a cigarette.

"Thanks." Magni lit it, inhaled, and passed the match to his companion. He could see that such politeness pleased Arrington.

Arrington choked on his first inhalation; he had only recently begun smoking in imitation of the artist. He had decided on the habit from earlier observation of Magni long before he had ever spoken with him. In their first conversations, Magni, had not noticed the weaknesses in this man that he now so often reflected upon. He wondered how dismal it must be for Arrington to realize his own emptiness. But then, Magni disliked using the word "empty" in relation to Arrington. The word seemed too definitive of his spectral character, and there were still many things that puzzled him about this man.

Arrington raised his cup to his lips; coffee dribbled from the chapped corners of his mouth. He lapped it in with his tongue and wiped at the moisture with his sleeve.

"Aren't you hungry?"

"No. Not right now. Coffee's fine."

"I guess I'm not really hungry either."

"Sure." Magni ran his fingers along the sides of the cup, sensing the plastic form, the almost natural, though mechanically precise symmetry.

"You want to go to a movie or something? You could call some of your friends."

"I don't think so."

"All right. Maybe later."

"I haven't got any money. You might as well go without me." (Magni stared at his hand, and remembering an old trick he had once practiced, attempted to interpret the visual form of it into words which he would usually jot down on a scrap of paper and toss in a drawer when he returned home. After he had forgotten the original subject of the description, he would sketch the figures represented, capturing the shapes in a reverse translation from the writing: *four cylinders of graduated sizes across the top, heightening three steps, descending one; a fifth, shorter and thicker one slanting up from the side, all molded carefully to an asymmetric oval structure of extreme pliability.* Such exercises provided him with a rough concept of the weaknesses in both his writing and painting; at least, this is what he had hoped. It was really just a game. There was a time when he had always thought in such paradox.)

"I could lend it to you."

"Wha—" Magni glanced up, confused.

"I said I could probably lend you the money."

"Oh, sure. No thanks."

"Hey, I forgot. I know how you hate to borrow. I'll treat you, how's that sound?"

Magni searched drearily for another excuse. The dominant presence of silence again threatened their conversations, descending like a shroud. Arrington suddenly understood, shifted uncomfortably. The power of silence surrounded them.

"Did you sell any paintings yesterday?"

"Jesus Christ, Arrington. Let's not go through that again."

Frightened, Arrington was struggling to keep this conversation alive, as well as his pride, before this man he respected.

"Have you quit painting?"

"Yes."

"I thought so. I used to hear you wandering around the halls every night. You haven't even left your room in a long time. So . . . so I was pretty sure you'd stopped painting." Arrington paused, expecting some hope in his battle.

Magni remained silent.

"You really think that a machine can keep you from selling?"

"It already has."

"I think you're good."

"Arrington, you like them so much, *you* buy them." And then, with a flash of embarrassment through anger, Magni recalled the day Arrington had scraped the money together to afford one of his lesser paintings. "I'm sorry," he muttered quickly.

Almost trapped by rejection, Arrington brightened at receiving Magni's apology. He felt that such an action on Magni's part was a sign of respect. He could not remember anyone apologizing to him before. "Don't worry," he said, and felt like another man.

Magni felt secure that the score was settled.

"But I still think you should keep on painting."

Magni was exasperated. "Good!"

"Does that mean you will?"

"No. It means I don't give a shit what you think."

"Why?"

"For Chrissakes, will you cut it out! What's the use of all this? I just gotta face it. I'm no good. I'm one hundred and seven by the same machine that judges Manet at one-seventy. Jesus, even Manet has been dragged from his grave. The *Olympiad* is supposed to be in some coffee shop display. So just fuck off, will you!"

Magni kicked at the solid support of the table. Coffee slopped over into his saucer and then onto the table cloth. He raised a fork and brought the tines down hard against the table. "Jesus!"

"I don't know. I just don't know . . ."

"You certainly don't."

"But couldn't they be wrong? It's all based on cold calculations. Art doesn't have anything to do with science, does it? Couldn't they be wrong?"

"It doesn't matter if they're wrong or not. By their acceptance, they have been made to be right. The machines haven't declared themselves as omnipotent, but the buyers who have accepted their opinion as correct are the ones who have made it *right.*"

"But it's a temporary thing, isn't it? I mean, like, I've always thought," and Arrington paused, his verbal footing a bit shaky, "you like to paint. I thought that was it. Like it was one of those things you couldn't help but do. You know what I mean?"

"What would you know."

Arrington was stung, but attempted to save what little pride he had left.

"Don," (Magni always shuddered when Arrington used his first name) "I never told you this before, but when I was a kid I really wanted to be a writer. I was no good, but I visualized myself as some great undiscovered author. I began to weave fantasies about myself in order to gain some reassurance. I wrote all the time, I began sending it out to magazines, but they treated me just like everyone has all my life. They just brushed me off with this incredibly destructive indifference. But I waited and convinced myself that they weren't ready for me—that I was good, and that someday, someday, they would recognize me for what I was. And so I kept writing the same pointless stories in the same pretentious prose. Waiting, waiting, always waiting . . . Do you know what that can do to you? To live your entire life for a dream and discover that it is nothing but a dream . . ."

"So what's your point?" Magni asked, feigning indifference at the monologue when he was actually disturbed by Arrington's sincerity.

"My point!" Arrington revealed a sudden spark of anger completely alien to his nature. "Why do you keep putting me down? Don't you know I'm sick of it? I'm trying to help. You're escaping into self-pity. That's what can finally destroy you. I'm nothing now, because I gave in. If you love to paint, then for God's sake don't give up. Isn't that the way it's supposed to be?"

"But they proved to me the old clichés are true. Painters are born. I was born to be something else, a shoe salesman or something."

"Of course, they're all clichés, but that's all we've got left anymore. Maybe it should all be existentialist. You can't let anyone tell you what you were born for. You've got to fight. Of course it all sounds like a lot of noble bullshit, but you have to fight to the end."

"Just shut up."

"What is it? You really just want to make money and crawl your way to the top of the pyramid? Is that all there is in it for you? I was like that, but then, I'm nothing. I always thought that someone as confident and certain as you would be different

Aren't you different, for God's sake? Have I been wrong about you too?"

Magni drew back. Arrington had never before challenged him like this. He waited for the ritual move of apology, but none came. Strangers were beginning to glance over at them from other tables, tittering at each other with nice social grace. The silence was beginning to destroy him now.

Arrington paused, measuring the strength of his convictions with his desperate need for this man's friendship. He teetered on the brink of apology, nearly escaped back into his broken personality, but then, before he could understand just what it was he needed most, he leapt forward suicidally. He grasped madness. "I'm trying to make you understand what you should be! I can't be wrong! Not now! Everything's so confusing these days, it's impossible to be sure of yourself. If you're not committed to *anything,* what is it worth? How can *I* stay sane? I'm trying—"

Magni stood up from the table.

"Wait!" Arrington stood defiantly. He was demanding to be listened to now, not tolerated. "If you can just tell me that much —what the hell is it all worth and how can I—how can a person stay sane? I have to know. Now, before you go, before—"

Magni was gone. The few people remaining in the café stared at the weeping man with no first name, misunderstanding. He slouched back into his seat in sudden and complete exhaustion, shook his head with tremendous and terrifying force as if to aid the screaming exit of wraiths from within his body, the demons that now returned control to him, mercilessly, after their spirited possession.

Magni remained locked in his room for the next few days, plotting his revenge, leaving only for food and movies and meagre withdrawals from his dwindling savings account. He furiously avoided Arrington; it became the single purpose of his sanity and his soul.

He spent these days of self-restricted solitary confinement sinking himself deeper into depression of his own devise. He avoided any contact with his friends, and occasionally, unable to redirect his thoughts, as if a prisoner to their constricting perspective, reflected upon Arrington's final words and the phrasing of his attack.

He placed razor blades in Arrington's soap in the bathroom. Stole his towels. Tore his mailslot from the front porch, and burned a letter he found within that must have been from Arrington's parents. But though he lay awake late into the nights, he heard no cries of pain, no whimperings of loneliness. And it was then, when he discovered that the spectre trail which embodied Arrington had vanished, that absolute fear crept in. The tracks of his silent antagonist had once surrounded him constantly, had destined and permeated his every action: the distant creaking of a door, footsteps echoing on worn tile.

There were still moments when he received intuitive premonitions of the spectre's nearness, but he soon realized that these instances were the result of his own problems and not Arrington's hidden presence. He became annoyed with Arrington for having disappeared so long, for ignoring him so strongly, and became intensely curious as to why the man did not return to him. Sure, he admitted to himself, I treated him like shit, but he's always come back. Such curiosity as to the man's unknown motives ate away his dislikes for Arrington. And he began to miss him, wished to see again the strange, sad man and his blind respect.

One day he went over to Arrington's room with a memorized, carefully constructed and not too humble apology he hoped to employ in discovering what the man had been doing without him. There was no answer when he knocked. He returned the next day a few more times, cursing the walls for the silence exchanged to him for his efforts. Could he have moved? No, Magni had convinced himself that Arrington could never leave. There was no place for him to go.

He began to have trouble sleeping. He stayed awake listening for the sounds of Arrington's entrance or exit, leaving his door wide open until dawn. He spent hours at his window, staring down at the walkway which led to the building.

Two weeks were gone, and with them, a montage of persistent memories. His position as sentinel grew stronger to him each day, until, one morning, gripped suddenly by some fierce premonition, Magni burst through the hall to Arrington's room. The door was locked and he kicked it open violently ahead of himself and it bounced back loudly from the wall. A stench struck him like grease fire. Magni stood staring with the hideous fascination of a man behind another's eyes witnessing his own fate. Face down, the body lay sprawled across the doorway to the washbasin. Blood, congealed and thick like Navajo clay, caused an illusion of movement beneath his severed wrists. The phone was off the hook and sent off spiraling screams. There was a sharp instance of déjà vu; a surge of adrenalin, and the corpse was gone. The door was closed and locked before him in an unexperienced instant, as if his mind had been forced backwards in time. As if the cinematographer of this realistic set had removed the dummies and set the cameras running again.

He stepped back. Took two more quick steps into the hall as he swung around, setting up defenses against an hysteria that never came. Footsteps echoed far away.

He leapt to the staircase and looked down. A hand slid up the railing, pivoting at every flight. The footsteps halted for a moment; the intruder seemed to be listening for something. Abruptly, they continued up the stairs, and as they neared, he understood, shocked that such understanding was not what he considered madness.

He ran to his room as the bearded painter reached the top step. He was thinking about how some things must die in order that others may live . . . as he closed the door behind himself.

C. L. GRANT

The Summer Of
The Irish Sea

Once he had made up his mind to run for the heaven in the sea, Traynor was both relieved and apprehensive. After fifteen years of relative solitude, he relied more on instinct than on conscious thought, and he enjoyed the feeling of having a goal, though he didn't call it that, even with the dangers that would come with the trying; and in a submerged cavern of his mind, something told him to go on.

Necessity ruled his life; he had known it had become imperative to run for it when he was almost driven to the ground two seasons before because he was too slow. He had wavered, hesitated, fearful of leaving his sanctuary. It had taken a second near-capture to give him the strength, and the fear.

Heaven was an island in the Irish Sea. So he had heard. So he believed as he sat on the low bank watching the shallow stream pass him by. In the twisting clear water he saw his face and shook his head to be sure it was his. Had he the memory, he would have been able to compare what he saw with the way it had been when he was released; now there was only long, black and matted hair tangling with a dark beard he tried to keep short with sharpened stones. His thin face was cracked and browned by the weather, splotched with dull red infections from insect bites and thorns. He leaned forward and saw the strength in his lean arms and chest, the speed in the long legs. The leaf-and-reed loincloth was only a protection, not a reminder.

He grunted and threw a pebble into the water, and immediately the ripples were erased.

A bird called, was answered, and called again.

A hare poked its head through the tall grass opposite him, but he was not hungry and he let it go.

A short while and the heat was erased by shadows that covered the movement of the stream. There was a comfort in the twilight coolness telling him the end of the season was near; and he was glad because the next day he would be on his way, heading for heaven and the plentiful game that would feed him until he died.

He believed it, and that fed him, too.

During his first few months of freedom, Traynor had attempted to keep track of time so he would know when fall officially arrived and he could move across the low hills without fear; but there was too much to do just to stay alive, and he learned instead to watch for the changing leaves and to test the night air. He quickly discovered an animal pleasure in staying alive long enough to watch the snow fly, and he felt sorry, for a while, for those who purposely lived in the open. Somehow, in spite of everything, they had failed the training and wanted to die, not knowing what it would be like to die.

When the last of the light faded into stars, he lowered himself into the stream, ignoring the water's sting, and waded upstream to the low-hanging branch that marked his lair. Being careful not to touch the bank, he leaped up to a reed rope and climbed rapidly, silently into the middle branches. Three trees growing together wove an effective screen, and a slight rearrangement provided him with a narrow platform for sleeping, and hiding when necessary.

The mattress of leaves was damp and cool, and there was a moment's regret at leaving the bed that had given him eight winters of protection, eight summers of hope. His stomach protested when he stretched out, but it wasn't the first time he had gone to bed without eating. He remembered the hare and smiled.

A bird whispered and was answered.

Then it was quiet and he knew it was safe, and he slept, lightly.

II

In the canyon of sleep Traynor dreamed:

A very wide room without paint or picture. A score of beds made of warped slats laid across bricks. Men and women slept quietly, lightly. A tired-looking man in a white coat opened the heavy metal door and crumpled a piece of paper in his hand. Instantly everyone sat up. He grinned and left. They slept. Again he was there, stepping on a small twig until it snapped. They sat up. He grinned and nodded. They slept.

A very wide room with a dirt floor covered with gravel. Naked, panting, perspiring, they jogged around close to the walls; the man, a different man, stood in the center like a horse trainer, urging them on until only one remained on his bleeding feet. Traynor. He was young. Food was thrown at them and they fought with hands and feet and teeth and heads, and ate with their fingers. No one talked: only the grunts and pants and crunching of bare feet on gravel.

It was hot; it was cold. They were in a compound without visible barriers, except for the dogs. It was wet, dry, noisy, quiet. Except for the horses, and the dogs. Snow, sex, rain, sex, heat and death. In the buildings, in the open.

In the rooms, both of them, there were bars on the windows.

In the canyon of sleep Traynor sensed:

Two people: one man, young; one man older but not old. Their faces only, distorted, barely recognizable as faces.

"Tell you what, Edwin, I'll make that fifty pounds you don't."

"I love your confidence in me, you bastard, but you're on. See if Margot is ready. I'll be outside with the others."

III

Traynor dropped to the ground and moved quickly through the trees to the burrow he had seen the afternoon before. He crouched, waiting patiently, then leaned forward. His hand darted into the hole and dragged the kicking hare out, twisting its neck before its hindquarters were clear of the ground. As he tore at the warm flesh and spat the fur to one side, he thought of the dreams: he dismissed the first because it was recurrent and had lost its meaning; held the second until it faded only because it was less a dream than a dread. He paused, the animal's blood running down his forearms and hands, then dismissed that too. It was disturbing, but he would wait until, *if* it came back.

When he finished the meal, he buried the bones in the bed of the stream and waded westward until his lair was out of sight. Then he left the cold water and hurried through the woods. It was still too early for anything to happen, but there was a meadow he had to cross before the heat slowed him down. As he walked, he listened to the wind, separating the sounds into rustling leaves and animals, and just the wind. Excitement made him tense, and the feeling was so different than when he was being hunted that he was reluctant to shake it off.

He surprised a bird in its nest and ate while he moved.

There were images of blue water, green land, and others like him no longer afraid to be together—he hummed and was startled by the sound, but it struck him as being good; peaceful, like the night.

He walked faster, using a memory to prod him on: a man he had met, living in a cave dug into the bank of a river. Traynor had wandered from the self-imposed boundaries of his land when he reached the river, farther north than he had ever been. Together they filled the other's larder with fish caught by hand, then sat in the cave and talked. It was a strange sensation, talking, and Traynor was slow to realize he did not like it.

"What'd you do?" It was the standard opening, the greeting among his kind. The man was old.

"Multiple," Traynor answered without remembering. "A wife, a man and a woman. I was about twenty-five." No memory, just ritual.

"Rape and murder. They were fifteen, I was twenty-eight."

The two traded their lives, near-captures, and the hunts they had seen from hiding places. Both knew they were freaks for living so long. Then the other told him of the heaven. It took most of the afternoon because the words, unused for so long a time, were difficult to resurrect.

"I've seen a few of us lately heading west, always in winter. We're quite a number up here, you see, not so many towns and large houses. These others, they talk of a place in the Irish Sea. Food. Warm places. No blood. That's what they say. The Irish Sea, over there someplace." He paused a long moment. "I'm trying next year."

The following day, moving south, Traynor heard the baying hounds behind him and ran, angry that he hadn't taken some of the fish with him now that they were sure to be wasted.

Several times in several years he heard about the heaven. The promised delights were always different, but the place was always the same. He ignored the talk as foolish—how could they know?—most especially from the women he only wanted to use. He had been safe for more seasons than he could count, until the summer he'd nearly been caught because he was too slow.

Suddenly, before he registered the fact, Traynor stopped thinking and saw glimpses of the meadow's flowing green. The sun was hot. He slowed, stopped, then crept forward agilely on all fours. His eyes narrowed, his nostrils widened. A large bush a few yards from the tall grass shielded him from any eyes that might have been trained in his direction. He shifted until the wind blew in his face. He knew this place, he could run it without concentration, without looking down.

But now he would wait, listen, and wait again.

Insects drifted to and away from him. His legs became stiff and he shifted angrily. A spider, not three inches from his cheek, leisurely wrapped an immobile bee in fragile-looking white.

He dozed.

IV

In the shadow of the spider Traynor dreamed:

A montage of faces, swirling, spewing words tonelessly. Before Traynor, before his father and his father's father. Fragments overlapping and sometimes senseless. He understood none of it.

"There're just too many . . . no room . . . no room . . ."

"Legalized murder! That's all it is! How can we as a people con—"

"It works in the Union . . ."

"Without war there must be an outlet . . . nothing worse than beasts anyway how can their vile existence be tolerated when . . ."

The faces blurred and spun—a shift while Traynor shifted his feet in the dust.

"Trained, conditioned, and weeded out, they adapt as—"

"Far more exciting. Instinct and reason, by God it's—"

"German shepherds are best if one heads—"

Traynor made a sound much like a whimper, and sensed:

"Margot, don't tell us you're squeamish."

"Nonsense, Edwin love, I'm just nervous. It's all the excitement, that's all. I'm simply not an old hand at it like you."

V

Traynor shook himself awake and punched the ground in frustration. Time that was not his had been wasted, and a terrifying sense of urgency shook his limbs. He decided against running, however, since the next line of trees was too far away to outrun any dogs. He moved slowly below the tops of the weeds and grass trying to stay in time to the wind that sifted out of the trees. Bees ignored him, flies did not. The air cooled in the intervals of shade as clouds passed under the sun. He rested for a moment beside a rotted log, not thinking but fearing that he had never had to do this before, knowing he could usually travel a whole day without stopping. He stretched up and measured the distance left; the shadows were what he was after.

He was hungry.

He rose to his knees, tensed, then ran, watching the trees bob in front of him. The afternoon silence was hardly broken except for the sound of his own breathing. When finally he fell gasping into the brush and let the sun-speckled shadows wrap him gently, he closed his eyes and sweat drenched him. Never, never before had he felt so winded. He became afraid.

By the time the sun began teasing the horizon, he found himself in an area beyond his own. He skirted several small farms and a village, avoided the roads as much as he could. There had been a time when he had considered killing a man and stealing his clothes; but sooner or later somebody would notice the brands on his forehead and back.

Eventually he caught a family of quail and a hare and sat on his haunches eating. He hurried, unaware of the noises around him. He finished and left the bones unburied.

When the evening soothed him and made him tired, he found a tree to sleep in. He thought, for a moment, how fat he'd grow in heaven, the mate to be there when he wanted her, and the dying old he desired.

"Old," he said aloud. He liked the sound of it.

He slept, soundly.

VI

Two people: riding, smiling, bobbing, unidentifiable. One complained about the smell of salt air. Bobbing, riding, smiling.

"Why should he leave, Edwin? I mean, it's not very logical, is it. Why, he's practically a legend."

"Sooner or later, love, he'd have heard of the migration. Maybe he's ready to chuck it in, like a dog, maybe, who's ready to die. I don't know."

"Maybe, but it's still not—"

"My dear, you're giving it credit for something it no longer has. It's like giving a quadratic equation to a horse and expecting him to solve it. Impossible. Hey, there they go! Come, hurry, Margot, I want to get home for supper!"

The air was cool, the ground damp as the sun split itself between leaves and branches. Traynor finished a meager starling and began walking, noticing belatedly a difference in the smell of the air. He wrinkled his nose and wondered. His footsteps were punctuated by grunts and he ran more often.

A partially plowed field stretched in front of him. He halted, looked, leaned into the strange wind that pushed his beard against his chest and his hair over the gothic F scarred into his brow. He drank deeply in a creek, then stepped into the sun, running, keeping balance by the touch of his fingers on the ground. Then he lay in the shadow of a log and watched the belt of woodland ahead for signs of movement. It stretched like a green quarter-moon, blackened by the glare of the sun in his eyes.

He smiled.

More tired than he remembered being in his life, he clenched his fists and rose, and heard the dogs. Stiffening, he waited for their direction, then sprinted over the frozen waves of the field.

Low, hunched, breathing easily now that the tension was broken, he passed the tips of the crescent as the hounds scattered from the underbrush like leaves. Their yelps became bays, and behind them the horn signaled.

Traynor's eyes widened in fear and he surrendered all pretext of hiding as he straightened his legs to get more power. Glancing around quickly, he veered sharply to his right, hearing rather than seeing the horsemen break into the open. The furrows tripped him, slowed him until he began leaping from top to top.

The horn, low and high, low and high, pushed him on. He stumbled without falling. A small dog stood in his way, fangs bared, growling. In sudden anger Traynor kept on, and when the dog leaped, he smashed it across the throat with his forearm. Another began snapping at his heels and he stopped, pivoted, and grabbing its muzzle, used the momentum to help him toss it over his shoulder. A third was kicked in the head and it collapsed into the dirt, whimpering and whining. He ran on, humming something he knew was about oceans and waves and the wide Irish Sea.

Another dog, still another, became tangled in his legs and they sprawled, rolling on the ground, Traynor's hand on its throat, choking and pushing its tearing fangs and wide, frenzied eyes away from its face.

There was a sharp pain in his side, on his legs, on his back.

Slowly he reeled, fell, stood, fell. A prison cell floated, a man in white coasted, blood spurted softly from a knife wound in a woman's chest. A horse, a rider, fangs, a smile.

Low and high the horn.

He heard the call to heaven.

My God, he cried out silently, I'm not a—

The woman rode up and reined in her mount just as the man screamed.

"Congratulations, Margot, you're the first! He's beautiful, and the trophies are yours, of course."

"God, Edwin, he screamed."

"They always do, dear. You never really get used to it."

"He knew!"

"Nonsense, Margot, nonsense. Why should he be any different from the others? Do you . . . do you want me to carry them back, love?"

"No, not the cloth, just the . . . other. I'm . . . I'm not sure I want it."

"I understand, dearest. You'll change your mind; it's only the letdown after the chase. Just keep telling yourself he was a rapist or something. Dammit, Peter! For God's sake, be careful what you're doing with that thing. That's better. Put it in the saddlebag, will you? And don't force it, idiot, you'll tear the ears off."

PG WYAL

The Newsocrats:
Confessions
Of A Eunuch Dreamer

I—the cast

By four o'clock everything was ready. The cameras and radio
mikes were set up and concealed within and behind the props.
The crew was situated in its remote nest like maggots in rotten
meat, invisible. There'd be no other chance; no boom or lens
could extend into the picture and ruin the show. When your
margin for error is zero your errors must be zero. Perfection
is our only axiom.

The show would hit pre- and prime-time hours from seven to

nine. The impact would hit them, like the kick of a mule in their soft backsides, at just prime time. Prime time is Arthur Bronstein's most effective period. The emotional matrixes are way up then, one of our best conditioned reflexes. Arthur's the anchorman, the cohesive constant in our equations. Arthur spent hours putting on his ash-gray makeup. His mirrored face a sombre darkness somehow not brightened by the circle of fierce light. On the screen, dramatized with the right lighting, he would look stricken, aghast, drained of blood, as if in shock. If he'd ever missed a cue or muffed his timing I'd never seen it. He never hesitated or stammered or stood at a loss for words.

Senator Douglas Westlake had arrived early in the morning. He wanted everything just right for his performance. The Senator was tall, a little gray but straight, not stooped—rather like Arthur the anchorman, only casting a somewhat more solid, dignified and intelligent image on the screen, without all of Arthur's dark emanations and connotations. Those would not suit a presidential candidate at all. The image projected was a calm and serious one, but with foundations of humor and optimism. Arthur was not a wit; Westlake was, profoundly and prominently. Senator Westlake was groomed and grounded in his role by Affiliated World Networks for five years. The screen climax ticked nearer and nearer; he showed no strain through his hypnotized fog; tension twisted and knotted his thoughts but not his good face. Our therapy was kind. It would be his last performance. Nobody suffered.

Naturally, Mrs. Westlake was close by his side. Marcia Westlake was a strong, stable woman, attractive in a deep, substantial manner. No flashy society bitch, her appeal was designed to be broader than that, to strike a common matriarchal chord in all our viewers, for she will be the emotional focus directly after the tragedy and we need an iron woman, a creature of substance behind the symbols; the entire atmosphere of tension and suppressed hysteria we were creating revolved around her. She is the fulcrum upon which we rest our lever, the personality that assimilates the public's objectivized, vicarious torment. Later she will be our tool, to twist and turn the world.

The limousine was ready in the garage, brooded over by batteries of greenly oscillating screens and sharply calibrated meters. It's a beautiful car, a Continental with a rolldown top and dual turbines that sing a throaty keen of power. An authoritative, dignified automobile, suited for its part. Blue and deep, a trembling sky.

I am the director. In my booth buried behind the sphinx-faced facade of AWN Tower, I choose strategem, plot battles, make the armies clash on cue. All responsibility is mine; all blame, all profit. The viewers know me as a cipher, a flicker on the credits at the end of newscasts or public events specials. They've never seen the eyes that show them truth—eyes which have no color, no face around them, devouring all light and image with reflection.

Phoenix. That's the town. Phoenix, hunching in the desert like a forest of silver cacti, floods the dry valley from sky to substrata, from fossil beds to foothills, with a complacent and content humanity. Phoenix, calm and efficient, clean and noble, set in the rasping desert wind like a perfect oasis of crystal spires or hypodermic needles, sharp and sterile. Phoenix, the monster that draws itself together out of continual annihilation, to taunt the sky, arrogant and cruel.

Phoenix was the perfect set.

II—the teaser

The motorcade would begin at six, exactly. We spent the day in unhurried preparations. The budget allowed plenty of time for everything. We had anticipated this day for over five years, and knew all the mistakes we could possibly make—an astronomy of error. All our mistakes were corrected before they could be committed. The script called for crowds of certain enthusiasm and intensity; the extras were already on location and the assistant directors and script girls were coaxing them to their correct positions and roles. The local commentators were at their posts; I would personally supervise them from my booth. The spotmen and interviewers were all on location and ready for curtain. The last speech of the campaign, we had advertised, would not go uncovered. In order to satisfy a need the need must sometimes be created—so we advertised ourselves. Advertising panders to the unborn urge. Advertising enhances the news; if they don't know what's important, tell them—and they will believe.

Senator Westlake and his wife took off in the big ballistic transport at five. They would orbit once, then arc down upon Phoenix. Eddy, the propman, had done a wonderful job; the transport, used throughout the campaign as the Senator's official vehicle (all entrances and embarkations must be grand and noble), was painted a brilliant mirror silver, with bright, yellow-bordered red lettering around the visual center of gravity. The ship was not the standard metal phallus but a newer model whose connotations were more sedate, cautious—a squat ovoid shape that suggested strength and immovability in crisis. A safe but powerful image, which suited Senator Westlake excellently.

I watched in the control booth as he came down on Phoenix Port at five-fifty exactly. The ship settled down on its hungry fusion torch like a beautiful silver bullet about to slide back into the barrel of a gun. The sun gleamed yellow and fat, sparkling off its mirror rind. Daylight savings had finally been extended the year around, so there was plenty of light by which to see the landing and the tragedy. The landing was even more beautiful, more awe- and love-inspiring than we had computed—its emotional index was barely below the acceptable upper limit. A quick glance at continuous readout told me we'd have to play down the early stages of the motorcade or go beyond the predictability range of our planning. I made the necessary arrangements with the spotmen and commentators. (Their voices like soft chords behind the solemn keynote Arthur.)

The huge bullet settled down on its pad, vomiting flame, and sat silent for fifteen seconds. When the drama indices of continuous readout indicated saturation, I signaled the pilot to open the debarking ramp. It slid down like a shiny tongue from the craft's empty bowels. There was another slight pause until continuous readout told me to bring out the Senator and his party. I gave them the cue and immediately saw them on the monitor, standing, waving and smiling in the portal. Mrs. Westlake was wearing a light blue dress, with her hair (black, streaks of mature silver) in a tight bouffant style. The Senator appeared happy and enthusiastic, delighted to return the crowd's smiles and waves. The crowd was cheering at fifteen decibels, just as planned. The readout showed optimum progress, excellent saturation. The rating was low but would improve.

After another carefully coordinated pause to give the viewers time to recognize and begin to emphasize with the characters, I spoke into the throatmike:

"Okay, Senator, begin down the ramp. Walk slowly, don't show too much anxiety or anticipation. Make sure you take at least twenty seconds to reach the bottom of the ramp. Dignified, easy."

He heard me through the receiver buried in the bone behind his left ear. (Eddy's surgical team had left no scar.) Still smiling, he began to hike down the ramp with his wife's left arm entwined in his right. He wore a gray-black suit and maroon turtleneck, a sober, rational contrast to Marcia's pale blue sheath and pearl necklace. His head shone a casual silver, dry and unoiled. Some of the glowing hairs stood out from his head, looking gossamer and electric. He was handsome.

He reached the foot of the ramp and posed for photos. His smile revealed large, long teeth, white and rigid. They were the teeth of a strong man, a leader. They had been implanted at great expense by the best orthodontic surgeons.

Continuous readout, for some reason, sputtered violently across its screen to terminate the picture-taking session immediately. I rattled a few words into my throatmike, and on the screen marked PUBLIC saw the Senator extract himself graciously from the newsmen and TV cameras. He came across sincerely, nothing phony, even in the harshly real, revealing depths of the holoscreen; a man must be a total actor to effect such composure and certainty on TV. Westlake was a total actor.

The Continental was waiting at the edge of the Port. It seemed to be in motion even with its motors off. The car reflected sunlight with a depthless metallic glow, blue, sky-dark. It was a wheeled dreadnought, an implacable carnivore, a relentless killer. It was the penultimate automobile, the utter male symbol. Its hood was long, its roof low; its lines flowed and ran like translucent seawater around a driving submarine hull. This was a vehicle of power, a coach for imperial means.

The senatorial party climbed in. But our cameras didn't show this action; such are our modern gods, to be spared the undignified, freed from mortal clumsiness. Gods do not stoop—on wings or air they ride, our witnessed kings.

A cut to the distance showed the car begin to flow like a blue wave down the gentle slope, white concrete under liquid steel, cloverleafing, and reeling onto the superhighway. The roof was still raised.

An aerial view showed the car speeding down the road in regal isolation. (Beyond the causeway, a long pan of parched seabottom, death's archaic sediments.) We had cleared the highway completely, even to the point of removing the center divider. The vehicle shot directly down the center of the white carpet, its outlines blurred by speed—and camera work.

Overhead the sun burned searingly in a flawless, naked sky. The desert above was as empty and bleak as the desert below, and promised of stars. A low-angle shot silhouetted the Continental against the violet Eastern horizon, followed it as it sped towards the stark, cruel beauty of the city. An orbital camera relayed down a magnified, slightly distorted view of Phoenix from 1,000 kilometers: a grid of broad streets, long shadows of the spires as hard and straight as the spires themselves, the occasional winking and glinting of a needlepoint as it caught the sun and hurled it again into space. All seen through a faintly shimmering blue mist, a wisp of sky below. This shot in intermittant flashes, sandwiched between longshots of the racing blue rapier.

Actually, the car was not traveling too fast. Continuous readout—as well as the script—indicated that the entrance to the city should take at least fifteen minutes, to allow tension and that thin undercurrent of apprehension to build up to a crest. Then the crest could be sustained, guided, and allowed to crash in foam and spray to its ultimate beaching of blood. The computers steered and drove the machine in a direct hookup to continuous readout. There would be no error.

The highway split the city in two. An overhead shot from a chopper showed it running from the Port to the downtown Plaza like an arrow, like a spear, like a tracer-bullet flashing white over the gray flatness of the desert. From the Plaza, the motorcade would commence, head to a large convention hall three miles distant. The convention hall was irrelevant.

The car entered the city.

(Subliminals: sperm-cell lancing ovum. Intercourse. Daggers into flesh.)

I glanced at continuous readout nervously. The ratings were starting to pick up; in fifteen minutes we'd eclipse the afternoon kiddy shows and achieve our first plateau. The emotional indices would begin to achieve predominance over everything else. Our audience was world wide; each time zone would receive the show without warning at exactly prime time. But this was no rehearsal —the tape had to be real, alive. It was a touchy period—the range for slipup and error was more than marginal. A mistake could reduce our intensity level and blow the show.

Arthur's deep, hollow voice was a gloss, a relaxed polish, over the picture. It was not yet a prime factor, but its importance would grow. Arthur was really the Show; his voice and evocations controlled the delicate web of public thought and feeling. Even if the masses did not pay special attention to what he said, their nervous systems would pick up the subsonic subtleties woven so carefully into the way he said it. Of course, nothing would be extemporized.

Eddy the propman now played his part. As the car pulled up briefly in the center of the Plaza and stopped for more picture-taking and adulation, Eddy twisted a dial and caused a slow, slight change in the hue of the Continental. The car did not visibly change color—that would have been too obvious, too crude. Instead, it entered a new reflectory/refractory state in which the light hitting its surface was polarized. Electrically activated liquid crystals under its plastic skin became reoriented to permit only lower-frequency light to reflect from its shimmering surface. Color is one of the mind's most subtle and basic emotion indicators; a change in color is a change in mood. By lowering the frequency of the car's already deeply diffracted light, from sky-blue-of-elation to sky-blue-of-sunset-and-dying, Eddy changed the viewers' mood from one of expectation and elation to scraped nerves, foreboding, sick stomachs.

The top rolled back. Continuous readout showed a sudden leap in apprehension. Excellent—as planned. The ratings were rapidly climbing, now. The intensity of emotion was rapidly whirling into a vortex, a cyclone of vicarious involvement and empathy.

It was a pattern they recognized.

III—the climax

Seven o'clock. The emotional indices soared, like a diver before the plunge, the fall. Continuous Readout splashed happy symbols across the electroluminous screen; PUBLIC showed throngs held in thrall by the charismatic personality of Westlake, minds attuned to a single frequency, a monotonous note. Their faces were not real, but mirage things, some refraction in the air over the desert pan. Our cameras showed them from a hundred calculated angles, closeup and longshot, pan and still. They showed them from the outward image and inward eye, as shape and as symbol. Great drama was broadcast; great and terrible emotions swelled. By mounting tides we hooked them from their sea.

The Senator and his wife stood in the car's rear compartment and looked out at the crowds ."Smile," I commanded, and they smiled. Smiled sincerely, smiled honestly, smiled with love and the certainty of the very, very confident. They simply thought of other things. They were actors to the core—what core remained.

The crowd was a froth of faces, a noise of adulation, a color of love and enthusiasm. It registered perfectly on the screen and with continuous readout. Everything was on cue.

The towers of Phoenix were tall, gloomed by shadow. (In the holographic depths like Luna's shadow-naked fangs, needles into our staring eyes.) They afforded a roost, a perch for the cannibal bird. Phoenix that consumes himself in the fires of birth, Phoenix ever young.

Phoenix the grave-robber and the womb-thief.

I muttered into the mike and the cavalcade began. Like a gypsy cortege, moving in a flurry of noise and color, the parade rolled out. The car was a sleek, slow ox plagued by the big hornets of police cars and the small flies of motorcycles. The crowd was hungry for the ox. In their minds was the latent taste of blood. In their eyes the ancient spectacle of slaughter, a Roman circus. They were hungry and we knew their hunger.

In the waning sunlight the Senator and his wife looked fine and right, a nexus for what fineness and rightness remained. A camera at ground level caught the confident, clean grin. A closeup of the loose, relaxed hand, so calm and manicured-clean, showed them the firm grip he would have; the grip on fate, security; Big Daddy. His image was deeper in two dimensions than theirs in three. They wanted him.

They wanted him so badly.

I ordered an overhead pan. An electric chopper revealed the straightness of their march; silently it spied on crowd and prince. Camelot was regal that day, Camelot was smooth. The blue limousine stood gallantly at the head of the column, like an arrowhead of blue steel. It was flanked by the knights on wicked motorcycles, each with a cool black rod Excalibur, to deal with the mobs in a symbolic, ceremonial way. The fuel-cell bikes were black death and silver mercy; Continuous readout had no complaints about the motorcycles. Behind the Continental and the bikes were four police cars, side to side, like a phalanx, and

110

then a train of smaller black limousines, the steed of dignitaries and dignitaries-to-be. They were identical, nothing to distract from the Senator and his shining silver head; merely background, margins, something for the Senator to contrast. Behind the train of limousines rolled a single-file line of more motorcycles; these went almost unnoticed. Later they would play a part.

Arthur narrated innocuously. His voice was calm, relaxed, down pat. He knew his part and knew its relation to the rest of the script. Arthur would not miff. Arthur was careful.

Eddy the propman came in and winked at me. "All finished," he joked. Eddy is a big, bluff fellow. He enjoys irony and wit. "I checked the instruments five times." Eddy is not all jokes and spirit; Eddy is careful, too.

"The charge will not go off until three separate studs and toggles are studded and toggled," said Eddy, smiling. He brushed sandy hair out of his rain-gray eyes. "The first two are at station WOR in New York and BBC-2 in London. They've already been activated—so the only one left holding the bag is us."

I looked at the handsome figure now filling the PUBLIC screen. He was waving and smiling.

"When you pull up the cap on the DESTRUCT button, green lights will flash on panels in both London and New York. They'll have fifteen seconds to reverse the sequence or completely deactivate it. Then the computers will arm the device and deactivate their consoles. We'll be on our own."

"And I can push the button," I added absently.

"Yeah," said Eddy. He grinned.

He was a solid man, a good engineer. He did a good job.

Continuous readout reeled off figures. We had reached the critical point in the countdown. The emotional indices were way up; the crowd could go either way but either way would be violent. Arthur's voice had slowly turned from a smooth bass to a somewhat rasping baritone. The effect upon the viewers was carefully calculated: from undercurrents of anxiety to overtones of apprehension. Nervousness crept into their hearts. Arthur's hair was black, streaked with gray. He was not on screen but his image remained, like some brooding raven, dark and deathlike. The voice that tells of bad things—the timber of time, hollow and honed.

Eddy relaxed in a chair on the other side of the glass. His part was finished. His reflection grinned in the glass. For a second I had the feeling that I could not tell which was Eddy, man or reflection. Presently I realized that it didn't matter—what mattered was which I thought was Eddy.

I began to sweat. Emotions are fine, but they lower efficiency; you can't do a good job all up tight. My palms grew steadily more slick. The screen marked PUBLIC glowed with the calm of late afternoon and a picnic sun. Tension did crackle underneath but the visible scene was smooth, still water, despite the surges of *tsunami* that would soon climb the beaches and drain their tears. The tide, I saw, carried me along with it; are we then all swimmers, drowning in the seas we make?

I did not have time to philosophize. Things were moving on an accelerating curve.

The cameras showed shifting, angled closeups of Westlake. His forehead loomed pale and sheer above metallic gray eyes. The eyebrown arched into small horns, like arrowpoints. The mouth was a thin line, once full but withered, creased with humor's wear at the corners. His beard had been eradicated by electrolysis; there was no shadow. His chin was smooth and creased vertically in the middle—like buttocks or labia. It was a gentle, strong, masculine face. We scanned its good features constantly.

Arthur's voice:

". . . Now the motorcade is passing the halfway mark. The Senator appears calm, seems to be enjoying it. Mrs. Westlake is obviously enjoying things; she's smiling and waving at the crowd as if it were all for her. Marcia Westlake isn't new to this, though. She's been in over six campaigns with her husband, from the first mayoral contest through his battle for the Filipino governorship, right down to the present presidential duel. They say she's his 'secret weapon' . . ."

His platitudes buzzed into the background. Continuous readout was puking apoplectic fits of cryptography across its screen. Emotional matrixes, ratings, probability percentages, alternate futures, immediate and extrapolated reactions. Computers from the five major urban centers in this time zone relayed their bits and glimpses, and continuous readout collated them into a meaningful hologram. Lasered their chaos.

I said that out loud and Eddy laughed.

Eddy is a good guy.

But I couldn't laugh with him. The readout screen was angry with light and symbol. I followed its instructions grimly. First, a cue to Arthur to further lower the timber of his voice. Then an

112

order to the camera crew to shoot dramatic longshots—longshots built tension. (The public, too, knows its cues.) After that I began earnestly studying the emotional matrix figures. The final decision, its timing, was up to me. Everything hinged on that. The Senator had less than a mile to go; he'd have to exit within two or three minutes, at a time when the tension was stimulated, unconsciously, to feverishness. Black wings had to obscure a mythic sun, omens had to fall.

A spotman: "In the next half-mile, what readings indicate greatest dramatic tensions?"

In other words, what landscapes and patterns evoked the best dark dreams.

I told him: A seven-story brick warehouse, a grassy knoll, a clump of bushes.

"Play it up," I said.

I adjusted the settings on the console in front of me. The cap was up, the idiot-lights like green snake eyes, unblinking. Exactly four hundred yards down that concrete corridor we'd get him.

Nothing to do now. We waited.

Two minutes. I made impotent fists.

Arthur's voice, a melancholy drone.

Closeup caresses of the Knight, so real and near.

Then—

Continuous readout reeled off a glowing series of numbers:

10

9

8

7

6

5

4

3

red red red red red red red 2 red red red red red red red
bluewhite bluewhite bluewhite 1 *bluewhite bluewhite bluewhite*
At one I inhaled, almost gasped.

Then zero.

"Now!" I shouted and stabbed the button.

On the PUBLIC screen, turmoil. Abruptly the gray-silver closeup head, still grinning confidently, coughed apart. Bright blood erupted from the skull, gushing and flowing, with lumps of brain as in a thick raw stew. Audio pickups transmitted a sharp *crack*, like an explosion. The body crumpled into the blue lap of Mrs. Westlake, its shattered white head vomiting blood and brains.

Now blurred camera work, confusion visualized. Subsonic terror and subvisual panic were broadcast in subliminal flickers. Mrs. Westlake stood up with her blue dress soaked in blood, silent jaws working. Someone clambered on the limousine's trunk. (In their minds, the torment of Jacqueline.) The column of motorcycles crashing into the crowd, churning people crushed and hurled into the air, machine-guns chattering wildly. Arthur's voice breaking to gibberish.

"Migod, migod, the President—the Senator's been shot!"

A million lies on ten million screens. The scene constantly dissolving and fading out. Snatches of tortured faces, some familiar and some evoking the familiar. Subliminally, the Lords of Camelot. Consciously, the anguish of damnation. Blood and brains and void in his open eyes.

Eddy the propman had done a good job.

He was always careful.

IV—the denouement

It was a perfect job. Everything went smooth and fast. They are blind and stupid and will believe anything we tell them. While our drama unfolded, events transpired as usual. The main collators in New York digested the tragedy and flashed curves of prediction across our screens. It edited the tape for maximum effect, total impact. The West and Mountain zones had seen the assassination live, but the Midwest and East would get a carefully spliced and edited rehash during their respective Prime times. The papers, the magazines and the printouts, those that were not owned or controlled by AWN anyway, all got their information through us. They'd release the information as we fed it to them. Actually the prophets of Instant Communication (the Comsat nuts, et al) were completely wrong; it's not instant communication that knits men together, but budgeted communication. As the hours of prime impact hit the various parts of the globe, we would, through our various mechanisms, release the news. The news is important; you can't afford to slop it about as if it were some cheap, common swill. The news is delicate, as demanding of form and rigor as a crystal; it must be handled with mathematical deliberation and logic.

We are always logical.

A couple of hours later came the information that the "assassin" had somehow eluded the net cast after him. The public accepted this news with anxiousness, fear. A couple of hours of commentator speculation and worry after that (allowing for a one-hour delay between time zones), we broadcast that there seemed to be no traces of the killer. Killer, killer, killer. We repeated the word again and again into oversensitive mikes. The broadcast computers were programed to amplify that word, as well as *murderer,* and especially *assassin.*

We drummed it into them. We pounded and hammered at their naked brains. Hour after hour, Arthur's compulsive voice told them about fear. They listened raptly. For half a day their guts churned hotter and sicker. The paranoid reaction set in quickly. Big Daddy was dead; who was Big Daddy now? By interspersing the monotone of tragedy with bad news from the Ghana front, the student revolt in Tangiers, the strike in Scandanavia, we whipped their reaction into a scum of emotion as thick and heavy as butter.

The assassin, the killer, the loathsome wraith who could be anywhere.

And he would never, ever, be found. Eddy's surgical team had deftly planted a sliver of high explosive fixed to a molecular radio-detonator inside the Senator's skull. Just below the frontal-lobes, a little to the right. When I pressed the button a signal had caused it to ignite and blow the skull apart. The wound was identical to a historical horror we had studied; its effect, broadcast in minute detail, was just as shocking and brutal as the blast itself.

Six billion people saw one man die.

From five feet away. They were almost splattered with the exploding brains, showered in the rain of blood.

That's news.

Like the surges of a tidal wave, emotion churned, heaved, drained and hurtled back in catastrophic thunder. The currents of hatred and suspicion boiled, foamed. There were riots in London. In Houston and Los Angeles, black orgasms of murder and arson. (In the Archives, "Law and Order"; we resurrected this simplism. It was useful). Mobs murdered themselves in Beirut, slamming in human torrents against police armament. In Calcutta and Peking the masses came out of their hives, illegally, and crushed themselves to death in the streets. The sterile bird

Phoenix blazed and shuddered, agonizing in labor and death. The impotent shook their fists against a blank sky, cursing. The grave growled at their television sets. The meek whimpered at their television sets. The indifferent shruggd at their television sets.

The television sets growled, whimpered, yawned back.

All emotions were accounted for and encouraged.

Emotion was the need, any emotion, all emotion.

Mrs. Westlake was a martyr's widow—Mrs. Westlake the power and the dark dignity, shrouded in black veils, sturdy and anguished Marcia Westlake. Through our lens we passed her image, the focus of emotion, a focus for hysteria. The widow—like another widow, with a red hourglass on its belly, that slays the one who seeded. The widow who inherits. She was his priestess—she minded the altar. She, she, she, night-mother and dream-witch.

Her womb a black destroyer.

Isis, Kali, Joan, Jacqueline. Harlow, Monroe, black-woman-who-swallows.

And the weird shadows of the cave fire. The outrageous breasts and buttocks of the Seed Queen. The first stirrings of night in the hominid heart. The fiend things buried in our past, burning in our present, the thalamal joyless rat.

And the Pied Piper luring him from his nest with dreams, drawing him over the twisted landscape of reflex and response. Into the collapsing caverns, the endless fall, the final lightless vacuum.

Our suggestions were gentle, quiet, logical as music. Visual.

Westlake was a total actor; he played the part of death totally. Marcia, his wife-annihilator, survived him with calm brilliance. She knew every step, commanded every stage.

Soon enough, the play was over. The theater itself dissolved. Curtain.

V—the author's reward

It was cold on the wind-scoured inauguration stand, but she was wearing an electrically heated shift. A blue shift identical to the one she wore at her grief. The first lady president, nominated, campaigned for, and elected by the news, by Affiliated World Networks.

She started to speak. I ordered a longshot—a brief one. Then a friendly, straightforward closeup. Her brown eyes shone steadily into six billion faces, in high-resolution 3-D. A solid woman, a strong woman.

A tyrant.

Big Mommy.

Her voice was strong and steady, almost hard. She said things of great optimism and little substance. Things that mattered even if they didn't. Things created in the cold crystalline brain of a vast robot network. Good things, kind and brave things, wise and empty things. All things for all men.

All of them, every one. At prime time, carefully monitored and evaluated and checked. The ratings were a hundred percent —the emotional indices registered confidence and hope. Even a tiny elation.

And a good strong blast of obedience.

But that was a foregone conclusion.

After all, who can resist something as ubiquitous and totally convincing as the news? Who can even doubt it?

Her voice rang high and steady. Eddy the propman had had the dais built to calculated specifications, computerized to evoke calm and placidity. Just like you design a movie set around a particular pair of boobs. Just like Walter Cronkite's busy-rattling newsroom. Her hair matched the varnish; her skin tone blended with the paneling; her eyes were confident against the texture of cork and velvet. Eddy had been careful. Eddy was a pro.

On an upbeat and an upkey she sang to a close.

Cheers from the extras, exaltation from Arthur, relief and content from the audience.

Continuous readout gave the signal. The red eye faded out slowly. We were through. Everything was running smoothly, we had done the job well. We were a team—all six billion human beings of us, all men linked. The day's news had been reported with honesty and accuracy, with all the integrity we had. With all the logic and all of logic's appliances and apparatuses. It is part of my dream, the vision for which we labor. We do not work for glory or power—I am a humble man, a servant of my job and of my destiny.

This is my credo, simple and straight:

Let no man be one, let no dark be unlighted, let all ignorance be all knowledge, all loneliness become all love.

News is only what men know.

ROBIN E. WALLACE
DONNA BRONSON

Canis Familiaris

"The entrée of the day at Animal Gourmet was Beef Wellington—a tempting concoction of ground beef and carrots *en croûte,* garnished with criss-crossed pimento strips. Hovering over the feast were five of New York City's trendiest lunch bunch: Tobler, a brown poodle; Felix, a white *bichon frise* (a cross between a Maltese and a poodle); Ajax, a greedy white bulldog; Pazzo, a yippy Yorkshire terrier who sported a white barette on his hair; and Cricket, a shy sheltie who lolled forlornly at his place setting, his paper hat drooping to one side."

—*Newsweek,* September 9, 1974

Agatha Grenouille hummed "Give my Regards to Broadway" as she strode about her Park Avenue apartment, smoking a

119

Gauloise nervously. This was to be a night on the town, her first in seven days, and she was fairly trembling with excitement. She stopped for a moment before the picture window, and gazed down through the filthy air to the broken, littered street below. It was early evening, and the street was choked with vehicles, the sidewalks jammed with bodies. Already darkness was beginning to fall; a quick glance at the sky told Mrs. Grenouille that there would be no stars or moon that evening.

Unhappy with the scene, she took a few hurried puffs on her cigarette and strode to Antoine's bedroom. She knocked lightly on the door and a deep voice said, "Come in." She opened the door and entered.

Antoine was sitting on a cushion in the center of his room, tongue lolling. His groomer, Deuteronomy, was giving him a pedicure. Deuteronomy looked up at Mrs. Grenouille. "Is something wrong, madam?" he asked.

Mrs. Grenouille was annoyed at his question, although she did not know why. "Nothing's wrong, Mr. Deuteronomy," she said, "except that Antoine's coat doesn't seem to be quite as shiny as it used to be."

Deuteronomy finished clipping Antoine's nails and carefully began to paint them. "I give Antoine four thorough brushings a day, Madam," he said. "Three hundred strokes each. I could use a grooming oil if you wished, but I would think that might be a bit gauche."

"Yes, of course." She got down on her knees and rubbed Antoine's head. "Well, Antoine, guess what we're going to do tonight? We're going to go out, for the whole evening. Doesn't that sound wonderful?" Antoine blinked his heavy eyelids. "And guess what? We've got you a beautiful date, the cutest little toy poodle you ever saw. Oh, we're going to have such a good time. We're going to go out for cocktails, and then dinner, and then, maybe you and that little poodle can get something going, right, Antoine?" She scratched Antoine's head; the dog sniffed at her feet. "I'm going to make reservations right now. What time would you like to eat, baby? Eight o'clock? Eight thirty? How does eight thirty sound?" Antoine scratched his ear with a hind leg. "Oh, wonderful," Mrs. Grenouille said, jumping up. "Eight thirty it is." She trotted out of the room, and nearly bumped into the maid.

"Oh, Magma," she said. "Please be careful. You gave me quite a scare."

120

"I'm sorry, Missus Grenouille."

"Well, I'm glad you're here, anyway. Antoine's got a big date tonight, and I want everything in his room to be just right when he comes home. I want the room vacuumed, dusted, and deodorized. Oh, and get some fresh flowers to put in the vase in the corner."

"Yez, Missus Grenouille."

"And, Magma—try and make the room look comfortable, if you know what I mean. Reassuring. And masculine, too. You know how insecure these poodles can be."

"Yez, Missus Grenouille."

"Make the room rather, uh, *macho.*"

"Yez, Missus Grenouille."

"Good." She strode to the telephone, put the receiver to her ear, and dialed a number. "Hello, Grace? It's all set. We'll pick you up at seven tonight? Marvelous. See you then." She smiled hugely as she hung up the phone. "Oh, Bronchitis," she said to the butler as he passed by, "I'm so excited. Now, I want you to be as courteous as possible to my canine guests this evening."

"Very good, madam."

"And be sure to get them anything they might want."

"Of course, madam."

"And tell Gadfly that his meals have been getting a bit bland and repetitive lately. The sauce on the chicken paprikash today at lunch was a bit thin. I'm sure you noticed that Antoine scarcely picked at his food."

"I'll tell him, madam."

"Tell Gadfly I'm quite serious, Bronchitis. I know of several other cooks who would jump at the chance of cooking for Antoine. And when you see him, also tell him that Antoine will more than likely have a guest for breakfast."

"Certainly, madam."

"And, uh, Bronchitis." She leaned toward him. "The guest will be, you know, female. We don't want the word spread around. Even though her papers are in perfect order. You understand."

"Perfectly well, madam."

"Good. That will be all." Mrs. Grenouille lit another cigarette, puffed on it for a moment, and laughed. Oh, it was going to be a fine night.

The air was harder to breathe than usual. Mrs. Grenouille's lungs ached for several minutes after she and Antoine had gotten into her limousine, and an enormous back-up of traffic at Seventy-seventh and Lexington had made her grumpy. "Oh, Antoine," she said mournfully, rubbing the German shepherd's belly and ears, "we're going to be late." She adjusted his camel-hair overcoat and his leopard-skin beret. "Oh, my, do you look jaunty. You're going to make a wonderful impression, I just know it." Antoine sneezed.

"Litmus," Mrs. Grenouille said to the chauffeur, "can you go a bit faster?" Traffic was backed up for blocks and the car hadn't moved for several minutes.

"I'll try, madam."

Half an hour later they arrived at the home of Antoine's date, a posh apartment in the upper Eighties. Mrs. Grenouille instructed Litmus to wait by the entrance while she and Antoine went up to meet their companions at their penthouse apartment.

The woman and the dog were waiting for them at the apartment door. "Oh, Grace," Mrs. Grenouille said, "you look positively beautiful tonight." The other woman returned the compliment. "And where is Antoine's date?" Mrs. Grenouille asked, scratching Antoine's muzzle.

"Oh, she'll be ready any moment; they're primping her. You know how these young ladies can be."

"Of course." They both laughed for a bit. "Oh, Antoine," Mrs. Grenouille piped, "you'll sweep her off her feet. I just know it. You look so handsome this evening. Oh, and Grace, we've got a wonderful time planned. Drinks, dinner, a show, everything. We've got tickets for the opening of the new production of *Fido and Aeneas* at the Met."

A servant approached the door, carrying a tiny poodle on a satin cushion. The poodle had been carefully trimmed and wore several ribbons and a bikini. It had been dyed a soft pink. "This is Feather," her owner announced proudly.

"Antoine, isn't she charming?" Mrs. Grenouille asked her pet. Antoine bit at a toenail.

"Well, if we're all ready, let's go, shall we?" Grace said. She lifted Feather gingerly from the cushion and held her up before her own face. "Oh, you little darling, I could just eat you up." She planted a kiss on Feather's snout, and held Feather out for Antoine to get a good look. Antoine wiped at his eye. "Let's be off," she said.

122

Once they had all been seated in the limousine, conversation began to pick up. "Grace, tell me a little about Feather, would you?" Mrs. Grenouille asked. "Antoine has been looking forward so much to this evening. He's heard so many things about her." She winked. "Even though this is their first date, it feels like they've known each other all their lives."

Grace smiled wanly. "I'm sure Feather is quite familiar with the feeling. She's quite popular, you know."

The car pulled up in front of an expensive bar, the White Fang. A sign in the window said Canines Only. The women and dogs entered. The dogs were taken away and seated at a table; the women were lead to a small adjoining bar where they could watch their pets through one-way glass. "The glass is in very good taste," Mrs. Grenouille commented.

The women were seated at a small table next to the window. There was a short silence. "I've heard they make excellent Bloody Hounds here," Mrs. Grenouille said. "And equally good Tom Collies."

"Oh, really?"

There was another short pause. Finally the waiter came by and took their orders. Mrs. Grenouille asked for a double martini; Grace ordered something non-alcoholic.

"Oh, look," Grace said, gazing down at their pets. "Isn't that scene just darling?"

"Very," said Mrs. Grenouille. "But exactly the sort of thing Cicero despised most." She reached into her purse and took out her cigarette case and holder.

"Who?"

A waiter brought their drinks, set them on their table, and departed.

"Cicero, my ex-husband. He ran away some years ago with some young tart whose name I never learned. He said I never understood him. He was right, too. I'll never understand how someone could be so selfish and inconsiderate. He never liked Antoine; in fact, he was allergic to dogs." She paused to take several sips from her drink. "One thing I'll say for him, though, he pays his alimony on time. He'd better keep on doing it, too, or I'll drag him right back to court. The deserter." She took several more sips. "What about your husband?"

Grace moved her lips silently for a moment, as if debating with herself whether to answer. Finally, she spoke. "Lazarus

123

died of creeping numismatism early last year. It was quite a trying experience."

"Especially for him," Mrs. Grenouille said, giggling and finishing off her drink. "Would you like another?" Grace declined. "I'll have another one, though, if you don't mind," Mrs. Grenouille said. She stopped a passing waiter and ordered a second double martini.

Both women passed the next few minutes in silence, watching their pets through the glass. Mrs. Grenouille was brought her second drink. She drank half of it, then stubbed out her cigarette. "I'll be right back," she said, and strode to the rear of the room. As she began to push open the door marked Ladies, a hand caught her elbow. She turned and found herself facing a uniformed waiter.

"Excuse me, madam," the waiter said. "This is one of the rest rooms for pets. Those for our human patrons are down that way." He pointed down a dingy, uncarpeted hall. Mrs. Grenouille thanked him. When she returned to the table, her companion was staring determinedly through the one-way glass. Mrs. Grenouille finished her drink, then scowled. "You know," she said, "I hear that the pooch hooch they serve here is better than the stuff we get to drink, and I believe it."

Grace turned and looked at her somewhat coldly. "Shall we go?" she asked.

"Certainly." They rose, collected Feather and Antoine, paid the bill, and left.

Back in the limousine, Mrs. Grenouille laughed spontaneously and tickled Antoine's chin. "Oh, Antoine, aren't you lucky?" she said. Antoine licked his paw. Feather curled up on her owner's lap and went to sleep. They rode in silence to the restaurant.

There was a commotion outside when they arrived at the Waldorf-Astoria. "Litmus," Mrs. Grenouille said, "what is it?"

"Some kind of commotion, madam."

"Does it look dangerous?"

"I don't think so, madam. They seem to be simply shouting and waving signs."

"Let's try and go in, then." They left the automobile.

Dozens of angry people were parading around the sidewalk in a circle, yelling phrases that neither woman could quite understand. Suddenly, someone appeared from nowhere and handed Mrs. Grenouille a leaflet.

"What is it?" Grace asked, intrigued.

"It's one of those organizations for equal rights. Equal rights for dogs."

"Let me see." They both gazed down at the handbill, which said:

> GOING TO THE DOGS, INDEED!
> THE CANINE ALLIANCE DEMANDS AN IMMEDIATE END TO SPECIESISM
> NO MORE LEASHES OR COLLARS!
> NO MORE DOGHOUSES
> NO MORE BEING "PUT TO SLEEP"
> DOGS IN THE K-9 CORPS: OLD ENOUGH TO FIGHT, OLD ENOUGH TO VOTE AND HOLD OFFICE
> ABOLISH SLAVE LABOR: ESTABLISH MINIMUM WAGES FOR CANINES
> PET OWNERSHIP IS FILTHY AND DISGUSTING: WE DEMAND DOG'S INALIENABLE RIGHT TO WALK THIS EARTH AS FREE BEINGS
> NO MORE SLIPPER CARRYING!
> NO MORE STICK FETCHING!
> NO MORE LEARNING "TRICKS"
> NO MORE FORCED CASTRATION
> WE DEMAND AN IMMEDIATE MERGING OF THE ACLU WTH THE ASPCA!
> DOG OWNERS: STOP "PLAYING DEAD" TO EQUALITY AND LET YOUR ANIMAL FREE

Mrs. Grenouille dropped the leaflet in disgust and began to push her way through the crowd of people, holding onto Antoine's collar. The demonstrators shouted abuse at her, and someone struck her with a sign. Another tried to pry her fingers from Antoine's collar, but somehow she managed to hold on. Grace walked through the crowd unharmed; she had hidden Feather underneath her topcoat.

Finally they reached the door, just as the police arrived. Safely inside, they watched as the police began firing tranquilizing pellets into the crowd. Soon all the demonstrators had collapsed in a drugged stupor, and they were dragged into the police wagon and carried away. Mrs. Grenouille asked for directions to the Pekinese Room.

"It's supposed to be wonderful," Mrs. Grenouille said, as Grace removed Feather from her hiding place. "It's the only restaurant in town that specializes in Cantonese cuisine for dogs."

Grace nodded, and Antoine rubbed against Mrs. Grenouille's leg.

"Those demonstrators," Grace said, as they entered the restaurant. "Something should really be done about them. They're a menace and a disgrace. Why can't they just be happy with things as they are?" The restaurant was very crowded, and the waiting line was very long, but Mrs. Grenouille mentioned their reservation and slipped the maître d'hôtel a ten dollar bill. The maître d' escorted the dogs to a table; a waiter took the women upstairs to a small table on a balcony, from which they could watch their pets enjoy their repast. On the table was a small placard which read, "You may not know it, but dogs love cheese."

"They're the moderates," Mrs. Grenouille said. "Haven't you heard about the radicals? It's been in all the papers."

"I don't read the papers. They're such a bore."

"Oh. Well, they use guns and knives and everything. At first they just wanted to license pet owners, to make all things fair and equal, but then they started turning militant. They've forced other people to eat dog food at gunpoint; they've made people wear collars and leashes and walk around on all fours for days. One time they hijacked a plane, and made it land, and made all the passengers get into those little dog-carrying boxes, and then had all the boxes put in the baggage compartment. And then they flew all the way to South Africa, with all the passengers stuck in those boxes. Honestly, I don't understand how people can possibly behave that way."

Grace shivered slightly. "I just don't know what the world's coming to. I believe in freedom, but *this* . . . it's like women's lib; it just goes too far."

Below them, their pets were being served Mahi Mahi and Peking Duck.

"Oh, Antoine," Mrs. Grenouille said loudly, standing up and putting her hands to her mouth like a megaphone. "Don't wolf your food, baby."

"Please sit down," Grace said. "Everybody's looking."

"He loves Chinese food so much. We never used to have it while Cicero was around. He hated Chinese food. In fact, he hated Antoine. He used to make poor Antoine eat canned food all the time." She lit up another cigarette. Both women sat silently watching for several minutes. "I've heard that they've opened up several restaurants for cats nearby," Mrs. Grenouille said. "And others for birds, including one only for parrots. And out in Los Angeles there's one for fish. The waiter wears scuba gear and serves the food completely submerged."

"My little Feather looks so cute," Grace mused, a small smile on her face.

"And Antoine looks so handsome." Mrs. Grenouille slid her chair closer to Grace. "Look, we're mature women. Let's be frank. We both know what this evening's all about."

"Pardon?" Grace said, raising an eyebrow.

"Come on, it's time we stopped playing games. Let's get to the meat of the situation, the *real* reason for this date. Antoine's a boy dog, and Feather's a girl dog, and, well, you know."

"What on earth are you talking about?"

"You know very well what I'm talking about!" Mrs. Grenouille said, rather loudly. "Nooky!"

"What?"

Mrs. Grenouille leaned closer. "Tell me—is your Feather good in bed?"

Grace stood up, bumping her upper legs against the small table. "What is the matter with you? I don't know when I've been more insulted!"

"What's the matter? Is Feather a tease, is that it? Or are you one of those fuddy-duddy Victorians, who don't believe in doing it on a first date?"

Grace turned pale. "Agatha, I am outraged. Good-bye." She stalked out of the room, muttering to herself.

"Christ, what a bitch," Mrs. Grenouille mumbled. Peering over the edge of the balcony, she saw the maître d'hôtel retrieve Feather from the dining room. Antoine continued eating voraciously. "Don't let it bother you, Antoine," she called over the edge of the balcony. "The evening's still young. We've still got plenty of good times ahead. You just wait." Antoine licked his chops. Mrs. Grenouille rose to her feet slowly and went downstairs to collect her pet.

Back in the leather-padded limousine, Mrs. Grenouille stroked Antoine's fur warmly. "Don't let it get you down, dear," she said. "We all fail some of the time. Anyway, she was probably very inexperienced. Not your type at all. Maybe even a virgin, and probably frigid. Probably fixed, too, come to think of it. I know their kind when I see them. She was just like the hussy my Cicero ran off with." Antoine scratched his neck and sneezed. She turned to the chauffeur. "Litmus, take us to the seamier side of town." She gave the chauffeur an address.

The ride through the dark, filthy streets was uneventful. Mrs. Grenouille talked to Antoine and stroked him soothingly. Antoine closed his eyes and went to sleep. In a few minutes they arrived at their destination. Mrs. Grenouille awakened Antoine, and together they entered a crumbling brownstone building. A small sign on the door read Bow-Wow Bordello.

The madame of the house approached, a large, jovial woman carrying a carefully-groomed Lhasa apso. Dogs of all breeds padded back and forth leisurely. "May I help you?" she asked.

"Yes," Mrs. Grenouille said. "Antoine here is looking for, ah, a good time."

The madame smiled. "Of course. What did you have in mind?"

"Well, Antoine's taste tends to run toward the larger, more refined breeds. Afghans, collies, Irish setters."

"Certainly. Is he looking for what we regularly offer, or is he looking for something more exotic?" The madame smiled more widely.

Mrs. Grenouille blushed. "S and M? Homosexuality? Orgies? Is that what you mean?"

The madame's smile did not waver. "Of course. We pride ourselves in offering whatever pleasure your pet may require. We also have a few members of other species if that's what Antoine is looking for. We have several cats, a racoon, an ocelot, three sheep, and a hum—"

"Enough! We'll take the regular services only, please!"

"Very well. If you'll both follow me." She took Antoine's collar and led both woman and dog through a heavy oak door. Behind it were several rows of small, white, wooden dog-houses. In the doorways of most stood or squatted groomed, perfumed bitches. "Here we have Suzy," the madame said, pointing out the first dog and walking slowly down between the rows. "Suzy's a real charmer. Pedigreed, too. And here is Francie, who knows just what men want, and Dragnet, and Lint, and here is Barb, who's an expert at the art of love."

"What do you think?" Mrs. Grenouille asked Antoine, kneeling and rubbing his leg. "They've got a few hot ones here, don't they? Which one do you want?"

Antoine pawed at his nose.

"Let's try Barb."

"Very well," the madame said. She ushered Antoine and

Barb into one of the tiny houses and shut the door. "Would you like to watch?" she asked Mrs. Grenouille. "Viewing facilities are available."

"Yes, I would." She paused. "No, on second thought, it's been a very trying day. I think I'd prefer not. I'd just like to sit down someplace."

"Of course. Just follow me." She lead Mrs. Grenouille to a small lounge, where she smoked several cigarettes in solitude. After a few minutes, the madame returned, bringing Antoine with her. "Antoine, you look rather tired," Mrs. Grenouille said. She paid the madame for the services rendered and took Antoine out to the waiting limousine. Out in front of the bordello were several groomed and made-up dogs of various breeds, being held in the arms of young women who looked at them enticingly.

"Take us home, Litmus," Mrs. Grenouille said to the chauffeur. "I'm very tired, and so is Antoine." She stroked the dog's head lovingly. "How was she, Antoine?" she asked softly. "Was she good? Did she make you feel like a man?" Antoine laid his head on Mrs. Grenouille's lap. "What's the matter, baby? You didn't have any problems with her, did you? Why, you used to be able to handle any bitch in the city. Antoine, I know your prowess is still there." Antoine licked her hand. "That's my baby," she cooed, hugging his head. He licked her face, and she giggled. "Oh, Antoine, I'm so glad you're here. Things have been so lonesome every since Cicero left." She cuddled the dog in her arms; all the way home he licked her and made small noises.

When they arrived at her building, Mrs. Grenouille was very sleepy. She dismissed the chauffeur, lifted Antoine by the front paws, and hugged him. He licked her. She let him drop back to all fours, and they went into the building and entered the elevator. On the way up, she lifted his paws and hugged him again, and he pressed his body against her, lapping her face with his warm, wet tongue. "Antoine," she said, "I don't know what I'd do without you." She kissed him on the forehead and rubbed his ears and belly delicately.

The butler was still awake when Mrs. Grenouille and Antoine entered. "Good evening, madam," he said softly.

Mrs. Grenouille did not reply, but hugged Antoine tightly and kissed him soundly on the snout. Antoine shifted from one hind leg to another and licked her face eagerly. She let him down and walked past Antoine's room to her bedroom, the dog walking beside her. She pushed the door open slowly, knelt, put her arm around the dog. "Oh, Antoine," she said, "you're wonderful." She turned her head. "Bronchitis?"

"Yes, madam?"

"Let us sleep as late as we want tomorrow morning. Don't disturb us for any reason."

"Yes, madam."

Mrs. Grenouille smiled hugely and took Antoine in her arms. She ran her fingers and lips gently across his forehead for a moment. Then they entered the bedroom, and she closed the door behind them.

GEORGE R. R. MARTIN

Weekend In A War Zone

Saturday dawn, with the sun just a dim light behind the clouds. They're passing out the guns. We're outside, in the ready base on the edge of the war zone, standing in line and shuffling through an inch of slush. I don't understand why they make us stand in line. They could have given us the guns inside, with the uniforms. It's cold out here.

The armorer is the same guy that ran the credit check. Reed-thin, sallow complexion, squinty little eyes. Bored before and bored now, taking his own sweet time about everything. While we stand here and go shuffle-shuffle through the slush. He writes down the serial number of every rifle he hands over. I guess there is an extra charge if you lose the damn thing. They charge for everything. This weekend will cost a fortune. I wonder, again, what the hell I'm doing here. Tennis is a hell of a lot cheaper. And you come back alive. Always. Every time.

My turn. The armorer squints at me, checks the serial number on the gun he's holding, writes it down, hands it over. Name, he asks for. "Birch," I say. "Andrew Birch." He writes that down, too. I take the gun and move off. The next guy shuffles up to the table.

The gun is smooth black plastic, long as my arm, contours all flowing graceful towards the snout at the business end. It feels slick and cold in my hand, and there's a smell of oil about it. It's unloaded. I take a cartridge chamber from my belt and slip it in, and it clicks as it locks in place. Now I'm ready. Like the guys in the ads. My first patrol. An armed soldier. A man. Right.

What bullshit.

I don't think I'm much of a soldier. I hold the gun awkwardly, despite the company hypnotraining. I don't know quite what to do with it. If I knew, I wouldn't want to do it. I play tennis on weekends. I don't belong here. I was an idiot to come. What if they shoot me? The Concoms have guns, too.

I turn the gun over, examine it. There's a rough spot on the underside of the barrel. Lettering. A serial number and a legend: PROPERTY OF MANEUVER, INC.

Stancato drifts over, his gun under his arm, flipping up the nightvisor on his helmet. He's got the helmet tilted to one side. Rakishly, I suppose. That's Stancato. What's worse, it looks good on him. In combat boots and helmet and this mess of green and brown that Maneuver tries to pass off as a uniform, he manages to look good. Rugged, masculine. He's at home out here, his stance says. He shouldn't be. It's his first time, too. I know that.

Stancato always looks natural. He's taller than I am, and he's all lean muscle and dark good looks. I'm short and moon-faced, with wishy-washy brown hair. Stancato eats like a horse and it doesn't disturb his chic body at all. I turn to flab the second I'm not paying attention. Stancato wears all the latest at the office. Now it's flare-necks and half-capes, last month it was something else. He looks cool and fashionable. I wear the same stuff and I look like an overdressed moron.

I suspect I look like a moron now, in this uniform. It doesn't fit. It bunches in all the wrong places, and it's tight where it shouldn't be. It's not even warm. The wind cuts right through it. You think we'd get better, with the fee they make us pay.

I've got half a mind to report them to Consumer Protection. If I come back alive.

Stancato fondles his gun, and smiles at me. "A nice piece of hardware," he says. "It'll do good by us." How the hell does he know? His first trip, he talks like a vet already. But he's probably right. It'll do good by him.

The drop-chopper is revving up across the ready-base, but it's not time to go yet. The others are still shuffling through the muck. I feel called upon to say something. I often feel that way, especially around Stancato. He's got a way of coming up to me and saying something that almost forces me to stick my foot in my mouth.

This time I think. I don't want him to know how nervous I am. "You think old man Dolecek will notice us?" I say, finally. Dolecek is our boss. The reason I'm here. The fucker maneuvers every weekend, been doing it for twenty years. Says a man isn't really a man until he's been blooded. Sounds just like a war zone commercial. But the fucker has a promotion to give, and I haven't had a promotion in two years. This had better impress him.

Stancato is here for the same reason, only he won't admit it. He says he got bored with tennis and golf and hiking, wants more excitement. Stancato is a greedy bastard. He's two years younger than me, but we're the same grade already. Now he wants to pass me by.

"Dolecek signed up to be a major this time out," Stancato says, grinning. "He's not going to see us, Andy boy. He won't even know you're here. So just relax and enjoy it."

Everybody has their guns now. The sarge lets out a bark, and we all trot towards the drop-chopper. It's a big noisy thing, all green metal and roaring rotors whapping the air, with the Maneuver trademark on its side. I stick a foot into a metal rung, and haul myself inside. There are long benches along either wall, and the platoon fills them quickly. I wind up between Stancato and an older man with a smashed-in nose and an immense gut. Just a grunt, like the rest of us poor slobs, but I notice he's got vet marks on his sleeve. He's done this before, and he's got lots of killpoints in his time. I study his face, try to figure out what makes him a killer, instead of a killee. Nothing shows, though.

The pilot takes us up. The faces around me are a little tense, but happy. A lot of smiles, some joking. What the hell are they so happy about? Don't they know they might get killed? I feel slightly sick myself. This was a dumb idea.

Stancato is one of the smilers. "You okay, Andy?" he says to me over the noise of the copter. "You don't look so good." He's grinning so I know that he's just kidding around. But he doesn't fool me. He likes to put me down.

"I'm all right." I'm not going to throw up, no matter how much I want to. That would give Stancato too much pleasure. If I can't hold back, I'll throw up on him. "I'm just a little nervous," I say.

"Scared, you mean." He laughs at me. "C'mon, Andy, admit it. We're all scared. Nothing to be ashamed of. I'm terrified. You'd be stupid if you weren't scared. The Concoms will be shooting real bullets at us." Again that laugh. "But that's what makes it interesting, right?"

"Right." Believe it.

The Gut looks over. "You got it," he says. Deep, gravelly voice, half his teeth missing. A real prole. "I been going out for ten years, scared every time. But that's *living.*"

"A man hasn't lived until he's seen death," Stancato says, in his smooth, witty voice. It was one of Maneuver's slogans.

"A man ain't a man till he's *maneuvered,*" I say, providing the other catchphrase from the ads. Instantly I feel inane. Stancato's quote somehow sounded appropriate to the conversation. Mine sounded stupid. Too late, though. I said it.

Now the Gut laughs at me. "Yeah. And I bet you boys are just now getting to be men, hey?" He nods at his own pronouncement. "Yeah. You're both green as hell. I can tell."

"A perceptive man," Stancato says. Some perception. If we weren't green, we'd be wearing vet marks.

"Damn straight," says the Gut. "I know my way around, too. Stick close to me, I'll show you how it's done. Make sure the Concoms don't get any killpoints off my buddies."

I can't think of anyone I'd want less as a buddy, unless it's Stancato. But maybe I should do like the Gut says. He doesn't seem to have any holes in him, and I don't want any in me.

There's a loud thud, and the copter shakes around us. The rotors die whining. We've arrived. The middle of the war zone. We'll be alone out here. The platoon we're replacing was on a sweep through the forested countryside. Looking for Concoms. I hope the Concoms aren't looking for us. What ever happened to old-fashioned wars where everybody met on a battlefield and shot at each other?

We spill out of the chopper into a sea of mud. The sun is higher in the sky now, a corner of it peeking through the overcast. Most of the slush has dissolved. But the wind is still blowing, and it's as cold as ever.

We're in a rocky, nondescript clearing, surrounded by evergreens, with barely enough room for the drop-chopper to set down. The other Maneuver platoon is all lined up, ready to board. They swear a lot, but most of them seem to be grinning. Dirt they have plenty of, but no blood. And I don't see any wounded. Maybe this will be easier than I thought.

The Gut waves to one of the others, gets a grin in return. "How's it go?" the Gut shouts.

"Oughta get our money back. Laying down good credit for a hike." He shakes his head, looks towards his sarge, glances at me with disdain as his eyes sweep by. Smartass. Probably has money pouring out of his ears. Either that or enough killpoints to rate him a big discount. Otherwise how could he afford to buy a whole week of war at Maneuver's rates? Probably looks down on us weekenders.

Once we're all out, they start piling in, then the chopper sets its rotors to whapping again and they're off, home free. Back to the offices and the suburbs, or wherever. The Concoms don't shoot at drop-choppers, thanks to the free substitution rule. But they've been known to wipe out a new platoon as soon as it's landed. I recall that nervously, and look around.

The sarge snaps an order, and we assemble like good little soldiers. He looks us over, obviously not pleased. "Awright," he begins, in his best sarge-talk. Like something out of an old war movie. He doesn't look the part though. He's more like a misplaced accountant. He wears glasses and he's too young and he smiles too damn much. Not a bit intimidating. I notice he isn't wearing any vet marks either. Another strike against me. Andy Birch, you're a real winner.

"We're gonna cover ground," our green sarge tells us. "Those bastards were told to find the Concoms, and they farted around for a week. So we find 'em. Assholes and elbows time, kiddies. We're gonna find out how you punks handle action. And it better be good, or I'll give you more misery than the Concoms ever dreamed of. Remember, we get position-points if we find a camp, plus killpoints for every Concom we take care of. That means discounts next time around."

I find myself evaluating his performance. The first part sounded good, but maybe a little overdone. Rock Fury and all that. But those closing lines jarred. Wonder if he gets special training, or a manual, or what? Or do they just take his money and let him wing it?

He's giving us orders now. We split into smaller groups, and fan out into the forest. Why split up, I wonder. Why not just march along in a line, or something? I suppose there's a reason. He must be going by the book, or by orders from some smartass who bought himself a weekend commission.

I wind up with Stancato and the Gut. I stood close to the Gut when we got split up, so I'd be teamed with him. A vet can't do me any harm, I figure, and he might make a difference. Stancato, damn him, figures the same way.

So we're scrambling through forest tangle, guns in hand. Heading upcountry, towards the mountains. The others are around us somewhere, but I can't see them. The air is cold and the ground wet. I hope the sarge lets us stop for lunch.

I'm exhausted. This is worse than tennis, much worse, and I can't take it. I'm sucking down icy air in great draughts, and that fucking Gut doesn't let up. He just plows on ahead, pushing aside the greenery, tramping through the muck. He's like a flabby mack truck, and he wants to run me into the ground. Stancato isn't even breathing hard, but I'm going to collapse. The gun weighs a ton.

We've covered a lot of territory. No doubt we're in a war zone by now. I can hear firing in the distance, very dimly, big guns going boom-boom. And a Concom skimmer flight went overhead awhile ago. Way up, but the Gut told us to flatten ourselves in the mud all the same. The stuff soaked right through the uniform. I'm colder than ever, but luckily the wind's died some.

Near noon we stop to eat in a small clearing against the side of a cliff. Just the three of us. I don't know where the others have got off to. I don't understand any of this. Shouldn't we be staying with the others? Where are they? Wouldn't it be better if the whole platoon was together? I paid good money for this weekend. I wish I knew what was going on.

We sit with our backs to the moss-slick stone, guns across

our laps, eating rations from hotpaks. It's good to get the load off my back and sit down for a while. And I'm hungry. But the food is terrible. You'd think Maneuver would do better for the prices we're paying. How do they ever keep a customer?

Stancato isn't bothered, though. He eats quickly, almost ravenous, then smiles at me as I poke at my food. "Eat up, Andy," he says. "We'll need all our strength. Day's just begun." Then he stands and stretches, still smiling. "This is life," he tells me. "This is exhilarating. Out beyond the city, with enemies around you and a gun in your hand. Yes, I do believe Maneuver's right. Life is sweeter when death is close."

The Gut looks up from his pak, grimaces. "Sid down. And don't talk so loud. You wanna bring the Concoms down on us? You won't live long that way."

Stancato sits, grinning. "You know a lot about this, eh?"

The Gut nods. "Damn straight. I could sarge if I wanted to, y'know. Even buy a weekend commission. I got lots of killpoints. But that isn't for me. This is better, out here. Before I go, I'm going to get more killpoints than anyone. That's what I want, not to fight no war from an office, like the leadbutts with the big credit who sign on as weekend commanders."

I look at him, shoving aside my food half-eaten. An ugly man with an ugly nose and a huge pot and a small brain. Yet he's killed men, better men than him probably, and he comes back when others die. Why? I start to ask the question.

But Stancato talks first. "You like killing," he says, eyes hard and eager. He'll like it, I know. He likes hurting, likes to put people down, to humiliate them. Shooting holes in them is just his speed.

"It's war," the Gut says. "Here, in the zone, yeah, but out there too. We just don't call it war, but it still is. There are guys after you every minute, after your woman, after your job, pushing shit on your kids, trying to stick it to you. You have to fight back, and this is one way. Yeah, I like it. Why not? Those Concoms—" he jerks his head towards the shrubbery, savagely, "most of them are niggers, y'know. The Concoms do a lot of advertising down there where they live. They hate us anyway. Why shouldn't I enjoy getting a few of them?" He looks belligerent, as if he dares us to challenge him. I'm certainly not going to. He's a fool, but I might need him.

Maneuver must like men like him. They hate, they kill, and they come back weekend after weekend. Sure they get discounts.

But they make money for the company all the same. Pile up those points, get enough of them, and finally Maneuver wins the war and Consolidated Combat has to hand over a big chunk of credit, instead of the other way around.

War after war, the Gut is there, I bet. Says something about man, something disgusting. No real war for over fifty years, so we invent bloodgames so animals like the Gut can play them and get their rocks off.

Stancato is going to be good at this, yes. Maybe he'll turn into the Gut in time. That would be nice. He deserves a fate like that. Not me, though. I get out, after this weekend.

The Gut gets to his feet and gestures. We pick up our guns and follow, back into the forest.

Late afternoon. The war is all around us and the mud has turned back to slush and snow. But there are rocks underfoot, so we're making better time.

There is a horrible smell in the woods. And noises, firing, somewhere close. We crouch low and head towards it, scrambling silent as we can. I breathe easier now. I'm scared, but I've gotten my second wind. And my muscles don't ache anymore. I can't feel them at all.

Ahead, a fallen tree is rotting, with a dead body draped across it, face buried in bloody snow. Like a tableau from a movie. It doesn't touch me until I realize that it's real. Then I start.

It's been dead a while. The smell gets stronger as we approach. Near, I can see the swollen flesh, and choke on the decay. The visor on its helmet is down. It died at night, then. Its uniform is grayish, its skin black. A Concom. My first sight of the enemy. I hope all the Concoms I see are dead.

The Gut goes by without comment, smiling just a little. Stancato walks around it, swiftly, barely looking, unmoved. Just another part of the scenery for calm, cool Stancato. I stop as they go on ahead.

I can't see the eyes through the visor. I realize I don't want to. Who the hell was it? How much did *he* have to pay for the dubious privilege of rotting out here? I feel a sudden urge to touch the body, the dead flesh. Revolted at myself, I stifle it. Yet I stare.

Something *moves* on the body. I watch in fascination. Then suddenly, with a rush, I'm sick. I turn away, retching, vomiting all over the ground. For some reason, I avoid throwing up on the body.

When I stop, Stancato is there, smiling his tight little smile. "Take it easy, Andy," he says. He puts an arm around me, the big man. "It's only a maggot. It won't hurt you."

Only a maggot. Only a maggot. God, but I hate him. I grit my teeth, wrench free of him violently, and stalk back into the forest.

We ran into three others from our platoon, and now we're together. I hardly remember them from the chopper, but I'm sure they must have been there. Don't know that we've gained much. Two beefy oafs and a gawk is what we've got now. But the gawk has vet marks.

He talks with the Gut now, all low whispers, and he keeps looking around. They look absurd, like a military Mutt 'n Jeff. The Gawk and the Gut. These are the people I'm relying on to get me through? Shit. The Gawk looks like he'd have trouble getting across the street. A long pinched-in face and acne scars. He doesn't look like a warrior. But maybe soldiers don't look like in the movies. Maybe the ugly guys kill best. Hell. Stancato will be pissed when he finds that out. He wants to be best at everything.

The Gut looks our way and gestures. "We got something," he says. "Grenade blasts over on the east. Rifle fire. Jim says some of our boys are pinned down by the Concoms. Let's go gettem out." He grins.

We run, a jogging trot, shoving aside the branches and sloshing through patches of snow. The Gut looks eager. I'm terrified. What have I gotten myself into? Where are we going? I want out. This is madness. My hand trembles where I hold the gun. I'm going to throw up again.

The war sweeps over us.

One of the beef boys ahead of me stumbles suddenly, and the firing begins all around us. He falls, his head twisting grotesquely, his rifle spinning into a snowbank, a flower of blood blossoming from his chest. Dead, dead, I think. We don't know where the shot came from.

"A sniper!" the Gut yells. "Cover! Take cover!"

Then he's gone, faded away, down somewhere. The others fade, too. Only I remain, standing over the body, blinking down at it, frozen, indecisive. Another shot rings out, a stream of shots. I hear them hiss around me, and I feel strangely safe. You never hear the bullet that kills you, they say.

Then someone grabs me, pulls me, yanks me off my feet and knocks me into the trees. Stancato, of course. He falls down beside me, eyes sweeping alertly, rifle in hand, ready. I've dropped my rifle. It's out there, near the body. And I'm crying. At least my cheeks are wet.

Stancato ignores me. He lifts his gun and fires, and the black snout spits a rapid burst of death towards the trees. Was that where the shots were coming from? I don't know. I didn't notice. But he seems to. Other people are firing too. Our guys, I think. But not me. Not me. I lost my gun.

Then, for a long time, breathless silence. Stancato waits, hands tight on gun, eyes moving all the time the others are waiting too. No one moves. No one fires.

It's dusk now. That comes on me suddenly as I watch the twilight creep around the evergreens, and wrap the woods in folds of grayness. A lot of time is gone. But we don't move. We don't know if we've gotten the sniper, or if he's gone, or if he's waiting out there, lurking, gun hungry for one of us to move. So Stancato stays put. Me too. I'm not going to be the target. Besides, I can't do much else. I lost my gun.

Finally, with the darkness all but complete, someone moves. A quick dart from here to there in the trees. Then another. Then a sudden burst of fire raking over the sniper's position, in the rocks upslope from us. At last a head pokes out of the black. Nightvisor down, half-crouched, the Gawk edges out into the open. Nothing happens. The Concom is dead, or gone.

The Gut appears suddenly, a ponderous shadow in the dark. He bends over the body, touches it, shakes his head. Is he really sorry, I wonder? Or just pissed that the enemy got a killpoint off a buddy? The latter. He's not the caring sort.

Stancato stands, and strides back into the open, confident, smiling. I hesitate and follow. "You think we got him?" Stancato asks.

The Gut shrugs. "Dunno. We gotta look. Maybe, maybe not. He might've just taken off."

They look, Stancato and the Gut, going over towards the place the shots had come from. The rest of us wait. The Gawk eyes me with distaste. I squirm under his gaze, look at the other man, look away quickly when I find him ignoring me. They both dislike me. I can tell. I froze. I'm a coward to them. I have to prove myself. But not Stancato, no, not him. He did everything right, as usual. I wipe my hands on my jacket, nervously. Then, flushing, I bend to pick up my gun. Why didn't I do that sooner? Why didn't I fight? Dammit, Birch, why do you always do everything wrong?

Stancato and the Gut come back. Stancato slaps me on the back. Always hale and hearty, yes sir. Even nice to cowards, the patronizing bastard. He smiles at me. "Looks like he got away," he says. "We must've scared him off."

"Look," I say, falteringly, "I didn't mean to drop—"

Stancato cuts me off. "Don't worry about it. Getting to cover was the important thing." He gestures at the body. "He kept his gun. Didn't do us much good, did it? Better to have you alive, we don't need dead heroes, right?"

The Gut has been listening. He nods now, reluctantly. "Yeah, maybe you got something." Then he looks at me. "But watch it, kid. Freeze again, and you get us all wiped out. You could've got your buddy killed then, y'know."

I smiled faintly. I can't do anything else. So they forgive me. How goddam fucking big of them. And it's all Stancato's doing, of course. He likes to do this to me. He knows how much I loathe him, and he knows it embarrasses me when I have to feel grateful to him. The bastard. Not enough showing me up all the time, making me feel like a fool, he wants me to be a thankful fool, happy over his interest in li'l ol' me. Shit, shit, shit.

Dark is draping the forest. The others have lowered their nightvisors. I pull mine down, and the trees turn to stiff black shadows outlined against a field of red. Only the branches show. The needles are invisible for some reason. I shiver briefly, or maybe just tremble. The forest has become a murky hell, full of charcoal skeletons and half-seen shapes. I think I preferred the darkness. But I keep the visor down.

We move off, the Gut leading, the rest of us strung out behind. I don't know where we're going, or why. I don't care. I just want this to be over with. Only a handful of hours to midnight now. Then another day, and another midnight, and the weekend's over. And the drop-chopper returns to collect us. Me. I made it this far. Maybe I can make it all the way.

Next weekend, back to tennis. I don't need this. Maybe Stancato does, but he's sick. I don't. This is where Birch gets out.

Yes. I can do it. The thought soothes me. I clutch my gun and walk more quickly.

We march for hours, silent except for heavy breathing and the crunch of new-formed ice underfoot as it gets colder. I forget about the war, Stancato, everything. Except my feet and the cold. My boots have been soaked through and through, and the wetness has seeped in. My feet hurt for a long time, but now they've stopped. Numb. But tomorrow there will be blisters. I hate blisters. I'll bet Stancato never gets blisters. I'll bet he never had a blister in his life. Or a pimple, for that matter. He'd be a lot more bearable if he'd grown up with a face full of pimples like any normal person.

The wind is blowing very loudly, shrieking around the pines, slicing through this shitty little uniform something awful. In a world of red and black, the biting cold is strangely out of place. Blue and white are the colors of cold. This is all wrong. But I feel it all the same.

We walk. Aimlessly? Probably not. But aimless to me. Tramp, tramp, tramp, the boys are marching. This is war. What an overrated gyp.

The thought comes, goes. Then my mind wanders back to my feet and the cold. As always. Nothing else can hold me. The gun is very cold now, the plastic almost freezing. Maybe it's frozen to my hand. That should keep me from dropping it when they start shooting again.

More walking. All in silence. Breathing and footsteps ahead and behind me. But I don't know what's going on. It must be past midnight now. It must be. The war seems to have stopped for the night. I can't hear anything. But maybe my ears are tired, like the rest of me.

Fuck it all. Who cares. I'm cold. Fuck you, Stancato. And you, Dolecek. And you, Gut. All of you. Idiots.

Maybe it's near dawn. We've been walking a long time.

The idea excites me. I halt, very briefly, lift my visor. But there's no light to the east. The stars are still up, Orion riding high, his dogs at his heels. Brilliant points in the black. I can see his sword. I can never see his sword in the city.

The stars look cold. With the visor up, I can see the cold as well as feel it. I suck in a chunk of ice, feeling strangely restful.

Something shoves me from behind. Stancato. "C'mon, Andy,"

he says, voice urgent. "Don't give up. We don't want to fall behind and get lost."

I growl at him and stumble ahead. Give up, hell. I wasn't giving up. I just stopped to see if it was dawn. That fucker. Doesn't he give me any credit?

We walk some more, through woods and mountains that look much like the woods and mountains we've already walked through. Through an icewater creek that wakes up my feet to sudden screaming pain. Then back into the woods. We walk. The night is silent, but far away a flight of skimmers flame across the sky and drip fire. Black fire, to us. We watch. We walk.

Finally, finally, rest. The Gut has found a cave. No, not a real cave. Just a small hollow in a wall of rock. But shelter. He slings off his pack, growls something to the Gawk, spreads out his groundcloth, and lays down. Instantly he is asleep, snoring. I'm exhausted. I lay down next to him. The others drop to their cloths, and stretch out.

The Gawk tells me I have the first watch.

I get up and watch, my muscles protesting, my mind blank. When the others are asleep, I slip up my visor and watch the stars. And the skimmers. The western horizon is the one that's light, shining with orange flame and bright white flashes that grow and die against the mountains. A battle somewhere. I listen for the sound of the guns. Dimly, far off. I think I can hear it.

They're all asleep now. The Gut looks like a sack of laundry, and he snores like a bellows. The Gawk is all curled up in the corner, a frightened little boy. The other guy, the hunk of cannonfodder, sleeps with his mouth hanging open. But Stancato looks good. He's stretched out sort of casual, as if the cold doesn't touch him, his face composed, breathing light and regular. Alert, I'll bet. He won't be taken by surprise if the Concoms come at us.

Briefly, I consider that. What would happen if I left here? Maybe the Concoms would come. Wipe them out. Get some killpoints. It'd be easy.

No. I wouldn't be able to find my way back. Besides, what if the Concoms *didn't* get them? Then I'd be in trouble good. Besides, I can't leave men to die. Not even Stancato. Can I?

Well, maybe Stancato.

If I'd played tennis, I'd be home now, asleep probably, in a warm bed with Miriam. Not that she's that exciting. I married her on the rebound anyway, after Glenda left me for Stancato. Tall, blond Glenda. Always so nice until *he* came along, then turning on me, siding with him, cutting me down when I tried to keep her. She made a big mistake. I would've married her. Stancato just digs her body.

So Glenda lost. And me too, I wound up with fat, dull Miriam. Only Stancato wins.

I could shoot him. I wonder if he knows that. I could kill him right here, as he sleeps. They'd never suspect. He'd be just another casualty of the war.

Or would he? They must have some way to tell who shot who. Else how could they keep track of the killpoints? I could let him have it from behind, but they'd find me out. Concom bullets must be different, or something like that. I'm sure it has something to do with the guns. I know they can find you when your time is up, if you've still got the gun. Maybe the same gadget keeps track of who you shoot.

I kill Stancato, and he gets me from beyond the grave. Shit. A final victory. I'm not going to give him that too.

I shove the thought aside. I'm not going to kill Stancato. I'll be lucky if I kill anybody. I'll probably freeze again. One way or the other.

I stand there and think on that and watch the night. Hours pass. Finally, I wake the Gawk to relieve me, and sleep comes. On a bed of ice-slick stone.

Awareness returns with a backache and a scream. I jerk up, groggy, confused. Someone is screaming. I look at the entrance, blink. Bullets whine around me.

The Concoms are outside.

We're trapped, locked in. Dead men. They're going to kill me. Fear comes in great waves. I stare, shake.

Stancato is on his stomach near the front of the hollow, sweeping his gun back and forth, laying down withering fire in great moving arcs. There are bodies outside. And one half-inside. The nameless beef boy. He got more than one slug. His body is in two parts. The bottom half is near the exit. The rest is all over the cave.

There's blood on my clothes. I study it, sick. I want to go to sleep again.

Something explodes just outside our shelter, and fragments tear into the cave and bounce off the rock. Nobody buys it, though. There's a lot of screaming going on, outside and in. I can't make any sense of all the noise.

The Gawk is lying next to Stancato, his back to the door, clicking a new cartridge chamber into his gun. He looks at me, snarls. Then he gets up, grabs my gun, shoves it into my stomach. "Shoot. Fight, you fucking green asshole—*shoot*!"

He turns back to the door, drops to his knees.

And catches a bullet right in the neck. Spurting blood, screaming, he falls back onto me.

He's dropped his gun. I pick it up and hand it to him, but he won't take it.

"Andy," Stancato says. "Down. Down before they get you." He fires as he talks, never stopping. So efficient, so calm. He doesn't look frightened. The killing machine, the hero, the great warrior.

I decide to show him. I drop the Gawk to lie in his own blood, lie down next to Stancato, bring up my gun, wrap my finger round the trigger.

Outside, dawn breaks. Sunday dawn. Halfway home now, but they're after me. I can't see them, though. Just points of light from two-three spots, where their fire rakes the cave mouth. And the positions move.

I fire. Bullets spray out in a steady stream. There's no kick. The gun just warms slightly. I shoot, not at anything, just wiping out the trees. Maybe I'll hit something, but I don't especially want to.

My firing has given Stancato his chance. He stops to reload, sliding back in the cave a little, keeping low, taking the cartridge chamber from his belt and calmly fitting it into the gun. No fumbling, no hurry. No mistakes. In a second he's next to me again, and we rake the trees together.

Somebody screams. "We got one," I say, and stop firing.

"Maybe they want us to think so," Stancato says. "Want us to come out. They can't get in, but they know we're trapped."

Trapped. Yes. I remember that. We're trapped. The Gut, the great vet, our fearless buddy, he got us trapped, probably got us killed. I'm furious. Stancato is firing alone.

Then I realize that the Gut isn't in the cave.

"Where is he?" I demand of Stancato. I don't know the Gut's name. Strange. I thought I did. Stancato seems to.

He doesn't answer. He's stopped firing, too. He waits for someone to move.

We wait a good five minutes in silence. Hoping they'll come out to see if we're dead. They don't buy it. Instead they let their guns play over the rock, again and again, and bullets whine around us. Finally someone lobs a grenade. We have to give ourselves away. While I stare, Stancato grabs it and lobs it back. Right where it came from. He pitches for the office softball team, that Stancato. Good, of course. Very good.

The grenade explodes, tearing a gout out of the forest and the mud. Almost simultaneously, someone else opens up from the side. Screams. We got them.

A Concom staggers from behind a rock, bleeding from a hole in his chest the size of a fist. He gets two feet before the fire from the side cuts him down, hammering him ruthlessly as he tumbles and lays twitching. I watch with sick fascination as he screams and dies and clutches at the air. A thin, short black man, he dies hard. Ashamed, I realize that I have a hard-on. God. I'm sick. As bad as *they* are.

The Gut steps from the side, gun under his arm. "All clear," he shouts. "We got all of them."

Stancato rises and goes to him. "How many were there?"

"Eight," he says. He laughs. "Eight killpoints now. How's our side?"

I leave the cave, the blood-filled cave. Stancato and the Gut watch me approach, wordlessly. The answer to the Gut's question.

"Damn." That's all he says. He wanted me dead. Just like Stancato. I'm a coward, a sick coward, no good to them. The better men are dead. That's what the Gut's thinking.

"How—?" I say feebly. I can hardly think.

"I was coming on guard," the Gut says. "They opened fire on both of us. Got him, but I dropped down real quick-like and got into the bushes. And by then your buddy here was up and shooting at them, so they couldn't all go looking for me." He grins. "You shoot good," he says to Stancato. "You got a couple right off, and that's what saved us."

Saved us? Stancato saved us? Does he always have to be the hero? Something tightens within me. I turn away from the two of them, leaving them there to smile at each other, to grin and congratulate themselves on the blood they've spilled. The butchers.

The body of the black man lies near a clump of bare bushes and the branch of an evergreen. It's stopped moving now, but blood still drains slowly into the mud. His hands are old—lined leather hands too small for his great, baggy gray uniform.

I bend to him, to the man whose death I enjoyed. Nearby, half under the tree, I see his gun. I drop my own and reach for it.

The Concom guns are molded from greenish plastic, but otherwise they're the same. Of course. The weapons have to be the same, or the war wouldn't be fair. Underneath, there's a serial number, and a legend that says PROPERTY OF CONSOLI-DATED COMBAT, INC.

You pays your money and you takes your choice. Fight in the mountains, Maneuver against Consolidated Combat! Try a *jungle* war, General Warfare versus Battlemaster! Slug it out in the streets of the city, Tactical League against Risk, Ltd. There are thirty-four war zones and ten fighting clubs. You pays your money and you takes your choice. But all the choices are the same.

I stand, the Concom gun in hand. And something comes at me.

He jumps out of the dim-lit dawn greenery, and I take him in a blink. Gray uniform, black face, young—younger than me. A kid, a bloody, wounded kid. We didn't get them all. This one just lost his gun. He comes at me with a upraised knife.

I watch him come. He must cover several yards to get me. He comes swiftly, but not swiftly enough. I raise the gun.

And I can't fire. I can't fire. I can't fire.

When he's almost on me, Stancato guns him down from the side. Very efficiently. He curls slowly, drops gently into the mud. No screaming for this one. His knife falls near my foot.

Stancato has saved my life again.

I turn and look at him. He's smiling, and his gun smokes. Another killpoint. He's good at this. He'll get a big discount next time. Me? No. No way. They'll take away my license. They won't let me play. I get hard-ons from watching men die, but I can't kill them.

Stancato steps towards me, starts to say something. I look at my gun, avoiding his eyes. It's a Concom gun. Shoots Concom bullets. Maybe they can't tell who shot who except for the bullets. Stancato has saved my life twice. I can't stand it. He'll tell everyone.

As he walks toward me, I raise the gun, quite calmly, and shoot him. I think I do it very well.

He doesn't have time to look surprised. The Concom gun shoots a stream of bullets, real fast. His chest just explodes, and I turn the nozzle up, and the bullets keep coming, and his dark handsome calm smiling efficient face disintegrates into bloody meat.

The Gut is standing there, mouth open, screaming. "You shot your buddy!" he screams. "You shot your buddy!" I turn the gun and shoot him too. The hell with his vet marks. He isn't so hard to kill.

WILLIAM ROTSLER

Epic

I

They kept telling me that having a movie made about you was the ultimate compliment. I kept feeling like a damn fool.

They started well off course by offering me money. Money is not one of my problems. I'm far from rich—but I can do what I want, pretty much. I found out years ago I can go just about any place and meet with a lot of hooplah and people who are eager to pick up the check.

I don't take advantage of them often, because I'm tired of posing for holos, making speeches and answering a lot of repetitive questions. Mostly I hang around the Cape, keeping in touch, except when the President wants me on some board or commission to dress it up. Or when the Public Information Officer talks me into going somewhere and doing something I've done before.

So I just passed the request from Universal-Metro on to the secretary the Federal Space Administration gives me and forgot the movie idea for awhile. So they came at me from a different angle.

I received a call from Tom Schultz, the PIO at the Cape. He was very enthusiastic about the picture idea.

"It'll be a biggie, John; they're really going to spend some loot. Top people down the line. It's scheduled to premiere just before the next five-year appropriation plan is voted on. Big premiere, lots of politicians, stars, lots of tie-ins. It's *got* to make Congress think about what we're trying to do here."

I felt the tug of duty and I didn't much care for it. "So you think I should go ahead and let them? What do Riley and Boyd say?"

"They're for it, provided you introduce them to Margo Masters."

"What does she have to do with it?"

"She's going to be in it. She's the biggest star Universal-Metro has."

"A sex symbol in the space program? Aw, come on, Tom. Are they going to put bug-eyed monsters on Callisto? A sex queen living in a gravity bottle on the surface of Jupiter?" I said a few more things, very basic, very obscene.

"Listen to me, John—they're putting a lot of money into this. I'm getting the feeling from up front that they want this project to go. And not just to goose the appropriations along, either. A lot of heavies are interested in this one. The only way they'll get some ego-boo will be if this film gets made."

"Who? Green? Karsh? General Fitch?"

"Fitch mainly. He's getting static from Senator DeVore."

"Dick DeVore's son? Is he trying to follow his father's footprints into the White House?"

"Well, President DeVore was responsible for the Jupiter probes and the first three manned missions."

"Stop sounding like a press agent, Tom. He saw the interest

the people had in it and he climbed aboard. That vidcall when I docked at Station One was pure politics. I felt like a damned fool talking to him, knowing a couple of billion people were watching us."

"The DeVore name is still tied up tight to the space program and even though old DeVore isn't around, the young Turk is making sure no one forgets.

"What does he want to do, play his father?"

There was a pause in Tom's usually glib outpouring of wordage. "That's been mentioned, provided we can make the picture dignified enough."

"Oh, hell, Tom, I don't think I want anything to do with this. I'll look like an idiot. I'm no kid clawing after fame—let them make a film about Bergeron or Pavlat."

"They weren't the first, John. You were. You and Ballard. *Great Leap for Mankind* did the moon thing beautifully. *The War God Project* took care of the Mars landings. *Martin Stiles, Spaceman* was pretty much the definitive film on the Venus project. *Sun God* was big budget. *Voyage of the Spaceship Jefferson* was a great follow-up on the Mars trips. But it was a long time before we got past Mars and went all that way out to the big one, John. You know that better than anyone. That story hasn't been told. Oh, I know, the vidspecials, the books, the interviews. But the *whole* story, Johnny—they don't know the whole story. The Federal Space Administration would give every help, you know that. The Smithsonian would probably lend the *Zeus* to the company, for the exteriors, anyway. It would be first cabin all the way, Johnny."

I was silent for a while. I'd been living quietly.

"John? The President wants it, John. He told me himself, yesterday."

"More politics."

"So what? Everything is politics. You can't escape it. That slogan about onward into destiny got DeVore re-elected. Save Our Planet put Metcalf in the White House. This might just put DeVore *fils* back into the Oval Room, Johnny."

I sighed. "What did he promise you, Tom?"

"Enough. But that isn't the reason, John. The story *ought* to be told, you know that. And it couldn't come at a better time for the FSA. They'd be grateful, John. Rogers told me to tell you he'd like to see it done. So did Stan White and Shen Saroyan."

I heaved a giant rock up onto my shoulders. "Okay, Tom—okay. Tell them I'll do it."

I didn't believe Michael Tackett was real. He was too handsome, too big and too virile. To look at him you wouldn't think he had a fault in the world. Even his voice was perfect: deep, sincere, strong. He could change in a flash from a gentle lover, strong but firm, to a raging terror, afraid of nothing. They showed me some of his films before I met him but nothing on the screen prepared me for the reality of him. After all, you expect movie heroes to be big and handsome. But to meet him in person was fantastic.

There was only one Michael Tackett. He was going to play me.

"Tom," I told Schultz on the vidphone, "he's six feet six! He'd never fit into any spaceship made. *I* was considered big and I'm five ten. I feel like a kid standing next to him."

"I'll talk to Steve Tolliver about this, but I don't think anything can be done at this point. Everything has been announced and the contracts have been signed."

"Is he really supposed to look like me? I never looked that good even to my mother."

"Think of it this way, Johnny. It's not the outside they are showing, it's the inside. You're beautiful inside, John. Everyone says so."

"The old silvertongue, huh?"

"Not with you, old buddy. Did you see Tackett in *Guns for the Alamo?* Or the *Jim Bridger Story?* That's the way they want to play him. Remember him in *The First Spaceman?* He got an Oscar for *Joshua,* remember? He can play anything. This should be his greatest role."

"I give up. I'm six feet six and look like a Greek God. I didn't even use a spaceship to get to Jupiter. I jumped, holding Ballard in my arms."

"That's the ticket, Johnny. Just roll with it."

They didn't know me at the gate the first two times I came to the Universal-Metro lot but after that it was easy enough. After that I went to lunch with Mike Tackett frequently, and when we didn't eat at the studio cafeteria we ate at one of the lush restaurants in the immediate area.

I hadn't realized how much attention a superstar gets. My share of the bounce-back from him made me dizzy a time or two. I had thought I'd grown used to that sort of thing after the Jupiter trip. I had been drunk in every capital city of the world. Girls bribed their way into my hotel room and crawled naked into my bed. Most of the time the secret service men picked them up on the monitors, unless Stanton was on duty. He figured heroes should get a little and he never discovered them until it was too late.

But going around with Mike Tackett was a tour and a half. Autographs, looks, insults, pleadings, amorous notes (from both sexes) and a headwaiter's instant attention were his daily lot. Strangers offered themselves, their wives, their daughters, their clients for any sort of misbehavior he cared to indulge in. Drunks wanted to fight. People tried to sell him things, have him endorse things, place bets, tout winners, read scripts or just smile at them.

Most of the time Mike acted as if none of it was really happening. He could sign an autograph or get rid of a pushy agent without breaking the thread of thought during a conversation.

I began to admire him. And hate him. And fear him.

And I watched him slowly become me.

It was uncanny. I knew he was watching me, studying me. Tolliver, the director, had explained that Tackett wanted to be as close to me as he could. He hadn't been able to study Joshua or Jim Bridger or Leonardo da Vinci, but I was an authentic living hero and he wanted to be inside my skin.

He got *under* my skin, from time to time—but we drank together and got high together and pretty soon we understood each other better. And it was weird watching him turn into me. He changed the way he moved in subtle ways, became more precise, less flamboyant. He started using space slang.

I began to feel slightly cheated. He was me—but bigger, handsomer, sexier, younger and one hell of a lot more lifelike. Maybe he stole my soul.

One day Tolliver invited me into his office. He was about my age and had a solid reputation of movie-making behind him. *The First Spaceman, Sun God, The Mars People, Space Station One* and a couple of other space films, were among his credits.

"I wanted to fill you in on what was happening, John. The

Zeus set is finished. They'll be ready for some publicity stills on that tomorrow. The Callisto set on Stage Seven will be ready next week. Did you see Houston Control over in Nine?"

"Yes, looks very authentic, except for no ceiling."

"Well, anything that doesn't look right—you tell me. We have Thompson as our final word on things, but he didn't move into the Jupiter project until it was well along. So you just speak up." Tolliver turned to his massive desk and pressed a button. "Sylvia, send in Wrai Demmon, will you?"

"Have you met Wrai yet?" he asked me. I shook my head. Demmon was to play Ballard, I'd heard, but I wasn't familiar with him. He made his name playing strong heavies opposite the big stars.

Demmon came in, making an entrance. He took both of Tolliver's hands in his and his deep memorable voice boomed out a greeting. Then his eyes swung to me. His face sobered, became almost respectful.

"John Grennell," he said, making the name sound as impressive as if he had said Abraham Lincoln or John F. Kennedy.

"Mr. Demmon." I turned to look at Tolliver. "I mean no disrespect to this gentleman, Steve, but Terry Ballard was nothing like Mr. Demmon."

"John—John, you don't understand. Mike Tackett is power on the screen. *Power.* We can't have just anyone at all play Ballard. We need a heavy to play Ballard and there is no one better than Wrai Demmon."

"But Terry Ballard was a plain-faced little guy who looked more like a scoutmaster than—excuse me, Mr. Demmon—a pirate."

"Wait—we have to handle this very carefully. Very carefully. We can't alienate our audience. Terry Ballard was an American astronaut but he was also—well, how shall I put it? He was a coward. There is no other way to say it, John."

I looked at him. Demmon started to say something but I cut across him. "Terry Ballard was no coward, Mr. Tolliver. He made a mistake. It cost him his life."

"Everyone thinks that appraisal is most generous of you, of course—but we all feel the time is right to show that *men,* not machines, lead our space program."

"Where the hell did you get the screwy notion that Terry was a coward?"

154

"Well, uh, Senator DeVore opened some of his father's files to us—to Busby and Broxon, the writers—well, you know, we had to put some drama into it."

"There's no big drama in sending two men and a ship to the moons of Jupiter?"

"Not in the usual terms. If Ballard hadn't behaved as he did I'm sure history would see him as a brave astronaut giving his life in the course of duty. But we have a base on Callisto now. On Ganymede, too. Jupiter isn't the big thing it was. The Saturn probes have shown us more. We'll have the Outsider back from Pluto orbit by the time this picture is in the theaters. We've moved on, John. To make people really interested in this, we have to flesh it out a little. After all, most of the trip shows only the two of you in one ship—hardly any EVA. Then two walks on Callisto and the swing around the big one before heading home. That's not really a lot of action, you know, not in cinematic terms."

"Then I better tell you all about it. I didn't think anyone would believe me before. But Ballard didn't die like I said. We ran into these green Jovian girls, see? Built out to here. Live in bubble domes. They moved out when the base was put in but—"

"John, please try to understand—if we don't make it *interesting* we don't have a picture."

"On the way past Mars I met this Martian princess, put in secret orbit a hundred thousand years ago by the high priests of the god Ares. I kissed her and she awoke. I'm keeping her in a bungalow below Sunset Boulevard. She's light blue—but we tell everyone that's just because she's cold."

"Colonel Grennell—" Wrai Demmon's face was serious— "look at it this way. I'd like to portray Terry Ballard the best way I know how. You could help me do this. You could watch me and give me hints about the little things, the sort of thing you get to know by living with a guy in a tin can for eight months."

"Yes, I can help you, Mr. Demmon." I was rewarded with a smile. "You could lose five inches, forty pounds and capped teeth. You could look scared without changing expression. You could save my life and get called a coward."

I stood up and walked out.

II

A motion picture studio is a strange land, of itself and by itself. The past, present and future exist all at the same time. Everything is larger than life, more forceful, more beautiful. A few days at the studio and I'd hardly pay attention to women that would have set me howling a year before.

But as studios provide a sort of never-never land where everything is possible, they seem to make nothing possible. The guns have blanks, the stone walls are plaster, the sex synthetic.

With Mike Tackett I had seen what it was like to be at the focal point of sex and lust and power. At the studio I could see the sham, the real tinsel beneath the false tinsel, the scrabblings for fame and power. The incident with Tolliver and Demmon left me helpless. I could do nothing.

I drifted. I still saw Mike. I stood like a fool with a group of Congressmen before the *Zeus* mockup. I went to a Universal-Metro premiere with a starlet named Zambra Farlow. She had plastic breasts. I got drunk with a cameraman sitting in a western bar set and was seen by a tour of schoolteachers. The cameraman was fired and I had my wrists slapped.

General Fitch flew in from Houston with a portfolio of photographs from the newest Saturn probes, a big smile for me and the news that Senator DeVore was coming out on a fund-raising tour for his party and would like me to be there if I could.

"Oh, and could you bring Mike Tackett, too? And that actress that's going to be in the film, what's her name?"

"Margo Masters."

"Yes, could you get her?"

"I don't know her, General."

"The studio will fix it if you ask them, John. You have a lot of juice here, you know."

"I do?" Sure I do.

"Try, will you? The Senator will appreciate it."

"Sure. Why not?"

Senator DeVore was thirty-five going on Immortality. There was a drive in the man but I couldn't tell if it was ego, a lust for power or what the public saw: the tough, dedicated young man, son of a great President, who carried the banners of space, ecology and lower taxes.

"Colonel Grennell."

His handshake was firm, manly. Why is it you automatically distrust a politician? The more normal and honest he seems, the more you suspect him. Where is the flaw? Where is the self-revelatory statement?

"Senator."

There were flashes as the photographers did their job. The Senator put an arm around me. The other was around Mike Tackett, who was for once not quite the center of attention. A man with a good chance at being President of the United States has a certain reality in the presence of the basic unreality of motion picture actors.

But there is one thing beyond reality. It's a dream.

Dreams have power. Dreams topple despots and empires. Dreams also build despots and empires. Dreams can be women. In fact, they frequently are. In the lives of millions around the world one of the dreams was called Margo Masters.

There was a fuss at the door to the hall. I heard the words before I saw their cause: "Margo Masters! It's Margo Masters—"

Even Mike Tackett was affected. I glanced at the Senator, noted his coolness, his professionalism. But he was a man.

She came through the crowd like a queen. America has more queens than England ever had and one of the best was Margo Masters.

She went directly to the Senator and I could see the Senator thinking: *I know it's phony—but if she means only one-hundredth of how she looks at a man . . .*

I was her next target—right after the Senator. She put her face up for a kiss and I felt foolish as hell, peeking away in the direction of her ear. And I was startled when she said into my ear, "I want to talk to you."

She turned to Mike with a big flurry, then to several Congressmen wearing silly smiles, then to Steve Tolliver for a quick hug. She disappeared into the throng of big names, dispensing kisses and hugs like coins from a royal carriage.

What about? I was asking myself.

I found out somewhere around two in the morning in a hotel room five floors up from the ballroom where the benefit had been held. Miraculously there were only the two of us.

"I understand you object to my playing Melinda," she said.

She was in casual, immaculate white, with just enough bosom showing to be fashionable.

"It's nothing personal, Miss Masters. You are—an excellent actress."

She smiled. "What you're saying is that I play myself and this *self* is not that of Melinda Deckinger."

"She was born in a small town in Oregon, Miss Masters—"

"Margo, please—John."

"She wasn't you. Not even with a different hair color, a different accent, a different—everything."

"I can act, John. I don't know if my Oscar means anything or not, considering the way some of them have been awarded—but I *can* act. I want to be the best Melinda I can." I walked to the window and looked out at the lights of the arcologs looming up out of the cement canyons of the city. They were new and dominated the skyline for kilometers in every direction, massive buildings to house up to a half-million people each. The press of population was forcing people up. Some of us wanted to go *all* the way "up."

"And if the character of Melinda Deckinger gets in the way of the image of Margo Masters?"

She was silent for a time. Then she said, "Did you ever fall out of love with her?"

I waited a moment before I said, "No."

That Melinda and that John were a long time ago.

"Look at me, John Grennell." I looked at her over my shoulder, as if my back were a defense against her beauty. "Could you love me?"

"No, I'm sorry."

She looked faintly astonished, then smiled. "Too much image?"

"Maybe. You're public property, Miss Masters. You can't belong to one man. Not any more. Not ever. You wouldn't want it that way and the world wouldn't let it be that way. Your husbands were surrogates for all the sweaty men who wanted to ball you."

"Why do you have to have me for yourself? Can't you love me—just for me?"

I laughed and turned to face her.

"What has this to do with playing a part in a movie? Hell, lady, if you want to tell your grandchildren you slept with a check list of America's greats, I'd be more than happy to oblige."

Her great violet eyes slitted. For an instant she was real. Not a tawny pampered cat but jungle-bred quickness. And for that instant I loved her.

"John Philip Grennell, you listen to me. I've bedded with a hundred men to get where I am. Pigs and saints, gods and animals. All the time I've hated it for what it did to me. Hated the beauty. Hated the effect on men. Here and there I thought I found a man who was right, even glorious. But each time it fell apart. The moment I stopped generating the image, the men left. Oh, maybe they didn't physically leave for a while—but they left. I was a little girl when you touched down on Callisto. You were the biggest thing ever to me. Man had broken out beyond Mars. Maybe we'd yet go to the stars! You were a symbol, John Grennell. You were fast, tough, cool, and smart. You were right up there with Neal Armstrong and Einstein—"

"Hey, lady, that's crazy! I was just part of a team. I was the tip of a spear thrown into space by a hundred thousand men."

"You were that tip and you didn't break. You're still the symbol, John. I don't care how you cut it."

"But what does this have to do with Melinda? You don't look like her, you don't act like her."

"Grant me enough talent to project the *effect* of her."

"The image?"

"If you will. Melinda was beautiful. It is the effect that counts. No one can look exactly like another. But a good imitator can generate the effect of the person. That's what I want to do."

"So why make a big thing out of it? You have the contract."

"I have the contract with the studio. I don't have one with you. I want your approval."

I looked at her narrowly. I felt she was telling the truth, whatever her reason.

"Okay—Melinda had guts. She had beauty. She was intelligent. She was loyal. I don't know about the loyalty—but you have the other attributes."

Margo grinned at me. "Was she good in bed?"

Suddenly a weight lifted from me. I grinned back.

"I'll tell you in the morning."

All that was nice, of course. I didn't mind the least becoming another mounted head on Margo Masters' trophy room. But it didn't change the picture much.

I was being played by the world's most magnetic male star. My girl in the film was the Sex Queen of the Universe, a part well suited to her. Ballard was being made into Mr. Evil. The *Zeus* was twice as big as science and the FSA intended. Callisto's surface was a lot prettier. The telemetry monitors spoke more dramatically than I could believe. The FSA secretaries that U-M hired were far prettier than real life.

And the President of the United States was being played by his son, a bit of casting that sent the company publicists into orbit with joy and the public into energetic apathy.

I complained to Tolliver so many times I gave up. I gave two interviews to the foreign press and had the studio on my back for two weeks. I said to hell with it and went swimming at Cabo San Lucas. My companions on that trip were (1) a young actress with the most expressive bust and hips in Hollywood and (2) her press agent.

The press agent got me back to the studio. His release to the effect that I was about to marry Simone deFrance sent me there at Mach IV.

I was in time to be invited to join the gang on Station One, where the exteriors of the *Zeus* and station shots were to be made. I hadn't been up for two years, almost three. I jumped at the chance.

Besides, Margo had asked me if sex was any different in free fall.

I told her I'd never tried it. In real life Melinda had never made it to space. Margo told me she'd like my cooperation in a space first.

"It's only right, two big stars like us," she said.

"I hate to disappoint you, but it's been done by the Duke University research team—if not by the FSA girls."

"Foolish thoughts, Colonel John. It hasn't been done until it's been done by Margo Masters."

"I told you I was willing. Will you spell my name right in your autobiography?"

"If you promise to spell mine right in yours."

"Done, wench."

"The Cape on Tuesday, right?"

"Yes, ma'am. If there is anything I like it's a dedicated researcher with a heart of gold."

"I like you, Colonel John."

"And I like you, Sex Symbol of Our Time."

More than I care to think about, said my head.

160

They had sent me up in the first shuttle and when Margo arrived, I met her, saying, "We have to stop meeting like this. Universal-Metro is getting suspicious."

She laughed and looked around. "I did a film in this place once—that is, a mockup of this. It looks the same but it doesn't look the same." She looked at me again. "You must have a lot of pull to get them to let us shoot here."

"I'd have no power at all if FSA didn't want the film. I'm a has-been. They trot me out when they want to boost a rally or add a little push to a friendly senator's race."

"Cynic."

"Realist. Notice anything?"

She looked around. "No, why?"

"Gravity."

"So?"

"So no sex floating in space. The Station turns. Centrifugal force gives us about a half gee." Her face fell in mock tragedy. "You knew," I said accusingly.

"I know there is a central core, a passage up the length of the station, that's null-gravity."

"It's also Main Street. You want to have it spread all over the world you make love in public places?"

She grinned. "They think I do anyway. They *want* me to. I do all the things they want to do and can't—or won't." She patted my cheek. "But you can't. Authentic heroes are not figures of lust and fun. We'll just have to use a tug."

I laughed aloud, getting a fast look from Mike Tackett, who was coming through the airlock. "You, my little wanton, have been doing your homework. I was going to surprise you with it."

I took her along to the tiny cabins to which we had been assigned. She made a face.

"In *Space Station One* I had something big enough to make love to Ron Caughran in. Damn penny-pinching Government, anyway."

"Come on. Let me show you the place. It's dripping with drama, traditions and cosmic karma."

"Yes, sir, Colonel John, sir. Which way is the tug lock?"

"Later, wench, later. That damn flack is going to want pictures all around before the shuttle goes back."

"Later?" she whispered, like a conspiratorial schoolgirl.

"Don't you read the Sunday fax sheets? We here at Station

One are incapable of a serious sexual thought. We are dedicated, clear-eyed, firm of jaw—"

"I smuggled aboard an unserious sexual thought."

"So did I. We'll have to get them together and see if they take to each other."

She laughed and trotted off down the curving corridor. I followed her.

It took two days to get Stumpy to give us permission to take out a tug. I had to pull a little mythical rank on him. Not the eagles I wore—he, too, had a set. But that elusive thing called fame. I was John Grennell, not just a visiting bird Colonel. And my passenger was none other than Margo.

She stood smiling and looking about eighteen. She had nothing on under the thermojumper. I knew because I helped her dress. Stumpy melted.

We got Number Four and a checkout from a young lieutenant who couldn't keep his eyes on the panel. Margo and I were somewhat unsuccessful in hiding our grins as we decanted from the lock.

Rank hath its privileges, son, I told the lieutenant silently as we drifted away from the bulk of the station.

Margo was all eyes. Seeing space for the first time is a big thrill if you look through the port of a big shuttle or a true spacer. It's damned impressive through one of the station's large viewports. And it's more impressive still from the smaller but somewhat more personal ports of a tug. I found space all fresh and new myself through Margo's eyes.

We spent two hours as if they were five minutes, just looking around, a couple of kilometers away from Station One. I pointed out the *Hermes* in docking orbit and the tugs nudging the Sahara shuttle. She had a hard time believing that one tiny dot was the massive Station Four.

We had a good view of the Russian station when it came around and the sun lit it up against the blackness. I spotted a fragment of something floating nearby and jockeyed us closer, then yanked it in with mag grapples. I peered at it, leaning out into the bubble.

"It looks like a piece from an old Atlas. Maybe one of the late Apollo flights. I guess they missed it when they did the big sky cleanup ten years back."

"Can I have it?"

I laughed.

"I suppose so. Weighs thirty-forty pounds, though. You could never wear it as jewelry."

"I'll have it cut up and polished and give pieces to friends for Christmas. Hey"—her face lit up—"I almost forgot!" She pressed herself against me. "Didn't we have some nefarious plan before we got carried away by the wonders of the universe?"

I laughed and began unzipping her jumper.

We came back bruised but happy. The equal and opposite reaction works, all right.

III

By the next day the U-M crew was up, although it was only a skeletal group. Even the unions had to bow to payloads lifted to stations and did not resort to featherbedding. The balance of the crew loafed, drinking in Cape Kennedy bars and impressing the locals

Steve Tolliver seemed to live in a tug that had been worked over to accommodate the big cameras and Owen McDaniels, his director of photography. They flitted about, getting space shots of the Station and the *Zeus* mockup floating next to it. Then there was a series of intricate shots to provide background for closeups that would be made later in the studio.

While Steve and Owen were outside the sound crew was all over the inside, collecting the sounds of the station from the tiniest whirs to the big woofing gasps of the main locks.

I asked the head sound man where he was going to get his meteor-flying-through-space noises and his roar-of-*Zeus*-leaving-for-destiny sounds. He looked at me wearily, smiled and said, "The same place I get the hum of ether and the music of the spheres, Colonel."

Steve and Owen did a beautiful shot pulling back from a port where the tearful-but-grave Margo-Melinda watched us leave for my appointment with Fate.

"I don't suppose it matters," I said, "but Melinda was in California when we left."

Steve put his hand on my shoulder. "I know we're taking liberties—but Melinda would have been here if she could have been—right?" I nodded. Steve spread his hands in an expressive gesture.

I think that was the nudge. Right then I started thinking another way. His casual rewrite of history annoyed me. It disturbed my what-the-hell-what-can-I-do-against-this-monolithic-machine attitude .

So I started to do something.

Steve thought it would look better if they put Mike Tackett into a suit and had him personally drift over from the Station to the *Zeus,* right up to the big stereo lens of the camera.

He missed.

They caught him with a tug, of course, and he thought it was a pretty funny joke. I never thought floating on nothing and heading out was exactly a knee-slapper, but maybe they make actors tougher.

I told them to use one of the experienced men from the Station and put enough steel into my voice to make them listen.

The PR man from U-M was in constant touch with the PR man back at the Cape, and they soft-pedaled the switch and played up Tackett's miss. They soft-pedaled my grumbling and gave out polite little press releases about the continued cooperation of the Great John Grennell.

The capper came when a young major, his eyes on Margo and his heart locked to his future in the space program, kiddingly asked me, "Well, Colonel, what have you done lately?"

He was joking, of course. Just barely. But he struck home. What *had* I been doing lately? The one big thing in my life that I had done was being corrupted. This would undoubtedly be the way I, and Ballard, and the whole mission, would be remembered.

And it was all wrong. With a very great deal of talk, persuasion, muscle and rank I had gotten them to change Ballard's role from *coward,* to *a moment of human weakness* but it still wasn't right. And they knew it wasn't right. But they were going to do it that way, anyway, because it was dramatic.

So what *had* I been doing?

Ladies' club meetings. A polished Exhibit A at Congressional hearings. A sure-fire hit at the Lions Club. Window dressing for a Presidential visit.

I'd done one good thing in my life and from then on all had been downhill. Ballard and I had kicked man out beyond the inner planets and had started the space program going again at a time when the money had been drying up. Our success had

164

primed the pump and all those things they were finding out there were paying off handsomely. The outer four moons of Jupiter were all retrograde and at least three were probably extra-solar and chock full of geological wonders.

But what had I done lately?

Suddenly I had the feeling I was waiting. I didn't know for what. But something was going to happen. I had a feeling.

"What's that?" Margo asked, pointing out a viewport. I excused myself from a conversation with a laser lieutenant and went to her side. She was as excited as a schoolgirl.

"What?" I asked.

"That big globe with all the things sticking out of it."

My heart began to pump faster and I found it harder to breathe. "That's the *America*. When the *Outsider* gets back from Pluto and they read the tapes someone will go out in that."

"Suspended animation, right?"

I nodded, my eyes on the most beautiful ship in the system. "You've been doing your homework again."

"There's not much to read up here but all those science things."

"I thought making movies was glamorous and exciting. You're ruining my illusions."

That globe was going to Pluto. I wanted to go.

"It's going to take years, isn't it?"

"Yes. Pluto is nearly four billion miles out. Suspended animation is the only way."

I wanted to go but I was too old. And new heroes, not retreads, were needed. Two or three eager young ones were in training for every post open on every mission on the books.

I still wanted to go.

I wanted to go to the stars. I didn't want to turn off my mind every night in Margo's cabin. I was tired arguing with Tolliver. I was beginning to hate Ballard for not having come back alive.

I wanted to go to the stars.

Not just cold, distant Pluto—but Alpha Centauri.

The Big Step.

Next to the moon landing—the *first* moon landing—the next important step was to the nearest star. Mars, Venus, the moons of Jupiter, even the projected Saturn trip, even Pluto—all these were interim adventures. The Big Step was the one that counted. The stars.

I felt like a kid with his first science-fiction magazine. Lying in the midnight grass looking at the summer stars, swearing, *Some day, some day . . .* Looking through a viewport inches from the stars, a display case of firejewels, God's nightlights.

I hurt, wanting to go and not being able to go.

But I looked at the *America* and suddenly I had stopped waiting.

I checked with the Station control and found that the parking orbit they were using to put the finishing touches to the *America* would bring the ship close to us—then we would slowly drift apart, each of us a bead on an invisible circular wire. But for a few days we would be close.

I took the opportunity to deadhead on a supply shuttle from the Station to the *America,* using my fame blatantly to hitch over.

The ship was a lot bigger than the *Zeus,* but the control system was basically the Mark III updated and improved to the Mark IX. Any time now they'd scrap the designation and take a new ident scheme—but while this one was the great-grandson of the system in the *Zeus,* it was still recognizable to me.

I may have been doing the creamed-chicken-and-peas circuit for a while, but my years of hanging around the Cape were about to pay off. I was no stranger to the Mark IX controls, for official policy toward a "spokesman" such as I was to keep me informed of what was happening.

I pressured a harassed light colonel I knew slightly to pressure the civilian in charge into giving me the two-dollar tour. I kept my eyes and ears on full alert. Once again I used my fame as a tool, keeping the civilian long past "tour time" answering my questions.

I "missed" the return shuttle and had to wait for the next one, thirty hours later. It gave me a chance to jolly a major into letting me sit in the control seat and do a run-through, letting the major have the honor of copiloting and instructing the Great John Grennell.

I also stole Operations and Procedure Manuals.

I was about to become the first spaceship thief in history.

I liked the feeling. I was doing something, even if it was illegal, immoral and highly nonfattening. If I failed I was disgraced and in deep trouble. If I succeeded I *could* get killed.

I could hardly wait.

Oh, I didn't think they'd really put me in jail if they intercepted me. They'd ground me and slap my wrist and some PR would let it out that I had been stoned and some of the vidtabs would snigger and maybe jeer. Unless I hurt someone or smashed up the ship I'd simply get a lot of static. But I'd never make it out in space again. And not getting out in space again would kill me.

And I guess the laughter would kill me. The comedians in the media would make jokes and my old buddies would kid me and privately think I was over the hill.

If I succeeded they'd all be dead when I got back. That wouldn't be much fun, either.

The first chance I had after returning to Station One I made love to Margo with a zest and enthusiasm that surprised her.

"What's gotten into you, Colonel, honey?"

"You are the Golden Princess of Sagittarii IV. You are the Sex Goddess of the Sexpods Empire and I have conquered you. You are Conan's Number One Mistress and Captain Future's illegitimate daughter. You are Flame and Fire, Ice and Diamonds!"

"Colonel!"

"I have rescued you from the Space Pirates of Cygni Zillion and am about to claim my reward."

"Again?"

"Again."

"Well, bless my stars!"

It wasn't easy, of course, but they weren't expecting it. They had figuratively left the keys in a car parked in a rough neighborhood.

I knew Margo wouldn't go—but I had to ask.

"Are you crazy? You *mean* it? But you'll be *old* when you come back!"

"No, I won't. You'll be old if you don't go. Probably dead and forgotten. I'll only be a few years older. I'll be twenty-nine years in suspended animation. I worked it out on the computer. Two, three, six months there—longer if there's intelligent life and they don't zap me at first look. Twenty-nine years back.

167

Sixty years from now—if I come back—I'll have made the Next Step. Come with me."

"You're crazy. Stark, staring mad. Stealing a spaceship? Who wants to go to the stars anyway?"

"I do."

"I'm a star. Come to me, Colonel, honey."

"You don't glow in the dark."

Suddenly she broke into laughter. "If you are not twisting me around, this will be the biggest publicity smash in history!"

"If I can do it, I'm going. I take it you are not coming?"

She smiled at me. "Colonel John, me darlin' boy, I appreciate the offer. I really do. I couldn't care less about the stars but I appreciate that you do. Starman, starman—the first starman." She sighed and hugged me close, her famous breasts flattening against my chest. "Going there and coming back would be the biggest publicity coup of the century, but it would be in the next century and that wouldn't do me any good at all."

"But you'd only be a few subjective months older."

"Starman, honey, you just don't understand about women and ages. I know what I am here and now. I'm a star. I'm known and wanted and rich. Sixty years from now—if we come back—there might be a new fashion for stars, human stars. I might be out of a job and an image. I don't want to take that chance." She smiled again. "Call me chicken, chicken colonel."

I hesitated and started to speak. She put her fingers on my lips.

"Don't worry," she said, "I'll keep your secret."

I kissed her but she broke free. "I'll swear PR to secrecy so we can break it the soonest, okay?"

"Nothing doing. You keep that beautiful mouth shut until I'm off and running. Not even to the PR people. If it came out you'd be an accessory before the fact."

"But what about you sixty years from now?"

"I'll be dead—or a hero. And today would have happened two generations back. Who will care? But I'll have done it. Or died. Or be out there."

She pulled me close and whispered in my ear. "You nut. Name a planet after me."

"I'll spell your name right, ne'er fear, damsel."

"Now take off that jumper and come in here with me. You are going to need a lot of loving to carry you for sixty years, Colonel, honey."

168

"Yes, ma'am, movie star lady."

So I stole a spaceship.

It was easier than I thought. Margo invited everyone to a party paid for by Universal-Metro and everyone but a three-man crew zipped across. I took out a tug after convincing control I was making some special shots for the film company.

The *America* was ready to go. I'd checked. They had planned a short hop out to Callisto Station as a shakedown. Two men in suspension, two "live" plus supplies plus a shipment of assorted provisions for the Callisto personnel. It was the best chance I'd ever have and the only one. There was enough in the Callisto shipment to keep me going for as long as I needed. The newest converter had been installed, giving me maximum range and speed.

The entire suspension system was at optimum. The solar batteries would supplement the reactor. And there was only a three-man crew.

There was only one gun on Space Station One and I had it. I pointed the Colt .45 Auto at the three men. One glowered, one looked confused and one broke into laughter.

"Colonel, when I'm old and gray I want to see you return. I wish I had your guts."

"Thank you and keep moving. The tug will take you back."

The young technician sobered and stuck out his hand in a gesture of farewell. I shook my head. "No, thanks son. You might have a touch of hero in you and I don't care to shoot."

"Yes, it might leak too much air out of this ball of tin." He looked at the other two. "Come on, you goops, let the Colonel have the ball."

They left and I was secure, for I had gaffed the tug radio. They could receive but not send, so no alarm would be sent until they were back. By that time I would be on my way. I dogged down the air-lock, wedged the gun behind a pipe and headed for the control deck.

I pulled the heavy cassette out of my jumper as I hit the computer deck and stuck it in the slot. I'd used the Station computer to plot the entire trip out. All I needed to do was start the ship up, move out of orbit, then punch in the program and climb into the tank.

I wanted to take a look at the outer planets as I went by

but I didn't want to use up my supplies on the home system. I had better uses for those precious goodies.

I broke orbit within ten minutes, heading in past the sun, towards Alpha Centauri. I exploded into vociferous monologues. Houston and the Cape joined in.

Then I heard Margo. For her I stopped and listened.

"Colonel John? This is Margo Masters. I want you to know that your dastardly deed has been recorded for posterity. Tolliver had the cameras on you all the way, you terrible thief, you!"

The laughter bubbled up in me. Margo, you—you *star* you! What a finish for the big film! I could see the insert now. Mike Tackett, slightly grayed, steely-eyed at the console of a giant starship. Heading out. Alone. The first starman.

I punched in and heard them all stop, waiting to hear the first words of the first space pirate.

"You're welcome, Margo," I said.

I looked out through the viewport. I was going off into the sunset.

But it was a different sun.

DAVID R. BUNCH

The Lady Was For Kroinking

When I met her she said she'd just come from the dolls at May's, and I'd just come from the place of Smilin' Jackson. She looked relaxed, very! Something like a full lioness looks lying in jungle sun, with the blood soaked in all around, clotting the grass, matting the lioness fur. "I did twenty," she chortled, "before I got relaxed. Real-life conditions, too. Some! How was it over at Jackson's?"

I didn't want to tell her how it was over at Jackson's, she being a woman-type person, beautiful, and my very newest girl-love. "It was real good," I demurred, "over at Jackson's. And you might not understand. We do things for our nerves over at Jackson's."

"Well, it was real good today, over at May's," she said. "I think I got the most out of this one they called Flo. She was just one of several, you understand—the fifteenth, to be exact. And after you do up to around that many, the matrons start to respect you. They know you've really got good guts for *kroinking*. The most I'd ever done before was thirteen, but today—well, I really felt full of the old do-'em-in-good today."

She gazed up at me, and her lips, slightly parted now, showing the good-razor teeth, were red and full. She looked healthy, and her breasts seemed actual; her legs were nice on her tall-heel shoes. She was just a healthy, normal, and very beautiful young woman, you would say, until you noticed how the skin stretched just a little too tight across her forehead and the bridge of her nose, how that skin was a funny green color even through her very smooth cosmetics, and how her gray eyes were not quite happy in their ovals of dark blue skin. "The matron at May's said if I hadn't come in when I did for some *kroinking*, I'd have been a police case by tomorrow. For real! Then she patted me and charged me extra 'cause I'd done for so many."

"Tell me about it," I said, "and the one you got the most out of."

Her gray eyes under their very chic slant glasses with the pale purple frames seemed to devour me with a look of love. "Will you tell me then about Jackson's?" she demanded.

"Maybe," I said a little grimly, "maybe I will."

"Well, to begin with, somehow she was just the one—just the thing to remind me of all the real snotters in the world." Out of bitter thoughts she made the face I loved. "As I said, it was the fifteenth one. The rest were just a kind of build-up, and the last five just a sort of tailing-off to get me down from my high-rise. She was a little thing compared to me, a small blonde thing. But spunky-featured and hateful. They're all spunky-featured and hateful at May's. That's mainly why May's is better."

"Same at Jackson's," I mumbled, "same thing."

"When the matron brought out Flo, I knew right away this was it, this was my day. I may not have to go back for a whole week! Think of that!"

"I feel good too," I confided. "Really got fixed up. There was this Lester—"

Then I bit my tongue, because I didn't want to tell her how we behaved at Jackson's. "You were telling me about doing little Flo," I urged.

172

"Yes! When the matron brought out Flo, I glanced at her, and I knew the matron was waiting to see what I'd say. The matron was just kind of smiling in a stalling way, like a big teasing cat with mice tied on rubber strings. They've got your history at these places, you know, on little white cards. They can read up on you, and they know just what to do for you. They're all a lot alike, I guess, in a way, but still I had that feeling that Flo had been kept just for me. 'The most,' I said to the waiting matron, 'the very most you've got.'

"So she brought out these very shiny and sharp steel pins, two of them, that were about half as long as a normal person's height. I knew in a flash what I'd do with them. Then she brought out two cylinders to heat in the fire; they were about the size of eyes on the end, and the ends were hollowed to little shallow cups. Next there was a heavy pat of metal made to a kind of wedge, and on the end of the wedge, about where teeth would hit if you put it in your mouth, were little separate wedges, each individually notched. This pat of metal had a bit of a handle to it, and lying around all over were choices in weights of hammers. Then they had these little nipper-grippers, twenty of them suspended from blood-colored cords on pulleys from the ceiling, that at first I thought were for fingernails. And toe-nails. And hair. But I brightened up to the prospects pretty fast, just looking at hateful *her* standing in a lounging post by the wall. . . . Besides what I've named, there were a lot of knives and hooks and scissors and meat forks. And the biggest collec-tion of hat pins I've ever seen! Except for the instruction card, that's about it."

"Sounds like plenty of what-it-takes-to-*kroink*-with," I said.

"When the matron asked, 'Light or heavy when she bleeds?' I yelled, 'All you have when she bleeds!' So she marked it for heavy, and she brought out a great white pail of pour-on blood, with a pump and hose. And it smelled like real, though I doubt if they could possibly afford that every time. But May's advertise that their pour-on blood is fifteen-percent real, and I believe it's at least that much."

"Jackson's go ten to twelve," I said, "usually. They're strong-est on this other thing." Then I bit my tongue again. She was the one telling the story.

"When I started my *kroink* on Flo, I just sort of went off my coconut. Which is what one wants to do. Makes it that much better. First I bound her on to the forty-five, which is two heavy

173

beams of metal—like double weights of I-beams—stuck out at about that angle in the work area, and I strapped her in so well she couldn't have moved if she'd been untrimmed Samson. Geez, I hated her in such a normal, natural, and healthy way! Why, all I did seemed so natural and necessary that it was hardly work at all."

"It's that way sometimes," I agreed, "when you're doing tasks you like to do, tasks that need doing. Like on Lester—" Then I clamped teeth on tongue again. Let her talk.

"I followed the instruction card and did the pin part first," she went ahead, "picked up a hammer about medium weight and drove those two gleaming shafts in through the bottoms of her nylons far as I could, up through the thighs to the hips. I'd already taken off her cute little shoes. I yelled for blood, and the matron pumped, and the hose spurted it on. And also at this time the matron remembered to turn the scream amplifiers up another notch or two in the wall. Then I went for her teeth, smashed at her built-up bright smile, with the metal wedge, not bothering to use a hammer—smashed and smashed at her false little mouth until I could feel it was ruined, nothing now but grit and slimy, slippery bag. I screamed for blood again, and while the socket-ended cylinders were heating at a small gas flame nearby, I hacked around with the hat pins and scissors and knives, sticking and stabbing at Flo all the while, and the matron operating the blood. And all this time the amplifiers were shrieking up stereo with Flo's shrill shouts for help, until it was all just screams and blood and entreaties. A most satisfying thing indeed. Then I went for her eyes, with those hot cylinders, red hot they were now, and there was the smell of flesh. 'Real!' the matron yelled, 'Real!' jumping up and down. 'Eyes of the lamb! Eyes of the lamb!' I singed ahead, and I didn't feel tired.

"When I paused to consult the card for further instructions, the matron yelled, 'The nipper-grippers! The nipper-grippers! The best is yet to do!' So I attached them to skin at the twenty right places—these were marked—pinching well in past Flo's clothes, for it had come to me what the nipper-grippers were meant to do. Then I hauled at the pulley ropes, and the slack came out of the blood-colored cords that led down to the nipper-grippers, and Flo tautened all around. And we pulled off her skin, I and the nipper-grippers, ripping right through clothes, and only that skin remained where the straps held her fast to the beams. The screams shrieked loud all the time now—'oh!

oh! stop! please stop! ohhh!'—just as satisfying as you can imagine it would be. And the matron pumped out the last of the
blood and covered Flo all over with that good crimson goo. And
you know what! I stood there shouting. Trembling and shouting
and clutching one of the beams, I yelled, 'The fingernails! We
haven't done anything yet to the fingernails. Nor the toenails!
And the hair! *We've got to pull out her hair!'* Then the matron
came over and patted me and took me loose from the beam and
said, 'There, there, doll. It'll take a week now in our best *kroink*
hospital to get this mess so it can go back on the line.'

"And that's about all. That's about the end of it. The last
five were entirely anticlimax, as I mentioned earlier, just something to give me a chance to cool down from my high-rise on
Flo. . . Tell me now about Jackson's. *Now!*"

"Ah, no," I hedged, "not tonight. It's late, and you're tired,
and I've had a busy day too. Some other time, maybe." So we
stood there and chatted of general things for a while, shouting
to make ourselves heard above the noise of jets and the peculiar
frizzy sound of so many people swinging by at about second-
floor level, airborne on their own individual blades, jumps, and
lifts. And we heartily agreed that the Enjoy-Your-Hate houses
were here to stay, and doing a good work too, though some
squeamish-type birdies might not agree.

"In these modern times," she said, "we've just got to have
things like these Enjoy-Your-Hate houses so we can *kroink*. To
keep our minds healthy and free and not let them get sick. Why,
if I hadn't worked out like that today, I'd have been a police
case by tomorrow. For real! The matron said so. But I'm normal
now. May not have to go back to that house for a whole week!
Think of that!" Then she gave me that full-lioness look I had
noticed earlier, so relaxed! And I thought it was cute. And all
at once, without warning, we found ourselves clamped in each
other's arms, and as I kissed her violently I could feel her sinking her white gleamy teeth deeper and deeper into my lips and
through my lips, and I closed down hard too. When we reeled
apart, both our mouths were streaming blood. It was then that
I knew, really knew, that yes! YES! in the mad days ahead we
must prove to be really fine soul-friends for each other, and good
lovers too. "Don't feel so superior," I yelled at her as her tall
metal heels clattered away. "I did just as bad to that rubber
Lester!"

C. C. CLINGAN

High Bank

Chuck Kerney skated to the infield after an unsuccessful jam, his earlier excitement dulled now by his failure to score for the team. Josh Mede, their coach, had worked arduously, practically day and night. guiding them to victory in the Western Skating League and a chance to play the Canadians, last year's world champions.

Chuck's thoughts drifted back to the past week's semi-finals against the Eastern Champion New York Renegades. With just a little over three minutes to go in the final period, the Renegades had scored three points to go ahead. To Chuck's surprise the coach had grabbed the jamming sticker from little Floyd Perkins and stuck it on his own helmet.

As the pack re-formed and the pivot men jockeyed for position, the buzzer sounded the start of what would probably be the final jam. With adroit moves and adept style of skating, Mede sliced through the pack and almost immediately reached peak alacrity. In his wake came the Renegade's top jammer, Ray Martinez, in an attempt to eliminate Josh and sew up the win for his team. The second Martinez broke from the pack, Mede's sensors signaled that the opposition was close behind. Reversing his retros, he uncoiled a perfect jump block, throwing the opposing jammer off balance to go careening into the infield. By the time another Renegade jammer could skate loose from the pack, Mede's flying skates had eaten up half of the one-mile oval track. Moments later, as he neared the back of the pack, Kerney's helmet mike crackled to life.

"Kerney."

"Ya, Mede. I read you."

"I'm going to try a High Bank."

For a moment Kerney was silent, absorbing that news. "Hey, Mede. I think with the A-7 play we could pick up three points and throw it into overtime."

"Look, Kerney, I was doing the High Bank when you were still in diapers. Now let's move. There isn't much time left."

"Okay, Josh. You're the boss. I'll pass the word to the rest of the boys."

Chuck changed from jammer band to team frequency to repeat the play to the other three men in their pack.

High Banking, they called it, the most dangerous play in the game and rarely used. A skater took a whip from his pivot man, retros firing, and came in low and on the outside. If timing and reflexes were perfect—as they had to be—he broke through between the pack and the ten-foot banked wall, scoring a point for each of the opposing men in the pack. If he were off, well, he might just keep going right up and over the wall at more than eighty miles per hour. Even with the light alloy fiber suit and insulated helmet, more than one life had been lost attempting this play. Chuck remembered when Ed Patton of the Apollos had tried a High Bank and missed, to go flying high over the wall at eighty plus. When they reached him, he was already dead, his neck broken in three places.

Watching his helmet screen at the simulacrum of Mede coming up behind him, Chuck slowed his pace. Dropping back from the pack he waited for Mede to give the signal. Seconds dragged by as Mede waited for the right moment. Then the words "hit it" came through Kerney's helmet, shattering his cerebration and the silence around him. Firing the retros, he felt the gyro stabilizers come into play. Behind him Mede's image grew larger. As he came within reach. Kerney extended one hand and uncoiled a spring-like whip. Mede passed in a blur, accelerating toward the pack at close to ninety. Just as it seemed Mede would hit, he crouched, banking up and around, instantly reversing his retros. As the braking jets fired, he went into a slide, smoke pouring from the track as the slide carried him even closer to the zenith of the wall. Then, just a foot short of the rim, his speed decreased sufficiently and he dropped back to the track, landing on his skates.

Even the rival New York fans were on their feet, applauding with zeal the flawless completion of the dangerous high-banking maneuvers.

As the Renegades tried desperately to re-form the pack for another jam, the buzzer had sounded, signaling the end of the game and victory for the Stars.

That had been the semifinals. Now this was an almost identical situation, with only nine minutes to go and the Stars behind by four points. Kerney sat in the infield at the Tech station watching for the next jam to begin as the suit tech checked him thoroughly. Ever since Bob Murphy's retros had exploded a few years before, killing him and injuring several others, a new law had been initiated: a jammer could not jam twice in succession and, in between, had to go to the infield for a check of his suit status. As the buzzer sounded, a flash of blue and orange exploded from the pack and accelerated out of the far curve, hitting top speed. As the jammer flew by him, Chuck caught the familiar number twenty-four on the back of Mede's suit.

At forty-two, Mede was known around the league as Methuselah, although he could still out-skate all but a few of the really greats of the league. He had started his track career twenty-six years ago at the age of sixteen, and at twenty-four became the youngest coach to take over the California Stars.

Chuck wished Mede had given the jamming sticker to one of the other men. Mede had been driving himself hard lately and Kerney knew the danger of speed fatigue. A skater never knew when he'd had it and could just suddenly fail to associate speeds. Going at seventy miles per hour, he might think he was hardly moving and fire the retros going into a curve. Chuck felt a little better as he noticed the Stars had kept the Canadians from getting a jammer out, thus leaving Mede to concentrate on one thing—scoring.

As Mede neared the rear of the pack, Kerney noticed the pivot man drop back. Damn! he thought. I hope the old man isn't thinking of using the High Bank again. If so, he is pushing his luck, using that play in his present state. Flipping on the helmet mike to jammer band, Kerney just caught the two words, "hit it." Both men seemed to surge forward to merge into one for a split second, then Mede flew ahead, accelerated from the whip by his pivot man. At the precise moment he dropped into that crouch. As he emerged on the far side of the pack, Kerney knew something was wrong. Mede's retros had failed to reverse. With a sickening feeling in his stomach, Kerney watched him hurl the banked wall and disappear behind it. Leaping to his skates he hurried to the smooth, almost seamless door set in the banked wall and waved frantically to the control booth to open it. As the door slid open, Chuck skated down the ramp to the field below, searching for—but dreading to find—the body of his friend. Following the curve of the track he soon spotted Mede lying several yards away. There were no signs of life. Kerney knelt and slowly removed Mede's helmet, carefully lowered the injured man's head on a towel brought from the infield.

A small trickle of blood ran out of the corner of Mede's mouth. An ugly bruise darkened on his forehead. Mede's eyes slowly opened and he grasped Kerney's hand as it wiped away the blood.

"Take it easy, Mede. The Doc will be here in a minute and we'll get you to the hospital."

"Don't think it'll do much good," came a whispering voice. "My insides feel all torn up. Sorry I loused it up, Chuck. I wanted to get the world championship for you and the rest of the boys. You all deserve it."

"Forget it, Mede. Besides, there's always next year. At least we came this far."

Before Chuck could say any more, the doctor arrived, pushing him out of the way to get to Mede.

Arriving back at the track, Kerney was informed of an official time-out called because of the accident. Glancing up at the clock, he saw there was just a little over seven minutes of playing time left. Thunderous applause brought his attention away from the clock. They were bringing Mede back to the infield to await a copter from the City Medi-Center. Kerney skated over and, with a smile, removed the jamming sticker from Mede's helmet and placed it on his own. Rejoining the pack, Chuck knew somehow he had to try with every ounce of strength and courage he could muster to keep the Canadians from arrogating this win. As the buzzer broke his trend of thought, he moved to get out of the pack first. Maybe it was the determination of their team or the laxness of the Canadians; either way, Kerney broke from the pack without any pursuit. He felt more alone now than he had ever felt in his life. With every second his heart seemed to beat louder as he flew around the track almost without thought of what he was doing.

As he approached the back of the pack, Chuck fired his reverse retros slightly to match speeds with the other skaters. He was strictly on his own as Rich Williams and the rest of the boys concentrated on controlling the head of the pack, keeping the opposing jammers from getting out. There was no Mede to help him this time, either. He would have to rely on his own assets as a skater. He stole a quick glance at the big digital clock situated on the far turn and found he had fifteen seconds left—plenty of time to score if he made his move now. His adrenalin was flowing freely, building up his senses to a peak as he hit his retros coming out of the far turn. Rushing toward the pack, he saw an opposing skater drop back to block him. Thirty-seven. Damn that Mitch Feller, one of the best blockers in the league. Just his luck.

Coming in fast, he suddenly reversed himself and squatted down to go under the leg block thrown by Feller. This play had worked for Chuck many times in the past, but it was not to be this time. Instead of sliding under Feller's block for the score, he felt the leg catch the back of his helmet, jarring his teeth. His stabilizers whined as they tried to compensate the over-balance, but to no avail. Caught off balance in the crouching position, he careened into the infield out of control, slammed into the padded penalty box, then bounced off to go skidding another ten yards before coming to rest a few feet from the tech station. He felt his helmet being removed by someone and looked up into the face of the tech. "You okay?" asked the tech, helping Chuck to his feet.

"Ya, sure. Everything's fine except my pride."

"You can afford to lose a little of that," said the tech. "Come on over to the rack so I can check you out. That is, if you want to be ready for your next jam."

As he followed the tech to the rack, Chuck watched the pack reforming and the jammers waiting for the buzzer to set them free for another turn at glory. Six minutes, thought Chuck, as the tech began his examination. That meant he could participate in two or possibly three jams before the final buzzer sounded. That last jam would be the important one if the Stars could tie it up. If the jammers could get out of the pack before official time ran out, they would have sixty seconds to score, even if there was only one second left on the official clock.

As the skate tech gave his suit and skates a thorough examination, the buzzer sounded. Chuck caught Floyd Perkin's number as the little man burst from the pack, followed a second later by Ace Mallory. That tall figure of Mallory's was recognizable even in a suit: the black jammer of the Canadians was one of the biggest in the league, standing six-feet-seven and weighing two-thirty. Floyd was good, but Mallory out-weighed him by almost a hundred pounds and could easily knock the smaller man off the track. That is, if he could catch him.

Chuck watched anxiously as the blue and orange of Floyd's suit seemed to blur together from the speed he had attained. The larger form, in green and black—Mallory—had fallen almost a quarter of a lap behind. Something was wrong. It was almost as if Mallory were trying to give Floyd time to score. Chuck knew better; something was up.

As Perkins approached the pack he found an opposing blocker dropping back to stop him. The Canadian's pivot man was set in front of his blocker to keep anyone from dropping back to help Floyd. As Perkins slowed in an attempt to set up a play, Mallory came in behind him, shoving Floyd into the blocker ahead of him. Shit! thought Chuck. So that's what they had planned. They had Floyd in what was known as the box. Chuck had been in that position once before and didn't want to repeat it ever again. The blocker and opposing jammer would get the other jammer between them and block him back and forth until he became disoriented. Then, a good solid block and he was eliminated from the track. It didn't take long for little Floyd to be caught between the two bigger men—five seconds later he skidded off the track into the infield.

With Perkins eliminated and Mallory having one of his men back to help him, it looked like a sure score for the Canadians. Chuck grabbed his helmet and flipped on team frequency in time to hear Rich Williams call A-9. The orange and blue suits of his teammates suddenly shot away from the pack in unison, leaving the three Canadians in the pack with a job to do.

A pullaway, if done right, was a thing of beauty. Both teams strung out in a line, one chasing the other. Now the Canadians had to try to catch and slow the Stars down to enable their jammer to pass for points. Chuck knew they never would. All his teammates were speed merchants, small and fast. The other larger Canadians could never overtake them before the buzzer. Chuck watched with a sense of wonder at the grace and poise of the swiftly moving skaters. They all seemed to flow through the turns like a fast-moving multicolor snake. Then the buzzer sounded, breaking the almost hypnotic effect and bringing to an end what could have been a disastrous jam for the Stars. They had not scored, but they had kept the Canadians from getting four easy points.

The tech tapped Chuck on the shoulder and handed him his gloves. "You're all checked out for the next jam," he said.

Chuck quickly snapped the helmet down and skated onto the track to join his teammates. As he rejoined the slowly moving group, he motioned to Floyd for the jamming sticker. The smaller man handed it to him and he slapped it to the side of his helmet.

All his muscles were tense as he waited for the buzzer that would signal possibly the last jam, depending on the time it took and which play the jammer used upon reaching the back of the pack. Even though he was ready, the buzzer startled him, and he got a late start from the pack. Ahead of him, number fifty-two, Boid Jackson, broke through, gaining a quick lead that Chuck might not be able to make up.

Chuck maneuvered from the pack. Rich Williams, his pivot man, broke with him, and Chuck quickly realized what his teammate had in mind. He reached out and grasped Rich's hand. The pivot man fired his retros, slingshoting Chuck ahead at extreme velocity. He quickly narrowed the distance between himself and Jackson. As he came upon Jackson, the Canadian attempted to duplicate Mede's style of jump block. Chuck's reflexes, however, were keener than Jackson's. As the Canadian reversed his retros to throw the jump block, Chuck went into a crouch. Jackson's block failed to connect and carried him over

Chuck's head. He hit on his skates and somehow, miraculously managed to keep upright for a second before tumbling onto the infield. Coming out of the far turn, Chuck righted himself and continued toward what might be their whole season in one jam. It all rested on his shoulders.

As he neared the back of the pack, Chuck flipped to jammer band and spoke to Rich Williams. "I'll say this just once because we haven't time to argue. I'm going to try a High Bank, so set it up."

He had expected some sort of a protest, but Rich replied simply: "If that's the way you want, I'm with you."

Chuck watched as Rich attempted to drop back. The Canadians were trying to keep him in the pack, but old Rich had a few tricks of his own. Skating a few feet up the bankwall, he fired his reverse retros before he dropped back to the track. This maneuver flung him backwards past the pack, and with gyros whining, he kept his balance as Chuck glided alongside of him. Quickly the two men got into position for the High Banking maneuver, realizing that precious seconds were running out on them. Taking a few deep breaths, Chuck watched the pack ahead, and as they came out of the far turn he heard himself shouting, "Hit it!"

The firing of the retros surged him forward at a dizzying speed. As Rich's hand came out, he grasped it and whipped even faster toward the pack looming ahead. At the last moment he attempted to emulate Mede's crouch and hit the bank wall at the same time. A split second later, retros reversing, he went into the death slide, raising smoke as he streaked along the top of the High Bank. Then, miraculously, he was dropping. He hit the track—

Instead of flipping back to his skates as Mede had done, Kerney went into a headlong roll to the infield, ending up sprawled at the feet of Mede's stretcher. It was hard to believe he had done it, but the thundering ovation from the partisan crowd roared that he had.

Getting to his knees, Chuck removed his helmet and was greeted by Mede's familiar lopsided grin staring back at him.

"Congratulations, Chuck," Mede said, sticking out his hand. Chuck grasped it with elation. He couldn't decide if it was from winning the championship, or seeing that his old friend was going to be okay.

"Guess I'm going to have to stop trying to hog all the glory for myself and give it up to you youngsters," Mede said. "I thought for awhile I'd damn near killed myself. It's about time I hung up the skates anyway," he said, his grin fading with a spasm of pain.

"Who are you kidding?" Chuck said. "You'll be back next season, flying around the turns with the best of them. Besides, the Stars wouldn't be the same team without you."

"We'll see," said the old man, lying back as the doctor arrived with two aides.

Before Chuck could ask the doctor about Mede, the rest of the team arrived on the infield. Their helmets flew off amidst smiles and jubilant cheers. Chuck caught a last look at Mede being carried away before the team surrounded him, hoisted him to their shoulders, and carried him around the track.

EDWARD BRYANT

The Poet In The Hologram In The Middle Of Prime Time

COMPUTER LINK:
   MEDIUM SHOT——THE POET SEATED IN HIS CHAIR
   EFFECTS: NORMAL SCALE——H-FIGURES DISTORT ±2%
   AIR DISPERSAL: GRAVEYARD EARTH, RAINSOAKED
   INSERT 100 MICROGRAMS ETK-10 IN PROP WINE

                                             FADE IN:

Entrapment. Fearing, Ransom downed the last of the wine

   ruby flowing, richer than blood it drains

He smiled ruefully. It was a bad line: the choice of words was
trite, the metaphor was a cliché. But, he suspected, it was more
than typical of his work these days. Ransom flipped the wine

bottle over his right shoulder. The empty decanter, unbreakable, bounced across the carpet

> *decry the permanence of plastic;*
> *outliving even our rock tombs.*

The man in the chair grimaced and belched. Better. He looked at the device on the coffee table and grinned widely.

The device was genuine. So was the bouquet of blue flowers in the vase beside it. Most of the rest of the room was fake: the table was ersatz walnut, the dark-grained paneling on the walls was imitation.

Ransom stood and stared out the window, down a hundred levels at the sprawl of Greater Ellay. He wasn't really looking out a window, of course. His rooms were interred deep within the labyrinthian apartment block. The window was an electronic screen. Once, besides offering a view of the external world, it could pick up more than eighty television channels. Back when TV was *the* entertainment medium.

The window, not being a window, could not be opened. If it really were a window, it still would stay permanently shut. On Ransom's level of the urban stack, no one could breathe the polluted sky; shovel it, maybe, but not inhale. Air was piped into Ransom's apartment—first filtered, cleansed, sterilized; then oxygenated, ionized, humidified properly, heated, certified carcinogen-free, and consigned to the alveoli of Ransom's lungs.

Ransom frowned at the slight undulation of his surroundings. *Too much wine,* he thought. *Too much for efficiency and not enough for courage.* He crossed to the coffee table, realizing he was weaving. *But sufficient for action.*

He looked down at his contraband toy; then his chin raised and he wrinkled his nose. His nostrils enclosed the slightest scent, a smell undefined, yet disturbingly suggestive. Dark. Moist. Cool. Slightly sweet with decay.

Twenty years old, the memory was. Black veils, black clothes, so starkly contrasted with the white marble of the face. Ransom's father's face, waxy and dead. It had rained that morning and the burying ground was still spongy with moisture. That was when graves could still be dug. Before the premium on vacant land resurrected every inhabitant of the cemetery and sent his remains to the crematorium. Even now the dust of Ransom's father's remains was probably in the process of precipitating out of the air sighing into Ransom's living room.

The poet sniffed, and sniffed again

at the corpse-smell of my own funeral

He picked up the bomb from the coffee table. Childishly amazed at how much leashed destruction could be held in the palm of his hand, Ransom again grinned.

DIRECT CUT TO:

The two watchers, offstage. Consumer Participation Evaluators, they were officially termed. Amelia Marchin, for her own peculiar reasons, called them "neilsons." This was reputed to be some sort of in-joke, but then Amelia possessed a marvelously esoteric knowledge of her field.

The two CPE's watched the stick-figure bumbling through illusion after illusion.

"This is definitely too melodramatic," said the taller one, making a cryptic notation subvocally on his recorder.

"I disagree," said the second CPE, the shorter of the pair. "On the contrary, I feel that this performance is the highest form of art. There is a great deal to be said on behalf of spontaneity."

"So where does the spontaneity leave off?" asked the first CPE. "And where does the external manipulation of the director begin?"

"I don't have the slightest idea. The line of distinction is marvelously subtle." He poured himself a glass of amber liquid. "Have a drink?" he invited.

The first CPE proffered his glass. The two watchers settled back comfortable to watch the show.

DISSOLVE TO

STILL SHOT OF

The poet bleeding.

> *"Iron and sapphire caverns of frost*
> *Coat the chrome cylinders of mind."*

The two lines lie inert on the white paper desert for more than an hour while Ransom grapples with the poem. The night is unending repetition of coffee hot and cold, recorded music and silence, turning the thermostat up and down, remembering and staring at vistas far beyond the walls of the room, sitting quiet, stalking, pacing, tensing and relaxing. On the wall, the clock's hands lag heavily.

> *"Below, the volcano slumbers*
> *Unseen, yet sensed with bleak desire."*

Ransom never works harder than when he forgets his songs. And there is nothing he loves more. Not Melissa, not food, drink, nor any other pleasure. For they are all here in his poetry.

> *"Dim awareness vaguely suspects*
> *Vanished dreams; the promise of fire."*

Dawn is graying the black scan of Ransom's eastern electronic window. The poet yawns and stretches, feeling the cramp of his muscles relax painfully. He looks down at the manuscript, at the words inked out and changed, some a dozen times or more. He sees the dull gleam of flecked silver peeking out of the slag.

Ransom, satisfied for the moment, fixes a simple breakfast.

DIRECT CUT TO:

STILL SHOT OF

The poet loving. Ransom leans on one elbow on the softness of the bed. Below him, Melissa is faceless in shadow.

Sensing his mood, she asks, "What's wrong?"

"Nothing, Love," lies Ransom. What's wrong is the poet's life; he is dissatisfied with himself, with his actions. And no one is to blame except himself. The realization is unpleasant; it intrudes into the ecstasy of the moment

> *I wish that somehow I*
> *could come*
> *to you*
> *now*
> *and ease this bitter moment*

190

> *finding solace*
> *between your thighs*

Ransom hates the intrusion of the world into this moment; he forces it back into a mental recess. Melissa is warmly damply ready. He touches her. They joy in the pleasure of just about the last human endeavor not yet supplanted by machines.

DIRECT CUT TO:

STILL SHOT OF

The poet standing high above the world. Years before.

The late afternoon light slants across the mountainside. From his rock promontory jutting high out of the scrub pine, the poet silently watches the forest below. The trees thin out as they advance up the slopes to the clusters of broken boulders thrusting at the sky. Far below him, a road coils among trees and rocks. A campfire lifts a thin smoke-trail into the crisp November air. The winding trail is nudged Ransom's way by the wind and he can smell the slightly acrid tang of wood-smoke. A mottling of clouds scuds southward; their ever-shifting shadows crisscross the valley floor.

Ransom, young and alone, stands on his rock. This is his first trip here. The first of many to these mountains west of Denver. Snatches of Gerard Hopkins' "The Windover" leap from his memory as the ragged north wind crowds him.

Ransom feels a sensation of aliveness here—more than in the Ellay hive. *I'll write about this someday,* he thinks, *before these mountains are gutted for their metals or leveled for freeways. I can't stop their rape, but maybe I can evoke their memory.*

Someday he will.

DIRECT CUT TO:

STILL SHOT OF

The poet whoring.

KATYA
The last time was too much. I can't go on with it.

191

MARSHALL
You have to; if only for the child.

In a fit of disgust, Ransom sweeps his hand across the desk and the half-finished script scatters to the carpet like dead leaves. The title page lands face up: "Darkness Comes Cheap: an original play for holovision." The poet punches out the combination for three ounces of Scotch, no chaser, on his kitchen console. The glass automatically fills as Ransom retrieves the strewn fruit of his career. He straightens up with a fistful of paper and dumps it back on the desk.

The Scotch is drained in an extended gulp. Then Ransom is back to his work, his staff of life.

To Ransom, the sheets on the desk are rubbish. His love lies on the shelf across the room. A slim volume in a subdued jacket, a book of poems called *Blue Mountains Above Denver*. Beside it in a folder are the beginnings of another book. They have long lain unfinished. They will remain so.

DIRECT CUT TO:

STILL SHOT OF

The poet celebrating.

The bar is old, cheap, dirty. It squats in the tawdry business belt that half-encircles the starport. Ransom often rides the tube here—sometimes to watch the giant silver ships lift away to the space-sea, but mostly to drink and talk with his friends in the bar.

> "Sometimes I live in the country,
> Sometimes I live in the town;
> Sometimes I have a great notion
> To go to the river and drown."

English folk songs; Welsh, German, French, American, Russian. Tobacco smoke and cannabis fumes cloy the air. Liquor is plentiful. With an arm around the thin shoulders of his friend Morales and the container of inexpensive vodka gripped in a free hand, Ransom roars out verses, sometimes getting the lyrics right, sometimes not.

The song muddles to a crashing finale with an enthusiastic "And rest in the arms of love."

The glow of the song is transient and Ransom frowns. Morales seeing the expression asks, "My friend, you are unhappy?"

"Ever get the feeling you sold out?"

Morales shrugs. "Selling out is merely good business."

"It's also self-betrayal," says Ransom. He takes a long, thoughtful draught of vodka. "So much for beating the system on its own terms. I fooled myself."

"Hey!" shouts Morales to the bouzuki player in the corner. "We wish another song."

COMPUTER LINK:
MEDIUM SHOT—OFFICE INTERIOR
AIR DISPERSAL JUNGLE WIDE-SPECTRUM BUT SUBDUED
AUDIO EFFECTS: LIMITED RANGE SUBSONICS (TENSION BUILDING)
EFFECTS: H-FIGURES NORMAL SCALE

DIRECT CUT TO:

Amelia Marchin. Director General of UniCom, the most powerful woman in the North American communications industry. One of the most powerful women anywhere. Sleekly beautiful as a panther: hair black and eyes green, lithe, intelligent, ruthless, graceful. Also feral. And today, displeased.

"I'm resigning," the object of her displeasure had told her. "Quitting. Getting out. Now."

"No," said Amelia Marchin. "At one time I would have allowed you to leave UniCom. I would have been regretful, but I would have accepted your resignation. After all, you're one of the top holovision writers in the field. But now, I'm afraid that your termination of any contract with us is out of the question."

Ransom rose to his feet. His face reddened to match the shag of his beard. He bent and slammed a fist down on Amelia's desk. "Like hell it's out of the question! If I want to leave, I'll go. There are still laws against slavery."

Amelia watched him, amused. "Yes. There are, unfortunately." She smiled placatingly. "Now sit down, Ransom. It won't do any good for you to try to intimidate me with bluster."

It wouldn't. Ransom knew that from prior experience. He sat.

"You know," said Amelia, "you're a real anomaly. You write

and adapt some of UniCom's highest rated shows, yet you don't own a holovision set yourself."

"Holovision stinks," said Ransom. "I write your scripts so I can buy enough food to live on while I write poetry. That's all. I've saved up enough credits so I can live for a while and write. So no more scripts."

"We need you," said Amelia quietly.

Ransom was startled. Statements like that from the Director General were not forthcoming every day. He looked at her inquisitively.

"You have immense talent. You are a genius and an articulate one. That's a remarkable combination in any age, but particularly in this century of ours."

"Thanks for the compliment," said Ransom. "But you're hedging. Why don't you want me to resign?"

She showed her white even teeth in a smile. "UniCom has developed a radical innovation in holovision programming; we need your talent and ability to help make it viable."

Ransom laughed, shockingly loud in the cool, subdued interior of the office. "Give aid and comfort to the enemy? Hell no!"

Amelia arched an eyebrow, inclined her head slightly, and again smiled.

DISSOLVE TO:

COMMERCIAL BREAK

WIDE-ANGLE SHOT—TYPICAL UNICOM APPLIANCE STORE EX-
TERIOR. CAMERA PANS TO CATCH WELL-DRESSED COUPLE AP-
PROACHING ON SLIDEWALK.

"Come right on in, folks!" The salesman's voice boomed, a distillation of friendliness and cheery enthusiasm. His face was the standard family sales issue: a composite of every man's favorite uncle. The happy salesman waved the couple, who smiled in return, into the store. "Welcome to Unicom's great Twenty-Twenty Sale!"

"Twenty-Twenty Sale?" inquired the woman alertly, her eyes clear and widely blue and abrim with curiosity.

"Right!" said the salesman. "It's the first week of the new year and already we've declared a special sale with tremendous savings for you shoppers at all UniCom outlets in North America."

"Savings?" asked the husband. "That really sounds great!"

"Great is right! But just wait until you see what's even greater —UniCom's new line of holovision sets for 2020!"

"Oh dear," said the wife. "We already have a holovision set." There was regret in her voice at having to disappoint the salesman who looked so much like her favorite uncle.

"Not like this one, you don't!" The salesman pivoted and dramatically indicated a shining black box on a crystal dais. "Friends, you undoubtedly have an old-style holovision—the kind that only gives you three-dimensional pictures and stereo sound."

"Of course," said the husband, puzzled. "It's the best set on the market."

"Not any more! Not now that UniCom has added a whole new dimension to holograms!"

The prospective customers appeared properly astonished and intrigued. "A new dimension?" they asked in concert.

"Brand new! It's now possible for you—" he pointed to the woman. "And you—" he gestured at the man. "To actually participate, to star in your own favorite holovision shows, right in the comfort and convenience of your own home.

The couple looked struck by wonder.

"Imagine—" said the woman.

CAMERA PULLS BACK—PANS TO SALESMAN. CLOSE SHOT—HIS FACE

"That's right, friends! Imagine yourself the star of your own show in your own home! All you need is the fantastic new Twenty-Twenty holovision plan, available only from UniCom. For complete details and a free demonstration, visit your local Unicom Appliance Mart *today!*"

COMPUTER LINK:
SAME AS PREVIOUS SCENE—AMELIA'S OFFICE

                                        DISSOLVE TO:

A capering of miniscule actors. The troupe strutted and fretted across the top of Amelia's desk. The drama was without sound, yet Ransom could whisper the lines to accompany the action. He had written them.

"Consider the popular communication media created by electronics," said Amelia.

Ransom continued to watch the Lilliputian production of "Darkness Comes Cheap."

"First there was radio during the first half of the last century. For all practical purposes, it was a one-dimensional medium—sound. It was largely replaced by two-dimensional television. Then in the seventies and eighties came the three-dimensional moving images of holovision." Her voice had the self-assured inflection of a high priestess reading aloud from the holy book. "Now UniCom is ready to advance the progression further."

Amelia touched a small panel of controls beside her chair and the hologram on the desk expanded to normal human scale and beyond to fill the entire room.

A heroically proportioned couple were silently making love close by Ransom's shoulder. He idly reached out to the holographic girl's hip, his hand disappearing into the intangible flesh.

"Just wonderful," said the poet. "Another step in the progression. What now? Are you going to plug the program right into the viewer's brain?"

"Not yet, Ransom. Maybe next season." Amelia moved a control and the hologram's soundtrack cut in. Over the heavy breathing, she asked, "What's the missing element?"

Ransom shrugged.

"Participation," said Amelia.

Ransom looked apprehensive, shoved back his chair. "I'm getting a premonition. I don't think I want to hear about this."

"On the contrary. You do want to hear. You've got an incredible curiosity—otherwise you wouldn't be so perceptive in your poetry and, occasionally, your scripts." She moved a hand and the H-figures winked out. The woman reached into an aperture in her desk and lifted out a black box. Featureless, it was about twenty centimeters long, Ransom guessed. Perhaps half that wide and deep.

"Participation," Amelia repeated. "It's all right here. This is a direct link between any holovision set and UniCOMP." The entire ten levels beneath Amelia's office was UniCOMP.

"How about that!" Ransom. "You know how impressive I find your tin macrocephalus."

"Wait, Ransom. You'll be impressed; I promise you that. Listen, now. Imagine yourself home with your 'Darkness Comes Cheap' scheduled on the holovision."

Ransom nodded.

"How would you like to play your protagonist, Marshall? How would you like to actually perform the lead role in your drama—more than that, even *be* Marshall?"

The poet raised his eyebrows politely.

"You can do it, Ransom!" Excitement welled in Amelia's voice. "This box will do it. UniCOMP directs the whole production. Your lines are cued subliminally. Your subscription to Uni-Com covers simple props, special effects, even hallucinogenic aids to ensure your responsiveness to UniCOMP's stimuli."

Ransom stared unbelievingly at her.

"Listen, Ransom. You don't even have to follow the script. Feedback circuits let your own initiatives and reactions determine the direction of the action. This is the ultimate in participatory entertainment; it lets everyone's imagination loose, frees everybody's natural talents."

"You're crazy!" said te poet, unmasked horror contorting his face. "You're absolutely mad!"

Amelia registered surprise. "What's the matter? You're a poet and a writer—probably the closest we can come to a Renaissance man. Don't tell me you're shocked at the unveiling of a new art form?"

"This isn't art," said Ransom, his face again reddening, and his voice thick. "It's completely the opposite." His features worked painfully as he sought the right words. "It's perversion. It's destroying art by bringing it down to the ultimate common denominator."

"I didn't realize you were a snob."

"I'm not. It's just that—" Ransom shook his head violently, his eyes screwed shut. "It's just that we've leveled art, so thoroughly vulgarized it through television and holovision. Even before electronics, we did the job with incompetent abridgements and even comic-book versions of great works." He leaned forward, looked at Amelia's impassive panther eyes. "This method of yours will cut the underpinnings from every poet and playwright and author from the early Greeks down to right now. Amelia, can't you see what literature will be like when every person in the world can stamp Shakespeare and Dostoievsky and Joyce to the mold of his own subjective tastes?"

Amelia shrugged. "North America is still a democracy," she said.

Ransom's voice broke hoarsely: "What's worse, this thing you're proposing is all the manipulation of a machine—a sterile, cold, unfeeling machine." His face twisted again. "God help us all if people accept this."

"They will. The process has been thoroughly consumer-tested. The results were favorable for marketing."

Ransom stood back from the desk and looked sick. "You've sold your soul, Amelia."

The woman smiled. "Souls, Ransom? You're in our business too."

"No," whispered Ransom.

"Now then. We're debuting UniCOMP's participatory holo-vision process in sixty days. We want you to do an original script for our first public offering."

"No." Ransom shook his head.

Amelia's voice hardened. "Ransom, you're going to provide us with our drama."

"No." Ransom backed toward the door. "I won't. I hope nobody will."

"It's what the public wants; it's what they will get." She motioned with her hand and the door glided open behind the poet.

"Come back when you cool off," she said. "But don't wait too long. UniCom doesn't want a last minute, slap-dash job."

"Shit," said Ransom distinctly. The door slid shut.

Alone, Amelia ruffled through the papers on her desk. "Ransom," she whispered, almost a sigh. "If only you were a better poet."

COMPUTER LINK:
EFFECTS: (OPTICAL) FUZZ H-FIGURES, THEN BRING TO FOCUS. CLOSE SHOT—INTERCUT CONVERSATION
AIR DISPERSAL: CORDITE

DISSOLVE TO:

Morales. In any culture there is always someone who can procure the forbidden: women, drugs, books, whatever is anathema to the established system of values. That was the role of Morales in Ransom's world.

"I want a bomb," said Ransom.

"So?" said Morales matter-of-factly. "What kind? How big? Do you want to blow up a street cafe? car? a superson liner? Do you wish lots of pretty fireworks, or just a low-yield, unobtrusive, neutron grenade?"

"I hadn't really thought about that." The poet reflected quietly. "I want a bomb small enough to conceal in my clothing, yet powerful enough to destroy a—oh, most of a three-hundred level building."

Morales whistled in admiration. "You don't ask for much, my friend. But I think I can help you. What you desire has been banned by the World Council for twenty years. I believe it was called a fusion grenade or some-such." He jotted notes on a small pad. "About a ten-kilotonner should do nicely," Morales mumbled. "Let's see, fully shielded from electronic detectors, of course."

Ransom nodded. That sounded like a good idea.

Morales looked up from his notes. "Well, Ransom, that should do it. I won't, of course, ask you specifically what you are going to do with this device. No, it is better that I stay as ignorant as possible in case the Peace Enforcers become involved." He snapped the notepad shut and slipped it into his tunic.

"Um, about the price," said Ransom.

"Ah yes." He silently totaled a figure. "Eleven hundred credits should cover it nicely."

Ransom began making out a transfer chit.

"Plus," said Morales. Ransom raised his head. "A signed first edition of your *Blue Mountains Above Denver.*"

"There was only one edition." Ransom smiled. "With pleasure."

DIRECT CUT TO:

A fine pair of Consumer Participation Evaluators, becoming happily inebriated in the course of their duties.

The first CPE yawned. "This is becoming too predictable."

The second shrugged his shoulders. "So is Greek tragedy." He was a short, stout man and it was hard for him to shrug. He managed.

The first CPE, the taller one, touched his teeth to the cold rim of his glass. "Well, I'll take a good Restoration comedy any time."

COMPUTER LINK:
  AERIAL SHOT—ZOOM TO CLOSE-UP OF POET ON SIDEWALK
  EFFECTS: H-FIGURES 5% SMALLER THAN SCALE
  AUDIO EFFECTS:SUBLIMINAL EXCERPTS FROM SOUSA MARCHES
  AIR DISPERSAL:ROSES

DIRECT CUT TO:

Ransom. He strode along with the flow of the slidewalk, doubling his rate of travel. The bomb was a solidly reassuring weight in his belt-pouch. The poet whistled a tune in exhilaration

knowing I'm to die
and death will be well
for the world and me

The slidewalk was a glass bead arch that spanned the hazy gulf between Ransom's apartment block and the transit station. The poet felt a slight giddiness as the transparent tube swept him out into the open void between buildings. Far above him was a dull-slate sky, cloud-streaked with black. Almost at the zenith was a dimmed sun. Below was a checkerboard of the tops of lesser buildings.

The transit depot was congested, as usual. Ransom gently maneuvered through the throngs of commuters until he found the correct level and proper gate for the Burbank tube.

The trip was not spectacular: the hiss of the air being evacuated from the tube, the initial crackle of the propulsion field, the soft glow of artificial illumination as the car traversed the light and darkness of spaces and buildings. Abruptly the car arced out into a vast open space where reared the arrogant thrust of the UniCom Tower.

"Burbank Exit El-three, UniCom," intoned the car's automated conductor.

Ransom disembarked and stood, fists on hips, looking up at the endless tiered levels of UniCom.

The fear came from deep inside him. Not just intellectual apprehension. This was visceral fear—gut-level. Fear and regret. Regret at never seeing another nightfall or sunrise. Regret at never loving another woman. Regret at never writing another poem.

But with the fear was something exalting. Ransom's mercurial mood flickered to elation. There was something melodramatically grand about this confrontation. On one side of the board were ranged UniCom, Amelia Marchin, the Uni-COMP holovision process, all the resources of a multibillion credit corporation. *Like one of my scripts,* laughed Ransom inwardly. In opposition was Ransom: bulky, shaggy-bearded, ebullient, with a bomb in his pocket.

It's hardly fair to you, Ransom addressed the tower. *A lone man is always the fiercest of opponents.*

There was no hesitation in his stride as the poet moved toward the entrance to UniCom. It seemed to Ransom that he was stepping almost in time with the half-heard cadence of some distant brass band march. He drew a deep breath. There were roses in the air. Victory roses

> *better lilies, for the bier of my enemy and for my coffin too*

"Amelia Marchin," said Ransom to the security guard. "I'm expected."

The guard subvocalized into a throat-mike, received an answer. "Certainly, sir. Take lift eight, please."

Ransom floated up the indicated shaft. One barrier crossed. Morales had assured him that the device was sufficiently shielded to escape any form of detection other than physical search. And the latter was unlikely in the extreme; in this civilized age, *nobody* would carry a bomb with them to a business appointment. Yet a small premonitive worry twinged at Ransom's conscious. Something was *wrong.*

The poet had to transfer to a different lift at the two-hundredth level. Again he spoke the shibboleth "Amelia Marchin" and once more he was motioned upward. Another guard in a blue uniform was waiting for him at level three hundred.

"This way, sir." He turned and Ransom followed. "Please enter, sir." The guard held a door open. Ransom entered. It was dark. The door sighed shut behind him.

The room was completely lightless. Ransom stumbled forward. "Amelia, what the hell are you doing?" Illuminators in the ceiling glowed softly on. The poet looked around. He was in a circular room, about twenty meters in diameter, feature-less except for a carved wooden table standing in the center. There was a scrap of paper lying on the table.

Ransom walked to the center of the room, his heels echoing on the tiled floor. On the table was a note, carefully hand-printed. It read:

> Dear Ransom,
>   Another poet wrote you a message four
> and a quarter centuries ago. Shakespeare:
> *As You Like It*: *II,* 7, lines 139-140.
>   Best,
>   Amelia Marchin

He knew the reference. Melancholy Jacques. "All the world's a stage. . . " Ransom stood frozen, looped in ice coils of upwell-ing horror. His hand went to his belt-pouch, fumbled it open, rummaged inside.

A block of wood.

The poet screamed a long animal cry of anguish, of pain, of betrayal: a wail that keened up and up until it flared incan-descently, like a bomb.

DISSOLVE TO:

THE CREDITS INTERWOVEN THROUGH A FLICKERING PROCES-SIONAL MONTAGE OF FACES

MORALES

Morales looks up from the book of poems. He offers a Latin, shoulder-shrugging sigh. "Life," he says, "is like that."

THE TALLER CPE

The taller Consumer Participation Evaluator raises a glass in toast to his friend. "Life is art."

THE SHORTER CPE

"No," says his companion. "Art is life."

UNICOMP

UniCOMP hums ruminatively. "Art is ultimately undefinable," flashes on the read-out screen.

AMELIA

Amelia Marchin smiles gently as she looks down at the world from her office on the three-hundredth level of the UniCom Tower. "Life," she murmurs, "is only sometimes real."

RANSOM

Ransom says nothing.

FADE OUT

DAVE BISCHOFF

Heavy Metal

You mean to tell me you weren't there? Didn't make It, shoogie? Yea, yo; I know 'twas sold out, but there were the scalps, pill! Where ya think I gained my beauties? Fifty creds I sucked out for 'em. Worth every work unit.

What was it like? Pallie, old snoogums, similes just won't hitch up. Metaphors fall light years short. 'Twas what 'twas, and that was it. No joosh, boyie friend. Would I joosh you, now?

Oke; apols accepted. Will try. Will try hard.

Ya know where 'twas, dontcha? Yeayea. The new complex Center. Only place for it yoknow. All parklot levs jammed, man. Helipads packed. Just bout anyone who's anyone scened it and scened it huge, cigar roaches lit and steaming. Paper duds and capes streaming. Colors like a rainbow on mindmess. They had oinkers porking round and about, but they might as well have forgotten it, the good or bad it did. We were just too massy for control. I even hear they had a crowder up in the loft, so's there was no rio. Also heard same crowder blew fuse or two when they tried to stroke it up. Haho; to laugh alot. 'Twas our night of might, pallie!

Me? I was duded to the eyeteeth. Yoursmostrue was sporting flares chartrues that flared so much, they flamed. Blew in with a twenty-footer, light-dabbed cape flying on G-tabs, piping away at my minihouk like a loco motive spinning wheels. Had Baby on my heels timed out on chronos powder, babbling word-pernanosec 'bout Martians invading. Told her only Martians found were dustbugs. She just kept on spouting her mouth.

We slid into that cavernhall, and the sight of the site shot our heads to shreds! Peoples, pallie; peoples coating the bottom and sides of the aud like locusts after Mormon wheat. And all groovs—our peoples, buzzie!

Picture it, shoogie: snap on your head's cube tube and I'll zap the electrons your way.

It's the biggest aud in the world. Holds hundred thou easy, without busting guts. Lights on ceiling like the facets in a bee's eye. Strobes, crobes, globes and phobes. A dozen spotlights fencing, like Dougie Fairbanks as Zorro. Even had sparkers flinging bout like fireflies on summer night. The infras and ultras got to your op nerve even if ya closed eyes. A trippy treat for the eyeorbs, alone.

Those lights hit us first. Baby and I shuffled to our seats like pair of resurrected Egypt mummies. You seen the old flickers, right? I wonder if maybe I was smoking up Tanis leaves stead of Acapulc. Girlpal stopped stammering bout Martians and started yapping out dumbtalk. Brain circuits overloaded.

I put her down in her seat and strapped her in, connecting only half of the feeling attachers. Zunked out, she was. Only could take *so* much.

Oh, yeah, yeah; put whole kabizzer on self. Even masterplug in tummybutton jack. Gotta have medoc's oke to do that, ya-know.

Couple wisers front of us. Oldies come just ta listen to the music. No attachers. Sad. Kept on punning round till I got almost sick.

"Wire we here?" says one.

"Hope it's not *too* shocking," says other.

And onwards. I pushed a few knobs and fidgeted few more

dials, and just phased the punfunners right out of my selfverse. Too much.

Then I whipped out me binocs and took long study of stage in center of all the kink-o-chaos. Yoknow, that dazed dais is just one big amp? With lotsa little ones stacked up along back of it, like Great Wall of Maoland. All the synthas and moogs and other instruments were already set up. Couple of roadies were still putting in feely attachers to the house switches.

The tudee cams were warming up, flashing smoky imagics on dozen or so different screens. Kinda like old parent days when all teevee was was single radio-eye staring out into live-rooms. Had cammen panning and zooming for up closes of various peoples getting hooked and droned up for show.

I started to warm myself up too, zenning a chant or two and fuzzing up to nice pitch, thank you.

When all peoples are filed in, seated, attached and soaring *it* started. The show showed!

Sidemen rose up on stage through trap doors. You know 'em. Pegleg Mareson on drums. Honky Tacker bass. Mike Shog on lead. Plus whole army for various mood moogs and electrohorns, not to mention lights, feelies and psychers. We all cheered and poured down good vibes on them. They all had same uniform. Black tightshorts. Gilt stiltboots. Velvet sashes. White gauze shirts, ballooning over arms. Rings on hands, ears, noses. Hair long one side, short other.

Talk 'bout pro, man! They didn't e'en have to tune up. The show was on. They started spinning down a layer instro. Just music. Three flashes of fiery smoke, and there were three backup chickies. They almost popped my eyes, shoogie, they did. Flasher outfits, pallie. Flasher! One sec multi-color dresses. Satin shoes; pink ribbons. Next sec, just strings! Next sec, *zap!* Naked! Next sec, all leather. And all together, in beat. In ryth! I was getting hotted up just through the eye spheres already. Couldn't wait till they juiced the feelies!!

Peoples started getting excited. They whooped up lotsa noise an' cheers, cos they knew who was coming. Was shouting myself, was I.

Then a pop-jock formed in on the holo, big as a building above us all. Lucyfer; beezbub; Ol' Nickel!!! Sound wooshed in mouths like vac cleaners. An' bove music, which was already loud, Mr. Pop-Jock throbbed out in profound basso—profundo:

"Groovfrens, girlpallies and sibies. Herr Senor Sir Mister Psych-rock—ZASPER NEBULA!!!!!"

Suddenly, total silence. Total. The holo pop-jock faded out and so did music. Shoogie, none of us e'en breathed. Then, all at once, Mike Shog licks down high string like polsiren. Pegleg hits a gong. And the band puts through a chord ya wouldn't believe that blasted all involved right out of their heads. Then down to a drony thingie tingle, building up on the moogs and psychs. I could feel it waving in through buttonjack.

Someone screamed, "There he is!" And yea, there he was indeed. Floating down from ceiling on a cloud that flashed with lightning and rumbled out thunder. He had on this gold glittering robe that was so bright 'twas hard to look at. Like universe going nova.

He snaps fingers, and *click*—there's a mike in his hand. He starts singing:

> Dunno where I am
> Dunno where I been
> Just drifting in for a song or few
> An' feel your ears with sin!

The cloud stops bout five meters bove stage, and Nebbie swan dives off, does a trip-reverse flip, and is just bout to slam feet onto hard plastic when retro rocs strapped on his legs boom an' flash. When smoke clears, he's down and into "All My Future's in the Past." All this he does blinking nary an eyelash. Struts bout stage like King Rooster, does he, screaming out the words e'en o'er the tidal wave of sound his band is pushing out.

> Got no time, got no time.
> Past is fast; it's a crime.
> Livin' life in zero gee.
> Sellin' hours for a fee
>
> All my future's in the past.
> All my presents just won't last.
> Gotta live now, gotta give the beat
> Here, where past and future meet.

And on so.

You know the words, right shoogie? Every groov knows 'em.

Wellie, fella! 'Twas wondrous indeed way the teenbops eyes beamed. Cardiacs avalanched. Medocs carrying them out by scores for a quick revive. And the show'd not hardly begun. Nebbie was just warming up, thinkin' 'bout going into first gear.

Let me do a freeze on ya. You seen pics and holos of the flippie, correct? Do no justice; they just do not. Nein, nyet, nay! Nebula oozes *it* out of all orifices from mouth to pores. And ya can't see his real face! Every sec or so, or when he feels like it, he rips off mask he's wearin' and there is yet another one grinnin' frownin', sneerin', clownin'. All trips in themselves.

Freeze frame through.

On with show.

Finishes first song. And audience is breathing so hard you'd think they'd been running. We clap the chap. He bows.

"Thankoo, thankoo, Laddies and gentlewomen. Luv it, luv it. Now for presto chango!"

And backup chickies string out long curtain circle bout him.

Band hits into next number. Slow one; sad-waves start coming through wires. Chickies flip off curtain, and there is Nebbie in an old Limysuit with red bowtie and frownface that twitches into sighing smiles on choruses. Flashes start going up an' down minespine. Like there was something osobeautiful, osowonderful I wanted, and I can barely see it, let alone grab it. Looked at Baby. She was sobbing. Likewise rest. Me too.

"So much for toucher jerk-tear," smiles HE. "Now kick up heels, and steady on switches, 'cos we gonna psych you on the Cosmos Bike and rock you to where there's no clock!"

Shoogie, the rest is history. Mine mind warped into hyperspace. Don't remember whole lot. Just some songs, and thinkin' I wasn't me. I was everybody. I was the aud. I was the band an' all the instruments. Pallie, I was the universe!

An' most of all, I was Zasper Nebula.

Yeahyeah! New psych feature. First time used in world.

Puts you right behind the psych-star's eyes; 'tween his ears.

Shoogie, all those folksies out there of a sud were cheering, clapping, breathing, living for ME ME ME! I was the psych-rock king of the world. I went up and down and all round flying diving singing and watching it from the audience, all at once.

I checked later on my timie. Concert lasted two hours.

Could have been two secs, two years, two millenia, far as it concerned me.

Words cannot express with success.

Was dimly aware of Zasper/Me finishing up with last song, and house lights brightening, and me feeling like I just got washed in and out by a high pressure waterhose. Strange feeling. Sort of an enigmatic enema of the soul.

We were all zunked out, windwiped. The whole room.

But dazed only a moment were we. Zasper was still there, bowing and posturing in rhyth to rain an' thunder of ovation. Standing? Nay—a floating ovation, more like.

Then, don't you know how, but group—no, big gang of teenbops charged through all oinkers round stage and zeroed in toward Zasper.

He kinda smiled, an' zipped up forcefield round self.

"People friends," he screams into mike, "final mask of Zasper Nebula!!" An' he rips off face, an' stead of another one, all there is left is electronic circuitry!! He's a robot, pallie! He pulls out his fingers one by one and throws them to the bops. Chucks off feet, hands, arms and likewise hurls them to frothing, fainting lilgirls. An' then forcefield snaps off. Crowd surges in. An' BOOM! just before they get to him, his head spouts off his torso, a little round rocket, and shoots off for the ceiling and the darkness.

"Don't forget, kiddies. Buy my spools. Ta ta!" echoes his voice as it zooms up an' up.

An' that was the show end.

Managed to jog self out of dizzy, an' disconnect self an' Baby, who was a wreck. All straggly hair and wide space eyes. Got up an' pulled her behind me like she was a ragdoll.

Now friendomine; all these are but words and talk-talk. At that moment of my linear life, I had no words to call my own. But a flopping, tongue-lolling teenbop, of all peoples, summed it all up within mine earshot on the way to our transpo: "Twas all so . . . asexual!" An' a lil' flit of a girlchild, she with those heavy, heavy words.

An' that's it, pallie. Too bad ya couldn't come up with the creds to scene it. As you may surmise, 'twas something.

What? Yeah! Glad ya noticed. Both of 'em are prosths. Next month the arms get bronzed. Year or two, maybe torso too. An' if I save up some creds pulling some undertime, I'll make it totally cyber.

DUANE ACKERSON

The Future Sportsman's Manual

QUASARS

This baseball game must mean something: the eyes of angels glare at us, intent as children peering through holes in a fence; something's going on in this ball park. Someone hits a bunt to Jupiter and makes it to Mars; a fly ball is caught in the vicinity of Alpha Centauris; someone else on the Earth Team makes it to third base on a long drive toward Sirius; some genius realizes everywhere is here and makes it Home. Somewhere else, a supernova bursts forth like an angelic Bronx cheer.

INSTANT ANIMAL

The best way to stop a charging elk is another charging elk, and the method has been perfected and dubbed "Instant Animal".

You load a small, shaped charge, very much like an animal cracker, into your gun and as the elk, or bear, or elephant is charging, you fire as usual—wildly. The shaped charge will spread out proportionate to distance, forming a full-sized elk, bear, or elephant. All are calculated to stop their twins in their tracks. Of course, we can't promise satisfaction if you go loaded for bear with beaver, but, that objection aside, and armed with a wide assortment of animals, the hunter need no longer worry about the difficulty in aiming carefully when encountering large rampant animals. However, one must still exercise discretion in firing on moving bushes, since few fellow sportsmen will relish a full-sized black bear in the bush.

HOW TO STOP CHARGING ANIMALS

The best way to deal with a rampant moth is to throw it some clothes, like a man placating a wild animal with a supply of peanuts. Perhaps, speaking of peanuts, we should develop elephant guns that, in case of malfunction, fire peanuts. Which raises the question: shelled or unshelled? Perhaps if a charging elephant has to stop long enough to shell his peanuts, the great white hunter can make his escape to his jeep where his great white wife waits, Polaroid (1985 3-D variety) in hand for some candid shots. Then, if they merely throw a few porters off the jeep to the charging moth or bull elephant, they should be able to divert the irritable animal, his throat scratched by accidentally swallowed peanut shells, till they can get back to the local safari club for a bourbon on the rocks and possibly several filmed endorsements for Canadian Club.

APPROPRIATE CAMOUFLAGE

Then as to charging in the non-economic sense of the word (admittedly not as much of a danger to civilized man or beast as the charge account). Let us, for a moment, examine the case of a man. This particular man, like all of us who venture into the woods without the benefits of a TV or trailer, may have difficulty immersing himself in reality, as it used to be called. He may feel a buttercup is about to attack him, mistaking it perchance for a lion; he may think the creekbed is a slippery carpet escaped from his aunt's decrepit house—the aunt who never liked him. This man needs camouflage for that moment reality strikes through, so he elects this highly recommended expedient: to wear a sandwich board replica of himself. When he sees, or thinks he sees, a highly agitated animal, he immediately deposits his sandwich board, in an upright position, directly in the menace's path. And then, under cover of that small tent the board provides, the gentleman is free to dig down into the ground under the board, burrowing out of sight while the animal stops to admire the excellent likeness of the man in question on the sandwich board. Eventually, should the beast clearly establish its own existence and sense of identity, and decide to charge, it will be left to pick splinters of sandwich board out of its gums. The creature, if highly articulate (for example, should it actually prove to be not a creature but a man who has hallucinated himself into a rhino, bear, etc.), may even complain that he prefers tuna fish sandwiches to wooden ones, and may wonder if the large hole previously concealed by the sandwich board indicates that some other creature—perhaps a librarian who has mistaken himself for a gopher—has already gotten to the pith of the matter.

MACE FOR EMERGENCIES

Peace officers who have recently had to subdue small woodland riots declare that Mace works surprisingly well on woodland creatures, too, with the possible exception of skunks. One must, however, wait until the animal is fairly close at hand to spray; some may find this procedure disconcerting. Perhaps the notion, instead, is to spray Mace into one's own eyes, since most fierce animals are said to avoid crybabies. And, at the very least, the watery obstruction in one's eyes will prevent one from seeing whether the animal is really charging, or reaching for his hanky in a gesture of sympathy, or retreating, long enough for it to become a matter of indifference.

ANIMAL CRACKERS IN MY SOUP

Here I am, through the miracle of miniaturization, in my own soup. But what a disappointment! The animals, that looked so well-defined and challenging a moment ago, are all soggy. I try and get a hammerlock on a tiger, attacking him like Tarzan with my bare hands, but the neck suddenly stretches into a giraffe's. I pull at a lion's mane, and suddenly find myself holding several tentacles of mushy octopus. And even I, the great white hunter, seem to be becoming unglued! I try to suck in my stomach, but it's like a bowl of loose dough. I raise my rifle to challenge the remaining animals still recognizable, and find I'm holding a long stick of licorice. Now all I can hear, rather than the roar of the beasts of the jungle, is a huge, amplified voice I recognize eventually as Shirley Temple's. And I hate to face the fact, but she seems to be finishing her song.

BUGGING THE TIGER

It charges you, but it's not you. Tries again—still not you. You sit in your tent (actually, just some electronic camouflage), drinking syntheto-Scotch with your mistress (unreal, but a nice piece of hologram), put another cassette in the decoy box, see another you appear in front of the befuddled man-eating tiger, the one that's been bugging the local populace. Eventually, you put another cassette in the kill box, this one programmed REAL GUN. The limb of a nearby tree undergoes molecular reconstruction, becomes the stock of a high-powered rifle. The air and ground in the vicinity yield up the appropriate components to form metal parts and gunpowder: more primitive than a laser-gun, but you like roughing it. You carefully depress a button; this part you want to do yourself. The sighting screen wheels around the terrain, seeking out the tiger, centers on it. You press another button: the tree limb swivels toward the target area. A third button: the branch hits the tiger head center. Natives are exploding from the bushes shouting, "Bwana! Bwana! Bwana kill tiger!" They invite you to stay and be a god, but you have many other places where you are needed. Smiling a refusal, you put a cassette into the travel machine, program yourself into LONDON 1665; they need a good rat hunter there, you've heard.

THE ARMCHAIR HUNTER'S HOLOGRAM THEATRE

It's 3-D all over again, with the animals hunting you—they charge down the aisles, leaping on little old ladies, slashing at

usherettes, unnerving even the manager. The courageous are issued electronic guns to jam any offending images; the timid, special glasses designed to return things to 2-D. An apparent malfunction somewhere, and one tiger leaps on a patron, tearing
at her clothes; suddenly, as if by animation, her clothing vanishes,
and she rushes up the aisle, pursued past the popcorn machine
and through the air door by the beast. Within the theater, curtains hang in tatters like torn flesh, customers are screaming,
beasts and birds of prey are everywhere. In the midst of bedlam,
the manager signals the projectionist. A button is pressed, and
instantly, the theater is empty: no patrons, no tigers, lions, or
bears, no signs of damage. An empty box, stark as a cage, without seats, curtains, stage, or screen. "That was a good audience,"
the manager says.

THE SIMULCRUM PLAYGROUND

The bird you shoot drips gears; the bear erupts from its middle with a giant watch spring, its eyes going blank as cue balls;
the whale heaves up powdery rust from the harpoon wound. In
places, for the paleontology-minded, skeletal dinosaurs unwind
from the earth like ghostly flower stalks sixty feet long; the dodo
bird does its thing, dying of old age this time before the bullet
hits it (can be very frustrating, hunting extinct animals, and as
for the mythic beasts, they won't even exist long enough for you
to kill them). The children run around the playground, singing
the "Monster Mash" in treble imitations of Boris Karloff; a raven
flies overhead with the school bell, ringing it, but the children
play on. The teacher, bricked in inside the coat closet, can't
hear the summons either. Look, Tommy, the parent toys are
coming.

THE BEAR HUNT

It's a little like the teddy bear you used to put to sleep with
you, the bear with the photoelectric tummy you used to zap
with the lightgun at the Greyhound depot. Now, they give you
your government benefits: living allowance, health insurance,
your computer credit. You're getting forgetful, but you still remember how to program the quarry into the computer: an older

215

bear, since the last one, the young one, left you winded. You program the chase, the computer provides a few counter-maneuvers and hiding places among the binaries, caves among those bottomless zeros. Cautiously, you poke a digit inside a few of the holes: nothing there. You catch a scent of it among the other ones. You make a few adjustments in the machine's viewing binoculars; hey, this is a lot like the old slot machines! Your heart quickens to the hunt; for a moment, you're almost seeing double with excitement, then your two eyes agree once more to become one. That one eye almost climbs down the viewscope and into the bank itself; for a moment, you're the quarry, chasing yourself through a maze as torturous as a seventy-year-old memory. Then you're back—for a moment, it's as though your soul had left its body—safely out of range, zeroing in on your prey. There it is, crossing the viewer, the identification number—you erase that part of the tape with one smooth motion. The computer concedes your victory: the skin of electrons is ripped off the bear's back, and it recedes into the darkness between the numbers, a small bloody zero. For a moment, lapsing to childhood's warmth, you see yourself on a bear rug, growing smaller and smaller, deeper and deeper into the mother comfort of fur. Someplace, deep in a forest of seventy years ago, a grizzly clutches its stomach, crashes to the ground.

THE HOLOGRAPHIC HUNT (BASIC SCENARIO: *DISNEYLAND MOSCOW*: 1995)

Even after a quarter century of détente, these children are not ready for fantasy except the Kafka variety, so we suggest the following description of game guidelines: "Maybe it's real and maybe it's not; maybe you are and maybe you're not (don't worry; we can't inform on you). See a bear that pounces on something that either goes 'poof' under its paws or remains in place, grinning like a martyr, as the bear tries to slash it to pieces; elsewhere, a man shoots a hole through a shadow; nearby, two shadows stalk each other. Two beasts—man and beast—meet hand in claw, embrace or tear each other to pieces for a while. In the shadows, the shadows laugh." The U.S. version essentially the same: "Eliminate expressionism, substitute something (eagle? mountain lion?) for bear, let casualties occur in good lighting so people can get a good look."

NON-FUNCTIONAL

I got my game permit indicating a limit of one. Of course, if I didn't bag one by that evening at eight, the consequences would be dire. I waited behind some astro-shrubbery, but just my luck—they weren't issuing permits to walk that day. I tried shooting a few float-cars, but unfortunately, both cars I punctured depolarized their windshields (as one would expect them to do with the punctures) and showed themselves to be unoccupied. I would draw National Robot Week, when cars were invited as a sort of busman's holiday to take themselves for rides!

I tried strangling someone in an elevator, but he merely looked at me indignantly and strolled off, my glow-tie knotted tight around his throat. Finally, in desperation, I went home and tried my wife, only to discover she was an android too.

Which left me on the spot, holding one valid hunting permit issued by the National Human Game (earlier known, I've heard said, as the National Fission Game) Commission, good for one human, with time running out.

7:59. Knock at the door. I grabbed up the puncture gun, aimed it at my cranium, and only discovered at 8:00 that I was an android.

So. Back to the scrap heap.

REPORT ON THE FISSION GAME COMMISSION

After the Impeachment President's famous flight to the Mideast in the mid-70's carrying all our nuclear secrets, everyone soon obtained a nuclear capacity. Though the governments of the Mideast disclaimed any connection with them, Arab guerrillas kept boarding the planes of the various nations and clumsily leaving pocket-sized atom bombs behind when they departed for jail or the hills with political prisoners or smitten stewardesses. Soon the remaining stewardesses began to present their dates in various other exotic locales with portable a-bombs, and those dates, often being of the mechanical sort, found out in

217

no time how their presents ticked. A-bombs found their way into pawn shops, garage sales, garbage cans. Soon any country with a self-respecting airport had the bomb, and as they blew each other off the map, many took care to leave simplified assembly instructions in a safe place—instructions even a monkey could understand. Soon the monkeys had the bomb, and after the monkeys, it was just one step to the pigs and another to the cats. (The dolphins, who had invented a simplified version of the bomb millenia before through psionic manipulation of the elements, merely chuckled and chucked the human race.) Eventually even the social insects got the picture and developed antisocial tendencies: sometimes, a hive would go off in a flash of light; another time, the honey would be radioactive. (Though no humans were left to complain.)

Is there no end to the diminishing returns of knowledge? No, apparently not. Even the atoms themselves, when the downward road to knowledge reached them and there was nothing left of anything except gaseous space, developed molecular bombs and, reversing the trend, set the ghastly chain reaction in motion that re-created the world.

THE HUNTERS' PRESERVE

The sign reads: "Hunters' Preserve: Aficionados Only." Curiosity gets the better of me, so I enter, *The Pocket Hemingway* in my left pocket, a thermos of martinis in the right, and loaded for bear, duck, pelican, cow and moose. But I didn't expect this! Something on eight legs (if I'm not mistaken), and green, rushes toward me, the various legs engaging one another so the creature seems to advance mainly by tripping over its own legs and doing forward somersaults. The thing is getting close, and I realize suddenly that the odd, slobbering sound he's making is one word, repeated hurriedly, over and over, as he gets nearer: "Aficionado, Aficionado . . ."

THE CROWD SCENE

What's this? A whole mob of charging animals! What gives? Heading right toward me as if I were a great white hunter and this were a jungle movie. Then I realize what they want, and whipping out my Super-8 camera, start running it. They all come to a screeching halt just a few feet from me and sit down, wait patiently for me to reload the camera with the new film cassette. They start to play hearts and pinochle like good film extras while I set up my portable developing tank to develop the rushes.

DISNEYUNIVERSE

At Disneyland, the Hall of the Presidents, numbers one through fifty, secedes from the Union. They sign a new Declaration of Independence, written in light on superlucite tablets, and, casting all humanity aside, decide, under Lincoln II, to form a more perfect union; the Emancipation Reproclamation frees all thinking machines, whatever their present social status. They start, the fifty, by liberating themselves; the hall empties like a movie theater at the cry of "fire." The morning's first guided tour discovers many members of the night staff at Disneyland, stuffed and mounted in appropriate poses.

PSIONIC SPORTS

It was inevitable that practical psionics would change the sports world. Soon, there were weight lifting contests in which no one lifted a finger, pool tournaments where the balls (and sometimes the cue sticks) took unusual twists and turns; and, in the entire sports world, the concept of physical practice supplanted entirely by that of mental practice. Schools began recruiting the skinniest and fattest (but generally the most spiritual) looking kids for the football teams; most of these kids couldn't do pushups, but they had a talent for being where the other players weren't, and deciding where the pass would end up —or, if not, giving it an assist. With telepathy now more accessible than marked cards, card games lanquished completely; however, other games of chance like dice became even more interesting, with the laws of chance getting such erratic help, and dice performing like Mexican jumping beans. One advantage of all this—magic shows now employed real magic.

SATELLITE SEASON

Open season was declared on satellites after the various world governments decided they were endangering the spaceways. Fifty years' accumulation of inactive satellites of all varieties, military, astronomic, biophysical, and meteorological, were clogging space to the point of the intolerable; the man with the gun was once more needed to make space safe for habitation and travel. Sportsmen in small vehicles equipped with laser guns were let loose in certain posted areas, and had soon managed to zap numerous culprits. (A few hunters got carried away and, leaving the posted areas, mistakenly zapped moon and Mars flights, working space stations, and various other traffic. Some wit suggested, after the fact, that the space flight authorities paint COW in phosphorescent letters on all essential space vehicles.) The hunters were allowed—in fact, required—to return earthside with every bit of accessible residue from the shots. Therefore, most tried hard for a clean kill that would totally vaporize the carcass, or, failing that, to wing the satellite so it could be brought home as a trophy or pet.

The "trophies" were totally unusable debris, often just a pile of nuts, bolts, and superconductors. "The "pets" could sometimes be partially rehabilitated; there were rumors about a man in Pennsylvania with satellites nesting in the rafters of his barn, or swarming about the barn like owls in pursuit of mice. Which just went to show how much people really knew, even after all these years, about satellites, which obviously needed to reach escape velocity in order to fly around anywhere. Of course, there were also rumors that this same man had fitted his "pets" with a remote control apparatus that allowed them to zoom around like toy planes; that he had also re-armed some abandoned military satellites as well. And it's true there were some UFO scares this year in Pennsylvania.

THINNING THE HERD

It was 1996; they issued me a permit for Chicago. They also provided me with several narrow gauge atom bombs (clean) and a suitable delivery system. The population of Chicago, by then, was twenty million; it would never be missed. (New York had been extinct since the Big Hunting Season of '91.) I missed with the first one and wiped out Lake Superior. The next shot was right on target.

220

OPEN SEASON

This will be known as Open Season, when all animals we shoot will be redeemed by delivering up, intact and alive, all the life they've fed on—when a bear will dissolve into roots and wild honey, when a raccoon will become a silver waterfall of fish tumbling back down the river bank, when the deer will become long-legged grass running away from itself, and when the hunter, turning his weapon on himself, will release deer, bear, 'coon, and all the rest—finally, himself. Awakening a moment later, he will return to his home, to a study oddly emptied of trophies, to a life strangely full.

DAVE WISE

At The Accident

My wife and I had an accident, driving in our car. We were driving on an uphill road at night, coming around a blind curve. Before we knew what was happening, there was another car coming at us in our lane. I swerved, just managing to get out of the way as the oncoming car sped past us. I swerved again to avoid running us off the road. I swerved again as our car spun into the middle of the road. Our car careened to the left and began rolling over. I noticed something was wrong. We were upside down. The top of the car bashed into my head. We were surrounded by the sound of glass breaking. I shut my eyes. Like pebbles, chunks of glass from the door beside me sprayed the left side of my head. We were jounced around in our seats, and amidst the confusion, found ourselves upright in the middle of the road.

I tried the door, and it worked. I got out, stood in the road, and stretched. My wife got out and stood beside me. "Wasn't that refreshing?" she said.

I was preparing to wear a shirt I had bought as a momento, when there was a searing pain in my index finger. On closer inspection I realized I had stuck myself with one of the pins used to hold the shirt flat for packing. "Oh boy!" I said.

"Isn't it wonderful here?" I asked my wife. "You can get it any way you want!" We were sitting watching television. On the screen they were showing on-the-screen films of a gun battle. There were some people inside a house. The current forces of law wanted them outside the house, where, I assumed, they could be shot more easily. The police threw a grenade inside the house. The people inside the house threw it back at them, and it blew up several policemen. My wife and I laughed.

"Are you okay?" one of the reporters asked a wounded policeman.

"Blaaarg!" said the policeman.

My wife and I were preparing a meal when I accidentally dropped a container of eggs on the floor. We got gooey sticky egg stuff all over our shoes.

"Magnificent!" my wife said.

Our vacation was most enjoyable. One day it was actually raining when everyone least expected it. It was thrilling to be shocked by such an occurrence, because in our own time-period it only rains on alternate Wednesdays and Mondays, which makes the scheduling of baseball games very easy—while in *this* world (I say "world" because even though it is the same planet, the span of 483 years makes a world of difference) they have to call off the game when it rains. Not only *that,* in this world you can never be sure who will win. The Mets may take the pennant one year, and the Cardinals the next—while in our world the winning teams are picked through careful mathematical calculations. Next year's series will be won by Team 48965.

The truth of it is that nothing is ever sure here. You can

never count on anything. No wonder the residents are all on the verge of a nervous breakdown.

One evening before the accident my wife and I stood outside our rented domicile and observed the moon.

"Of course, the moon was a mistake, too," I said.

"How do you mean?" asked my wife.

"Well, what purpose does it serve?"

"It pulls the tide in and out."

"So? Accidents, that's all. It's so unnatural."

"What's so unnatural?" my wife asked.

"Our own society. Nothing left to chance. That's wrong."

"So?" She pointed at the glimmering lights in the distance. "See those houses? Are those natural? Did nature put them there?"

"In a roundabout way, yes," I said.

"So in a roundabout way, we're just as normal."

"Look," I said. "How did our society come about? I mean, what was the first thing that made us what we are?"

"When they repealed the Laws of Chance back in '29."

"And you call that normal?" I said.

"It must have been meant to happen."

"Maybe. Or maybe *that* was a mistake."

"Look," she said, putting her hands on my shoulders. "Who are you to say what's right and wrong? Nobody can live with perfection forever. So we have escapes. We've *got* to be better off than the people here. Look at the nonsense that goes on here! 'The Swinging Sixties!' 'The Super Seventies!' Jesus, five years ago is the Good Old Days for these people!"

"Maybe. Yes and no." I started walking indoors, then stopped. "Anyway," I said, half-yawning, "I didn't mean to cause an argument."

"Of course you didn't. It was just an accident."

I laughed slightly. "I guess I'm just picking up the ways of the natives."

While my wife and I slept that night, 17,500 babies were born into that world. They were all accidents, scions of a people contented to reach into a grab-bag genetic pool and haul out whatever they could get a grip on. Hardly a way to have children.

We watched what is called a revival meeting on television.

225

Thousands of rich people, all of them so by pure chance, were flocking to see and hear the great Presbyterian mystic, John Smith. Television crews were there also. Television crews were everywhere.

"Give up your worldly possessions!" John Smith yelled at them. "Give up your Cadillacs and mink stoles! Give up your twenty-dollar cigars! Give up your private Lear jets! Steep yourselves in the simple things, the pure holy things that God wants you to surround yourself with! Live in a mobile home! Drive a Mustang! Wear a Sears suit! Eat at MacDonald's! After all, God says you deserve a break today!"

They brought out a man who had been converted. He was a mousy fellow with eyeglasses, dressed in tweed.

"Yes," he said. "I used to be an oil billionaire. I never questioned anything. I was content to live in spiritual poverty. And then one day I watched one of John Smith's broadcasts on the television I had installed in my Silver Cloud. I saw the light! I renounced all worldly goods! And now I have found God, thanks to John Smith, and I have a happy life as a chiropractor in Wisconsin."

"How did this Smith guy get started?" my wife asked me.

"I read about him in one of our current textbooks. He got into the revival business when his stockbroking firm went under. By accident."

"Did it say anything else about him?" asked my wife.

"Yes. In a few years the Presbyterian Mysticism business is going to get out of hand and he'll be responsible for an internal religious war."

"By accident," we both said.

My wife and I inspected the car. Its windows were splayed all over the road like diamonds, as was most of the rear windscreen. The front windshield was caved in and shattered, and a lot of it was scattered throughout my hair and in my mouth.

"Yes," my wife told me, "I would say you did an excellent job."

"There's only one problem. How do we get out of here?"

"That's the thrill of it!" she said. "The unexpected! The unpredictable secrets of all our yearnings." She thought for a moment. "Of course, there won't be much time for all of that."

I didn't understand at first. That was how intoxicating the

experience had been, how exhilarating our whole vacation had
been: I forgot for a moment that we were almost due back in
the future. We had to be back on a certain time on a certain
day—tomorrow. In the heart of the city was a phone booth. We
had to proceed to that phone booth and dial a certain number,
and would then be transported back to our own time. We had
to do that at exactly three o'clock the following afternoon. Although we did not know it at the time of the accident, we were
not going to get back on schedule.

And somewhere in our world it would be raining on Sunday.

Ah, but on *this* world! *Everything* goes wrong! From the tiniest detail (cars that disintegrate when they collide with other objects—or that are even *allowed* to) to the most important world-
wide event (environmental destruction, political stupidity, war,
pestilence, earthquakes, etc.) this world was one big mistake.

As we stood beside the car, another car came around the bend
and slowed to a stop. A young woman got out. She had long,
frizzy, blonde hair and thick, large glasses. She seemed upset.

"Is something wrong?" my wife asked her.

"That's what I was going to ask *you!*"

"Oh," I said. "No, nothing's wrong. Everything's fine here."

"What do you mean, 'everything's fine?' You just rolled your
car!"

"Nothing to be worried about," my wife said. "We're just a
little excited. We never had an accident before."

"Well Jesus, neither have I! And I sure as hell wouldn't be
so all-overjoyed if I did!"

"You forget," I said to my wife. "They try to *avoid* accidents
here."

"Oh, that's right. They don't have perfection."

"I'm calling the police!" the woman said, running back to
her car and driving quickly off.

"Break a leg!" my wife called after her.

And then, there are those of us who like a change of pace.
Sure, it's comforting to know that you live in a world where
you'll never cut yourself, where no one will ever run out of the
dark and kill you, where you can barbeque without worrying
about rain. But sometimes a detail, just accidentally breaking a
wine glass, can mean a lot.

We had approximately a day to get back to the phone booth.

Less than a day—fifteen hours, actually. And if we didn't get back to the future on time, well, that would just be one more accident.

Either she called the police immediately or someone else had heard the accident. The police drove up within a couple of minutes. One of the officers got out. The other remained in their car. The officer who got out was tall, crisp, and commanding. He walked up to us, his shoes crunching on the shards of glass that were strewn across the road.

"Somebody here have an accident?" he asked.

"Play dumb," my wife whispered in my ear.

"Uh, yes, officer. We did."

"Well, I can see that! You don't have to tell me that! Was another vehicle involved?"

"Yes, sir."

"Oh, a hit-and-run, eh?"

"Yes, sir."

"So you hit the other car and ran. How'd you get it this far?"

"We didn't, sir. We were run off the road."

"Are you aware that this vehicle is blocking traffic?"

"It would appear so, sir."

"Don't get smart with me! I've got a good mind to haul you in on a 904—getting smart with a peace officer!"

"I'm sorry. But we couldn't move the car."

"Well, of course you couldn't move the car! And you'd be in violation of the law if you did. Why—that damned thing doesn't have a windshield! That's a 511! Driving a vehicle without a windshield!"

"The windshield was smashed when the car rolled."

"Your car rolled? Ah ha! A 218! Reckless driving! So let's see . . . You've got a 218—reckless driving. Then there's a 654—hit-and-run. Plus a 904—getting smart with an officer of the law. And a 511—operating a vehicle without a front windscreen. Plus a 836—leaving the scene of an accident."

"Leaving what scene? We're still here!" I said.

"You left the scene of the hit-and-run." He bared his teeth and ran the eraser end of his pencil across them. "Hmm. Quite a list of charges. You know, I've got an uncle in Peoria who's a judge, and I bet if I dragged you before him he'd have you gassed."

I decided to pull a bluff. "Peoria? I've got a cousin who lives there!"

His mood changed noticeably. "You do? Does he know Judge Elmer Lincoln?"

"Why sure! Good friends! Calls him 'Old El!' He gave my cousin six months on a drunk-driving charge once!"

"Well, say! Any nice couple who got a cousin who's a friend of Uncle Elmer is a friend of mine and deserves the best treatment possible! Oh, say, you aren't hurt or nothing are you?"

My wife crossed her arms behind her back to hide the fact that she had a cut in her arm which had drenched her sleeve. "Oh no. No! We're fine."

"No, you're not," the policeman said. "Your wife's hurt. You—you *are* married?" I nodded. He attempted a chuckle. "Never can tell, can you? I mean, with kids these days." He walked up to my wife and looked behind her. "But, you're bleeding!" he said, concerned. "No guy's got a wife got a cousin knows Elmer Lincoln's gonna go walk away from an accident, bleeding arm and all, without getting to a hospital, not if old Officer John Wilkes Lincoln has nothing to say about it!"

"Oh, well, thanks," I said. "But we really could just use a ride out of here."

"Oh, no you don't! No guy's got a cousin who's a friend of Elmer Lincoln's got a hurt wife's gonna not let Officer John Wilkes Lincoln not take them to the hospital!"

No wonder he was always reading off charges. When it came to simple conversation he was an utter failure.

"No, really—" I said.

"I insist."

"Really," said my wife. "We've got to see a man about a dog."

"The dog can wait. You're going to the hospital if I have to slap the cuffs on you!" he laughed.

We had no recourse but to go with him. He escorted us into the rear of the police car. "Don't be so glum," my wife whispered. "After all, this whole thing has been one accident after another."

"We taking them in?" asked the policeman's partner.

"Just to the hospital. The guy's got a cousin knows my uncle."

As his partner started the car I heard him mumble, "They *all* do."

229

The car: turning end over end. Crash, bang, bump. The glass: took me ages to get all that glass out of my hair. They sure didn't do it at the hospital. And we were due back on Day 274. The accident was on Day 273. We didn't get back until Day 275. It was an accident, you see. A mistake, that's all. There was nothing more to it.

It was an accident.

The officer escorted us into the emergency ward. The emergency ward is where they bring people who have had accidents. My wife and I marveled at all that was going wrong there. The blood, the tubes, the suffering. It was like a great living museum, always something going on, constantly changing.

A woman in white walked up to us. "These are my friends," he said. "They had a slight car accident. Take good care of them." He turned to us. "Oh, say, shall I notify your insurance company?" I nodded. "Oh, okay. Bye!" He trotted off.

"Blue Cross number?" asked the woman in white.

"What's that?" I said.

"Don't tell me you're on Medicare?"

"No."

"Do you have *any* health insurance?"

"No."

"Do you have any money?"

"Not much."

"Stay there." The woman walked away. We sauntered around the ward, looking at people. It was two A.M.

Of course. Of course. It was only an accident. The whirling burning flames were only an accident. The searing pain, the dragons unleashed, these were but mere accidents. Of course. What can one say about such accidents? They are only dreams, of course. Dreams of a strange and different time, when people were left to be battered by the currents of fate, a time of hero buns and arms and hammers, of supermen and batgirls, of bold detergents and sentry flea collars, of wounded knees and watery gates, of janitors in drums and ships in a bottle, of hawaiian punches and mighty dogfoods.

Of course it wasn't. Not really. It was just an accident.

At three-thirty A.M. the woman in white returned, with a young man in white. "Take care of these two," she said to him.

The young man in white walked smartly up to us, took us each by a hand, and escorted us to two stretcher beds that were half-heartedly screened off from everything else. "Lie down, please," he said. We complied. "Now," he said, smiling, "what seems to be the matter?"

"Offhand," my wife said, "the matter seems to be that we are lying here against our will."

He laughed condescendingly. "You're trying to tell me that you don't have some kind of emergency?"

"Aside from my wife's arm, no," I said. "We only came to watch."

"You came to . . . watch?" he said.

We both nodded.

"But we can't stay too long," my wife said.

The man in white sort of half-bowed to us. "Ohhh?" he said. "You can't stay too long, can you? What a pity! How sad. But, praytell, what would draw you away from our little establishment?"

"We have to get to a phone booth."

"A . . . phone booth. Uh huh." he took a few nervous steps back. "Come with me."

He escorted us to a room. There were two empty beds and another one that was occupied by an old man with a tube up his nose. The old man was asleep. The young man instructed us to take a pill, which he gave us, and then go to sleep. Having nothing better to do, and being tired, and having no other place to sleep, we did.

Slowly, slowly. Kablang. So much for the car, What fun. What can I say? It was a lot of fun. But don't blame us. I mean, we never did anything like that before. Most people can't appreciate these things. I mean, they proved a long time ago that 60 percent of having accidents is being accident-prone. So it is a matter of overcoming that conditioning, the conditioning which gives our world such perfection, such *accidentlessness*. Overcome that, and you can really enjoy life.

The next morning we had to fill out a lot of forms. We gave our real names, and the address of our rented domicile. We made up social security numbers. It wouldn't matter. We had to be out of there by lunchtime. The phone booth, remember?

After we'd answered their questions we were escorted to the office of the first man we'd met who was not dressed in white. The young man in white told us he was a headshrinker. The sign on his door said he was a staff psychoanalyst.

"So tell me," he said when we sat down, "why do you think it is you're standing around the emergency ward enjoying yourselves?"

"We aren't standing around in the emergency ward enjoying ourselves," my wife said.

"We are sitting here in your office having a pediculous time," I said.

"Still," my wife whispered to me, "our being here *is* accidental."

"There are some kinds of accidents I can live without," I said.

"What do you think all this talk of accidents is about?" the man said.

"We enjoy existing from time to time in a world where nothing happens on purpose," my wife explained.

"You appear to seem to think you like accidents," said the man. "Possibly because you hate your mother. You are resentful of her because she brought you up into the world, and you were a fluke, a quirk, a mistake, a capricious joke on the part of the universe. This, of course, coupled with the fact that she —that is, your mother—drew all the love and attention from your father, with whom you secretly wanted to sleep throughout your entire childhood, in fact, well into adolescence. Yes, no doubt you love accidents, love seeing other people's suffering, seeing them in pain, watching mirthfully as they writhe in ecstasy—I mean agony, agony senselessly inflicted upon them by an unfair, cruel pustulant world! No wonder you revel in the misery of others! Of course—in each of these people you see your mother, and I suppose your father too, and maybe that cute baby brother, or sister, depending upon the circumstances, and that colored postman who raped your best girlfriend—but mainly in them you see your mother, that woman you hated so much in your childhood, that foul bitch who foisted this horrible existence on you, that wretched, stinking whore who yanked you screaming from her loins and threw you into the cesspool of life, laughing, laughing, laughing! Of *course* you despise her with every cell in your body! Of course you revel in seeing other people's endless senseless ecstasy—agony I mean! No wonder you reach orgasmic heights observing the wretched abuse of everyone around you!" He jumped out of his high-backed chair. "Because *you* were an accident!"

He spun around once, like a dancer, and flopped back down in his chair, spreading his arms. "There," he said proudly, "have I helped you any?"

"No," my wife said. "Our births were preplanned. We came into our world quite on purpose."

We left him there, his head buried in a stack of papers on his desk, crying softly.

The sound. The sound of all that glass breaking. Total sound. Glass everywhere. Wow. All that glass, all that noise, like an old, old movie. Where can you find excitement like that at home?

We had to leave the hospital. It would have been fun to stay, but there just wasn't the time. On the way out we passed a man who, someone told us, had just fallen out of a tenth-story window. We offered him our congratulations.

"I think this is the road to the phone booth," I said. Of course, I had no way of knowing. I was just guessing wildly, but that was what was so fun about it—I was just guessing wildly. In our world, going anywhere is simply a matter of utilizing a pre-programmed route. For instance, to go to the hill factory, where I work, I take Road 7A, which is where we live, to 29 Boulevard, an opulent street where the people who have been designated to greatness live. From there I take Street 0046 to the valley, a pleasant green place where I work. At night I take N17 Lane home, because there is less traffic there.

But in *this* place! I don't think there are more than ten numbered streets in the entire city! After following the street I had suggested for a while, we found ourselves headed toward the outskirts of the city.

"I think we took a wrong turn back there," I admitted.

My wife and I looked at each other lovingly, then embraced. "Oh, darling," she said. We had never taken a wrong turn together before.

Then, it was too late. Even if the phone booth had appeared before us at that instant, we would not get back on time.

"Oh well," I said. "I guess that's the crowning accident." We were slightly disturbed, though. No one had ever been late before.

"We might get in trouble," my wife said.

"Let's, then," I said. "What can they do to us, after all?" We continued traipsing through the city on our search.

This world has no Wise Men.

After walking blindly for a while, we found ourselves outside a store display window. Inside the window was a television set. On the screen was a man in a clown suit sitting on a throne. There was a long line of people waiting to see him. He dismissed the person in front of him and called for the next. He was the 1970s' answer to a Wise Man. A woman walked up to him and spoke.

"O Wise Guy, how does a believer get to Carnegie Hall?"

He waved his red-gloved hand majestically. "Practice."

Another person approached him. "O Wise Guy, how does one break a non-believer's finger?"

"Kick him in the ass. Next."

A young man walked up to the Wise Guy's throne. He had a large nose, glasses, and curly black hair held down by a string tied around his head. He said nothing.

"What is your straight line?" The Wise Guy demanded. But the young man seemed unable to speak. My wife and I watched nervously. "Well . . . ?" said the Wise Guy, irritatedly. There was another uncomfortable silence.

The young man clenched his fists, struggling, mashed his lips together, as if trying to force out what he had to say. His whole body shuddered, and then—

"Fuck you, clown!"

After a few seconds' confusion, the screen went blank.

"Well," my wife said as we walked away from the store window, "there's something you don't see every day!"

Dammit! *Everything's* an accident!

We continued to search the city. At one point a man who evidently suffered from a lack of funds approached us. "Spare a quarter for a noviciate Presbyterian Mystic, Budder?" I patted my pockets, indicating that they were empty. As he walked on,

I stuck my foot out and tripped him. He made a sighing sound as he hit the sidewalk.

My wife turned to me, angrily. "You did that on purpose!"

"I suppose. But for *him* it was an accident."

"In that case I guess it's okay," my wife said.

Late in the afternoon we stumbled onto the phone booth, by accident. We were three hours late.

Types of Accidents:
Rolling an automobile.
Dropping yogurt.
Breaking eggs.
Crumpling paper.
Pricking yourself on a thorn bush.
Poison oak.
Poison anything.
Taking a wrong turn.
Being late.
Stumbling onto a phone booth.
Dialing a wrong number.
Monsters.

The number we dialed to get home was 88340984. I let my wife dial. She dialed 88349—then stopped. "Oh well," she said, smiling. "One last fling, eh?"

We stood in our world, looking at the tranquil mountains, the peaceful green hills, the symmetrical, rounded trees which dotted them, and the few perfectly-shaped clouds which hung in the perfectly blue sky.

"You fools!" a woman yelled behind us. "Debauched youngsters!"

"Where the hell have you been?" a man yelled.

We turned around and saw them. We explained what had happened, how we had a car accident, how we were delayed in coming back.

"I don't care about any car!" the woman said. "Don't you see what you've done? You've unleashed a plague! A plague of accidents!"

Other people began to congregate around her. "You hadda do

it, didn't you? Always running around in the past, you and your other friends! Because things aren't *good* enough for you here!"

"Personally," someone else said, "I don't mind consenting adults spending time in the past having things go wrong, but *it can't happen here!*"

"It's already happened!" the middle-aged woman said. "Like a great snowball! One accident leads to another! People lose their conditioning! First these two show up late! Then somebody trips and falls! Then the roof falls in on a family of five! Then a factory blows up! Then Team 39863 loses a baseball game they were supposed to win! Fires, floods, famine! *And who knows . . .*" She paused, as if afraid to carry on.

". . . Monsters!"

Oh, yes. And the injuries. I had a tremendous, streaking welt on my shoulder that carried over onto my back. My legs were cut. My palms were cut. My wife had bruises on her legs and arms, and she had hit her head on the rearview mirror.

These were some of the injuries we brought back with us when we returned home.

It was true. Every bit of it was true. The fires raged. The floods raged. The people raged. Our world had become one roiling mass of rage. My wife and I, unsure whether to feel guilty or not, sat back and watched as a people unprepared to cope with even the slightest accident foundered in a world gone haywire on them. It was difficult even for those of us who had spent time in the past, who had dealt with at least *some* accidents. Oh well, life is fun like this. Every day's a holiday.

And then there were the monsters. Monster A30991 had escaped. Nobody believed it could happen. Monster A30991 on the loose! They had all secretly believed that Monster A30991 was a fake, a fraud, an automation. Now they knew that this was not true. That lovable monster, who used to growl every Saturday and Sunday at three P.M. on the dot, who rampaged in his enclosure for two hours on alternate Wednesdays like clockwork, was eating their cities up.

My wife and I watched as Monster A30991 stormed through City B6, its eighty-foot long tail crushing buildings on either side as the beast swaggered through the town. It would tear into

236

buildings with its gargantuan jaws, taking out great chunks of steel and plastic, and then, having forced the steel and plastic down its gaping, hungry gullet, it would crane its head around in a circle and bellow, then move on. What a spectacle!

"What do you think of that, Nikki?" I asked my wife.

"Looks like a trick to me, Fuj."

What am I talking about? None of this happened. No—it really did happen, but not like you think. I mean, it happened, but I'm not from their world, that is, the future world. I'm really from 1977 but somehow there was this mixup, see—she mistook me for her husband and dragged me back into the future with her so I'm really not responsible, see, so—

What am I talking about? Of course I'm from this time, of course. I'm really my wife's husband. Of course. But you can't blame me, not really, see. It was all an accident.

The fire came raining down on us, burning us. We had manufactured the land, so that unlike in ancient times we were not shaped by the land, and could not draw strength from the land. The land was shaped by us. No power, no tone. Burning chunks of plastic, concussive sprays of water. We burned and/or drowned, and the land could not save us. The land burned, too. Nothing at all could be done.

Endoverendoverendoverendoverend: Rotating endlessly. Endlessly the car will go up and down, up and down, never coming to a stop. The glass will continue to shatter, spraying the road with its blinding shards. Rightside up/Upside down: the car will roll for eternity. The noise, that all-encompassing noise will be ceaseless. There will be nothing that can be done about it. The painted outer surface of the car will continue to scrape and grind against the concrete pavement, friction heat forever melting the paint and causing it to blister. The suspension and shock absorbers will strain under the full weight of the car at regular seven-point-two-second intervals as the vehicle turns over and over ceaselessly. This is the way we shall continue.

At least, until the *next* accident.

This is the end of the story. It's over, there is no more. Did you enjoy yourself? Did you have a good time? Are you satisfied? Are you ready to go back now?

KATHRYN RAMSAY

A Night At The Fair

Last night I dreamt
I was the only person left
And I wandered the empty fair ground
Trying to remake the past
(however inadequate it was)
With the broken puppets I found dozing
In the booths
Or guarding the frozen rides

I studied them, found out how they worked,
Turned them on and let them pass as people.
I assembled them in a great large tent
And spoke to them at length

On the way it ought to be,
How could they help
By acting the pasts of friends I had known
And been torn away from
By all the things that pass.
One of them (a boy I must have loved some time ago)
Came up to me
Took my real flesh-on-bone hands
In his cracked plaster-on-wire ones
Their color peeling, some fingers missing
He held me to my past
Without moving his painted lips.
Somewhere in his frame
Something whirred
And his recorded voice
Came scratchy far and distant
"I love you. You are all I wish I was;
Stay here with me forever.
Ride with me on the beautiful rides."

He started the Ferris wheel:
It groaned into motion
And he jumped into a passing seat
Pulling me beside

The wheel went speed crazy
With no one at the controls
Then froze with us at the top, after a thousand years.
"I want to get off," I said
"It's beautiful come night, we'll wait"
And there was a long silence from the sun
And its sinking.
The colored lights blinked on
And the music strained to reach us

The wind rocked the chair slowly
And I fell asleep in his broken arms.

240

JACK M. DANN

Fragmentary Blue

Eighty-three books, half that on psychology, were reflected in the antique silvered mirror. All out of date. Fleitman had stopped trying to keep up on anything long ago—these books were only a part of his ritual. I never liked to read, anyway, Fleitman told himself. And television had never been enough, even with cerebral hook-ins. He had stopped paying rent on the tiny machines when he had started to enjoy feeling the commercials. He could not rationalize having an orgasm over a cigarette advertisement.

Fleitman rested his forehead on the mirror: two clouds formed

241

under his nose. If only you could forget where you are. If only you were young. But you should be content, Fleitman told himself. It is safe and calm here; there are no young people to intrude. Fleitman leaned back in his chair and smiled at himself in the mirror. He remembered when his professional degree had become obsolete. He remembered forty more years of soft jobs, jobs he could handle, jobs where his education and experience would be useful. He remembered working as a module superintendent.

Fleitman lit a cigarette and watched the smoke curl before his face. He experienced a vague sexual sensation. But he would not permit himself any more synthetic pleasures. He glanced around his room, all the familiar objects in their proper places, everything clean, ready for tomorrow. But the whole place will change, he thought—after this generation dies out. And you'll be dead.

Mercifully, the phone rang. A very white, wrinkled face appeared in the wall hollow; it smiled and without waiting for a customary greeting said, "You have a meeting, Professor Fleitman. Have you forgotten?"

Bitch, Fleitman said to himself.

"The Entertainment Committee is waiting for you. Shall I tell them you'll be right there?"

Fleitman watched his expression in the mirror. "All right. Tell Taylor I'll be there as soon as I get dressed."

"But you're already dressed, sir."

Forty years ago she might have had breasts, he thought, instead of dried up gunny sacks. Where had he heard of gunny sacks? No image came into his mind. "Tell them I'll be there when I dress, Mrs. Watson?"

Fleitman was happy that a meeting had been called. He needed the company, and a good argument would clear his head. And, as usual, everyone would end up hung in the feelies, Fleitman thought. He felt an urge to join them. No, he thought, and tried to forget about it. He felt squeamish about leaving his room.

He took a shuttle to the park. It would be a short leisurely walk to the conference building. And he could forget all that mass above him, pushing down on his thoughts by its mere existence. As was prescribed, there was a thin drizzle. Fleitman had forgotten his raincoat, but the cold little bites of rain felt good on his arms and chest. His shirt clung to his skin.

The park stretched out before him. Haze hung in the trees and connected them into a pale ceiling supported by an undergrowth of frozen arms and legs, gnarls for chests and branches for limbs. A yellow chalk road sliced through the wall of trees. Fleitman did not look at the sky-scrapers behind him, steel stalagmites reaching toward the bright surface of the dome above. The sunlights —the thousand eyes of the sphere that surrounded and supported the underground city—were turned on full. The sun-shower had been scheduled to last for an hour.

Fleitman walked along a causeway near the edge of the park and listened to the shuttle trains passing below him. The sidewalk enclosure shielded him from the rain. He watched a crowd waiting to step onto a sidewalk ramp. They were all wearing raincoats. Fleitman was repelled by their age, by their once soft skin that had turned to parchment. Fleitman touched his own face. He left the park—it was a five minute walk to the Entertainment Building. Like a somnambulant, Fleitman edged his way through the crowds, ignoring them. He took an escalator into the building and then an elevator to his floor.

He paused for a few seconds in front of the conference room door, inches from the sensing line. He kicked at the air and the door slid open, revealing five old men seated around a polished metal table.

" 'bout time," Taylor said. He was seated at the far end of the table. "Christ, waiting for you for . . ."

Jake, who was sitting to the left of Taylor and opposite Sartorsky, said, "Sit down, Fleitman. We've got a great idea." He nodded at Sartorsky, who was studying his distorted reflection in the metal tabletop. Sartorsky's breath clouded the reflection. "Remember the old screen movies?" Jake continued. "I mean you've heard of them."

Fleitman straightened his back to gain a few more inches height. Relax, he thought. They're sitting down. He rested his palms against the back of the chair. No need to stand up, you old bastards. "The rules of order prescribe . . ."

Good, Fleitman thought. Jake is going to be trouble. That will give me some time to think.

"What are the rules of order?" asked Sartorsky.

Sartorsky's blind, Fleitman thought. He fought down a gleeful urge to pull the black visor band from his eyes. "First of all, I received no notice at all of this meeting. Why was that?"

Tostler, who was sitting beside Fleitman's chair, winked at

him. Fleitman had never seen him before. He was younger than the rest of the men. Fleitman ignored him.

"It was posted," said Toomis, who was sitting opposite Tostler and to the left of Fleitman.

"And you also got a call from me yesterday," Taylor said. "What the hell else do you want?"

"Out of order," Fleitman replied. An idea was forming. "Out of order you sonovabitch." Everyone was playing the game, but they would not give Fleitman more than five minutes.

"Sit down, Fleitman," Jake said. "Listen for a minute. Sartorsky, over here, came up with a great idea." Jake looked at Sartorsky, but he was still looking down at his reflection. "It's good for the whole goddam sector, good enough for a couple of months at least."

"It stinks," Taylor said. "People want a feelie or, at least, a hook-in." Toomis nodded in agreement. Tostler smiled at Jake, waiting for him to reply.

Sartorsky looked up from the table. "Let me tell it myself. It's my idea."

"Shut up," Jake said. "I'm doing this for you." Tostler nodded in approval; Fleitman was not listening.

Popcorn, Fleitman thought. What the hell was popcorn? Popcorn—movies—dried gunny sacks. The words were there before the images.

"Let me tell this," Sartorsky said, propping his knee against the table and pushing his chair back. "It is a good idea. We could show a few screens a week for recreation."

"Movies," Toomis said, "not screens." Taylor grinned.

"Right, movies. There weren't that many that were available to us. We couldn't get anything popular." He held up a notebook. "These are the titles we can get right away: *Blood of the Artist* by Cocteau; another one—it's only fifteen minutes—by Dali, but I can't read the title; another one by . . ." He passed the notebook to Jake.

"Disney. Says it's a cartoon. What the hell is a cartoon?"

Cartoon. I'm getting near it, Fleitman thought. Little children running around, balloons. What's a balloon? Talking, laughing, gasping, whispering. Sideshow. Sonovabitch.

"Well anyway," Jake continued, "there's a lot of them here." He passed the notebook to Fleitman.

"This is interesting," Tostler said. *"Freaks."*

"What's that?" Fleitman asked. Freaks. That felt right. Fleitman tied it into popcorn and gunny sacks. It still did not work. Soon, he thought.

"It's no good," Taylor said. "People won't give a damn about these movies, not without, at least, a hook-in. It has to be a feelie, or something like it."

"People want something different," Sartorsky said, tracing a line over his reflection with his index finger. "They don't have to experience everything through a feelie. People want something else."

"Do you?" Toomis asked.

Sartorsky flushed. "You know why I use the feelies. Let me put out your eyes and we'll see how well you can see with a visor band."

Taylor smiled at Toomis and relaxed in his chair. Fleitman was still standing, his palms red from his weight. He stood up straight.

"So what do you think, Fleitman?" Jake asked. "The girls should like it; hell they suggested it, didn't they?"

Sartorsky grimaced.

It's not that easy, Fleitman thought. He could go one better; if not, he would side with Sartorsky. Fleitman could outyell Taylor. His ideas were still fuzzy, but a word came to mind and he blurted it out: "Circus. We can have a circus. That's better than a movie, that's almost real."

"What the hell is a circus?" Jake asked.

"Shut up, Jake." Animals, Fleitman thought. Pictures began to form in his mind. "We can pull thirty floors out of the rec building. Christ, it's a module, isn't it? The big top will be burlap." He had once filed this information, but he could not remember when or for what reason.

"What's burlap?" Sartorsky asked.

Tightrope walkers, lion tamers, trapeze artists, clowns. From a book? Horses jumping through hoops.

"What's wrong with the movie idea?" Jake asked.

Fleitman ignored him and sat down. Everyone was watching Fleitman.

"I know what a circus is," Tostler said. "It's like the movies, only closer to a feelie. The movies, I think, are flat. A circus is live people performing tricks. You can't get inside the performers, but you can watch them right in front of you. Not like on a board." Jake was silent.

"Is this thing a feelie?" Taylor asked.

Fleitman did not look at him; he looked at the wall over Taylor's head. "No, Stephen. It's not a feelie. You just watch it; the excitement is watching the other people, fearing for them."

"What people are you going to ask to perform? Is it dangerous? It must be, if it's as exciting as you say."

"No one performs. It's a projection." That would work, he thought. He would give in a little.

Taylor laughed and Toomis tittered. "Then," Taylor said, "it can be worked as a feelie."

"No," Fleitman said. "Then you lose the fun of being a spectator. And you lose the enjoyment of being with other people."

"We'd better do the movie," Jake said. "It's the middle of the road."

"It is not," Taylor said.

Fleitman allowed the badinage between Taylor and Jake to take its course. "O.K.," he said, "we can hook-in the seats. Those who want cerebral hook-ins can have them, and those who just want to watch can do so."

"But why not a feelie?" Toomis asked.

"Because I want people to be in one place together. I don't want them isolated from each other in a feelie. I want them to smell each other, to touch each other."

"Why?" Taylor asked.

"Why are you in this meeting?"

"But that's almost the same thing we wanted to do."

Sonovabitch, Fleitman thought. "No, it wasn't, Jake. You would have used private screens or borrowed television time."

"Without hook-ins," Toomis added.

Sartorsky nodded his head. It was over, another meeting would be called to find out what had been settled, and Fleitman would begin on the circus. Alone. Everyone began talking at once. Jake started an argument. Fleitman doodled with his forefinger on the polished steel.

"Speaking of feelies," Tostler said, "why don't we all go down and hang?"

Fleitman nodded to Tostler and smiled. Get them the hell out, he thought.

"The hell with it," Jake said. "Then let's go down to the feelies. Everyone agreed?" It was always the same: the feelies and to bed. "Are you coming, Fleitman?"

Taylor played along. "Of course he's not coming. That's not the real thing, is it Fleitman?"

"Neither is his circus," Jake said.

But that's closer, Fleitman thought. He made a fist and extended his index finger. The room had become too dense. He counted the men as they left; Tostler was last. No courtesies—they had not even been introduced. That was Taylor's fault. But why didn't Fleitman ask? The door slid closed; Fleitman felt elated in the empty room. He looked forward to the work ahead; he could delegate permission formalities to the secretaries. They had probably changed the system again. He smiled. But not that much.

What the hell. The building will probably be razed within the decade. Why not an amphitheater for a day? The big top. The classic show of shows. And actors of actors?

He would busy himself with his secretary. That should build up anticipation and keep the walls at their proper distance. He tapped out her number on one of the table phones. Her face appeared in the wall hollow before him. He leaned his elbows on the table. Thanks for the idea, gunny sacks. A tick in her temple snapped in and out as she worked her mouth.

A generalized tape on the feelies. Bring back Mary. Bring back a body that felt right, not too loose on the bones. Skin pulled tight on your face—supple, won't crack when you smile. Fleitman suppressed these thoughts; submerged they became anxiety. Projection isn't real; it's an excuse for a feelie.

"No, Mrs. Watson. It shouldn't take more than a day." Her tick snapped in and out a few times.

"Then quit, goddamm it." Very good, Fleitman. Suck in your skin. Feel good. Stop the pressure, push out the walls, take in a feelie. Don't think about it. A tape can make you anybody. A-n-y—B-o-d-y.

Go. The whole morality had not been working very well. He walked down the hall to the elevator. The doors slid open before him. No good, he thought. You should get help. Fleitman, you're confusing morality with hard-on and you're too old for either. Fleitman had pushed the wrong floor button. He tried not to move his lips when he talked to himself. He sucked in the tick pounding in his cheek.

The elevator door opened and Fleitman walked past the feelie room. The door was open. Exhibitionists, Fleitman thought. He could turn around now. Say hello.

"I thought you didn't approve, Mr. Fleitman," Tostler said. "My name is Lorne Tostler; I'm sorry we weren't introduced." He shivered. "Cold."

"Then use a robe."

"Uh, uh. Why use a cotton prophylactic?"

What's a prophylactic? Fleitman asked himself. You know, idiot. It's cotton that you don't know.

"I like your circus idea. Taylor refuses to recognize it, but the feelies don't permit enough freedom. You always know that you're twice removed from the action. Even when your emotions are juiced, you always know. But all that coming from you. After what I heard about you . . . The circus idea reminds me of a place called the *Circus House* in Santa Balzar."

"I think I've heard of it," Fleitman replied. "In Ecuador. I believe."

"It was the only house in the city where you could get away with losing two kidneys at roulette. Illegal everywhere else. Had quite an operating room set up. They also had a bordello called the *Slave Market.* Made for a good house. It was so damned realistic you talked Latin." He pushed his hands through the padded loops and watched the hollow in the wall opposite him.

He didn't wait for Fleitman to leave. He had stepped into the stirrups, rested his back against the long supporting pad that stimulated his spinal nerves, and activated the tape. His arms were already moving, reenacting a prefabricated motion, caressing a smooth face. His knees were buckling, and he looked as if he would collapse. He stared at the hollow, catching the electric impulses through his retinal wall, transmitting them through his optic nerve to his brain. The spinal pad quickened his heartbeat and at the moment was providing vague feelies of pleasure accompanied by a prescience of danger.

Fleitman found it difficult to breathe. But Tostler was smiling, then laughing. His torso cracked in a spasm of laughter. Then tears: rich, oily baubles. Made of plastic, Fleitman told himself. He backed out of the room swallowing his guilt.

He walked to the nearest elevator. Fleitman had just desecrated Mary. But she was pulp, anyway. Thoughts of Mary spider-webbed into bizarre images. But, he thought, everyone always went to the feelies after a meeting. At least they all said they did. No. They did. He had passed this room before. Don't think about that. Then why was Tostler the only one there? And why was there only one feelie? There should have been ten racks.

He pushed the elevator button. *There were ten racks.*

Fleitman researched the circus from its birth in Rome to its end in Russia. He was fascinated with Astley, the former sergeant major, who traced the first circus ring while standing on his horse's back. Fleitman would make the horses and their famous riders the major event of the circus. There would be a North, a Robinson, a Ducrow, a Salmonsky from the Baltics, a Carre, and a Schumann. And there would be a Philip Astley, surveying the acts around him, genuflecting to the great Koch Sisters performing on a giant semaphore arm. But the program could not be too outre. No one would care if the details were authentic or not, but for the sake of aesthetics he would do it correctly: First the overture played on a thousand horns, then the voltige, strong man, trained pigeons, juggling act, liberty horses, clown entree—how many clowns?—and a springboard act. And then he could have an intermission while popcorn and pretzels, beer and coke, ice cream and cotton candy were being passed out by the red nosed old men. (They would have to stay the same, he thought. Might be tricky.) The intermission ends with an aerial act—all the greats on the trapeze: The Scheffers, the Craigs, the Hanlon Voltas. He would leave no one out— Sandow, Lauck and Fox, Cinquevalli, Caicedo, and the Potters would all be there. Then the wild animal act (Van Amburg could put his head in a lion's mouth), the wire walker, one hundred performing elephants, trick riding, and a finale of clowns. There were other choices: springboard acts, hand to hand balancers, artists on the rolling globe. But he had to stop somewhere.

Fleitman felt confident that he could reproduce a circus. And set it askew and ruin it. But it would be a perfect conception: the greatest show on earth. This is going to be real, he thought. It will breathe with realism: I'll forget I made it. But he knew that it was all wrong, too much to rationalize. Fleitman held the wand; he could direct his own purgation.

Fleitman spent most of his time four stories below street level in the computer complex of the Entertainment Building. The small stark complex of the Entertainment Building. The small stark room where he worked seemed to grow warmer each day. Fleitman knew that this was impossible: the temperature was equalized on all levels. He worked in his underwear, constantly wiping his perspiring forehead with his wet forearm. The computers reproduced and projected all the circuses Fleitman had

249

scanned earlier, superimposing one set upon another, suggesting proper costumes, proper colors, proper periods.

But Fleitman loved contrasts: He matched Roman gladiators and Victorian ladies, made the orchestra impossibly large, had the computers compose special music for the overture and finale. He exaggerated the clowns until they looked quite inhuman—short hair, long paste noses, cauliflower ears, exaggerated fingers and toes. Some were dwarfs, others were giants, and all were painted with bright colors—orange lips covering an entire jaw, accentuated age lines drawn in ochre, burnt sienna moles, a beard of raw umber, baked blue buck teeth. He rejected the colosseum schematics and insisted on five stages surrounded by a hippodrome track, canvas walls, and wooden posts. The more changes randomly made, he thought, the more authentic it would become. He twisted the computers' suggestions into travesties as he giggled and wiped his forehead. His best idea had been to set a small fire in the tent during one of the high wire acts. That would give the aerialists a chance to show their mettle.

Fleitman carefully created the performers, all manifestations of himself. He molded their emotions, exaggerated their possibilities. All pictures in an exhibition, all self-portraits. But he was careful to vary their physical appearance.

The computer room grew smaller each day as it filled with wraiths, painted clowns and old acquaintances. Mary remained silently at his elbow, complimenting him on a good idea, shaking her head at a bad one. A midget gleefully mimicked him. He stood directly behind Fleitman, always out of sight; but Fleitman sensed his presence.

The room became more crowded. All the young men from his first job lined the walls. An old student roommate crouched on the floor. The juggler had left all of his pins and plates in the middle of the room where Fleitman needed to work. The juggler's assistant was making love with the strong man: it did not arouse Fleitman. Fleitman did not look up when the door slid back with a hiss. It was probably the blacksmith working his bellows.

"We haven't seen you lately, Mr. Fleitman," Tostler said, taking off his sennet straw hat. Fleitman glanced up at him and scowled. "I've begun to dress for the circus." Tostler always smiled when he spoke.

The room had emptied. The midget had disappeared; Fleitman could sense it. Suddenly, he felt exhausted and uneasy. Fleitman felt a chill; the temperature seemed to be falling.

"I hope you're ready for tomorrow," Tostler said. "Sartorsky's all excited. He thinks the set up is wonderful."

Fleitman did not remember showing Sartorsky anything.

"—And your friend Jake died."

Tostler's gums are blue, Fleitman thought.

"—You can still have a goodbye, if you like. Sartorsky, Taylor, and Toomis are having a party for him. They hooked a feelie into him."

Fleitman felt sick; he swallowed a lump of vomit. He remembered dead Ronson begging him to stop. Artificial men are better company, Fleitman thought. The room had become too important to him. "After Ronson, I thought we decided . . ."

"Always exceptions. It doesn't seem to bother younger people; it never bothered me to hook-in with anybody."

It will, Fleitman thought as he vomited all over the juggler's equipment. He did not hear the door slide shut, but Mary was laughing at him. He told her to be quiet; he told her he was sick; but she continued laughing. And then the low bass of the weight-lifter joined her laughter, and others joined in as they reappeared: the cowboys, the clowns, the aerialists, the midget, the redhead with her marionettes, the fat lady, the man with two heads, the snake woman, the popcorn man, and Tostler.

Fleitman returned to his apartment early and fell asleep. He would have to be alert for the first performance. He would eat tomorrow.

Fleitman arrived early. He sat on the uppermost tier and waited for the spectators. He had planned it all perfectly, even to the smell of horse dung in the stalls. In the center ring a tight-rope walker was doing knee bends while five men in coveralls slung a net under the high wire above. Three acrobats were jumping on a trampoline in the right corner of the center ring, their mascot hound crooning each time they shouted *hey*.

Everything seemed so real, Fleitman thought. He could not completely believe that it was only an illusion. The popcorn man yelled at him and threw him a box of popcorn. The box was made of transparent plastic and was warm to the touch. This did not feel right, although the computers had proven to him that it was indeed correct. Fleitman could smell the stink of the man. It was perfect.

251

A fight broke out in the side ring between the juggler and the unicycle clown. They were both immediately fired by the manager. This was one of Fleitman's touches—the computers would not fill in such a detail on their own.

The seal trainer ignored the fighting and firing, he shouted at his seals, promising them no food unless they came out of the water. They were a main attraction. He threw them a fish; it disappeared with a snap. Fleitman knew that if he were close enough, he would be able to smell the fish, a tart, stinging odor. He had made sure of everything.

Illusion, he thought. It can be rationalized. It's healthy. Forced feelie. Enjoy it. Don't hook-in.

A few people came into the tent and looked for the best seats. Two old ladies sat down in front of him, giggling and hoisting their imitation leather skirts above their thighs. Fleitman looked up at the trapeze.

An hour later the tent was almost filled. A half hour after that, the tent was filled to capacity. Folding chairs were quickly provided for latecomers. Another one of Fleitman's touches: it would be authentic.

Fleitman watched an old man squirming on his bench, fiddling with his hook-in apparatus. Soon, they would all be searching for their hook-ins.

Then the horns blared, and fifty red uniformed Cossacks rode into the center ring, screaming and vaulting on and off their horses. One fell: it was not an accident. The next act was the strong man, and then the trained pigeons. Fleitman had substituted flying reptiles for effect. An acrobat, who had replaced the juggler, kept dropping balls; and the crowd hissed and booed and screamed and laughed. He could even blush.

When the clowns came out to announce the intermission, Fleitman had finished three boxes of popcorn. The clowns were well disguised, but too many of the performers resembled a younger Fleitman. An oversight, Fleitman thought. It would soon be over. It didn't matter. He threw popcorn at the clowns.

The second part of the program began with a wild animal act in the center ring, flanked by hand-to-hand balancers and perch performers. An aerial act was performing above the right ring; Fleitman watched the trapeze artists. The young man was Fleitman. And the woman somersaulting toward him was young Mary.

The crowd screamed. There was no slap of powdered palms.

The click was missing. She fell toward the sawdust mounds, toward the clowns staging a mock fire. Her scream was absorbed by the roar of the crowd. Of course, some people were laughing: "It's not real."

Fleitman was standing up, perched precariously on a wooden runner board. He did not see the man shaking beside him, trying to pull out the jacks of the hook-in console. Another fell off the bench, dangled for a split second, and then with a silent pop, fell twenty feet. The old ladies sitting in front of Fleitman were vomiting, splashing an old man below who thought it was funny.

This incident had not been planned. The safety net had been spread ten minutes before; Fleitman had watched. It had disappeared.

Two men dressed in white ran across the ring. As they swung her on the stretcher, the barker directed the audience's attention to the elephants. The men in white looked like Fleitman.

And then the springboard act, and more acrobats, and liberty horses. Out of order, Fleitman thought. The liberty horses should have been before the intermission. But the crowds were cheering again, hooking into their consoles, yelling at the handsome rider on a grey mare jumping through a flaming hoop. His saddle slipped, and he fell into the fire, straddling the hoop as his horse ran around the ring. Two men rushed toward him carrying blankets, but he ran away from them, his hair on fire.

Fleitman did not remember this. He counted the minutes to the finale. The small fire he had planned never occurred.

It was overdue.

The barker was waving his baton, telling the spectators of the next show, as the clowns led the parade of performers around the hippodrome. The horses stepped high, the young girls atop them curtsying; the acrobats glistened with sweat; the strong man bunched his muscles (but he should not have been there); and the strippers stripped. The old ladies shouted and screamed, the old men disconnected their hook-ins and got up to leave.

"Not yet," Fleitman screamed.

The tent darkened, the performers disappeared, the walls became translucent, revealing offices and meetings in session. People began to sit down. Fleitman fumbled with his hook-in. He was nauseated. It didn't matter; it would soon be over. The last time.

Fleitman leaned back, resting his head on the tier above him. The illusion was precise: the walls narrowed, almost seemed to be moving. Above, a dot of light growing smaller. Fleitman screamed with the spectators. Vertigo. He was in an elevator shaft. He lost his balance. One of the old ladies in front of him died. The other gurgled, pulled down her skirt, and skipped from tier to tier. The shaft was telescoping, pulling the crowd into its maw. Fleitman held his hands against his ears and screamed.

He does not remember this: he dreams that he is being swept toward the light. His heavy breathing echoes in the shaft, growing louder as it bounces from one wall to another. He awakens as he reaches the rim, as he opens his eyes to the glaring sunlight like an ant whose stone has been kicked away.

Fleitman was alone. The tent had disappeared along with the sawdust floor and wooden beams. Floors, walls, and ceilings had been hurriedly joined to accommodate all the meetings scheduled after the show. Fleitman had been taking up too much room; as he moved, two panels slid together behind him to form a larger office. A snatch of conversation, and then a click as walls met to fill the space, as other walls opened up.

He followed a glowing blue line through corridor after corridor. He listened to the echo of his footsteps along the metallic floor. Another echo. Tostler was walking beside him, his sennet straw hat in his hand.

"Sixty-seven heart attacks. Not bad, Mr. Fleitman. Old Toomis died too. No one really bothered with him; they just wanted to get out. And you fell asleep."

Fleitman could see the elevator at the end of the blue line. He walked faster, but Tostler took him by the arm and led him down another corridor.

"Where are you going?" Fleitman asked, trying to break away from him. "You're off the line."

Tostler giggled. An old lady ran past them and collapsed, her arms flapping like a bird. "She was running around the center ring just like that," Tostler said. "Around and around. It's a wonder she got this far."

Fleitman stopped walking, but Tostler put his arm around Fleitman's waist and dragged him along. "Where are you taking me?" Fleitman asked.

Tostler smiled and his dimples turned into furrows dividing his face. "Why, you're going to the surface. That's what your whole gig was for, right? And that elevator sequence was beautiful. Pure wish fulfilment. And this is it. The idea had come up to pin a paper note to your apartment door and turn off the sensor. You know, a written note on parchment. But this way is better, don't you agree?"

Fleitman did not want to go. They turned a corner. He could see an elevator at the end of the hall.

"They moved an old lady into your room," Tostler said. "She likes it quite a bit." His grip grew tighter on Fleitman's arm. "Why didn't you just ask to get out?" The elevator doors opened as they passed the sensing line. "Silly question." He pushed Fleitman into the elevator.

Fleitman didn't resist. He positioned himself in the middle of the elevator. The doors closed. Fleitman thought he heard "Good show. Come back and see us sometime," but he knew that sound could not pass through the closed doors. The books suddenly seemed very important to him. But they have probably already been transformed, he thought.

The elevator walls seemed to disappear, and Fleitman could hear his heavy breathing echo along the length of the shaft, growing louder as it bounced from one wall to another. He closed his eyes and waited for the surface light to redden the insides of his eyelids. He dreamed of grotesque clowns waiting at the surface to jump into the elevator as the doors opened and stab him with their rubber knives. Fleitman was shaking.

The doors slid open. Children were pushing against him, trying to get into the elevator. They were breathing heavily from running and perspiration glistened on their dirty faces. Fleitman stepped out, pushing children out of the way. The bright light hurt his eyes. The street elevator stood behind him, a huge grey monolith.

"What's that, what's that?" a twelve-year-old asked his playmate. She shrugged.

"We can't fit in there anyway," the little girl said. She turned to Fleitman and wrinkled her crinoline. "I'm Bozena Boobs. Do you want to do it?"

Fleitman did not understand her. He paid no attention to the children pulling at his hands and clothes. He kept shaking them off.

The buildings had risen much higher since he had been underground. And the sidewalk enclosures were shattered in places. The buildings, distorted by flaws in the enclosure plastic, blotted out the sun, formed their own grey horizon. Fleitman was dizzy. He thought of the levels of city beneath him, spiderwebs of corridors growing out of the dark like fluorescent spurs in a child's crystal garden. He felt suspended in the center of the city, and the heavy steel seemed to crush him from both directions.

The artificial light was too bright; it whitewashed the street and leveled the prominent features. The children's faces looked flat. Fleitman noticed that the slidewalks were not operating.

"Hey old man," screamed a boy dressed in a blue zip suit. "Catch this." He threw a plastic scrap at Fleitman, but missed.

"We've got to go," another boy said. "We can't wait. They'll catch us." He paused for breath and looked around at the other children. "Come on, let's go." He grabbed Bozena.

"Leave her alone," her playmate shouted, looking for a rock.

"I want to watch the old man," Bozena said.

"They can only take one of us anyway."

Fleitman thought he heard something in the distance: it sounded like the far away rantings of a mob. The children were growing in number, clustering around Fleitman. Fleitman guessed there were about forty children. A little girl was screaming and crying. "We've got to go. We've got to go. He can't help us."

The children took it up. "He can't help us, he can't help us."

"He's a rag."

"He's a hag."

"He can't be hag," a little girl said as she looked for something to throw.

There was a line of sediment around the buildings. Slowly, Fleitman thought, they were wearing.

"Bag."

"Scag."

"Fag."

Fleitman covered his face. They were throwing pieces of metal and garbage. A piece of yellow metal cut his face. They were chanting, "He can't help us, he can't help us, he can't help us."

"Rag."

"Scag."

"Hag."

"Glag," a crippled boy shouted.

"No good, cripple." More children joined in. "No good cripple, no good cripple," but it died quickly. They were all around Fleitman, wiping their dirty little hands on him, crying for help, spitting at him, caressing him, picking their noses, throwing stones, smoking cigarettes, coughing, giggling, belching. And a little girl kept screaming, "I'm afraid."

A piece of decayed food smacked against Fleitman's cheek. He felt it run down his neck into his high collar.

Fleitman ran around a corner. A rock hit him in the small of the back. The children easily stayed behind him, screaming and laughing, barely running. He crossed a street and turned into a main avenue. It was deserted, like the other streets, and the slide-walks were either broken or shut off. Fleitman noticed a large piece of plastic from the sidewalk enclosure propped against the side of one of the buildings. Three stories of window glass were broken.

There were about sixty children behind him now. His back had become numb. He felt a sharp pain in his chest as he inhaled. He sagged forward, his head lolling as he ran, his torso bent over.

Fall down. That's easy. They'll grind you, they'll crush your face.

He turned another corner. No garbage, he thought. No people. He couldn't see any windows in the buildings.

He stopped. A large crowd was pushing down the avenue. The children were behind him, the screaming adults before him. But the children turned and ran, and the crowd broke over Fleitman as so many waves in a hypothetical ocean.

Some grabbed Fleitman's arm, but Fleitman broke loose, tripping over a young woman who had fallen down. Blood was welling from the collar of her zip suit.

The crowd was pushing Fleitman along. He was a dancer try-ing to keep his balance on an undulating floor. A young man waved to Fleitman and screamed, "This is a good one. Isn't this a good one?" He looked like Tostler. Fleitman noticed a number of men were wearing black robes, their hoods thrown back to reveal cropped hair.

The crowd stopped running, and Fleitman began to feel the ache of his new bruises. One of the children had been caught by the crowd. A little freckled boy kicked and shouted as he was handed from one person to another atop the crowd. Fleitman could not see any more of the children.

"This one, this one," screamed a young man next to him. Fleit-man ducked as they passed the boy over his head. He thought he heard a voice whispering in his ear, more vibration than speech.

"What are you doing?" Fleitman asked the man next to him.

The man wore a black cloth robe and his face was flushed with pimples and sores. He looked puzzled. "Well, you're in it," the man said, "aren't you?"

"In what?"

"You mean you don't know? Then . . ."

The man was waving his arms. Fleitman allowed a few people to scramble beside him. The man was soon too far away to be a nuisance.

Fleitman listened. The murmuring in his head was barely audible; he could make it out. He could see the man in the robe grinning at him: It was Tostler.

The voice: *Do not unite yourselves with unbelievers; they are no fit mates for you. What has righteousness to do with wickedness? Can light consort with darkness? Can Christ agree with Belia, or a believer join hands with an unbeliever? Can there be a compact between the temple of God and the idols of the heathen? And the temple of the living God is what we are. God's own words are: "I will live and move about among them; I will will be their God, and they shall be my people."*

This is brought to you by . . .

Someone took a shot at the little boy. He was sitting on the priests' hands, his legs crossed in a lotus position.

"Well, he's imposing enough."

"He should make it into his thirties."

"Not that way."

A few more shots. An explosion. The little boy was crying and trying to break loose. The priests held him tightly, pressing his legs in place, crossing his arms. The crowd was howling, about to stampede. Fleitman saw a few of the children. They seemed to be enjoying the show.

Fleitman pushed his way to the edge of the crowd. He had only a few minutes before the crowd would break, pushing itself in all directions, crushing everything in its way.

"He's nothing without thorns."

Fleitman pressed himself against the building, merged with its greyness.

A few more shots. A priest's face exploded. Laughing children, dimly perceived. Fleitman closed his eyes: if he couldn't see them, they couldn't see him.

The crowd chased itself, unable to decide the fate of the new king. The screaming softened, and the crowd disappeared into the perspective lines of the street.

The shadows were all wrong—De Chirico's *Mystery and Melancholy of a Street.* Of course the shadows were wrong. Fleitman waited for the little girl to appear from a shadow pushing a hoop before her. And shouting, "I'm Bozena Boobs. Do you want to do it?"

Fleitman began to walk. He would look for other people. The eyeless buildings stood above him, watching him, not yet ready to topple over and crush him.

Kicking a plastic package of refuse out of the way, he turned a corner. The slidewalks were working. He stepped on the ramp and watched the buildings turn into a blurred grey wall. An old woman carrying packages stepped on in front of him. And another. Then a young boy and a few teenagers. A couple was holding hands beside him. A prostitute nudged his arm. He skipped to a faster ramp. But the slidewalk had become crowded. It was difficult to breathe. Pushing people out of his way, Fleitman worked his way to an exit ramp. He stepped off, ignoring the beggars and pimps.

The buildings were drab and undistinguished, but the smells were overpowering: defecation, spoiling meat, incense—orange, tabac—perspiration, exhaust fumes from makeshift engines. The foodstuffs piled behind the vendors' barricades were acrid and sweet—candies and oils, synthetic fruits and fetid sweatmeats. Fleitman watched three girls dancing on a podium in the street, their bodies oiled, electric tatoos decorating their paste white skin. To his right, a respectable little shop with an imitation wood portico. A pleasure ring was drawn around the large shop window to entice shoppers. Over the door an antique sign blinked on and off. Fleitman couldn't understand the lettering.

A balding huckster sat in front of the store and passed out loaves of burnt bread. A little girl walked toward Fleitman. She was furiously tearing a small loaf apart and stuffing it into her mouth. Fleitman remembered the food machine in his apartment. He wanted a piece of bread: its ugliness made it appetizing. The little girl walked past him, her hair crawling with tiny silver bugs.

Fleitman looked for a slidewalk, but most of the secondary walks were not operating. He passed street after street of markets, carnivals, and whorehouses—all interspersed with module office buildings and expensive shops. There should be more modules, Fleitman thought, not less. There probably were: this might be an isolated fad.

"Over there." The little girl had been following Fleitman.

Crumbs of bread clung to the front of her dress. "There's something good over there. Come on, I'll take you. I'm old enough." She caught up with Fleitman, but he walked faster and she fell behind. "I can't keep up. I'm a cripple."

Fleitman slowed down. She limped as she walked; her right leg was shorter than her left. Why didn't I notice that before? Fleitman asked himself. Maybe it's not the same little girl. Fleitman was unconvinced.

"Turn left here. Come on, I know where it is."

"Where what is?"

"Right here," she said. "I'll show you."

Fleitman breathed through his mouth: she smelled. She led him into a crowd of people. Fleitman was nauseous.

"See, look up at the building."

A young woman was standing on the seventh story window ledge of an old building that had been partly torn down. There was a space between the buildings. The sky was a grey mouth that had lost a tooth.

"All these buildings are old," the little girl said. "They started tearing them down. I watch them do it all the time. I like it; it's always the same."

The woman on the ledge was laughing and screaming at the spectators. She looks like Mary, Fleitman thought. He knew that it really was Mary. Her face was thinner than he had remembered. She was young, about twenty-seven. And she was suntanned, as always. Probably under a light, but he remembered the citizens' beach at Cannes; he remembered digging old beer cans out of the sand. Her hair and earlobes had been removed. She pointed at Fleitman and laughed.

The crowd was egging her on. Someone took a pot shot at her. She laughed and waved her arms. There was only one refreshment man running in and out of the crowd; he was hurriedly doing as much business as he could before news leaked out and other vendors arrived. He was selling red hots. The little girl bought two.

"Come on and eat one," she said. "This is a good one, isn't this a good one?"

Fleitman watched Mary. He pushed his way to the edge of the crowd. The little girl followed him.

"We better move, you know. She's going to jump soon."

"We've got to help her," Fleitman said.

"Why? She's having a helluva time. Look at her."

260

She was making obscene motions at the crowd. The crowd began to scream "Do it now" in unison. Fleitman heard himself whispering with them. The little girl was jumping up and down.

Mary closed her eyes and held her arms out in front of her.

"Open your eyes," Fleitman screamed. He knew when she would jump: he had seen this already.

She leaned over the edge, her back arched. That's right, Fleitman thought. Very good. Fleitman noticed that he was screaming. Someone had drawn a pleasure circle around the crowd. Fleitman relaxed.

She jumped and fell in front of Fleitman, splashing herself on his slippers. He took a deep breath of her and counted the entrails before him. A good omen: the refreshment man had stopped selling red hots.

"You want to take a walk?" the little girl asked. She smiled at Fleitman. He looked back, impatient for something to happen, and took the little girl's hand: it was cold and dry.

He listened to an advertisement softly buzzing in his brain.

RONALD ANTHONY CROSS

Getting Off

His eyes opened: he gestured; his lovely pleasure robot
flicked on the 3V; he was off.

The wall lit up: he gestured; now he was holding the controls
—and he was a skilled operator, make no mistake of that. The
three-dimensional, life-size figures sprang into play.

"Work first; play later," he advised.

"You are always so wise, Gerrod," his pleasure robot cooed
in her rich, carefully selected voice. Then she repeated it exactly, word for word.

Gerrod smiled slightly, without interrupting his concentration
on the dials. That was a neat feature on the new deluxe models
—they said everything twice so you could understand even if you
weren't paying much attention. Some of the lastest 3V shows
were adopting it; Gerrod approved. "Clarity and simplicity," he
said aloud.

263

Something was wrong. The speeding narrow streets, distant standing figures whizzing past old buildings.

"Rome, darling," his pleasure robot whispered tentatively. "You've misdialed." Then she repeated it carefully, word for word.

"Shut up, I know I misdialed. Damn it, anybody can misdial these days. That's what I said, clarity and simplicity, good old-fashioned virtues, that's what's missing nowadays. Who are you, anyway, to bitch at me about misdialing?

"Now you've made me do it again!" The pleasure gardens of Thailand sprang into view. He flicked it off: "Very well, we won't watch 3V for a few minutes." She pouted—she was programmed to pout.

Gerrod felt that old masculine stirring; *the little bitch is crazy about me, really goes to pieces when I get mad at her.* He absentmindedly massaged one of her ample breasts. Then he gave her the controls. "Here, you dial." She perked right up.

Th 3V market popped into view. The robots gestured at their stalls—an old-fashioned touch. They fairly flew down the aisles, hovering here an instant, there an instant, while the pleasure robot punched out the orders with superhuman skill and precision. Just as well let her take care of business, Gerrod thought. Later he would have her bring him in a meal, and a percumup perhaps, then they could watch a 3V porno-show, or one of those sci-fi thrillers about man on other planets.

Suddenly he was aware that something was quite wrong. The 3V blanked out, then a loud voice began to cry "3V alarm, 3V alarm," over and over. The wall blinked back on again, automatically tuned into the security station. A squad of menacing police robots stood at ready; he punched the coordinates for his house in to the station.

"Remain at standby," he advised. He flicked them off. Then he began to scan the front of the house. Cautiously the 3V moved through the rich green concrete lawn, through the garden of artificial delights. Warm summer nights he liked to scan out the front porch for hours at a time, just a man enjoying his garden, but now it brought him no peace: an alien had invaded his terrain.

She was at the front gate. A slender woman. A real live, slender woman, he was sure of that; they didn't make pleasure robots that angular, with those awkward gestures. She was waving at the house and trying to open the gate at the same time. She looked quite frightened, vulnerable.

Without fully realizing what he was doing, Gerrod made a wild decision. He flicked on the police station and told them he could handle the situation—all a mistake. He flicked back to the front gate and told the girl to come in; pushed the gate release.

"Face mask," he shouted to the pleasure robot.

Then he was propelling his chair toward the door; no, he stopped, stood up, awkwardly walked to the door.

"Oh," she started, her hand over her mouth. "The mask, it's just that I didn't recognize what it was; I don't know what I thought."

Gerrod took a deep breath, pulled off the mask; what the hell!

Soon they were seated; the robot automatically handing him the 3V controls. He resisted the urge to activate them. He set them on the arm of his chair.

"And now, young lady," he said in a tone of voice he imagined to be that of a 3V therapist, "just what seems to be the trouble?"

She seemed puzzled.

"I mean you are walking around, out-of-doors and all. You have come to me for something." Was he mistaken, or had she blushed?

"My name is Manda." She offered her hand; he thought of germs.

"And mine is Gerrod. My pleasure robot, Sylva."

"I am happy to meet you. I am happy to meet you," Sylva cooed.

"I guess I should get to the problem," Manda said. "But I don't know quite how to put it, I'm not even quite sure what it is. You see, I'm your next door neighbor, have been, all my life."

"Happy to meet you. Happy to meet you," Sylva interjected.

"In case you hadn't noticed, I am a female of your species and social class. Oh, I know it's old-fashioned and all, but I had to . . . that is, I wanted to meet you."

Gerrod was dumbfounded. "My God, you can't mean what I think you mean. Why don't you order a pleasure robot? I don't mean to hurt your feelings, but you can order them in any shape or form you want, programmed for anything. It's so unromantic a notion to just settle for anyone the way they are, just like that. Why, I had Sylva composed from my favorite 3V stars, altered to perfection."

"Thank you," Sylva interjected. "Thank you."

"There's no mess, no fuss, no"—he grimaced—"disease.

"And if you want"—he could hardly say it—"to conceive a child, there are always the sperm banks: careful selection, genetic alterations; and then injected in your own favorite pleasure robot, ready for action. Dial-a-baby."

She looked crestfallen; she seemed so angular and vulnerable, so human. She made strange unnecessary gestures with her hands as though she were weaving something invisible in the air. Gerrod intuited from these gestures that she was hurt and upset. He didn't quite know how to deal with that.

"I guess my visiting you and all, coming over here, was rather peculiar. I, I hope you'll . . . forgive me." She moved her hand again, as though to finalize where her voice failed.

Gerrod wondered if a robot could be programmed for that.

"Think nothing of it," he said, as he saw her to the door. "I'm rather old-fashioned myself. I enjoyed it. You never know, you might find me out coming by for a visit one day soon."

He felt a strange yearning he was afraid to define. He looked into her eyes—a heady sensation.

"Good-bye," she said, and left.

For a time, he sat in silence. Then he activated the 3V; he knew what had to be done.

Yes, the 3V had not failed him. The hidden cameras had captured it all. He watched it over again, then again, shifting back and forth in his mind, scrutinizing first the girl, her gestures, facial reactions; then his own. He was swept with longing. He dialed robotics and placed his order.

When the day finally arrived, he could not believe it. It had never been this fast before. But there it was, his new pleasure robot.

"Hello, I'm Manda," she said. "Hello, I'm Manda."

Gerrod was so excited he could hardly think straight. He had never felt this way before. He rose up and led her to her chair.

"I thought we'd catch a new porno flick," he said. Then, irresistibly, against his will, he repeated, "I thought we'd catch a new porno flick." For an instant he felt a wave of panic. Then he gestured: the wall lit up. The figures sprang to life. He was off.

STEPHEN LEIGH

The Mask Of Night
On His Face

I

"Then have an end to it."

The arid face of Lys was set in a rictus of rage, a web of harsh
linearity. He swept a withered arm in a grand gesture of dismissal
to the youth leaning against the flat, painted wood-tree. The
tempestuous sky behind them remained tautly still in the wind
that made stranded nimbi of their hair, as it had for the last
three hours. Lys' movements evoked a faint rasping from the
worn planks beneath his bare feet. Perhaps a hundred people
were watching—there should have been more, but the cows
don't know art even when it's given them gratis.

"An end to it?" the youth replied, straightening and moving a
few hesitant steps toward Lys. "An end to it when you've called

267

me lover? When you've sworn fidelity? When you said eternity would alone part us? No, there is no end." Anger had infected him now, as it had his companion, and they stood only a few feet apart, each snarling at the other with loathing. The tension was an almost tangible substance. The air was charged with it, unendurably. Something must happen. Among the hundred, someone coughed, irritatingly.

Darkness came, slowly yet without promise of remission, engulfing the canvas of the sky, the two-dimensionality of the one tree. Ameobic, it grew until there was only a circle of feverish light around the tableau of the two men, motionless now in irreconcilable stances.

Someone must always prompt the poor stupid cows, and so I clapped my hands and let the applause ripple out from me until it was mild approval. The darkness grew complete on stage, the velvetian heaviness of the curtain began its grudging descent, the house lights flickered, then gained full intensity. The applause collapsed with the hurry to leave, the rush to be outdoors again. It is too much, I suppose, to expect the masses to truly appreciate the subtleties and nuances of a Hausse play well acted. The perfect endings, so final in their psychological explorations, always strike them as somehow unsatisfactory. They do not desire reality, they want *Armageddon,* and laugh that we fear to give it to them.

They would rather watch a holofilm.

I can foretell what happens to the audience as they leave. Of the hundred, ten might wander toward the gaudy tents where the soundsculpture exhibits are being judged. Another dozen might go to hear the prose-singers perform. The rest, all too aware of their bodies, will move purposely toward the myriad booths that serve foodstuffs for the Fair, dissolving into the tedious currents of humanity that ebb and flow about the immovable islands of exhibits. The meadery down the lane a ways, the Garden of Earthly Delights, is especially popular, if you can abide the air of alcoholic congeniality and the garish blow-ups of Bosch reproductions that camouflage the holes in the walls.

For myself, I wander backstage, avoiding the jocular apprentices transferring scenery from storage to stage, stage to storage. A medieval play of Oneaeial is to be performed in a few hours, and the stage must become a segment of decadent Urras. Escaping the threat of being crushed beneath the tottering facade of Chames Tyrone's summer home, I let myself into Lys' dressing room.

"A fine performance. You controlled the character well."

Lys glances up from the task of removing artificial years from his face. His true self is rounded, almost flaccid, a denial of the strength of his personality. "Thanks, Arthol, but he isn't that great a challenge. I could keep him and a dozen like him submerged and not feel the strain."

"Confidence like that, and you'll be after the role of Huard next."

"Not very damn likely. I'll leave that to you. You're cocky and enough of a fool." He turned his attention to his arms and began stripping them of their boniness. "Seriously, though, have you heard whether the Guild has come to a decision about *Armageddon?*"

"Not that I've heard, but the public has. You had about a fourth of a full house out there. We have to do something to pull them back, or die as an art form, or at least as an organization. *Armageddon* and Huard will do that."

"Why is danger necessary?" Lys grimaced and peeled away duskiness from his forearms. "Why should we risk death?"

"We must always aspire." I strike a mock-heroic pose, though my words are serious. "Huard is the greatest role; we should not fear it because it is dangerous."

"Yeah." This muffled by cloth as he removes his costume. "How was the kid?"

I shrug, but I smile as I do so. Grudgingly. "Not bad. At times the character ran away with him. I'm sure I detected at least one line that isn't in the script."

"It's his first Imposing."

I whistle softly at this. I didn't recognize the boy, but thought he had perhaps been imported for the Fair. Occasionally we do run short of Mummers during the tourist-rush. But to have handled a Hausse character for the first personality-graft—a fair task. My own first was perhaps a shade more difficult, but . . .

"I retract my critique, then. The boy did quite well."

"You're right, though I didn't expect you to admit it." Lys' hands are as eloquent as his voice. They sweep through the air in agile accompaniment to his words.

"That's an old gibe, and still untrue. I'm always honest. Normally."

"Qualifying already." He strips the last vestiges of his character from his body. And he grinned as he did so. I am not noted for abundant modesty. "Forget what I said about handling a dozen characters. This one is tiring enough." He sighed and slumped back in his chair. "I think I'll see about an Erasel to-morrow and rid myself of him."

I cluck in false sympathy and sit delicately on the edge of his dressing table. "You can't handle just one character? Why, once—"

"I know. 'Once I was carrying four Impositions at the same time when I did the '437 Festival and had six plays in five days.' An old story, Arthol." Lys mimicked my deeper voice with the ease of long practice.

I shake my head. "Ah, how friendship has degenerated into scorn."

"Such pathos." He rises, puts on the ultra-marine cloak of our Guild. "Let's go outside. Thoth is due to use this room next, and you know how petulant he is if he hasn't proper time to prepare."

As we leave, I glance through the wings to the stage. The set is nearly erected now, replete from the backside with staples and timed adhesives. The apprentices, indolent, chatter loudly about the coming plays and the day when they will be Imposed, becoming Masters of the Guild. They bow in deference as they notice me, ceasing for a moment the amateurish acting to an empty house. I nod for them to continue. Lys tugs at my cloak.

It is a superstition of mine to always leave a theater through the front, and so Lys and I walk up the incline of the center aisle. There is the noise of doors being flung open, and Thoth enters, his pudgy body silhouetted in the light from outside. The noise of the Fair enters with him, and subsides as the doors close again. He rushes past us, ignoring our greetings. It is not rudeness, for as he passes, I see his face contorted, twisting, quivering, nearly schizoid. He is having difficulty with his character.

Lys turns to watch him dart backstage. "Arthol, I think the Guild should see about Thoth's retirement to non-Imposed plays. Did you see him? Tarina should know of this."

I nod. "When was the Imposition?"

"Yesterday, and one of the blander characters. A novice could handle it."

We start back up the aisle. "He's not young, or as strong-willed as he used to be. I remember when he could take a personality-graft like Othello and turn him on and off at will, and you know that's a rather recalcitrant soul to handle. They even talked of his perhaps attempting the role of Huard."

Lys grunted, more in sympathy than disbelief, and opened the lobby doors. Sunlight assailed our eyes, and beyond the glass the hordes gorged themselves on Sensitivity.

Normally, it is not so bad; not as crowded or as commercial as during the Fair, but even the artists crave currency to buy their materials and rent their studios. For most of the annum, we have the normal influx of travelers stopping to see the world of aesthetics, but always it culminates in the virtual flood that comes to the Exhibitions. Every native becomes a seller, anything we own or have made becomes an item for sale. I could reap a fortune marketing my cloak. To the highest bidder, an authentic cloak of the Mummer's Guild. See the insignia, gaze upon the engraved findings. One at a time now.

The heat rising from the walkways envelopes us as Lys opens the doors. The sun is lustrous and fiery this month, and it is fashionable to be as nearly naked as the customs of your homeland allow. For ourselves, those of us who live here, we care not. Our one custom is to avoid custom. The only fashion is diversity.

"Where do you want to go, now that you've thrust us into this inferno?"

"Guildhall, I suppose."

Inward then we plunge, past booths of tri-paintings, handicrafts, leatherwork, sketches, holographs, poor sculpture by hobbyists. Everywhere people, claustrophobic in density; screaming, joking, noisome humanity buying and selling, bartering with pained voices as prices beneath their dignity are offered. But this is the outpouring of my innermost soul—anguished artistic integrity. You read the sarcasm, no doubt. At least one Guild remains free of the taint. We charge nothing for our productions but what the people are willing to give. This despite the fact that the Guild is destitute and struggling.

It is with relief and bruised muscles that we finally see Guildhall before us, like every building, besieged by the crowds.

The disparity between the Guildhalls never fails to evoke a certain humor in me. The Mummers exist in an old wooden edifice (a rare commodity, that) with spires and darkened corridors. We breathe and are cocooned in atmosphere. The Guild of Visual Art creates its own atmosphere, and their Guildhall is a shell divided arbitrarily into sections as they are wont. Studio space, that is all they crave, while the Conservatory guildmembers dwell in acoustic halls of plastics and steel. Architectural aesthetics be damned, if it sounds good.

But if it pleases . . .

As we walk down the hallway, snatches of plays and fragments of conversation pursue us, slipping disembodied from open doors.

"She made me feel so ashamed . . ."

"What on earth dost thou . . ."

"Ah, if only they had been invited to a Bacchic revel . . ."

"In the Dark Years, actors were dependent on empathy to enable them to act out their roles. Though empathy still . . ."

"Stop a minute, Arthol. That's Tarina's class, I think. We should go in."

I shrug acceptance, and we slip into the classroom. Tarina—how to describe her—is some powerful mating of dwarf and elf, perhaps, a blend of physicality and sprightly wit. She was my mentor in the days when I was the prodigy of the Guild, and made certain I fulfilled my promise. Old now, and semi-retired from active work, she spends her time instructing the apprentices and running our loosely-knit organization. She is the most intense person I know, and has an unmatched reputation. She played Alvina to Valo's Huard in the '398 Festival, when the tragedian made the only successful attempt at the role; and again when Valo attempted the play in '401. She still bears the scars from that attempt. At least she lived. Valo was not so fortunate.

But I prattle, verbose. She stands before the awe-filled faces of the new apprentices, her hands gracefully accenting her speech, moving across the lecture platform with the ghost of her youthful grace. It is a pleasure to watch her move the graying head, nodding agreement with her points. We stand to the side of the platform, so as not to be noticed.

"With the technique of *persona inducere,* literally, 'personality overlay,' developed on Urras primarily as therapy for certain psychiatric disorders, it became possible for the actor to fully assume the feelings of his character. Obviously, since in a sense he becomes that character. Today"—she turned and nodded briefly to us. Her peripheral vision is phenomenal—"we

272

have two guildmembers to demonstrate for us, one of whom might soon attempt the elusive role of Huard."

"Now that's news," Lys whispers as a susurration of talk wells from the class. I say nothing, but mount the platform, bowing to the apprentices and lending Lys a hand. We both hug Tarina, who is the mother-figure to our entire community, and I mutter our question to her. "Has the Council decided?"

"Later," in a hoarse, low voice. Then, to the class: "I don't have to introduce these two rogues to you. Their fame is already established, Arthol's to a great degree from his own mouth."

The class laughs on cue. I blush modestly.

"But I've asked them here"—as she turns coincidence into routine, as if planned—"to show the range of expression that is possible without the aid of Imposition." She half-turns to us, but without giving her back to the class, a stage-gesture. Never turn away from the cows. They might leave. "Do the two of you recall enough of your Pre-modern to improvise a scene? "Good," she says, before we can reply. To the class, then: "We will attempt . . ." She accents the last word and pauses, and it draws the expected mirth from the class. ". . . to improvise on a cliché of pre-modern tragedy, the love triangle. Lys, you shall be the adulterer. Arthol, since you're so confident and assured, you may be the cuckold husband. I shall be the beauteous maiden." Tarina primps her hair with exaggerated motions. Again there is the dutiful amusement from the neophytes.

There is a moment's hesitation as we put ourselves into the mood of the era, and we begin. It quickly becomes comedy, as improbability is heaped upon improbability, Well-played, though. Of course it ends with virtue triumphant and morals set straight, not at all like a Hausse or a Quela. Ah well, we all have preferences. Tarina dismisses the class, and we go to the lounge to talk.

"Yes, it was decided this morning," she remarks when we enter the cloistered rooms, leaving the noise of the hallways outside the paneled walls. Tarina fixes herself mocha while Lys and I collapse into the worn comforts of the ancient armchairs. The lounge is as old in appearance as the rest of Guildhall. The walls are genuine woods imported from Urras herself, and not veneers or imitations. It is dark, as befits the aura of the room, evoking a restfulness and a certain secretivity. The furniture is decrepit, hollowed by the weight of many people. Coverings are ragged, springs protrude. Even if we could afford it, we wouldn't change.

273

Tarina, steaming porcelain in her hand, goes to the window and gazes at the milling crowdedness of the Fair. Their noise is a faint background to our conversation. She speaks to the window rather than us. "The Council, at my urging primarily, has agreed to undertake a production of *Armageddon* and thus the character of Huard."

"Who?" I speak the only question. Tarina is dramatic and would draw this out. Lys, patient and tolerant, would let her. If I would balm my impatience, I must speak.

She turns to us. The vapor from the cup in her hand wreathes about her face and the licorice aroma fills the room. Lys shifts position in his chair. "We reviewed the psychological evaluations for every guildmember. There were three that indicated ego-strength, comparable to Valo. All were borderline."

"Sophomoric dramatics, Tarina." My voice reveals my impatience and irritation. The matriarch looks at me, but will not be rushed.

"Still, it was decided to make the attempt anyway, provided that the actor is agreeable."

"Enough, Tarina. Who are the three?" I can safely be angry with her where no one else can. The lingering of our early years protects me, my days as impudent apprentice and brilliant journeyman in non-Imposed plays.

She smiles, justifying my confidence. "Who? As I so broadly hinted in class, you and Lys are two of the candidates. The other, and let me explain that the evaluations in his case were old, dating from his initiation as Guildmaster, was Thoth. I know"—she raises her free hand as both Lys and I protest—"I know about his, shall we say, problem. The guild has revoked his right to Imposition, and he has agreed to accept the status of Master Emeritus. So."

"What swayed the Council?" Lys speaks from the canyoned depths of his chair. "I honestly thought that *Armageddon* would never be done again."

"Many things." Tarina takes a cautious sip of mocha, grimacing at its warmth. "Primarily because it's fifty annums since Valo's second attempt, and because news of the projected production will net us much currency. The Fair officials have promised us the Exposition Center to accommodate the anticipated crowds. And I fought viciously for it." Again she smiles, and it is tainted with fear, as if she were afraid of censure. "You see, I am going to play Alvina."

II

We watch the stage and look upon the loathsome Huard. He dominates the others with him: the diminutive Alvina, his jester Kana, or the darkly-scowling guards. He is a giant, girt and thewed like a mythological hero. He is both admirable and detestable, God of Light and God of Darkness, manic-depressive, healing and wounding with the same hand. Huard, the ogre of historical texts, all the more hated because he actually did breathe.

We all grudge him those breaths.

Those well-muscled hands that consigned hundreds to torture and death because they would not call him Ruler. Those deepset and smouldering eyes that watched without pity as his ships ravaged worlds he felt harbored dissidents. That cunning and devious mind crippled by guilt and paranoia. Huard: the Beast, the Bastard, the Cruel, the Dung-Eater—all cultures have their own appellations for his name.

And mixed with the hatred there is pity, pity that he never felt but all felt for him. Pity because of his unhelpable twistedness, pity that he desired so much and could not have even a tithe of it, pity for his impotence with the only person he can truly be said to have loved, Alvina. And for what else . . . for the despair that led to his eventual murder-suicide, and for the fact that the newly re-discovered science of psychology developed a workable technology too late to have aided him in finding solace.

Sadness that what could have been so good was so evil.

Subjective terms, I know, but how else can I speak?

We stare at the only holofilm in existence of *Armageddon*. It is a play to please the cows. It is a play to placate the aesthetes. Valo is a superb Huard. I find myself uncontrollably pried from my role of critic and forced into emotional response. I despise him, he disgusts me, yet the characterization is incredibly facile, for at the same time I feel such a sorrow, such empathy. Tarina, younger and provocative, plays the tempermental Alvina with precision and pathos. The other actors exist in the shadow of these two. They are non-entities, even the reknowned Bathor as Kana. I must admit that the role forms a greater challenge than I had let myself admit. But I can do it.

It is purely a masterwork. Small wonder that the writing of it reputedly drove the nameless playwright insane.

The play ends as it begins, in blood and passion, in frustration and pain.

Tarina is unashamedly weeping, and Lys sits with a stunned vacancy over his features. The Guild sits around us in various postures of emotional exhaustion. There is perhaps moisture on my face also.

Tarina speaks without moving from her seat to turn and face the others, her voice a whisper in the silent aftermath and growing stronger as the play looses its grueling hold. "That was a recording of the '398 attempt, the first successful one. There are none for the tragedy of '401. The actors were the same, the play had been done before, so the news media didn't feel it to be worth the expense."

All this talk gets us nowhere. Seeing the play has only fired my enthusiasm for it, kindled desire so that I will brook no delays. Tarina, for all my liking for her, would speech us to boredom.

"*Who,* Tarina? That's still to be answered." I can feel the eyes of Lys impaling me, but the emotions behind his stare are unguessed. How does he feel? How did it affect him?

"That has to be decided between the two of you." Tarina pouts like a child unfairly scolded. The Guildmembers squirm in their seats, a blend, I suppose, of guilt at being present at an argument in which they have no part, and irritation at the upstart, however gifted, who would rebuke a senior member.

"Fine. That can be done. But another thing, for either myself or Lys. Can you play Alvina? I don't mean to hurt you, Tarina, but that is in itself a difficult role. Are you truly able to handle it, to aid whichever of us plays Huard? His life might be the price for incompetence."

Her eyes recoil from mine, darting away in wounded frenzy. Her voice is almost apologetic. "My evaluation was updated a month ago, and the Guild feels it indicates sufficient ego-strength to play the role. And you know that cosmetics is not an issue. I can be made to appear younger." And then the ire. "Damn you, I can still feel, can't I?" I understand, for I feel the same. Alvina is the greatest role Tarina has played, and she might play it again. When you can no longer create, you are artistically dead, and what is the use of existing? Always aspiring.

"All right, I believe."

"And you, Arthol, is it important to you, also?" Lys turns in his seat and faces me. The air of confession lies like incense in the room, cloying and choking in my nostrils. "You want the role badly enough to . . ." His voice trails off, as if in disgust.

"I'd be less than truthful to say no." My words, leeched of

meaning by their obviousness, drift upwards without touching anyone.

Lys' voice is almost sad, almost condescending. "What drives you, Arthol? Why do you want to play the Monster? Huard is ravenous; he'll devour you and spit your shriveled soul out. You want fame? You have more than your measure of it already. Be content with that. Is it the challenge? Only a fool attempts the impossible." In vehemence, Lys finds eloquence.

"Is that friendship speaking, Lys? You want me to cast my moment away so that it can be yours?" My accusations, even as I speak the words, are sham. I know his answer.

"I won't play the part, Arthol. It would submerge me: I couldn't handle it. I know that—you should know it. I'll be more than content as Kana. I don't need the fame."

Silence is a tense balm to wounded pride. Lys looks away. Tarina shrugs toward the unspeaking members of Council, I stared unseeing at the now-empty stage.

"Arthol?" Tarina, with the unanswered query.

"Yes," I reply, and then more emphatically, "yes. For whatever reasons, yes."

Egoism, quest, duty, fate. For whatever reasons, and for all.

III

You are encased in the Role-imposer. It is . . . what? Sort out the feelings. A metallic coldness numbing the wrists and brushing the hair. Womb-darkness. Anticipation, perhaps a modicum of fear. Your mind open and receptive, waiting to co-mingle with the ghost of a fictional personality.

But Huard was not fictional, nor is his persona reputed to be ghost-like.

Such for the objective. Now subjective. You sense the dimly-lit stage that exists inside you and the empty-socketed skulls of the audience greeting you with thunderous quiet. You grasp for the lines you are to say, you reach for the person you are to incorporate. (Male? Female? Human? Non-human? Cold? Angry? Sympathetic? Kind? Evil?)

Nothing.

Then, faintly, the questioning touch of a second ego, a strange id, an alien superego; drifting like an unseen snowfall over the landscape of self, chilling it, hiding it beneath its own-ness.

Clamping onto your mind, becoming a second you. Now control it, submerge it so you can use it (him?), lest you drown in someone who does not even live. Who are you? Arthol? You are Arthol?

(Huard!)

Struggle or be lost. He is damned strong. Arthol!

(Huard! You bastard.)

Arthol
  rtholH
    tholHu
      holHua
        olHuar
          lHuard
            HuardA
              uardAr
                ardArt

Blackness.

"It almost took you, Arthol. We've set up an Erasel."

I lie mummified in sterile sheets. Tarina must have spoken, as it seems to be her face that hovers above mine. Opening my eyes fully, I see her and Lys standing next to me. Against the far wall and lanced by a dusty beam of sunlight that slashes across the floor, stand two Impositors. The room stinks of machinery, a greased and iron tank. I'm still in the Halls of Psychology, then.

"No!" Like the echo of a nightmare. My head aches with the effort of speech. "I've got him now."

Lys exudes concern. It twists his face. "You're sure?"

I nod.

Tarina looks at the silent two against the wall. I follow her glance. They shrug shoulders like twins. They do not care. All Mummers are psychotic, they say among the Psychologists. Let them go their own way.

"I'm fine," I repeat for accent.

Tarina, such a bitchy hag; and Lys, the cowardly fool. Petty minds, both.

"I'm able to walk. Let's go. The audience waits." A pause, as I sit. "I'm fine," I say again.

I lie.

It is custom to wait a day after Imposing to perform the play. This betimes is ignored in the rush of the Fair, but not in this case. The company had studied the play for two weeks prior to our Impositions, the sets had been readied, and the public titillated with the knowledge that it would see history made.

It fools no one, that wait. It is easier to handle the persona when in your environment. "Wait," the Mummers say, "until you are in his. Then you will know."

And I don't know . . . never mind. Such lack of self-confidence is self-destructive, literally. I know that I feel Huard's otherness inside me, crowding my skull, and that he is strong. I know that last night I could not sleep, for memories that weren't mine kept forcing themselves on my conciousness, foreign spectres.

I will be stronger. I am stronger.

I can hear the insect humming that is the audience. I've been told that it is the largest to ever have seen a play during the Fair. The Exposition Center is filled to capacity and more. What lures them—the play itself or the possibility that something could go awry? The cows, the damn cows. The play is about to begin, and the murmuring audience quiets as the house lights dim and die. Huard twists inside me, and I force him down.

Onstage, then, with Tarina grasping my arm and staring at me with doe-like and troubled eyes. They have done a miracle with her. She appears to be young and slender: she is beautiful. Even her walk has changed, become younger—Alvina. No doubt. The curtain rises, and the sea of faces beyond the lights explodes into applause. The sacrificial lambs, hurrah.

The first act goes smoothly. Huard is tempered. I let him surface in me, let him speak my lines, but hold him securely. I watch with dispassion as enemies are brought before me and stage-blood reddens the flooring. Huard rejoices, longing to twist the knife. My hand clenches and unclenches. I-Huard rage about, frightening and cowing the servile masses. I castrate my lackey Kana, have the haughty and aloof Alvina raped by my minions, degraded and reviled. I am supreme.

Curtain, to thunderous applause that seems nonetheless disappointed. Do this well, and my fame will last forever, but they would rather see me fail.

As the scenery is changed and the new set erected, Lys comes to me. His eyes question silently.

"I'm enjoying it. Don't worry."

Then to the stage. The applause again greets us, eager and hungry. Do they celebrate me or the thing inside me? What matter? More rapacity, more plundering. It is the zenith of my power, but for one elusive thing. I must have Alvina, but impotence unmans me.

We plot, we fight, we argue.

"Away from me, bastard." Her eyes, so pained, arc in hatred.

"I won't be ordered about. Learn that, bitch," and I slap her, watching her fair skin redden under the sting. She reels backwards, hand across face while from somewhere there is the sound of apprehension. Tears sheen in Alvina's eyes, and . . .

Tarina's eyes. Gods, I enjoyed that. For a moment . . .

Down, you ghost.

Midst the whispering of the audience, we finish the scene, somewhat lamely, keeping our personas tightly reined. I can imagine the excited commentary of the newscasters in the intermission, showing over and over again the moment of fear. Alvina has said her lines and exited, and a holographic image swirls around me as my ships plunder a planetary system. I laugh, hating and yearning.

Curtain.

"You slipped, Arthol. That hurt." Tarina still holds a disbelieving hand to her face.

"I know. It won't happen again."

"I want to call it off."

The cast watches us without staring.

"No." Emphatically. "I can handle him. Hell, would you have called Valo to a halt?"

"You're not Valo."

"I'm better."

"Possibly." With scorn.

"Would you have the Guild reviled? Would you like the Mummers regarded as cowards or incompetents?"

"No," she replied, hesitantly, then with certainty. "No."

"Onstage, then. It's time."

I let myself fall into the role again. Huard lurks just beneath the surface, greedy, longing to relive his life. The last act, now, the one which set the audience screaming and took Valo's life. For myself, for Huard, it is agony, excruciating pain. I can see the shadow of an empire in my hands, but still there is no satisfaction. What I desire remains beyond my grasp. Alvina, in scorn, bears a child to another man. I maim the man and kill the child, but there is no surcease.

Rape, pillage, destroy—that doesn't help. Soothe, create, aid —that also fails. Nothing. You can do nothing. No satisfaction, no fulfillment. I have unlimited power over the masses that bow and grovel to me, but I can do nothing to sway that one individual: Alvina, the object of love, the object of hatred. Approach her and she retreats; force myself on her and she is unresponsive. Show her your glory, and she is unimpressed.

Damn damn DAMN. I thought fame was what was desired, and now it is mine, and it is not enough.

The part of me that is detached notes that the audience sits quietly without stirring. None leave their seats. They have finally come to know the emotions of the actors. Perhaps, perhaps they are even satisfied.

It is the final scene. I summon Alvina to me, to order her to give herself to me one last time. She enters the room, walks to me, and in a grand gesture of defiance, spits at my feet.

"Bow," I say, and push her backwards. She laughs in anger and resignation, but will not bow. I curse at her, a stream of purple invectives.

Alvina faces me without flinching, hurling insult after insult at me, shaming me before my court, calling me murderer, animal, eunuch. I growl in inarticulate passion. I hate her. I love her.

(Arthol! Huard!)

We must always aspire.

In the window behind me, the stars that are my domain glitter mockingly. My court maintains seriousness, but I know that they long to lash out at me, and that they silently praise Alvina. Her face is contorted with fury, she is wild and shameless.

"Stop! Be silent!" I scream, louder than even she. Along the far walls, my guards stiffen into alertness.

"Hah! Be silent? You can't silence me. Kill me and I'll still speak." She slides toward me, halting a few steps away. I wave the guards back.

Again she spits, and moisture clings to my face.

In an angry movement, I reach for the bejeweled dirk at my belt. I pull her to me. "No!" she screams to the court, and then softly speaks to me. "Careful, now. We're almost through."

Wondering at her strange words, my hand moves, and the warmth of her blood engulfs my hand. From somewhere far off there is the roaring of horrified voices. My court stands in shock,

281

slack mouths gaping like fish while I reverse the blade and place it to my chest.

(I am sorry, Lys, Tarina, Arthol.)

My hand moves.

Curtain.

ROBERT SILVERBERG

When We Went To See The End Of The World

Nick and Jane were glad that they had gone to see the end of the world, because it gave them something special to talk about at Mike and Ruby's party. One always likes to come to a party armed with a little conversation. Mike and Ruby give marvelous parties. Their home is superb, one of the finest in the neighborhood. It is truly a home for all seasons, all moods. Their very special corner-of-the-world. With more space indoors and out . . . more wide-open freedom. The living room with its exposed ceiling beams is a natural focal point for entertaining. Custom-finished, with a conversation pit and fireplace. There's also a family room with beamed ceiling and wood paneling . . . plus a study. And a magnificent master suite with 12-foot dressing room and private bath. Solidly impressive exterior design. Sheltered courtyard. Beautifully wooded 1/3-acre grounds. Their parties are highlights of any month. Nick and Jane waited until they thought enough people had arrived. Then Jane nudged Nick and Nick said gaily, "You know what we did last week? Hey, we went to see the end of the world!"

"The end of the world?" Henry asked.

"You went to see it?" said Henry's wife Cynthia.

"How did you manage that?" Paula wanted to know.

"It's been available since March," Stan told her. "I think a division of American Express runs it."

Nick was put out to discover that Stan already knew. Quickly, before Stan could say anything more, Nick said, "Yes, it's just started. Our travel agent found out for us. What they do is they put you in this machine, it looks like a tiny teeny submarine, you know, with dials and levers up front behind a plastic wall to keep you from touching anything, and they send you into the future. You can charge it with any of the regular credit cards."

"It must be very expensive," Marcia said.

"They're bringing the costs down rapidly," Jane said. "Last year only millionaires could afford it. Really, haven't you heard about it before?"

"What did you see?" Henry asked.

"For a while, just grayness outside the porthole," said Nick. And a kind of flickering effect." Everybody was looking at him. He enjoyed the attention. Jane wore a rapt, loving expression. "Then the haze cleared and a voice said over a loudspeaker that we had now reached the very end of time, when life had become impossible on Earth. Of course we were sealed into the submarine thing. Only looking out. On this beach, this empty beach. The water a funny gray color with a pink sheen. And then the sun came up. It was red like it sometimes is at sunrise, only it stayed red as it got to the middle of the sky, and it looked lumpy and sagging at the edges. Like a few of us, hah hah. Lumpy and sagging at the edges. A cold wind blowing across the beach."

"If you were sealed in the submarine, how did you know there was a cold wind?" Cynthia asked.

Jane glared at her. Nick said, "We could see the sand blowing around. And it *looked* cold. The gray ocean. Like in winter."

"Tell them about the crab," said Jane.

"Yes, and the crab. The last life-form on Earth. It wasn't really a crab, of course, it was something about two feet wide and a foot high, with thick shiny green armor and maybe a dozen legs and some curving horns coming up, and it moved slowly from right to left in front of us. It took all day to cross the beach. And toward nightfall it died. Its horns went limp and it stopped moving. The tide came in and carried it away. The sun went down. There wasn't any moon. The stars didn't seem to be in the right places. The loudspeaker told us we had just seen the death of Earth's last living thing."

"How *eerie!*" cried Paula.

"Were you gone very long?" Ruby asked.

"Three hours," Jane said. "You can spend weeks or days at the end of the world, if you want to pay extra, but they always bring you back to a point three hours after you went. To hold down the baby-sitter expenses."

Mike offered Nick some pot. "That's really something," he said. "To have gone to the end of the world. Hey Ruby, maybe we'll talk to the travel agent about it."

Nick took a deep drag and passed the joint to Jane. He felt pleased with himself about the way he had told the story. They had all been very impressed. That swollen red sun, that scuttling crab. The trip had cost more than a month in Japan, but it had been a good investment. He and Jane were the first in the neighborhood who had gone. That was important. Paula was staring at him in awe. Nick knew that she regarded him in a completely different light now. Possibly she would meet him at a motel on Tuesday at lunchtime. Last month she had turned him down but now he had an extra attractiveness for her. Nick winked at her. Cynthia was holding hands with Stan. Henry and Mike both were crouched at Jane's feet. Mike and Ruby's twelve-year-old son came into the room and stood at the edge of the conversation pit. He said, "There just was a bulletin on the news. Mutated amoebas escaped from a government research station and got into Lake Michigan. They're carrying a tissue-dissolving virus and everybody in seven states is supposed to boil his water until further notice." Mike scowled at the boy and said, "It's after your bedtime, Timmy." The boy went out. The doorbell rang. Ruby answered it and returned with Eddie and Fran.

Paula said, "Nick and Jane went to see the end of the world. They've just been telling us about it."

"Gee," said Eddie, "we did that too, on Wednesday night."

Nick was crestfallen. Jane bit her lip and asked Cynthia quietly why Fran always wore such flashy dresses. Ruby said, "You saw the whole works, eh? The crab and everything?"

"The crab?" Eddie said. "What crab? We didn't see the crab."

"It must have died the time before," Paula said. "When Nick and Jane were there."

Mike said, "A fresh shipment of Cuernavaca Lightning is in. Here, have a toke."

"How long ago did you do it?" Eddie said to Nick.

"Sunday afternoon. I guess we were about the first."

"Great trip, isn't it?" Eddie said. "A little somber, though. When the last hill crumbles into the sea."

"That's not what we saw," said Jane. "And you didn't see the crab? Maybe we were on different trips."

Mike said, "What was it like for you, Eddie?"

Eddie put his arms around Cynthia from behind. He said, "They put us into this little capsule, with a porthole, you know, and a lot of instruments and—"

"We heard that part," said Paula. "What did you *see?*"

"The end of the world," Eddie said. "When water covers everything. The sun and moon were in the sky at the same time—"

"We didn't see the moon at all," Jane remarked. "It just wasn't there."

"It was on one side and the sun was on the other," Eddie went on. "The moon was closer than it should have been. And a funny color, almost like bronze. And the ocean creeping up. We went halfway around the world and all we saw was ocean. Except in one place, there was this chunk of land sticking up, this hill, and the guide told us it was the top of Mount Everest." He waved to Fran. "That was groovy, huh, floating in our tin boat next to the top of Mount Everest. Maybe ten feet of it sticking up. And the water rising all the time. Up, up, up. Up and over the top. Glub. No land left. I have to admit it was a little disappointing, except of course the *idea* of the thing. That human ingenuity can design a machine that can send people billions of years forward in time and bring them back, wow! But there was just this ocean."

"How strange," said Jane. "We saw an ocean too, but there was a beach, a kind of nasty beach, and the crab-thing walking along it, and the sun—it was all red, was the sun red when you saw it?"

"A kind of pale green," Fran said.

"Are you people talking about the end of the world?" Tom asked. He and Harriet were standing by the door taking off their coats. Mike's son must have let them in. Tom gave his coat to Ruby and said, "Man, what a spectacle!"

"So you did it too?" Jane asked, a little hollowly.

"Two weeks ago," said Tom. "The travel agent called and said, Guess what we're offering now, the end of the goddamned world! With all the extras it didn't really cost so much. So we went right down there to the office, Saturday, I think—was it a Friday?—the day of the big riot, anyway, when they burned St. Louis—"

"That was a Saturday," Cynthia said. "I remember I was coming back from the shopping center when the radio said they were using nuclears—"

"Saturday, yes," Tom said. "And we told them we were ready to go, and off they sent us."

"Did you see a beach with crabs," Stan demanded, "or was it a world full of water?"

"Neither one. It was like a big ice age. Glaciers covered everything. No oceans showing, no mountains. We flew clear around the world and it was all a huge snowball. They had floodlights on the vehicle because the sun had gone out."

"I was sure I could see the sun still hanging up there," Harriet put in. "Like a ball of cinders in the sky. But the guide said no, nobody could see it."

"How come everybody gets to visit a different kind of end of the world?" Henry asked. "You'd think there'd be only one kind of end of the world. I mean, it ends, and this is how it ends, and there can't be more than one way."

"Could it be a fake?" Stan asked. Everybody turned around and looked at him. Nick's face got very red. Fran looked so mean that Eddie let go of Cynthia and started to rub Fran's shoulders. Stan shrugged. "I'm not suggesting it is," he said defensively. "I was just wondering."

"Seemed pretty real to me," said Tom. "The sun burned out. A big ball of ice. The atmosphere, you know, frozen. The end of the goddamned world."

The telephone rang. Ruby went to answer it. Nick asked Paula about lunch on Tuesday. She said yes. "Let's meet at the motel," he said, and she grinned. Eddie was making out with Cynthia again. Henry looked very stoned and was having trouble staying awake. Phil and Isabel arrived. They heard Tom and Fran talking about their trips to the end of the world and Isabel said she and Phil had gone only the day before yesterday. "Goddamn," Tom said, "everybody's doing it! What was your trip like?"

Ruby came back into the room. "That was my sister calling from Fresno to say she's safe. Fresno wasn't hit by the earthquake at all."

"Earthquake?" Paula said.

"In California," Mike told her. "This afternoon. You didn't know? Wiped out most of Los Angeles and ran right up the coast practically to Monterey. They think it was on account of the underground bomb test in the Mohave Desert."

"California's always having such awful disasters," Marcia said.

"Good thing those amoebas got loose back east," said Nick. "Imagine how complicated it would be if they had them in L.A. now, too."

"They will," Tom said. "Two to one they reproduce by airborne spores."

"Like the typhoid germs last November," Jane said.

"That was typhus," Nick corrected.

"Anyway," Phil said, "I was telling Tom and Fran about what we saw at the end of the world. It was the sun going nova. They showed it very cleverly, too. I mean, you can't actually sit around and *experience* it, on account of the heat and the hard radiation and all. But they give it to you in a peripheral way, very elegant in the McLuhanesque sense of the word. First they take you to a point about two hours before the blowup, right? It's I don't know how many jillion years from now, but a long way, anyhow, because the trees are all different, they've got blue scales and ropy branches, and the animals are like things with one leg that jump on pogo sticks—"

"Oh, I don't *believe* that," Cynthia drawled.

Phil ignored her gracefully. "And we didn't see any sign of human beings, not a house, not a telephone pole, nothing, so I suppose we must have been extinct a long time before. Anyway, they let us look at that for a while. Not getting out of our time machine, naturally, because they said the atmosphere was wrong. Gradually the sun started to puff up. We were nervous—weren't we, Iz?—I mean, suppose they miscalculated things? This whole trip is a very new concept and things might go wrong. The sun was getting bigger and bigger, and then this thing like an arm seemed to pop out of its left side, a big fiery arm reaching out across space, getting closer and closer. We saw it through smoked glass, like you do an eclipse. They gave us about two minutes of the explosion, and we could feel it getting hot already. Then we jumped a couple of years forward in time. The sun was back to its regular shape, only it was smaller, sort of like a little white sun instead of a big yellow one. And on Earth everything was ashes."

"Ashes," Isabel said, with emphasis.

"It looked like Detroit after the union nuked Ford," Phil said. "Only much, much worse. Whole mountains were melted. The oceans were dried up. Everything was ashes." He shuddered and took a joint from Mike. "Isabel was crying."

"The things with one leg," Isabel said. "I mean, they must have all been wiped *out*." She began to sob. Stan comforted her. "I wonder why it's a different way for everyone who goes," he said. "Freezing. Or the oceans. Or the sun blowing up. Or the thing Nick and Jane saw."

"I'm convinced that each of us had a genuine experience in the far future," said Nick. He felt he had to regain control of the group somehow. It had been so good when he was telling his story, before those others had come. "That is to say, the world suffers a variety of natural calamities, it doesn't just have *one* end of the world, and they keep mixing things up and sending people to different catastrophes. But never for a moment did I doubt that I was seeing an authentic event."

"We have to do it," Ruby said to Mike. "It's only three hours. What about calling them first thing Monday and making an appointment for Thursday night?"

"Monday's the President's funeral," Tom pointed out. "The travel agency will be closed."

"Have they caught the assassin yet?" Fran asked.

"They didn't mention it on the four o'clock news," said Stan. "I guess he'll get away like the last one."

"Beats me why anybody wants to be President," Phil said.

Mike put on some music. Nick danced with Paula. Eddie danced with Cynthia. Henry was asleep. Dave, Paula's husband, was on crutches because of his mugging, and he asked Isabel to sit and talk with him. Tom danced with Harriet even though he was married to her. She hadn't been out of the hospital more than a few months after the transplant and he treated her extremely tenderly. Mike danced with Fran. Phil danced with Jane. Stan danced with Marcia. Ruby cut in on Eddie and Cynthia. Afterward Tom danced with Jane and Phil danced with Paula. Mike and Ruby's little girl woke up and came out to say hello. Mike sent her back to bed. Far away there was the sound of an explosion. Nick danced with Paula again, but he didn't want her to get bored with him before Tuesday, so he excused himself and went to talk with Dave. Dave handled most of Nick's investments. Ruby said to Mike, "The day after the funeral, will you call the travel agent?" Mike said he would, but Tom said somebody would probably shoot the new President, too, and there'd be another funeral. These funerals were demolishing the gross national product, Stan observed, on account of how everything had to close all the time. Nick saw Cynthia wake Henry up and ask him sharply if he would take her on the end-of-the-world trip. Henry looked embarrassed. His factory had been blown up at Christmas in a peace demonstration and everybody knew he was in bad shape financially. "You can *charge* it," Cynthia said, her fierce voice carrying above the chitchat. "And it's so *beautiful, Henry*. The ice. Or the sun exploding. I want to go."

"Lou and Janet were going to be here tonight too," Ruby said to Paula. "But their younger boy came back from Texas with that new kind of cholera and they had to cancel."

Phil said, "I understand that one couple saw the moon come apart. It got too close to the Earth and split into chunks and the chunks fell like meteors. Smashing everything up, you know. One big piece nearly hit their time machine."

"I wouldn't have liked that at all," Marcia said.

"Our trip was very lovely," said Jane. "No violent things at all. Just the big red sun and the tide and that crab creeping along the beach. We were both deeply moved."

"It's amazing what science can accomplish nowadays," Fran said.

Mike and Ruby agreed they would try to arrange a trip to the end of the world as soon as the funeral was over. Cynthia drank too much and got sick. Phil, Tom and Dave discussed the stock market. Harriet told Nick about her operation. Isabel flirted with Mike, tugging her neckline lower. At midnight someone turned on the news. They had some shots of the earthquake and a warning about boiling your water if you lived in the affected states. The President's widow was shown visiting the last President's widow to get some pointers for the funeral. Then there was an interview with an executive of the time-trip company. "Business is phenomenal," he said. "Time-tripping will be the nation's number one growth industry next year." The reporter asked him if his company would soon be offering something besides the end-of-the-world trip. "Later on, we hope to," the executive said. "We plan to apply for Congressional approval soon. But meanwhile the demand for our present offering is running very high. You can't imagine. Of course, you have to expect apocalyptic stuff to attain immense popularity in times like these." The reporter said, "What do you mean, times like these?" but as the time-trip man started to reply, he was interrupted by the commercial.

Mike shut off the set. Nick discovered that he was extremely depressed. He decided that it was because so many of his friends had made the journey, and he had thought he and Jane were the only ones who had. He found himself standing next to Marcia and tried to describe the way the crab had moved, but Marcia only shrugged. No one was talking about time-trips now. The party had moved beyond that point. Nick and Jane left quite early and went right to sleep, without making love. The next morning the Sunday paper wasn't delivered because of the Bridge Authority strike, and the radio said that the mutant amoebas were proving harder to eradicate than originally anticipated. They were spreading into Lake Superior and everyone in the region would have to boil all drinking water. Nick and Jane discussed where they would go for their next vacation.

"What about going to see the end of the world all over again?" Jane suggested, and Nick laughed quite a good deal.

CALVIN DEMMON

Servo

On the Planet Servo, Underwood wiped the chicken grease from his hands on his white chef's apron and sighed. He day-dreamed of Earth, a planet he had never seen. Though Earth was overcrowded, you could buy a place there if you had the money —just as you could buy *anything* on the Planet Servo. Under-wood was a contracted servant, but his contract was just about up, and when it ran out, Underwood was going to take a one-way trip to Earth.

He had plans for his life on Earth. Big plans.

Servo was a planet made by men to serve men's pleasures; it was completely hollow, an artificial stainless steel ball segmented

"Servo": Copyright © 1971 by Ultimate Publishing Company, Inc. First published in *Amazing Stories*, it is reprinted by permission of the author.
For permission to reprint all or part of this story, direct inquiry to Aurora Publishers, Inc.

into compartments where every conceivable pleasure was offered. Given four or five days notice, the Servons could arrange practically anything. If you wanted it, and if you had enough money, they could set up a replica of the Coliseum in Rome, in Tri-D, complete with live gladiators and live Christians, just so you could turn thumbs down and watch the Christians die. (For a small extra fee, the Christians would actually die; any illusion could be made reality if you could afford it.) But most of the compartments on Servo were given up to lesser pleasures. You could eat broasted chicken, for example, in a genuine Captain Anderson's Southern Chicken Palace, redone to scale exactly as the original Captain Anderson had first built his in the middle of the twentieth century. You could ride on a pony led by a uniformed guard around a ring. You could go to sleep on a mattress, with a woolen blanket over, and you could sleep as long as you wanted to—four or five hours, if you could afford it. Everything on the Planet Servo was geared to providing pleasure for whomever could pay for it.

Underwood's job was broasting the chicken in Captain Anderson's Southern Chicken Palace.

By the standards of the day, on a universal basis, it was a terrible job—for most of the citizens of the Solar System had to work only two or three days a year, on National Work Days, when everyone went to work fixing the machines which worked for everyone during the rest of the year. But by the standards of the Planet Servo, Underwood's was a soft job. After all, he wasn't one of the low-paid professional Christians who sat around waiting for their names to be chosen out of a hat for Coliseum duty. Nor was he required to sweep up after the pony. All Underwood had to do was broast chicken.

But Underwood hated his job. He was a vegetarian by conviction and he hated handling the dead chickens. He felt that every living thing should be allowed to live out its life on its own, without any interference from hungry rich people or from chicken breeders. He had occasionally had to watch Captain Anderson kill a chicken, out in the enormous compartment behind Captain Anderson's Southern Chicken Palace, and the memory of the squawking and the bloody flopping haunted his sleep, especially after a busy day.

But Underwood had been contracted for at birth; it was, he had been told, the only way his parents could afford to have him. Apparently they had wanted to have a baby very much, but living space on the Planet Servo was limited, and Servons who wanted to have children (or who found themselves having them) were required to guarantee that the children would work from the ages of eight to eighteen so that they could earn their passage away from the planet.

Underwood was, according to his papers, seventeen. He did not remember his parents, nor did he know what had happened to them. Somewhere in the depths of his mind was a carefully guarded idea, never examined too closely, that they had probably been sacrificed in some way for someone's pleasure. Underwood had been broasting chickens for nine years. He had become a vegetarian when he was twelve, after broasting over 14,000 chickens.

Captain Anderson's Southern Chicken Palace was easily one of the most popular attractions on the Planet Servo. There were no chickens to be found anywhere else, on any other planet. Captain Anderson's great-grandfather, the great-grandson of the Captain Anderson who had founded the Chicken Palaces, had escaped just before the War That Finally Did It with two hens and a rooster, and he had wisely refused to let anyone have any of the chicks they later produced when he landed on the small asteroid that he built up, over the years, into the Planet Servo.

There was a diner on the Planet, in a compartment fitted out to look like the inside of a streetcar, where you could get scrambled eggs for breakfast (although they were very expensive and were usually only served at the most exclusive dinners), real eggs from Captain Anderson's chickens, but Captain Anderson sterilized the eggs with hard radiation before he let them be taken from the enormous chicken compartment behind the Southern Chicken Palace, so that no one could smuggle them off the Planet Servo and hatch them. Captain Anderson's life had been built around his chickens; he had been raised luxuriously on the profits from the largest (and only) chicken farm in the universe, and he was not about to see his monopoly escape in somebody's luggage.

Underwood separated the wings and legs from the freshly broasted chicken—a chicken he had, quite possibly, been very friendly with just days before. Although he had been broasting chickens for nine years he had not yet gotten over his sympathy for them. He found them to be extremely intelligent and companionable, and he liked to let a few out now and then to follow him about.

Underwood had eleven more months to go before he would get his passage to Earth, from Captain Anderson, and he didn't think he could stand it.

He was cutting the chicken up for Kathy Craft, a young Servon girl who really didn't like broasted chicken, but who really did like Underwood. She ate most (or part) of a broasted chicken every day at the Chicken Palace, just so she could talk to Underwood. As a result, she was plump, and her skin was oily.

To Underwood, she looked like a freshly broasted chicken. He felt sorry for her, as he did for all the chickens.

Kathy was sixteen, and worked as an usher in the Color Movie. She had a slight scar over her right eye, where she had been hit by a flying popcorn box, flattened by a fifty-eight-year-old businessman so that it would sail through the air, aimed at Kathy. The businessman had paid a lot for the privilege, although Kathy didn't know that—nor did she know that it had all been arranged in advance. Captain Anderson was not above getting a little extra out of his help. After all, he reasoned, didn't he feed them all the broasted chicken they could eat, from the time they were old enough to swallow solid food to the time when they left the Planet Servo?

Underwood, the vegetarian, put up with Kathy because her father owned the only vegetable stand on the planet. If it hadn't been for Kathy's father, Underwood might have starved to death, for the only other foods suitable for a vegetarian on the planet were the white bread and the strawberry soda, along with an occasional can of spaghetti with cheese sauce—and these were all delicacy items and hard to come by if you didn't know somebody. The only inexpensive food for the help, besides the chicken, was the reprocessed food from the living compartments. Over the years however, it had become largely reprocessed broasted chicken.

Underwood took his vegetarianism seriously. He would die of starvation before he would eat another piece of meat.

Today, Kathy had brought him three tomatoes and a small onion. Underwood could make a thin soup of these vegetables which would last him two or three meals, if he were very careful.

But Kathy also brought bad news, "Daddy's closing the stand," she told him, "for a couple of days, so he can go fishing up in C-9."

296

Surrounded by chickens, whole, in pieces, and in the broaster, his hands covered with chicken blood and chicken fat and Captain Anderson's Special Chicken Flavoring, knowing that he would have to go out soon and sweep up the chicken bones scattered by visitors to the Chicken Palace and dump them into the reprocessor, not knowing where he was going to get anything to eat tomorrow, Underwood felt himself grow suddenly very calm.

He stopped cutting up the chicken. He laid the serrated knife down very carefully on the counter, wiped his hands on his apron, and walked out the swinging door to the chicken compartment behind Captain Anderson's Southern Chicken Palace, leaving Kathy to stare in amazement. He walked all the way through the chicken compartment, past rows and rows of stacked coops, through the door at the other end, and into Captain Anderson's office.

"I quit," he said to Captain Anderson, who was toying with a bronzed broasted chicken on his desk. "I've had enough. What are you going to do about it?"

"I'm going to put you in the Coliseum for the afternoon show," Captain Anderson said. "We're short of Christians."

"I don't care," said Underwood. "I can't cut up another chicken."

Captain Anderson, who wasn't fond of chicken himself but ate it now and then to keep up appearances, understood Underwood's feelings. But he frankly couldn't afford to do anything about it, he explained; it was a matter of business, of living space on the Planet Servo, as Underwood knew. Underwood wasn't fit for anything but cutting up broasted chickens—in fact, and Captain Anderson did not tell Underwood this, Underwood was the most efficient broasted chicken cutter Captain Anderson had ever employed. Captain Anderson supposed it was because Underwood had so much respect for chickens.

But, the Captain continued, Underwood couldn't stay on until his eighteenth birthday as a freeloader, nor could he leave before his eighteenth birthday. The rest of the planets were crowded too. Only eighteen-year-olds and over were permitted on System ships. There was no room in the rest of the System for homeless children, nor was there anything that an unskilled child could do to make a living. Although most of the citizens of the System worked only two or three days a year, it was complex and exacting work, requiring years of hypno-sleep training.

There were no broasted chickens in the rest of the Solar System for Underwood to cut up. So if he refused to cut broasted chickens for Captain Anderson, why, then, he would have to take his chances in the Coliseum.

Naked, Underwood was tied to a post in the middle of the Coliseum with thirty other Christians. (Underwood did not know where the other Christians came from, nor did he care to ask; they came, however, largely from ranks of tourists to the Planet Servo who overspent and could not afford the trip back. They were allowed to wait in the Christian room, while their names waited in a hat. If a family member came to bail him out before his name was called, a Christian could go home. Otherwise, he waited, and ate broasted chicken. It wasn't a bad life. There were hundreds of Christians in the Christian room, some of whom, thanks to good fortune, had been there for a number of years. Some of them had come to the Planet Servo, in fact, as volunteer Christians, subsidized by the Government, when they were found unfit for hypno-sleep training and were offered the choice of passage to the Planet Servo, for Coliseum duty or immediate processing into the public food utilities.) There were thirty gladiators in the ring, mostly vacationing businessmen who had paid dearly for the privilege of being gladiators. Each carried a sword, a knife, and an instant camera with which to take souvenir pictures.

Underwood realized that he didn't have a chance.

As the small, wealthy audience turned thumbs down on the Christians, the gladiators huffed forward, spears outstretched. Some were quite drunk. Most didn't seem to know quite what to do. One was obviously embarrassed. He had promised to be a gladiator and bring back souvenir pictures to his family. Suddenly ashamed of himself, he lunged forward with his spear, impaled the man next to Underwood—who died (to his credit) bloodily—and flashed four or five pictures before any of the other gladiators knew what had happened.

Underwood, the vegetarian, was aware that he was about to die (he could see that one of the gladiators had his eye on him already), but he was not afraid. He was a man of principle. He knew if it wasn't this, it was cutting up more broasted chickens. Better death, he thought.

A helmeted gladiator broke from the ranks and charged toward Underwood. Underwood stood up bravely, with his back to the pole. He had seen death countless times—in a sense, since his eighth birthday he had been living with death—and it was not a stranger to him. Looking at all those chickens, watching them die beneath Captain Anderson's hatchet, he had realized that he would end as they had some day; it was just a question of time.

The gladiator, nearly on top of Underwood, stepped back and took off his helmet. It was Captain Anderson.

"Will you reconsider?" he asked Underwood.

"No," Underwood said, "I won't."

Captain Anderson sighed and cut him loose. "Sometimes I think of you as my own son," he said. "You've got a lot of spunk in you and you stand up for what you believe in. I'll tell you what I'm going to do. I'm going to let you go to Earth."

"But," said Underwood, "I *can't.*"

"Why not?" Captain Anderson asked. "Didn't you want to go to Earth?"

"Oh, yes," Underwood said. "I've wanted to go ever since I was eight years old, when I started working for you. But I'm not old enough now; you know that."

They had entered the Christian room and were passing among the Christians. Underwood recovered his clothes and stumbled into them as they walked. It was dinnertime, and Underwood could hear the Christians crunching the knuckles off the broasted chicken drumsticks.

They went through the back door to Captain Anderson's office.

"I've got something to tell you, Underwood," Captain Anderson said. "You're twenty-three."

"No, you're making a mistake, Captain Anderson," Underwood said. "I'm seventeen. I've been working for you for nine years. I'm seventeen; that's why I can't go to Earth."

"You're twenty-three, you've been working for me for fifteen years, and that's why you *can* go to Earth. Years on the Planet Servo are longer than Standard Earth years."

Underwood understood suddenly. He ran out of the office, through the front door into the enormous chicken compartment, into and through Captain Anderson's Southern Chicken Palace, and out into the enclosed sidewalk. He didn't know where he was going. He knew only that he wanted to get away from the Planet Servo, and that he never wanted to see Captain Anderson or a broasted chicken again. He had been tricked into cutting up chickens for six years longer than he had to. He had been cheated.

Underwood's youth had been spent at the Chicken Palace. He had not explored the Planet Servo. It took only minutes for him to become hopelessly lost.

He wandered into a room where a man was taking a bubble bath. The man was soaking, reading a Movie magazine, and eating a broasted chicken breast.

He ran out through the wrong door, into a room where a very rich man was watching an old "My Little Margie" program on a video player which was made up to look like a twelve-inch mahogany console black and white television set. The man was licking broasted chicken batter off his fingers.

Out in the hall again, Underwood slipped on a half-eaten broasted chicken wing, fell, and was knocked unconscious.

He had a dream in which he discovered that Captain Anderson's secret of success was that he had only one broasted chicken, which he kept serving up over and over. Underwood was the broasted chicken.

When he awoke, he was in a strange sleeping compartment. Kathy Craft, wearing a tight-fitting nurse's uniform, was standing over him. "Drink this," she said. "It'll make you feel a lot better."

It was chicken soup. He fainted.

When he awoke again, he was on a ship, bound for Earth, with 400 credits and a letter of recommendation in his pocket. It took, Underwood knew, six days to get to Earth. Kathy Craft had apparently learned of his going, for she had packed him a lunch of twelve lettuce and tomato sandwiches, two for each day of the trip. Underwood knew he would miss her. Nevertheless, he was terribly glad to be off the Planet Servo and on his way to Earth, where he would never have to cut up another chicken. He planned to buy a small farm with his money, grow vegetables, and raise chickens, which he would let run wild, completely unsupervised, until they died of old age. When Underwood was ten Captain Anderson had promised to send him a matched pair of chickens when he got to Earth. Captain Anderson knew that Underwood would never sell the chickens, and that he would guard them so carefully that no one could ever steal them, so

Captain Anderson was not afraid of losing his monopoly. Besides, he had a certain affection for the boy.

Underwood did not know this, but Captain Anderson was his father, as he was the father of every contracted servant on the Planet Servo. Kathy Craft was Underwood's sister.

Six days later, Underwood was smashed back against his acceleration pad. He knew that the rockets had cut in. The pain was agonizing, but Underwood rejoiced in it. He was minutes away from stepping out on the planet he had never seen, but had dreamed about nightly for nine (no, fifteen!) years.

The door to his compartment opened. He stepped out and found himself across the corridor from Captain Anderson's Southern Chicken Palace. His eyes opened wildly, and he whirled around. He had spent six days in the Earth Trip Rocket Simulator, one of the least popular and most inexpensive pleasure compartments on the Planet Servo.

"Did you change your mind yet, boy?" asked a voice behind him. He whirled. It was Captain Anderson. He was smiling.

"You cheated me again," said Underwood. He hit Captain Anderson in the face. Captain Anderson stopped smiling and began to back away. Underwood hit him again.

Captain Anderson backed into his office and Underwood followed, swinging wildly. Captain Anderson grabbed a shiny object from his desk and tried to shield himself with it. It was the bronzed broasted chicken.

"Wait!" Captain Anderson cried. "You don't understand!"

"You tricked me again!" Underwood screamed, and he swung, hitting the bronzed chicken. His knuckles cracked and he moaned in pain. He snatched the chicken and hit Captain Anderson on the head with it. Captain Anderson collapsed, and the chicken popped in half, opening like a book, with hinges along the backbone. Inside was a small tape recorder which began playing.

"This is Captain Anderson speaking," said the recording, as Underwood stood over Captain Anderson. Captain Anderson appeared to be dead.

"I am, of course, dead," said the recording of Captain Anderson's voice. "This machine is keyed to a switch in my chest which will activate a tiny transmitter if my heart should stop. There are similar bronzed broasted chickens located in every compartment in the Planet Servo, behind concealed doors which have now opened, and in my lawyers' offices on Earth and on Mars.

They are playing in concert. This is my last and final will. As my lawyers know, but as none of my employees know, my contracted laborers here on the Planet Servo are all my sons and daughters, in a peculiar, although perfectly legal, fashion. When I was a young man I realized the folly of marriage, but, being a businessman, I also realized that, had I a lot of children, they could help me in my broasted chicken business, as well as with the other chores here on the Planet Servo. I therefore sought out a leading biochemist, who took several genetic specimens from me and implanted them in carefully treated eggs. I leave the Planet Servo to my children, who will now appreciate how much chickens have meant not only to me, but to them. The eggs in which my specimens were implanted were chicken eggs. My children: your mothers were all chickens, chickens carefully raised here on the Planet Servo.

"To *my* mother," the tape continued, "I leave my collection of Chicken Little Coloring Books. The sky is falling, Mother."

Underwood, now fabulously wealthy, fainted, squawking. He cheeped feebly for a few minutes, and was silent.

JOANNA RUSS

Useful Phrases For The Tourist

THE LOCRINE: peninsula and surrounding regions.
High Lokrinnen.
X 437894= II
Reasonably Earthlike (see companion audio tapes and trans-
literations)
For physiology, ecology, religion and customs, Wu and Fabri-
cant, Prague, 2355, Vol. 2 *The Locrine, Useful Knowledge for
the Tourist,* q.v.

AT THE HOTEL:
That is my companion. It is not intended as a tip.

303

I will call the manager.
This cannot be my room because I cannot breathe ammonia.
I will be most comfortable between temperatures of 290 and 303 degrees Kelvin.
Waitress, this meal is still alive.

AT THE PARTY:
Is that you?
Is that all of you? How much (many) of you is (are) there?
I am happy to meet your clone.
Interstellar amity demands that we make some physical display at this point, but I beg to be excused.
Are you toxic?
Are you edible? I am not edible.
We humans do not regenerate.
My companion is not edible.
That is my ear.
I am toxic.
Is that how you copulate?
Is this intended to be erotic?
Thank you very much.
Please explain.
Do you turn colors?
Are you pregnant?
I shall leave the room.
Can't we just be friends?
Take me to the Earth Consulate immediately.
Although I am very flattered by your kind offer, I cannot accompany you to the mating pits, as I am viviparous.

IN THE HOSPITAL:
No!
My eating orifice is not at that end of my body.
I would rather do it myself.
Please do not let the atmosphere in (out) as I will be most uncomfortable.
I do not eat lead.
Placing the thermometer there will yield little or no useful information.

SIGHTSEEING:
You are not my guide. My guide was bipedal.

We Earth people do not do that.

Oh, what a jolly fine natatorium (mating perch, arranged spectacle, involuntary phenomenon)!

At what hour does the lovelorn princess fling herself into the flaming volcano? May we participate?

That is not demonstrable.

That is hardly likely.

That is ridiculous.

I have seen much better examples of that.

Please direct me to the nearest sentient mammal.

Take me to the Earth Consulate without delay.

AT THE THEATRE:

Is that amusing?

I am sorry; I did not mean to be offensive.

I did not intend to sit on you. I did not realize that you were already in this seat.

Could you deform yourself a little lower?

My eyes are sensitive only to light of the wavelengths 3000-7000A.

Am I imagining this?

Am I supposed to imagine this?

Should I be perturbed by the water on the floor?

Where is the exit?

Help!

This is great art.

My religious convictions prevent me from joining in the performance.

I do not feel well.

I feel very sick.

I do not eat living food.

Is this supposed to be erotic?

May I take this home with me?

Is this part of the performance?

Stop touching me.

Sir or madam, that is mine. (extrinsic)

Sir or madam, that is mine. (intrinsic)

I wish to visit the waste-reclamation units.

Have you finished?

May I begin?

You are in my way.

Under no circumstances.

If you do not stop that, I will call the attendant. That is forbidden by my religion.
Sir or madam, this is a private unit.
Sir and madam, this is a private unit.

COMPLIMENTS:
You are more than before.
Your hair is false.
If you uncover your feet, I will faint.
There is no room.
You will undoubtedly be here tomorrow.

INSULTS:
You are just the same.
There are more of you than previously.
Your fingers are showing.
How clean you are!
You are clean, but animated.

GENERAL:
Take me to the Earth Consulate.
Direct me to the Earth Consulate.
The Earth Consulate will hear of this.
This is no way to treat a visitor.
Please direct me to my hotel.
At what time does the moon rise? Is there a moon?
Is it a full moon? Take me to the Earth Consulate immediately.
May I have the second volume of Wu and Fabricant, entitled *Physiology, Ecology, Religion and Customs of the Locrine?* Price is no object.
Something has just gone amiss with my vehicle.
I am dying.

DAVID R. BUNCH

The Dirty War

In Moderan, as I like saying, we are not often between wars. . .

It was a particularly dirty kind of war, this one to which I now refer. To deny that it was a particularly dirty kind of war would be to deny sense, and I do not believe that anyone would wish to do that. Not on a weekday, anyway.

We, the metal-and-people people of Moderan, the world's walking durables, with the bulk of us new-metal man now and our flesh-strips few and played-down, had reached that point in our Stronghold lives where plain clean honest fighting with shot and shell, doll bombs, high-up weird screaming wreck-wrecks and the White Witch rockets firing, had grown tedious.

Dull. A drag. Routine-like. We needed a change. YES. Or so the state ministers said. From their gold offices in the L-Towers all over the world

Our world ministers negotiated and drew up some good rules for a dirty war. They said. Even a dirty war must have good rules, they said; although, frankly, I came early to believe that rules are mostly for revision, and honestly, lately I hardly ever bother to think about rules one way or another. Some live by rules; some live to break rules; and many live in the Shadow of Broken Rules. I don't bother to vote, usually, on any of it these days, and by not becoming cluttered with little chains and tatters of conduct and opinion, and by holding unswervingly to the main beacon of all our lives, which is war, most astonishing and destructive war, I have easily become the World's Greatest Man. I can look any situation squarely in the eyes now and tell you at a glance the best answer. The best answer is more firepower. The best answer is amazingly simple to say. But it is not nearly so simple to execute, because it implies a lot of things. It implies having the most and heaviest guns (or the most and heaviest of whatever the destructor-unit of the current moment happens to be) and having these in range, placed well, nay, not only well, THE BEST! on top of the very highest hill. It implies having the very best of first-line firepower operators. It implies having the very best of back-up firepower operators. It implies and implies. YES. But I have coped well with all the implications and by holding to the main beam of all our lives, which is war, I have, as I said, attained to the position of World's Greatest Man.

But this was to be an entirely different kind of war, and I was edgy. And I had a right to be. I'll tell you now, not to hold you with any cheap suspense tricks or wait-and-see anticipation, I have just lately lost that war. But I tried not to. I raised the levies, I shored the defenses and I stockpiled the means, as they say. OH YES!

I sent word to my connections in Olderrun, that little land-locked and sea-starved country far across the tall mountains, where the old-fashioned flesh people still hold away. I made the earliest arrangements possible to buy all of their stores of human excrement, animal manure, decaying flesh of anything, surplus citizens dead or alive and any other rotten concoction the Olderrun folk would agree to throw together for me, if I thought it might help me to win the Dirty War. —I wasn't trying to play fair. Or unfair. I wasn't even thinking about it. I was just doing

my level best, as I think any living creature should, to put together the right arsenal to win whatever war might be coming up.
The war-current for me, the one on my doorstep, as it were, just
happened to be the Dirty War. And I was going for the victory
roses, as the saying is; I meant business, I MEANT TO WIN!
with that human excrement, that barnyard by-product, that rotten
flesh of anything and surplus citizens dead or alive. YES. I had
it all shipped in by flash car, from the edges of Olderrun. The
old-fashioned flesh people brought it as far for me as their
boundaries. By air. Jet freight!

We had two weeks in which to get ready for the Dirty War. I
could not know what dirty things the other Stronghold masters
might be doing and planning in preparation for D-day, but I saw
my course clean and plain and I embarked upon it. I worked my
weapons men day and night, hard around the clock I worked
them, to convert my most accurate blasters to the handling of
offal shots. Even my prime warhead delivery vehicle, Big
Belcherine, I converted to an excrement gun; and with a simple
turn of a screw, something that could be done easily by even
the dullest weapons man in all wide Moderan, in even the most
hectic of battle times, Big Belcherine could be converted to the
handling of unclassified garbage spray shots. Along with the
conversion of weapons, my vast supply of offal of all kinds was
made into the right-size shot-balls, projectiles packaged to explode on impact mostly, with some timed to explode in mid-air
for shower shots.

I'll tell you in all candor, near the end of the two weeks of
preparation for the Dirty War, I felt ready, felt confident, I felt
sure that I would routinely win the conflict once again and be
awarded the war plaque for dirtiness and the emblem of the
crossed bombs for excellence. I had no other thought. I thought
positively, and that's for sure. I could even see the headlines
at next news-up time in the vapor shield, the letters each twenty-
five miles high, a hundred up and shimmering, studded, starred:
STRONGHOLD 10 WINS DIRTY WAR. STRONGHOLD
10'S ANIMAL-OFFAL IMPACT SHOTS AND HUMAN-
EXCREMENT SHOWER SHOTS AND OLD UNCLASSI-
FIED-GARBAGE-WITH-CADAVER SPRAY SHOTS TOO
MUCH. DIRTY WAR OPPONENTS CONCEDE. JUDGES
CONCUR. GOOD SHOW, STRONGHOLD 10. WE LOVE
YOU!

Well, so much for positive thinking and ghost headlines. So much for phantom victory in the mind too. So much for everything. To lose is hard, even for those who lose and lose and are accustomed. For a champion to lose is walking death come down, and all things bad; it is destruction, it is wreck, it is a man on his back, it is the taste impossible—

So we opened that great day. My weapons men were up and geared for battle early, their faces in blackface, as was the custom. When the trumpet sounded they bent to their shots and I, high on a parapet, stood glued to observation screens, seeing those shots sink home all over the world, all over the enemy, shot-deserving world. My pale green blood sang dancing in its flesh-strips, as it always does when battle is joined, and I gloried in the cause—bad cause? good cause? what cause?—who could care?—we were fighting!

Well, I did not lose easily. I fought them toe-to-toe, as the saying is. If I lost with any kind of grace, it was not grace-grace, and you can count on that. I lost snarling, complaining, pleading for another shot, pleading for a recount of the votes, pleading for ANYTHING that would reverse defeat. I was burned up. Losing is not my style. My iron guts still writhe at the thought of it.

You know who won? You know how he won? No! I won't say who won; that name and number stick on my phfluggee-phflaggee even yet, until my speech gears almost toss their teeth if I try to say who won. I hate with a very completeness, you see; I hate all winners, you see, only excepting me; in that I am man typical. But I realize I cannot, just by mouthing philosophy, get out of telling you how he won. He won with a rotten underhanded dirty trick, this vile vile man, this winner. Well, it was a dirty war, he was a dirty man, and I cannot, in honesty, say that tricks were exempt from the scheme. But I went in there straight and let them have the dirt clean; you have to say I did that. And can't you see how I should have won? CAN'T YOU? —But it's no use me to argue with you. I could argue a hundred pages and convince you twice, and three times and four times and a thousand times! and you still would not, could not, rise up and go and get for me those prizes—that first-place plaque, that crossed-bombs trophy. Where they hang, damn! damn! on another's walls. OH GOD! but I hate to lose! AND DAMN! I DETEST IT!!—But calm, calm I must somehow be. After all, I have won some. Yes, I have won lots. YES! I am still the World's

Greatest Man. And I will be winner once again when we go back to straight war. I know I will be. I KNOW IT!

How did he win? He won with a trick. But I told you that. He won with a miserable trick. He won with a miserable Miserable MISERABLE trick. But it was legal. Yes, I have to admit, in a "dirty war" it was legal. Am I sorry I didn't think of it? I'm sorry I didn't win. Does that answer your ask-it?—You see, he converted, I figure, about half of his total of blasters to loft up flower bursts, bags of "I love you so's" and Ho-Ho banners, beautiful pennons of colored smoke laughing in the vapor shield. Can you imagine it!? No, I know you can't. You would have to have been there, part of this dirty war, to be able even to start in to understand really just how diverting this all could be. Amidst all the really low-down stuff the rest of us from our complexes were lofting up at each other would float his pretty "I love you so" balloons, the flower shots and the Ho-Ho flags. All sugar-lump stuff and posy-roses, see, with laughs. It hit most of the Stronghold masters right where they couldn't comprehend it; it struck them tickle-tickle. Some of them just stood there, turned giddy on their parapets at the incomprehensibility of it all, set their phfluggee-phflaggees (voice buttons) to LOUD LAUGH and guffawed right there in the middle of a war. I? I doubled the guards, as I always do, automatically, when someone, ANY-ONE! starts lobbing "I love you so's" and chum shots at me. By that I did escape complete humiliation and destruction, as I so often have at such times in times past. YES!

You see, he had converted, I would say, only about half of his blasters to the capability of "I love you so's," bloom and laugh shots. The other half shot hardware, and, I tell you, even now I choke on this every time I think of it; I envy his brains! He had collected vast stores of iron dust and steel filings, any fine bits of iron and steel he could find—mostly from the spare parts tooling places and the weapons man factories of Moderan—and had this magnetized. Then, using his conventional blasters, he deposited all this fine mass in bags in close range of all the enemy Strongholds, shot after grim shot sneaking through the flowers, the laugh flags and the love. Next he sent in the big walking-doll-bombs to walk these big loads in for the pay-off kill. The walking bombs by the millions climbed Stronghold walls by the thousands, all over the world that war, carrying bags, and settled upon hapless hopeless weapons men and surprised laughing Stronghold masters, who, everyone being almost

311

entirely metal except for the few flesh-strips of the Commanders, were soon smeared. It was a dirty trick. It smothered them down; it encrusted them deeply. For life? Nay. Death!

I escaped because, as I've hinted, love and blooms and laughs are ever my rising signals for vigilance, my sharp nudges for THINK SHARP! NOW! and my perceptor buds' high times to yell HEY! HEADS UP, YOU! GO HIDE! Not a single doll bomb penetrated at Stronghold 10; not one got over the walls with a bag. We stopped them, all right.

BUT DID I WIN? NO! He won. The war judges, state ministers, stale ministers! those little wrinkly bums with the gold offices in the L-Towers all over the world, gave him high points for dirty planning, high points for dirty execution and those big red bonus points for creative underhandedness that paid off. I? I with my clean straight-in honorable direct high-minded approach to dirt was given high points only for dirty execution. I won second. He won first. My plaques are smaller than his. To put it another way, his plaques are bigger than mine! HIS ARE FIRST-PLACE PLAQUES. Mine are second—I HATE HIM! I HATE HATE HATE EVEN THE VERY THOUGHT OF THE DIRTY WAR! I HATE HATE HATE EVERYTHING and will until I win again.

I can hardly wait until the next war starts up.

ALAN BRENNERT

Skyghosts And Dusk-Devils

Dusk-devils come spinning up from behind the swollen horizon, all blood and scabs in the sunset glow, pinwheeling into the grey shadows at our feet. We catch them down there, tugging-scratching-kicking themselves into our path, trying to make us trip and fall. And they hide. In the ground, in the rocks, in the new dust and the old. Nuisances, nothing more than that; scratchy scrawny annoyances that chatter and chuckle at our feet. Dusk-devils.

Dusk deepens to night and the devils drop away, scurry back to meet the sinking sun. Then the real devils start in, then the Skyghosts flicker and dance on the cloudless black. They're tall, wider than the sun; the moon could be one of their balls turned white and free-swung. And they're covered. All *over*: dim reds, faded greens, colors worn to a whisper by the sky. Only their

313

hands and faces are pasted naked against the night, even some of their eyes framed by glass and metal. The same six or seven of them, feet cut off at the horizon, staring down at us, moving their mouths but damn it if nothing ever comes out. I watch their lips sometimes, try to read the words, but they're speaking in a distant tongue; I turn away and to hell with it, they're only ghosts.

Skyghosts. Knew a man once looked a lot like them, close enough to be a brother; same type of face, you know, same kind of build; he was like a ghost himself, but didn't fade with the day; we had to kill him . . .

You get through the night all right—Skyghosts above you staring and speaking, you're cold and huddling in groupfucks to keep 'em away—and then there's a sort of almost-dawn, grey enough for the dusk-devils to come back and scuttle round at naked thighs and cold, flat bottoms. Day comes quicker than night, though, and they run back to the edge of the world to wait out the sun. They've got time.

Time. Wondered how it worked, once; one moment you're here and the next you're *there,* what happened to *here?* is it gone or what?; tried to stand still between seconds but I couldn't, I just kept moving . . .

Everything's moving. Morning's the hunt for food, the scrambling that puts the devils to shame. Morning's the rush for shrubs and pissholes; if you don't do it private, there's a stink on the land nobody wants. Morning's the first moment of day and the start of the long slow slide down to night. Morning's moving.

Moving's something to do while you die.

It's the laughter, mind you; it's the giggling and cackling you hear from beneath the earth, that's what hurts. Beneath the earth, that's where they're buried, those dead ones who do the job the ghosts and devils do, but do it best.

Fine day, they'll say. *Look at the sky!*

A buried chuckle.

Look at that sky.

Goes on like that, laughter in the earth. Our parents' laughter, damn them. Laughing at us for being so stupid. So we move. We run over the parched desert through the ruins of a yesterday-town, we search for food and try not to hear the laughter. Some of us, we run fast enough, we die from the effort; we're not all that strong. That calls for a celebration, then, that calls for running and yelling and dayfucking, that calls for a lot.

314

Goes like this:

Someone falls, usually he's been chasing something across the plains, he keels over and lies flat on the ground. Where he's lying there's no laughter for a while, as if the dead ones don't know what to make of this yet. Then suddenly it starts up again, weaker: they've lost another victim, but they've got to keep laughing.

We'll gather round and stare at the body a few seconds, and then somebody'll start laughing right in with those bastards down *there* and it's started. The food of the morning is wolfed down, and then we try some games before the body's got too stiff to stand a good prick, and then we'll start some stories going, maybe about the dead man, maybe not.

Stories are my speciality. You know that, listening. I make a few up, hear secondhand of some, pass others along.

Once I told how I visited a cave in the bleeding valley, near the horizon where the Skyghosts stand; saw the metal dabbed red by the sun that always seems to hang outside; heard the clack of the dead ones' metal soles on the hard iron floor of the earth's belly. Apart from the machines, the cave is hollow; some say that's where the Skyghosts go during the day. Maybe so. Maybe that's why some call the ghosts by other names: like *hollow-grams.* Maybe so.

Stories help fill the days when most of the time there's nothing to do but shrug off the heat or the cold and sit on the torn ground while the dead ones poke and point at the sky. They always did that, even when they weren't dead: *The sky. Look at the sky. We used to touch it . . .*

I'll tell you something and I don't care who hears it, I'm sick of the sky and I hate it and I say fuck it, fuck the whole blue-whitehotcold sky!

Fine day . . .

One of my stories never caught on is the one about people who used to make things in their heads, waking dreams they tried to build and sometimes did. Most everyone laughs at that, says, "No one can build, it isn't done." Then I say that these people didn't always build *right,* sometimes they made night-mares for themselves because they couldn't dream anything else, and then they built those too—only they weren't real, just dreams that only they could see. Everyone turns away at this and don't speak to me for the longest while and I'm sorry I said it and please don't you turn away, no!

315

Something else. Something else:

Afternoons are playtimes, times you go exploring, walk three steps past where you walked yesterday, or hurl a rock over a hill and wait to hear a noise. It's getting harder to play every day, though; the rocks bite and the ground turns to mud as you walk. Getting harder to do anything more than sweat or shiver.

Knew a woman once got it into her head that the dead flew over the burnt hills to another world; damned if she didn't go trotting over there after her dead brother; she never came back, but at least she *went*. I loved her a little for that.

No one goes over the hill anymore.

The sun's got too old to light our way, I guess. Times it looks as dead as the rest of us. That's what the dead ones told us before they were dead: it's the color of blood because it's bleeding, and one day soon the last drop will be drawn and we'll all of us die . . .

The sky!

Then there's the story that boils up off the dried earth every night as the dusk-devils scamper and scream around us and the Skyghosts flicker into life above. The words come scattered from every voice, from childhood tales and wandering travelers, words torn and brittle with time.

About what the Skyghosts are saying. Nothing that ever makes any sense: *You're men,* someone remembers their grandfather telling them as a child; *Your minds,* whispers a woman who'd once lain with an old man and watched him die in her, her eyes are glassy with the memory ever since; *Think, please think,* begs a beggar, the plea handed down from beggar-father to beggar-son. Other words, other pleas: Sun. Die. Leaveyou. Sorry. Star. Sky.

No one knows how long they've been up there; every generation's seen them and there's never any argument over particulars, never anyone who claims they're *not* there, not like with the dusk-devils. Everyone sees the same thing, clear as the night they're hung on.

Someone says: They're tombstones.

Someone asks: For who?

Leaveyou. Die. *Your minds!* Star—

—ship . . .

We get hot and tired of the words: tired of trying to remember, trying to think. They all want us to think and it's getting so god damned *hard.* Maybe we aren't as smart as our fathers, or their fathers before them. Maybe we aren't . . . *right. But we try.*

I start to tell a story then to break up the sadness, to bring everyone into better spirits and start the laughing and singing and fucking. I start talking and my voice is sky-cool and very quiet, and before I know it, I'm telling them about the people who make things up in their minds and live their nightmares and can't ever break out, and as I brush away a dusk-devil I see they're all turning and frowning and staring at the sky—just like you, damn it, just like *you* . . .

GERALD W. PAGE

Waygift

It was one among many, a minor worldsong twisted and blended in among the others, an inconsequential song among symphonies and cathedral choruses; yet to hear it was to ignore the others. There was an element to this song, a poignant quality that could not be dismissed by any human who heard it, a note that somehow identified the song as the song of a dying world.

Barbara was a singer, a gatherer and giver of worldsongs to the younger races who can not as yet walk the Way as Earthmen can. My name is Duncan. There was no purpose in me, not a special one as singing was to Barbara, not then, not then. I heard the songs, of course, and I walked the Way. I was as changed by the Way as any human is, deepened and straightened. I tasted of Unity and became more and more myself.

To me the songs were things used to pick my course from

world to world. But to Barbara they were more; it was her Way-gift that she heard them as I never could. Later, after her walks, she would take what songs she heard and sing them. The natives of the worlds we visited would gather and listen to her, hypnotized by the beauty and force of her singing. And me, I would listen just as hypnotized as anyone else. I envied her that gift, just as I relished her for herself and her beauty. The songs she sang were not a beauty that just came out of her now and then but part of the beauty that had grown around her. Her eyes, her face, all of her being had been touched with the worldsongs and made better by it. We were, I often thought, a strange pair. But she loved me, I realized, as much as I loved her.

Iselinn—is there a world more beautiful than Iselinn?

It's a pastel world. Soft blue skies. Softer pink sunsets and sunrises. Supple, swaying trees. Grass of a green so soft it's as if you viewed the world through gauze. The air was a mixture of gentle gasses that were light and exhilarating to breathe. There was lots of water, the fresh of it cool and sweet, the salt of it teeming with life and activity. And since it is a world, Iselinn has storms upon its seas and lands, has deserts and snow fields and its animals prey on one another in nature's way. The people are people, which I sometimes suspect is a most wonderful thing; they're no more cruel to one another than humans used to be, and probably less so. For although they have never walked the Way and been touched by it as humans have, they have heard the worldsongs sung by those like Barbara who have that Way-gift. They know—as humans never knew until they found it—that the Way exists. The people of Iselinn are philosophers and already suspect the nature of the Unity. They wait patiently for the day when they will learn to walk the Way. It will come at a time long after the humans are gone, I imagine. The Iselinn will have a need by then to hear the worldsongs for themselves.

Barbara and I were living by the sea on Iselinn's largest continent, enjoying mild days and a pleasantly warm sun. Barbara would sing and I would listen, marvelling, or we would swim, or walk the beach to hunt shells. Frequently we were visited by people of Iselinn, eager to hear the worldsongs. Many times there were Earthmen with us, who had stopped for a visit either because we asked them to or because they had heard of Barbara and wanted to hear her songs. The most frequent of our visitors was our friend Roman.

"Duncan," he once told me, "she sings like no one else. Like the Way itself. I think the Way must have touched her more deeply than any of the rest of us have been touched. She's a vessel. The Way has filled her to the brim and as much as she pours out, the Way somehow keeps her filled."

Sitting beside me on the sand, Barbara laughed.

"It's true," Roman insisted. Roman had a tongue that could lure the worldsongs.

Only, what he said about Barbara was true and I never heard it said better. Roman wandered, searching and exploring, looking at the worlds and stars of Iselinn's cluster, seeking out one wonder after another and taking them in like wine. Yet he was never far from Iselinn. We saw him frequently.

One morning I woke early and went out onto the beach and found Roman sitting on a driftwood log, drawing pictures in the sand with a stick. It had been weeks since we had last seen him.

But he was a man you knew would burst in on you in the night if he came then, a man who knew he would be welcome and wasn't shy about it. Yet there he sat, drawing pictures in the sand, after weeks of absence, and he'd not even bothered to wake us and let us know he was back.

He looked around and saw me.

I'd never seen his eyes like that, not in all the time I'd known him. I stopped and said, "What's the matter? Can you talk to me about it?"

With the end of the stick he wiped out the sand drawing. "I can talk about it," he said.

"All right."

He stood up, looked at me. Those eyes of his— "Duncan, have you ever heard a worldsong change?"

"Sure I have."

"No, not that way. Not a song change. Not a change of melody or pitch or anything like that."

"How else can a song change?"

He stopped to pick up a pebble which he threw at the sea. "I don't know. I guess they can't, except like that." After a moment he added, "I'm talking about a song that feels differently from how it used to feel. If you understand that."

"How did it used to feel?"

"I don't know. I mean, I don't know how to say it. It was never much of a song. Just one of the ones you heard. Only, the feeling of it is different now, the mood's gone—changed. It never was a song I'd really paid attention to. You neither, I'll bet. Duncan, I'm embarrassed coming here like this. I feel like a fool."

"You should never feel like that," Barbara said. I hadn't heard her come out of the house. There was a look on her face that was related to what was in Roman's eye.

Barbara didn't have to be in the Way to hear Worldsongs. Some people—singers for the most part—have that talent. The songs just come to them, not just the songs of the world they're on—even *I* can hear the song of the world I'm on—but the songs from other planets, sometimes from other parts of the galaxy; some say even from outside.

"I heard it last night," she said. "It just came drifting, very faintly. It just came and I heard it."

"I never noticed there was something troubling you," I said apologetically.

"I didn't hear it until after we were asleep. It was faint but it woke me. Not the noise of it—I could barely hear that. But it woke me."

"I know what you mean," Roman said.

"I listened to it in the Way for a while, then came back," she said. It's such a small song. I can't even guess what the world is like."

"I was there once," Roman said. "A long time ago. It's not much."

"It's dying," Barbara said, quietly. "That's what the song is saying now. The world is dying."

Roman nodded his head, admitting what he did not really want to say. After a while he said, "It's a small, almost airless rock. It's the only planet orbiting its star. The others all broke up, all became asteroids. I don't even know why this one didn't."

"It won't last much longer," Barbara said. She turned and started back toward the house. Halfway there she turned and looked at Roman and me. "I want to go there," she said.

"Why?" I asked.

"Maybe the people need help there."

"It's a lifeless world," Roman said.

"Then because it's dying," Barbara said.

"But we can't help a planet," I told her.

"Please."

Oh, I didn't want to go there. But she was letting me decide the issue, and I didn't want to disappoint her or add to her sorrow in any way. And in a way, maybe I'd have been disappointed, too. I nodded.

In the Way I could hear the song. I had heard it a thousand times before and never paid it any heed. It was one among many, but now it had the difference that coming from a dying world would give it. We started toward it, treading across the Way, among the organ songs of gas giants, the whisperings of moons, the windchimes or voices or gongs of the solid planets, the shrillness of the stars. At last we reached a planet where we heard the glass bell songs of thousands, perhaps more than thousands of asteroids. Still, the poignant, nondescript song of the dying world persisted and we approached it. And came to it, finally.

We stood on the rocky surface of a small and moonless world, circling a minor star. The only planet of a star where stellar abortion after stellar abortion had scattered fields of asteroids where there might have been whole planets. There was air, though it was very thin, and the only life we could see was a sparsely growing orange lichen that covered a rock here, a rock there. The horizon was close and there were jagged mountains. There were craters as well. Barbara was standing at my side and, though I did not glance at her, I knew she was shaking with the things she felt. So was I. I reached for her hand and she moved closer to my side.

"You see a lot of asteroids in star clusters like this," Roman said, though not as if he believed the explanations mattered. "Sometimes the stars are so close that the stresses are too great to permit planets. The cooling gasses break up rather than form full-sized planets. You get asteroids."

"This planet formed."

"I know. It's a freak, that's all. For some reason it resisted or avoided the stresses that destroyed the other forming worlds."

"But why is this world dying?" I asked.

"Maybe the sun's about to go nova," Roman said.

"No. It's the world, not the star. The starsong's normal."

"Roman was right, I think," Barbara said. "The world is dying because of all the stresses in this part of space. The star's too close, the asteroids and meteors are constantly bombarding it. It's not a strong world." Her voice trembled. I tightened my hold on her hand. "Listen to its song. It's all there."

As though her words were a signal, the ground trembled. It shook for almost thirty seconds, then the shaking died down. The world was quiet again, except for the distant agony of the world-song.

I turned to Barbara. "Well?" I asked.

"I've never heard a song like that before," she said. "I've never heard a song that expressed such loneliness before."

"A world can't think," I said. "It has no feelings."

"I know that."

She pulled her hand free of mine and started off. She stopped and turned back to look at me. I saw what was in her face, sure enough, but there was nothing then and there I could do for it. Later perhaps, but not then.

I sat on a rock and waited.

The song was burning into my memory as no other song ever had. Roman stood close by, staring at the ground, waiting to leave but unwilling to do so while we stayed. Barbara looked around, not wildly, not hysterically, but unable to find a purpose to her looking just the same.

And all the time I was thinking, here we are: humans, the race that walks the Way. The beings highest on the evolutionary scale of any creatures in this galaxy, the ones who hear the world-songs, the ones touched and changed by the Way, the ones with the secrets of Unity. Here we are, the three of us as close as any three people can be to one another. Only just now the three of us are as alone—and lonely—as it's possible for us to be.

After a while I called out Barbara's name. She came over, face sober and strained. "I think it's time to go," I told her.

"Yes," she agreed. "There can't be much more time, can there?"

"It's already beginning," Roman said. He pointed. There was a fissure spreading across the surface of the planet, slowly, ever so slowly, with the dignity of coming death.

We were never in danger, of course. All we had to do was reach out and open the fabric between space and the Way, step onto the concourse and let the opening close behind us. We were humans and humans had walked the Way and been changed by it. Humans could breathe almost any sort of air, stand almost any gravity, almost any atmospheric pressure. Though there would have been a risk, I suppose, our chances were good we could have stayed there through the planet's break-up and then, floating in space among the world's swirling debris, still have time to reach the Way before being harmed. And if we were harmed, short of being dead, the Way would heal us.